HOUSE OF FURY

Evelio Rosero

House of Fury

a novel

translated from the Spanish
by Victor Meadowcroft

A NEW DIRECTIONS
PAPERBOOK ORIGINAL

Manufactured in the United States of America
First published as New Directions Paperbook 1622 in 2025

Library of Congress Cataloging-in-Publication Data
Names: Rosero, Evelio, 1958– author. |
Meadowcroft, Victor, translator.
Title: House of fury / by Evelio Rosero ;
translated from the Spanish by Victor Meadowcroft.
Other titles: Casa de furia. English
Description: First edition. |
New York : New Directions Publishing, 2025. |
Identifiers: LCCN 2024043482 | ISBN 9780811234580 (paperback) |
ISBN 9780811234597 (ebook)
Subjects: LCGFT: Novels.
Classification: LCC PQ8180.28.07 C3813 2025 |
DDC 863/.64—dc23/eng/20240923
LC record available at https://lccn.loc.gov/2024043482

2 4 6 8 10 9 7 5 3 1

New Directions Books are published for James Laughlin
by New Directions Publishing Corporation
80 Eighth Avenue, New York

For Mireyita, Melba Yolanda, Fabiola, Peri, and U.

All that I have said will come true.

                              —Tiresias

HOUSE OF FURY

PART ONE

1

URIELA CAICEDO, THE YOUNGEST of the Caicedo Santacruz sisters, was leaning over a balcony festooned with roses
and tuberoses when she spotted, advancing like a timid
mouse between patches of sunlight, her Uncle Jesús coming
up the tree-lined street. Too late, she wanted to withdraw
from the balcony, leap back and disappear: her uncle waved
his hand in greeting, and it was as if another invisible hand
were forcing her to remain on the balcony, flushed, caught
red-handed in her crime of bad manners. She had spent a
good part of the morning leaning over that balcony, waiting.
What was she waiting for? For whom? Nothing and nobody;
she was merely digesting, perplexed, the news of that Friday,
April 10, 1970: the Beatles had broken up. And, just when
she had decided to go to her bedroom to get dressed for
the party—guests would soon be arriving to celebrate her
parents' anniversary—she discovered her uncle's shadow
beneath the trees, in that street with no shadows save for
those of the tidy mansions of that Bogotá neighborhood.

*Well, Uncle Jesús surely wasn't invited to the big family cele-
bration, who would invite him?* she thought.

Her uncle came to a halt below the balcony, exuberant in
his decrepitude: he was wearing a gray suit that was too big
for him, a tatty suit that had once belonged to the magistrate
Nacho Caicedo, Uriela's father, and he was moving his wide
mouth without emitting a sound, as though chewing a tough
morsel or adjusting his dentures to begin speaking. And,
indeed, his voice did ring out in that deserted street, almost a

3

threat, but also a plea, in any case the voice of a hustler, Uriela told herself, mesmerized by that pair of serpent's eyes that lay in wait for her, ten feet below the balcony. Her uncle had his hands buried in the pockets of his coat, and he twisted them inside, clenching and unclenching his fists as he spoke.

"Uriela, do you remember your dear old Jesús?"

Uriela nodded, leaning farther forward: she saw the wind ruffle the few hairs on that yellow skull, saw the nostrils of his hairy nose flare, and she smiled, because she had no other option, and yet her smile was sincere, the smile of a seventeen-year-old, and her voice a kind of sympathy:

"I could never forget you, Uncle Jesús."

"That's true," he replied, spreading his arms and revealing, intentionally or not, the intricate stitching on the sleeves of his coat, worse than a scar. He had a raspy voice, like someone suffocating: "We saw each other exactly a month ago."

Uncle Jesús was in his fifties, with flat, pointy ears; hair poked out from inside each ear like tiny cotton plants; they were big ears, like radars, yet he complained of deafness, or deafness assailed him whenever it was convenient not to hear; his mouth was as wide as an ear-to-ear grin, his jaw very long and sharp; his neck was that of a bird; his skin, the color of café con leche; he was clean-shaven and baggy-eyed, and his fingernails resembled claws; small in stature, though not *too* short, half-bald, by turns sly, then meditative, then sly again, he lived off visiting his relatives from month to month and demanding what he termed his family honorariums. A tribute that proved inescapable even to Doña Alma Santacruz, Uriela's irascible and respectable mother, sister to Jesús, and much less to Jesús's other siblings, or his working nieces and nephews, or the occasional family friend—none could avoid offering Jesús his payment for existing.

Uncle Jesús was one of a kind; one morning, he had told

4

the La Caridad hospital to phone two of his nephews: he'd died of a heart attack, come deal with it. The nephews arrived there almost contrite, and yet, at the top of a staircase, Uncle Jesús had appeared, revived, arms spread out like a cross, his gruff voice demanding a hearty breakfast and a boozing fit for a king. His nephews had indulged him, refusing to be left behind: from then on, they had referred to Jesús as "No Hope."

Officially, Jesús Dolores Santacruz handled tax returns, and he claimed to live off that, off bookkeeping, on a street in the heart of Bogotá, opposite the Ministry of Finance, with a folding table, a stool, and his typewriter. Yet he was so bad at preparing declarations, and so cynical with his questions to his regulars, as if accusing them of avoiding taxes on a treasure trove, that his meager clientele very soon abandoned him.

All this after having been rich and admired as a young man, when he had worn a felt hat and dressed in monochrome, enjoyed a different girl every month, taken friends out for chicken on Sundays, and hit the booze come rain or shine.

One of the things that caused Señora Alma Santacruz to suffer panic attacks were these visits from Jesús, the youngest of her siblings. Why? Nobody knew. She—who wielded a firm hand over her husband, six daughters, three dogs, two cats, and two parrots, and who imposed discipline on an army of employees shared between the house and the farm—seemed frightened of him. Or did she loathe him? A joke buried deep within the family maintained that Jesús had been adopted: he wasn't even afforded the luxury of bastardy. Alma Santacruz's family all had light skin and blue eyes; the men were distinguished for their stature, their foresight in business, their sound judgment, and the women for their beauty and the very fine voices

5

with which they sang boleros; slim and dreamy, they danced the waltz as competently as the tango. In her youth, Alma Santacruz had been a beauty queen in San Lorenzo, the town of her birth, and her sisters were princesses. But, in terms of both looks and character, Jesús, the youngest, was completely different from the others: pug-nosed, small, sallow-skinned, he wasn't practical or successful in the least, but rather a troublemaker, a gambler, and a womanizer; in his youth, he'd been a faithful reader of the pamphleteer José María Vargas Vila and an absolute devotee of the death poet Julio Flórez, whose most lurid verses he would recite from memory:

> *They sawed through his skull*
> *squeezed out his brains,*
> *his now cold heart*
> *they ripped from his chest …*

So, when it came to the Caicedos' big party, Señora Alma Rosa de los Ángeles Santacruz hadn't imagined or hadn't remembered that Jesús even existed. And how could this be? She'd been preoccupied solely with her wedding anniversary.

Alma was sitting in bed, as was her husband, one on either side; she was fifty-two, her husband sixty; they had woken up in each other's arms, more due to the Bogotá cold than to tenderness; they even simulated a hasty amorous encounter, as though humorously parodying those they enjoyed in their youth. To celebrate their anniversary, they had initially planned to travel to Greece, a country they had yet to visit, but, having grown tired of customs and airports, they invented this monumental party instead; now they were going over the various friends and relatives who would be joining them that day; if the pair were guilty of coming up with that party, at least they were happy culprits. And they had just been preparing to have breakfast brought up to them in bed, when Italia—the fifth of their daughters, nineteen, and two years older than Uriela—burst into the room and stood staring at them in silence. She didn't so much as say good morning; she merely stood petrified in front of them, in her pajamas, with long tears dampening her face as she bit her lips until drawing blood. Her parents stared at her in disbelief, still half asleep. Was this a nightmare? What was Italia doing crying her eyes out in silence? She was supposed to be the happiest of their daughters, the most beautiful one, coveted, accommodating, affectionate and effusive, with the clear eyes of an ox.

"What's the matter with you?" asked Alma Santacruz, as her husband, the skilled magistrate Nacho Caicedo, wheezed and put on his slippers.

"I'm pregnant," replied Italia, and started crying again.

2

"Uriela, aren't you going to invite me in for coffee? It isn't easy crossing half the city, under your own steam, with the sole aim of greeting your family and inquiring after their health, my feet hurt, my head is burning, something's gone wrong with the rhythm of my heart. How is Alma, how are your sisters, is the magistrate up yet? Come, Uvita, come down and open the door, and lead me to the kitchen, I need a broth, I'm not asking for the dining room, the kitchen is good enough for me, the broth will taste the same."

"This isn't a good day to visit mamá. She's celebrating her anniversary today, there's going to be a party, with guests arriving, and you already know, Uncle Jesús, how anxious she gets when she sees you. Tomorrow would be preferable."

"A party, a celebration? Oh, Uriela, why so formal? Why not call me plain old Jesús?"

"You already know, Uncle, that in Bogotá we adopt formalities in accordance with our mood, in accordance with the weather, and in accordance with accordances."

"What's with this *you already know, Uncle?* What should I know? I need a coffee, at least, and a few gold coins to pay for the bus, to buy some bread, is that too much to ask? Just go and inform your mother that someone who shares her blood has arrived."

"It isn't convenient, Uncle, it's for your own good. I would be mad to take her news of your arrival."

"Did you say mad or glad? 'I would be glad' sounds far better to me. Ah, if I were still the man of old, the owner of a trucking company, I'd surely be the first to receive an invitation; but a wicked woman put a curse on me, and my twelve trucks tumbled one by one into the abyss. I never recovered, I was pursued, asphyxiated, turned into what I am today, another starveling of this country. What harm could it do to invite me into the kitchen? I repeat that I won't ask for the dining room; your house is as big as a village, it has two floors, an attic like a bedroom in which your old Jesús could quite easily live out his days, a patio with a shrine and a ping-pong table, two gardens: one out here and the other behind; two entrances, the front door and the one round the back; I'll come in through the garden and present myself at the back door, you give me something to eat, offer me two or three gold coins, which I presume you must keep in your money box, and I'll go. You scratch my back and I'll scratch yours, Uriela: with whatever measure you use, it shall be measured back to you. You're a kind girl, sincere, you tell the truth, you're famous for it, but I too am speaking plainly, my legs are trembling, my heart aches, can you see the carotid vein in my neck? It's a blue vein that swells up from time to time, I can feel it throbbing, it's ready to burst, now, now, it's true."

With his index finger, Uncle Jesús was pointing to a spot on his neck. Uriela had leaned farther forward:

"It isn't visible from here," she said. "I can only make out the yellow stain on your shirt, is that mustard?"

"Oh, Uvita, it's mustard from the last hot dog I ate, a whole year ago."

"Then go to the back door, Uncle. We'll meet there, I'll let you in. You can have that broth, that coffee, and I'll give you the gold coins you request, which isn't much."

"God bless you, U," said Uncle Jesús, slipping into the garden with a single leap.

Marino Ojeda was the guard of the street on which the Caicedo home was located. The inhabitants of that opulent residential neighborhood employed a guard to bolster the security of their streets; on the corner, there was a booth, a narrow metal cubicle in which it was only possible to sleep standing up: this was where the guards took shelter from the cold, drank coffee from a thermos, and mustered the energy to resume their watch, walking up and down the street during the night or the day, before being relieved. Ojeda had been assigned the daytime shift, although he would have preferred the night. He was a corpulent young man with indigenous features, a caressing gaze, come to the cold of Bogotá from his village on the coast; he'd been the guard for less than a month and had yet to meet Uncle Jesús, becoming suspicious of him the moment he saw him turn the corner. He had followed him at a prudent distance, shielding himself behind a tree, then watching from there as the man spoke to the youngest of the magistrate's daughters; he watched but didn't hear them, concluding that the young lady had sent a beggar on his way; and, when he saw the beggar hop like a rabbit into the garden and head toward the back door of the house, Ojeda hurried to intercept him and set things straight. That's what he'd been hired for.

But that wasn't the only reason he was getting involved: since the day he arrived, he had been infatuated with the maidservant who worked at the magistrate's house. It wasn't the first time Marino Ojeda had become infatuated. Garrulous and jovial, during his three years of working as a guard in different Bogotá neighborhoods, he had become infatuated on three separate occasions, with identical results: three children Marino Ojeda would never acknowledge, because it was none of his concern, he thought, and even if it was his concern, there was nothing he could do about it: he barely got by. And now another adventure was beginning that dazzled him like never before, because he had never met a more beautiful girl, he claimed, than Iris Sarmiento, the Caicedo family's errand girl, blonde and petite, but with wide hips, and blue, frightened-looking eyes. He had already managed one or two conversations with her, when she would come out to run errands. And Iris Sarmiento appeared to welcome the guard's attentions. At seventeen, the same age as Uriela, she had never had a boyfriend, and now Marino Ojeda had set her dreaming.

Ojeda soon caught up with Jesús in the garden, just as he came to a stop outside the back door. He asked him who he was, where he was going, and why.

"And what's it to you, fuckwit?" the pointy-eared head turned to face him. "You have no idea who I am, dirty louse; don't think that I'm scared of the pathetic rifle you carry; when you were a pup, I was already barking; I know more about life than all your grandparents put together; I should

10

give you a sound whupping; what pigsty did you crawl out of, swine? Scarecrow, scum of the earth, if you want to keep your job as a watchdog, you'd better start running now—and away from me."

Marino Ojeda was taken aback. It was a long time since he had heard this type of choice vocabulary, having spent a year in the Riohacha prison for stealing a grilled chicken. The two men were busy sizing each other up when Uriela appeared at the door.

"It's alright, Marino. This is my uncle Jesús."

In an exaggerated show of gratitude, Uncle Jesús made a deep bow and raised Uriela's hand to his lips. Uriela withdrew her hand, bristling with genuine cold: she recalled the time she had brushed a frog's skin on the farm, damp and smooth, like ice. Behind Uriela, Iris appeared, expectant. She was carrying a mug of hot chocolate and a tamal Santafereño for Marino, because it was a custom for families to take turns serving refreshments to the guard. Uncle Jesús snorted; he glanced at the guard for the last time, with offended dignity, and entered the house with Uriela.

Iris and Marino were left alone, seemingly dumbstruck with happiness.

3

Inside the enormous kitchen, it wasn't only the lifelong employees who could be found—Doña Juana the old house cook, Lucio the gardener, the sexagenarian Zambranito, who, as well as chauffeur, served as electrician and plumber—but also the team of cooks and servants hired to attend the guests that day, guests who, in Juana's words, would turn the house on its head and then leave it for dead. Maids and waiters were coming and going, dressed in uniform. Uncle Jesús gawped:

it's a party, he thought, *and one of the good ones, where anything can happen, from the celestial to the diabolical.* His mouth had dropped open, and he wondered, alarmed, if he was drooling, for he had started to be assailed by that debility, against his will. *I'll need some inspiration*, he thought.

He was aided by the silence of the servants, aided even further by Uriela's brief introduction:

"This is my uncle Jesús."

"A greeting to all who toil and prosper in this house," proclaimed Uncle Jesús, in a powerful voice, drawing on inspiration. "Good day, Señoritas; beauty becomes more beautiful still in young maidens at work; the smell of garlic and onion on your hands is the most seductive perfume. You will be blessed with many children. And good day, Muchachones, energetic youths; respect the girls, strive to serve those who serve us, love them as though they were angels; do not be wicked, do not overwhelm them with looks worse than bites; court them with respect, and then may God bless you, as it should be. And good day also to the one or two old-timers like me, who I can see doing the work of three or even six, old cooks who sweat worse than their saucepans, sorcerers of meat and milk, no less magical for being old, I am Jesús Dolores Santacruz, accountant by trade, brother to Señora Alma Rosa de los Ángeles, light and heart of this family, good day proletariats of all countries. Workers, unite!"

Following a stunned silence, the voices responded in unison to the greeting, but no one considered returning to their tasks; this being appeared to come from another world. Even Uriela was surprised by the greeting. Yet she composed herself:

"Some broth, some breakfast, whatever my uncle Jesús requests: pretend he's the first guest to arrive."

"Thank you, Urielita. I've never heard more generous words."

Solemnly, as though not feeling the pangs of hunger, as though playing hard to get, Uncle Jesús sat down at the head of a long bare table, surrounded by other tables covered in plates and cups and glasses, all brimming with fruit and birds and ham. *Food for a century,* he thought, enraptured. Only then did he discover that, at the opposite end of the table, there sat some kind of ghostly shadow. It was the house gardener, holding a half-finished cup of coffee, it was Don Lucio Rosas, in his fifties like Jesús, his mouth open like Jesús, with the same surprise in his eyes—or in one eye, for the other was missing: he wore a black patch over his left eye.

Uncle Jesús seemed not to appreciate this stranger looking at him with his single, uncertain eye; he didn't greet him—*not even the faintest acknowledgment,* thought Uriela, stunned, *what an infernal uncle.*

The employees resumed their duties, hurrying to and fro, on tiptoe, soundlessly.

"Well!" Uncle Jesús brought them all to a standstill once again, raising his voice. The servants listened in: "Sitting at the table with a stranger who is lame in his right leg and missing his left eye is a sign of good fortune!"

Uriela couldn't help but laugh.

"Uncle," she whispered, "stick to what we agreed. Eat and then go, here you are." She placed an envelope of money in his hand.

"Sit down beside me, U," grunted Uncle Jesús, as he slipped the envelope into his pocket like a magic trick. "It isn't good to eat alone. He who eats alone, dies alone. But he who eats with a lame, one-eyed stranger eats doubly alone."

13

Uriela shook her head and sat down resignedly beside her uncle. In that moment, she recalled how she had never had a proper conversation with him, except during that brief Radio Nacional odyssey, a century ago, when she was ten years old and her uncle had taken her along to the *Know-it-all Bunny* competition for children. These days, her uncle was nothing but a tramp who came to visit every month, shutting himself in with her mother and then leaving the house. Who was this Uncle Jesús? Why did he offend people with his words? Lucio didn't have a limp in his right leg; it's true he was missing his left eye, he wore that patch …

Lucio Rosas, who as well as being a good gardener also had his pride, corroborated this:

"Mister," he stated, as if on the point of exploding, "I've been this family's gardener for twenty years. I live on the Melgar farm. Today, Señora Alma has tasked me with spreading roses and tuberoses throughout the house. That's why I'm here, mister. I'm missing an eye, yes. But I'm not lame."

"You might as well be," replied Jesús. "I don't say that to offend." And he looked around, serenely: "How does a man of this Earth lose an eye?"

There was a mortified silence. The question, its absurdity, the way it was phrased, surprised everyone, and it saddened Uriela.

The gardener had not been anticipating this line of questioning, but he plucked up his courage:

"My work itself snatched my eye, mister. It was ten years ago, when I was using the motorized lawnmower for the first time. A stone skipped up at me. A treacherous stone, mister, hidden in the grass. It took my eye, burst it. That's how a man of this earth loses an eye."

This response satisfied the waiters, who exchanged quick glances. Some smiled, and this did not go unnoticed by Jesús.

"No," he countered. "You had a debt to pay. And you paid it. You paid it with your eye. It was destiny."

This time, it was the gardener whose jaw dropped in disbelief; he stared straight ahead, believing that he found before him a wretch of a man, a poisonous insect:

"If it wasn't for the respect I bear for Magistrate Caicedo and his wife, who gave me work and lodging on their farm, who are the godparents to my child, and if it wasn't for the presence of Señorita Uriela, I'd … "

"I'd?" coaxed Jesús, then immediately ignored the threat. "Listen everyone. Stop rushing around. You need to stop and think from time to time. When a person works like you do, they don't think. Why are you yawning?" he asked suddenly, looking at the head cook Juana, Juana Colima, the old house cook, who had stopped for a moment, hands on her hips, to listen. "When you yawn, your soul gets out, Doña Juana, cover your mouth when yawning; and if you fail to cover it, trap your soul with your fingers and swallow it down again, or you'll be left soulless."

The old cook hadn't opened her mouth to yawn, but rather to gulp. She was already well acquainted with Jesús. That man—she summarized it in three words—gave her indigestion. She forced a smile. Lucio the gardener finished his coffee. Without a word, he left the kitchen and made for the inner garden of the house, to a hiding place in the greenhouse that was his lair.

Uncle Jesús wasn't smiling.

"Uncle," said Uriela. "Aren't you going to eat?"

For a maid had already set a bowl of broth down in front of him.

"Please remember that I'm not starving," he hissed under his breath. And then, addressing everyone: "Well, if you insist, I don't want to be rude, here I go!"

He raised the bowl between his trembling hands and polished off the broth without any fuss, before the perplexed eyes of the servants. He gulped it down like a convict subjected to hunger torture.

He must be crazy, thought Uriela, *he's going to burn himself.*

Because the broth was steaming and spilling from his mouth, dampening his neck. Then he trapped the chicken foot at the bottom of the bowl, paring and polishing it in the blink of an eye. And, without taking his eyes from the ceiling or the heavens, as birds do when they drink, he ended up licking what was left in the bowl and requesting seconds, which he chewed and swallowed all in one go, then burped, grunted, and stood up.

"Now I'm leaving," he said.

Then he faltered.

Discreetly, the employees resumed their tasks like milling ghosts. Uncle Jesús headed for the door, hesitantly. Suddenly, he turned back to everyone and spluttered:

"I think I'm dying."

Uriela closed her eyes, then opened them again. Why did these things always happen to her?

"Uncle," she said. "I'll see you to the door."

"Don't take me just yet," Jesús rebuked her. "First let me sleep. A brief nap and then I'll follow my path to the end of the world."

And to everyone's astonishment, he made for a corner of the kitchen—a nook by the base of an oven—curled up on the floor, and fell into a deep sleep—or at least, that's how it appeared.

The old cook Juana Colima realized that Niña Uriela couldn't handle her uncle: she'll never be able to wake him, she repeated to herself, disappearing up to madam's bedroom in a flash to warn her in secret. She entered confidently, not even noticing Italia, slumped in a chair in front of her father. Juana Colima approached her mistress and whispered these winged words in her ear:

"Your brother Jesús is here, he said he was dying and lay down to sleep or die under the oven."

Never has a woman's scream been as great as the silent scream let out by Alma Santacruz.

"My god," she cried. "This is all I need today!"

4

At that moment, Francia, the eldest Caicedo sister, having recently turned twenty-seven, was in her bedroom, sitting at a desk presided over by a framed photo of Rodolfo Cortés, her fiancé—an engagement only her sisters and bosom friend Teresa Alcoba were aware of.

She was poring over documents required by the notary to effectuate her name change, the first of the magistrate's daughters to rebel against her name. She had yet to consider what alternative she would choose, and didn't much care whether it was Lucila or Josefa or María; she simply wanted to change her name as soon as possible, to rid herself of the absurd name Francia, born of who knows what passions, what outlandish quirk of her father's brain—*for there are some quirks that aren't actually outlandish*, she thought.

The magistrate Ignacio Caicedo had been able to come up with no better names for his daughters than the countries and cities where they were conceived—at two-year intervals.

Francia was called Francia, because it was in France that Nacho Caicedo and Alma Santacruz celebrated their honeymoon, in the soft beds of Paris and the burning ones of Marseille. The second sister had been the result of a rekindling of passions in Portugal, and was called Lisboa; the third was called Armenia, capital of the Quindío department; the fourth, Palmira, a city in Valle del Cauca; and the fifth, Italia. Uriela escaped being named after a city because, on the eve of her birth, her mother had dreamed the Archangel Uriel had visited her with news of a surprise from God, which would arrive in the form of an illuminated flower. With the result that, on the day of the baptism, and to the astonishment of Monsignor Hidalgo and the magistrate, Señora Alma insisted on the name Uriela. And thus Uriela was spared, by a miracle, for otherwise it would have befallen her to be named Bogotá.

This notion, this fancy—which some relatives defined as temporary insanity—of baptizing his daughters with the names of countries and cities did not appear out of character for the magistrate. As a young man, as with the majority of young men of his generation, he had fancied himself a poet, and being a poet entailed nothing more than distinguishing yourself from the rest, for better or worse. Of this sickness, the only poetry that remained to the magistrate was the selection of his daughters' names. For the rest, he was a diligent lawyer, like each and every one of the country's lawyers—as Ignacio Caicedo himself confessed—who study less for the purpose of applying justice than for making a mockery of it. Even so, the injustices he practiced weren't too aberrant, and he passed for an honest criminal lawyer, author of a doctoral thesis that was lauded by the College of Lawyers: "On the Legality and Necessity of the Expropriation of Indigenous Lands by the State." He was a friend to important political figures, including an ex-President of the Republic. He was a politician himself, a member of the Conservative Party, and, on the day of the assassination of the Liberal firebrand Jorge Eliécer Gaitan in 1948, the deadly mob had been on the brink of crucifying him, literally, "at a port on the Pacific coast whose name I do not wish to recall," he would say.

Ignacio—or Nacho—Caicedo had a well-earned reputation for eloquence, for being a philosopher and a soothsayer: he took advantage of any occasion to reveal what the world would be like in ten, twenty, fifty, and a hundred years. His speeches at the Supreme Court of Justice were intelligent and applauded not only by Conservatives, but by Liberals too; he pursued conciliation on the benches, the good of the people, and was always praised for such efforts, precisely because his efforts never bore fruit, but—as he himself put it—one had to persist in order to keep up appearances.

Although Francia would not have time that Friday of the anniversary to complete her application for a name change, she made herself a promise to do it the following Monday, first thing: *I don't have many hours left of being Francia*, she thought, *and then I'll be called I don't know what, but something that suits me.*

On top of her desk, there was a small yellow envelope with her name and address. She hadn't noticed it until that moment; it had a postage stamp dated the week before; *what an oversight on Iris's part*, she thought, *not delivering my correspondence into my hands, it could be news of a death, and me left not knowing, after a week's delay—but how melodramatic of me, who would die?*

Francia, slim and delicate like her sisters—all of a spiritual slenderness, accentuated by their melancholic eyes—had graduated in architecture in December of the previous year. While completing her degree, she had dreamed of going to do a master's and a doctorate in Canada, but her boyfriend and fiancé Rodolfo Cortés, a biologist who'd also recently graduated, had intervened. According to him, the first step toward attaining happiness was to get married, and the second was to have children and live in Cali, in a house with a pool, near his parents' home. The dream of a master's and a doctorate had gone up in smoke.

On the flap of the yellow envelope was the return address of Teresa Alcoba, Francia's best friend, who now lived in Cali. This intrigued her, because Teresita only ever communicated by telephone. She opened the envelope, instantly recognizing her friend's handwriting, and read, avidly. The short note was accompanied by a folded newspaper clipping. The smile on Francia's face faded as she read:

> Forgive me, dear Francia, it is my duty as your friend to make you aware of the truth—do not suffer.
> Suffer only what is necessary.
> This too shall pass.
>
> Teresa

The newspaper clipping unfurled before her eyes like the vile body of a deadly snake, which suddenly propelled its head toward her and sank its teeth into her soul: there was a photo of Rodolfito Cortés, her fiancé, in a dress suit, those large amphibian eyes peering back at the camera, with his name underneath, in printed letters:

> Newly graduated biologist Rodolfo Cortés Mejía tonight announces his marriage to Hortensia Burbano Alvarado, graduate of the Apóstol Santiago College, at Club Colombia in Cali. Attending will be the governor of Valle, father of the bride, His Excellency ...

She was unable to carry on reading. The newspaper clipping fell at her feet. She went pale, glacial, observing in disbelief how night came down all around her, first over her eyes, then inside her.

And then she fainted.

5

The early arrival of the brothers Ike and Ricardo Castañeda, nephews to Alma Santacruz, was providential. Their aunt gave instructions for them to be immediately shown through to the small parlor, a private chamber to one side of the dinalone.

The two brothers had arrived on their motorcycles; they were the same pair Jesús had once requested to be phoned from the hospital, with the lie about his death. They were contemporaries of Francia and Lisboa, but, unlike Francia, they hadn't finished their degrees and never would: they each enjoyed roles at the Ministry of Justice, where they had already been recognized as Doctors of Law. This standing, as well as their posts, which would have appealed to genuine lawyers with experience, was a gift from Magistrate Caicedo, who occasionally used his influence to assist family members, lavishing upon them roles of great responsibility. These uses and abuses of power did not bother the magistrate: they were something that needed to happen, something anyone in the country would have done in his position.

Ever since childhood, Ike Castañeda had suffered from a mad infatuation with Francia, an unfettered idolatry, he claimed, and he'd arrived at the party early in the hope of catching her alone: in the immoderation of his love, he wished that day to ask her to marry him. Ricardo, his lieutenant, felt an obligation on his part to find himself hopelessly in love with Lisboa, the second of the Caicedo sisters, a shy nursing student. Ricardo was Ike's confidante, backing and seconding his brother, acting as his messenger and secretary, and was eternally grateful for Ike's advice on defending his cushy job at the ministry, where, following precisely this advice, he had joined the union; Ike assured him that this would prevent them ever getting rid of him, that even the biggest imbeciles, the most inept, could not be laid off once they had joined the union, adding that it was a good idea to divide their forces: Ike would work by the side of the bosses, Ricardo among the subordinates, and in this way they would cover each other's backs like spies and counterspies—*like in the movies*, thought Ricardo, captivated.

Alma Santacruz entered the parlor, distraught; she was still in her bathrobe, and her face was so full of remorse that her nephews assumed someone had just died, surely the magistrate—who else could it be in that family of six unsacrificed nubile sisters? They grew uneasy, for without the magistrate's patronage, life would become difficult for them at the ministry. But on discovering the reason for their aunt's affliction, the brothers laughed in unison, reassured: it all related to that No Hope, no one else. What needed to be done? Impatient but wary, they listened to their aunt, whose reputation for being quick-tempered was legendary. Their Aunt Alma, as generous as she was authoritarian, seemed genuinely distressed. They tried to glean the absurd meaning behind her words:

"Jesús said in the kitchen that he was going to die, and now he's asleep or dead in the kitchen, or he's playing dead and sleeping, with him you're never certain; he intends to remain in this house, in the middle of the party, and he's more than capable of taking to the dance floor with Monsignor Hidalgo, who will be arriving soon. Here are the keys to the station wagon. You'll find him in the kitchen; if he doesn't cooperate, if he doesn't wake up, carry him to the garage, by kindness or by force, put him inside the station wagon, and take him far away—very far away—from Bogotá. Well, not too far, but outside Bogotá, maybe Chía or Tabio, you

22

choose, and pay for his hotel and meals for three days. He mustn't return to this house today, that's the fucking point. God and I will know how to repay you."

And she handed Ike a wad of cash to cover expenses. Ike pocketed the wad but protested:

"Can't Zambranito take him, Auntie? Zambranito is the chauffeur, after all."

"I don't want anyone finding out about this decision; let this episode remain between blood. Zambranito is taking the Mercedes to pick up Adelfa and Emperatriz, who are my sisters, as you may well recall. And Adelfa is bringing your sisters. Are you scared?"

"Never," snapped Ike, his mood soured. "I'm just worried we'll be late for the party."

"Late? You'll be back in time for lunch, your plates will be waiting for you. The party starts this afternoon, and Cecelito's orchestra will deafen us from three onwards. It's no more than an hour from here to Chía; if you add another hour for the return journey, that's two hours, a breath in a lifetime. Now get moving, you layabouts, pick him up and get rid of him."

Señora Alma handed the keys of the station wagon to the disgruntled Ike, the elder of the Castañedas, and she traced the sign of the cross over the brothers' heads, as if blessing not only their heads but also the dangerous task they were undertaking.

Ike and Ricardo raced to the kitchen.

6

There was that No Hope, in the fetal position, beneath the loitering servants—and beneath their skirts, discovered Ike, admiring the number of young women in caps and aprons who were all curious to discover if the dead man would be reborn: their vaporous skirts flew above the dead man, and you might even believe, thought perceptive Ike, that this cunning uncle was keeping half an eye open, rising to glimpse that which he would never devour.

"Alright, Uncle Jesús," he said, "we're going for a little trip. If you feel bad, we'll take you to the doctor, help us to help you, come on now."

There was no response.

Ike started gripping him under the armpits, Ricardo by the legs. A whisper of admiration spread around the kitchen: the maids were in the front row, their mouths open, their eyes wide; farther back were the waiters, and, much further still, Uriela with Doña Juana and Zambranito. Uriela wanted to know what her cousins intended to do with her uncle, wanted to spy on them without being discovered: Ike and Ricardo struck her as a pair of strange clowns, and weren't they also in love with Francia and Lisboa, how similar they were, she thought, what ghouls.

Though not dealing with a big fat man—more like a sack of bones—after only three steps the Castañedas could go no further with the corpse. Just like a corpse, Uncle Jesús had gone limp, making himself heavier. Juana's eyes expressed laughter and sadness at the same time:

"Where are you taking him?" she couldn't resist asking.

"To the garage," replied Ricardo, looking around as though expecting someone to help them. Zambranito, the sexagenarian chauffeur and handyman, wasn't listening: he knew that hammering in a nail wasn't the same thing as carrying a dead man. The waiters stood still: this wasn't what they'd been hired for. Doña Juana sighed; her curiosity would not be satisfied: she wanted to know where, outside the house, they were taking him, what country—for she was convinced that there was no country from which Uncle Jesús would not return.

Again, the brothers strained; this was now a humiliation they endured. It had never been their intention to demonstrate their weakness in this way, publicly. "Are you seeing this, Ike?" moaned Ricardo, wearily.

"Excuse me, I can help," came a cavernous voice, arriving from who knows what coldness.

It was the gardener.

Lucio Rosas advanced as quickly as he did calmly, leaning down and gripping the corpse, lifting it with just one arm and throwing it over his shoulder.

To Ike, it seemed his uncle Jesús opened one eye, in terror, but remained motionless, more dead than alive. In this way, they headed to the garage, the two brothers behind Lucio and the dead man, in a slow procession. The gardener set down the corpse, laid it out on the back seat of the station wagon, and turned to the brothers.

"All set," he said.

"Lucio," said Ike, "are you working at the moment? You see, I've just had an idea."

"No work, sir. I'm at your service."

"Come with us, Lucio, in case we need your help with taking him out."

From inside the station wagon, there came the sound of something moving—the dead man? Yes, it was the dead man, listening to them.

As one, the two brothers jumped into the front of the station wagon. In the back sat Lucio the gardener, with Jesús's head in his lap. The Ford's motor purred into life in the garage, the air becoming suffused with bitter smoke, and Doña Juana herself opened the doors to the morning light, she opened them looking radiant and rejuvenated. "Let them take him," she yelled through gritted teeth, "let them take him to hell!"

7

Twenty years earlier, in 1950, Lucio Rosas had not been a gardener; he'd been an Oster blender salesman, from door to door.

Aside from his wife, whom he'd recently married, Lucio had two passions: cultivating medicinal plants—plants he talked to—and hunting: from time to time, he would go out hunting, the old shotgun slung over his shoulder and a straw hat on his head, like a mythical duende. He also talked to the turtledoves, after hunting them, because talking to turtledoves and plants seemed preferable to talking to himself, and in the year since they'd been married, he and his wife appeared to have said everything they had to say to each other; they were mute. They enjoyed going to the movies, and liked the crime thrillers best of all, but once they left the cinema, they wouldn't even exchange impressions, that's how mute they were.

They lived on the second floor of a rental house in a working-class neighborhood. In those days, there was still a clear-water river, forests, and blue mountains around the back of the neighborhood. The song of the turtledoves in the thicket called to him: shrewd birds, not at all easy, they would swim zigzaggingly through the air, dancing, and then glide and swoop and rise, almost mockingly. He didn't care about the Andean sparrows, or the weasels and shrews, much less about the sparrowhawks or blackbirds or spot-flanked gallinules or guinea pigs. He had an understanding with turtledoves. On their winged trail, he would be spurred to

26

rise early and set off into the mountains surrounding the city, which were damp and alive. In contrast to the forests, Bogotá itself still lay in devastation. Two years earlier, in the wake of the Liberal firebrand's assassination, the people, now lacking an intellect to channel them, like a river that bursts its banks, had dedicated themselves to getting drunk and setting fires, and still the city had not recovered: everywhere, there was scorched brickwork; Bogotá sounded like a ravaged heart. That's why Lucio Rosas would lose himself in the mountains: to forget Bogotá.

He would hunt, but one morning he had become deflated. In a clearing in the trees, sitting on a rotted trunk, his shotgun lying defeated on the ground, he began to feel a deep sadness, as if he understood that this day would be a bad one: remembering this later, he would be shocked that he had sensed his impending tragedy. But instead of fleeing from the premonition, he had allowed himself to be drawn in: he didn't feel like killing another turtledove, what for? Better to let them fly. He'd had his soul's fill of turtledove meat; his wife didn't know any more ways to prepare it, she kept serving it in brine, in stews and roasts and hot pots; he liked it best with onion sauce; but he'd grown fed up. "If only I could hunt a deer," he lamented, returning to his home in the sleeping neighborhood.

The house he lived in had three floors, all rented to families. He lived on the second floor, with his wife and plants. It was an ancient house, the kind with arabesques on the ceilings and a back gate once used for horses; each floor had a balcony; just as he did every time he climbed the muddy slope, like an involuntary greeting, Lucio Rosas raised his eyes up to his balcony, and it was there that he discovered him: a perching thief. Without thinking twice, Lucio gripped his shotgun and took aim.

The gunshot woke no one, as tends to happen in this city accustomed to gunshots. There were no witnesses, and it seemed impossible to prove that the thief was a thief: he was from the neighborhood, one Josecito Arteaga, a cobbler by trade. Josecito's widow made her accusation: her husband was many things, but a thief wasn't one of them.

No one contradicted her, despite the fact that the whole neighborhood knew that Josecito Arteaga *was* a thief. He may have been a cobbler by trade, but he was also a thief—or else he was a thief by trade who also cobbled on the side. More than one person had had an ironing board or a chair or a suitcase stolen by Josecito; it's likely people felt sorry for him, and that's why there were never any complaints: Josecito Arteaga was just an innocent citizen of those parts. Lucio Rosas couldn't pay what the widow's lawyer was demanding, in settlement, and was now staring into the abyss of who knows how many years of jail time. He was immediately fired from his position as a salesman. Regrettably, the public defender assigned to represent him was the worst news of all: from the start, he gave the case up for lost, asking Lucio if he'd ever considered the possibility that the thief robbing his house might not have been a thief at all, but rather his wife's lover.

"I'd have killed him even worse," said Lucio Rosas. "I'd have killed him twice, mister."

He said this without irony, employing his customary frankness.

And his response was overheard by the lawyer Nacho Caicedo, who had been visiting the prison. Nacho Caicedo, twenty years younger and more compassionate, not yet a magistrate, listened in on the gardener's words. And he liked what he heard.

He took on his defense pro bono, expounding before the jury on the tremendous irony, the terrifying reality, of a neighborhood in which nobody—not even out of mercy, or simple caprice, or even to overcome their fear—absolutely nobody had decided to come forward and report the fact that the deceased was a thief through and through: *the neighborhood thief*. Yet at last, he had stated during his defense, a number of compassionate souls had testified. Just as there exists a town fool, so too there is a thief; sympathy for the widow should not preclude justice; there is only one justice, and it travels in one direction, and while it's true that Colombian justice may limp and limp and never arrive, one day, sooner or later, it would arrive, let there be no doubt about that; Lucio Rosas was innocent; he had suffered damages, injuries, and he deserved compensation from the State, as well as a public apology.

There was to be no compensation or apology, but Lucio Rosas emerged a free man. His benefactor went further: in light of the fact that Lucio had lost his job, he asked him what he did and what he was good at, hiring him as the gardener for his farm in Melgar. Lucio Rosas would be grateful for the rest of his life; he would have died for Magistrate Caicedo. He had not only gained new employment, but would be moving with his wife to the farm, with lots of trees and plants and fine weather.

But there was one cloud in his sky: the gunshot and the death of Josecito Arteaga. He could never rid himself of that. This is why, when Jesús asked in the kitchen how a man of this earth loses an eye, responding that it must have been to settle a debt, Lucio Rosas had been shaken to his core. Was that wretch of a man referring to his destiny? Could he be aware of his past? Did he know? Of course not, but even so, that big-eared fiend, why had he said what he did, why did he have to say that?

Lucio Rosas shuddered again inside the station wagon, with the head of that wretch of a man in his lap.

8

And the dead man awoke. He sat up. It was time to resuscitate.

"What's going on with this world?" he asked. "Where am I?"

The two brothers turned to face Uncle Jesús.

"So you're awake, dead uncle," said Ike, and pulled over to the side of the road. "Great, because we need to talk."

"What am I doing in the station wagon? When did you bring me here? I was in the kitchen with Uriela, I think I got vertigo, I fell asleep, who is this man?"

And he warily examined the stony, one-eyed man sitting next to him, as though he had never met him before.

"There's no turning back, Uncle, it's perfectly simple. We're following orders. In brief, my aunt Alma has given us a one-way ticket for you, my dearest uncle, to the end of the world. She told us to take you to Chía—or was it China?—and to leave you in a hotel for three days, all expenses paid. Why? So you don't make an appearance at the party, Uncle, so you don't mess things up."

"What's this about me not messing things up," huffed Uncle Jesús, "since when have you been so disrespectful toward me? I'm your uncle, your mamá's brother, in case you'd forgotten, ingrate."

"You're the last person in the world I should be grateful to," responded Ike. "Nobody is grateful to you, but you should be grateful to the world. Listen, Uncle, I have a proposal, and I'm being serious. You may be an uncle, but we all know what kind of uncle you are, and how you always go around putting your foot in it. This time, it's Aunt Alma's anniversary we're talking about, and neither she nor I want any trouble. Listen, don't interrupt me. We've come with Lucio, my aunt's gardener, do you recognize him? It's just occurred to me that he should be the one tasked with taking you to Chía. Aunt Alma gave me this"—here Ike extended and waved the wad of cash before Jesús's eyes—"to pay for your hotel, hopefully for three days. She recommended I not give you a centavo. I'm handing the money to Lucio—here you go, Don Lucio, receive this as an order and take my uncle to a hotel in Chía or to the moon, but somewhere far away, and for three days."

Uncle Jesús observed the scene, horrified: Lucio Rosas stowed the money in his pocket.

"The highway's not far, you can see it," said Ricardo, point- ing with his finger. "There you can catch the bus to Chía. You can't miss it."

"Never," yelled Jesús, indignantly. "I'm not moving from here!" He rolled down the window to let some air in and crossed his arms.

"Uncle," said Ike, "if you're canny, if you're intelligent, as you've led us to believe you are, you'll get out of this car with Lucio, then you can convince him to let you stay in Bogotá, but well guarded inside your home. That way, he can pass the hotel money on to you, into your hands. You'll obviously have to give a cut to Lucio, who agreed to carry you from the kitchen to the station wagon and who, one way or another, has had to suffer you. But a word to the wise: if you take that money and don't keep your end of the bargain, showing up at my aunt's house, I swear to God that I'll hat-whip you out of there myself, because you'll have made me look bad, get it? I'll warm your backside with kicks myself, uncle or not.

I won't be the first nephew to have dealt with his mean and stubborn uncle. Now get out and decide. Get out the both of you, because we don't have fucking time, they're waiting for us at my aunt's house."

"This isn't very fair," Uncle Jesús had begun to protest, sinking farther into his seat, when Ike jumped out and raced to the back door, behind which his uncle was taking shelter, hauling him out by the underarms in one go and leaving him there, sitting on the sidewalk.

"You get out too, Lucio," he yelled.

Lucio Rosas climbed down from the station wagon, impassive. Uncle Jesús, as surprised as he was shaken, was still trying to say something when Ike spoke again. He was now incomprehensible:

"Lucio, take this monstrosity to Chía or to the other side, but take him and make sure he doesn't come back, and remember: these are my aunt's orders!"

Ike got back in the station wagon and pressed his foot down on the accelerator. The tires screeched. *Like in the movies,* thought Ricardo, turning to look out of the window. On the increasingly distant horizon, he could see Lucio approach Uncle Jesús and spread his arms, as if to prevent him escaping. Uncle Jesús wasn't going to escape, thought Ricardo: he was all too aware who was holding the money, and, furthermore, he would start talking, become inspired. Would he convince Lucio? he asked himself, before replying: *he'll convince him.*

Ike Castañeda was only thinking about Francia, his venerated cousin. They hadn't seen each other in a month. A month ago, in the parlor, he had kissed her on the mouth for a few mortal seconds, without any opposition.

Lisboa and Armenia Caicedo were already dressed for the party. They had convened in the second-floor sitting room, where the house's largest mirror hung.

"You're a princess," said Lisboa, gazing into the mirror.

"Who are you talking to," asked Armenia, "me or your reflection?"

Both were decked out in floor-length gowns, their hair gathered at the nape, their shoulders and arms bare. They laughed, contemplating each other, and then, arm in arm, still laughing, ran down the long corridor toward Francia's bedroom.

They found her lying on her back, passed out, one hand covering her eyes as if only recently returned to life.

Palmira, the fourth sister, had just arrived, and Lisboa—who was a nursing student after all—instructed her like a doctor to fetch a glass of water and some aspirin. When Palmira returned, they had already lain Francia down on her bed, her head between pillows.

She was weeping furtively.

Her sisters sat down on either side of the bed. When they asked her to explain what had happened, Francia merely pointed to the newspaper clipping on the floor. Palmira read it aloud, as Armenia and Lisboa shook their heads in disapproval. Francia took sips from her glass of water, having refused the aspirin. She had a lost look in her eyes. She seemed to have grown skinnier and always appeared sadder than she actually felt, without meaning to. But this time, her sadness was truly destroying her.

"But who could have imagined it," said Armenia. "What a little son of a bitch that Rodolfo is, with his toad face, what a sissy!"

"I ask that you please refrain from using that foul language," ordered the eldest sister, horrified, her voice hoarse, "I have a stomach ache." And she told them to pass her the newspaper clipping, tucking it under her pillow.

Although not bearing a strong resemblance to each other, the Caicedo sisters all displayed the same tinge of sorrow in their gaze. It wasn't quite tenderness, but almost. A tinge of melancholia that, from one moment to the next, could become a mortal joke, a reinvigorated attitude—from one second to the next—of the eyes and eyebrows; those who had dealings with them, friends and boyfriends, were unable to explain it. That facial expression, thought Uriela, that curious reticence, which invited you to defend them—"but who asked you to defend me?"—hadn't come from their mother, who had an imposing gaze, but rather from their father's family, a sinuous line of lawyers of which Nacho was the greatest exponent, the pinnacle, the model. Uriela considered her father to be "the greatest specimen of his family." Three of her sisters, Armenia, Italia, and Palmira, were already studying law, convinced by her father that it was the profession the country was most in need of, and would provide them handsome benefits. Uriela was only just finishing high school and hadn't decided what degree to take. This was her tragedy: she could be good at anything, and yet, for that very reason, believed she was good for nothing. In fact—and this was a secret kept to herself—she didn't want to continue studying; it seemed to her that both her primary and high school education had been nothing but a waste of her time.

And yet, the six sisters diverged from that sinuousness. They were transparent, in their own way. Ten years separated the eldest from the youngest. They were happy about their

34

parents' anniversary party. Not only would their cousins be coming, but there was also sure to be some new face appearing amid the family tedium for the first time. Nevertheless, Francia's fainting spell had crushed their plans. They thought she looked deranged.

"I'll call myself Abandonada," she was saying. "No. Better Repudiada. Or Despreciada Caicedo Santacruz. That's what I'll change my name to."

"Don't be silly," said Armenia. "What we should do is beat the shit out of that scumbag. I thought I heard our cousins Ike and Ricardo arriving. Just tell them to snap the limbs of that little lamb and you'll have your revenge served cold, Francia."

"Get her out of here!" said Francia, waving her hand as if shooing a mosquito.

They all laughed.

"What outrages me," Francia continued to herself, "is discovering that he lied to me. And he'll be coming, he's coming to the house, to this party, he has the gall to come here without a hint of shame. Only yesterday, he was asking me about the best present for papá, who's done him so many favors, even getting him that wonderful post at the Ministry of Health, helping him buy the Renault 4 … he said we were getting married, I ironed his shirts, I used to iron them … "

Francia started crying again.

"Maybe the announcement is a lie," whispered prudent Palmira. "Maybe someone paid for that announcement so you'd get sick like this and throw it all away."

"No," said Francia. "He's a pig. The announcement is real. He's been different for a while now, he won't even touch me … you understand what I'm referring to?"

They all laughed.

"What a brute," said Lisboa. "Would he dare to come?"

"I'll give him one hell of a greeting," Francia assured them.

"Don't worry about that. But don't any of you go getting involved."

"It's up to you," said Armenia. "But let me know if you need me. I can help."

"Let's not sink to his level," said Lisboa. "We should simply slam the door in his face. Say you're not welcome in this house, get lost, slimeball."

"You too, Lisboa?" said Francia, with a howl of warning. "I'll handle my own affairs. This fainting spell was a trick of the heart, I'm not setting any store by it. I'll handle my own affairs, because they're mine alone, nobody else's, you all keep out of it."

This admonition from their eldest sister relaxed them all. Things were defined now. Francia would know how to handle it.

And, as if nothing had happened, they continued to lean their faces, their dresses, toward the long mirror in Francia's bedroom, tirelessly, in search of their own image, speculating on the possibilities of the dance, the live orchestra. What music would they play? *Today's the day I'll meet somebody, it must be,* Lisboa was thinking to herself. That's when they discovered that peerless Francia, the eldest, the most even-tempered, the most practical of them all, was sitting on her bed and eating the newspaper clipping whole.

She was chewing it, her eyes submerged in a deep fury, her body hunched forward, her hair tangling between sharp fingernails.

"Don't eat newspaper," came the voice of Uriela.

When had she arrived?

She was the youngest of all the sisters, but her voice sounded like the oracle; they listened to it because it told plain truths.

"Ink is toxic, and the stuff they use in newspapers is pure bile, it could make a hole in your stomach," she said.

Francia immediately began expelling the newspaper clipping as though vomiting it up.

"Italia," concluded the magistrate, his broad hairy hand on his daughter's shoulder, "you aren't the first, and you won't be the last. The only thing to keep in mind is that we're with you. You'll have the child, your child, my first grandchild; we'll love that child here, we'll protect it. You've told us that your friend … what was your friend's name?"

"I call him by his surname."

"Which is?"

"De Francisco."

"De Francisco," repeated the magistrate, shrugging—*the "de" is a mere appendage*, he told himself. "And where does your De Francisco live?"

"In El Chicó."

El Chicó was a neighborhood one tier above the one in which the Caicedo home stood. The magistrate nodded, gravely:

"But what is his name? You aren't telling me that couples these days call each other by their surnames."

"Porto."

"Almost Oporto, like the wine region?"

"That's why I call him by his surname."

Father and daughter were avoiding looking at each other.

"And Porto's papá, what does he do?"

"He's owner of the Pollo Real grilled chicken chain," said Italia, with a hint of sarcasm.

"Well," said the magistrate, "you can find one of those chickens on every corner."

Porto de Francisco, nineteen years old like Italia, a first-year law student, was supposed to break the news to his parents first thing in the morning; he had agreed to this with Italia, to reveal the truth to his parents at the same time, just as Italia was doing at that moment, and yet Porto de Francisco would not and did not dare, preferring to carry on sleeping.

Italia was aware of this, for she had phoned Porto that morning, and he hadn't answered. Such cowardice, when they had both agreed to confess everything at the same time, combining their cosmic energies, they said, to declare that they would be keeping their child, such cowardice led her to finally discover where she was, the exact position in the world where she found herself: *alone*.

That's why she was crying.

But it wasn't the only reason.

She didn't want the child.

She didn't know who to turn to for help.

Where not to have that child.

Because, by the looks of things, her parents hadn't even considered this possibility. They were abandoning her, handing her over to that child, for the rest of her life.

PART TWO

1

For the Caicedos' big celebration, Cousin César could think of no cleverer notion than to arrive riding on a white mule. As it turned the corner, the mule rang out like a carnival: it was wearing a cacophonous necklace of cowbells, with small tinkling bells on its mane and knees, and carnations in its ears; it held its head high, its hooves clacked, its tail flicked up, its brow shone, and all along the street house-wives commented on its progress, from window to window. Kids sitting in the gardens spied on the procession, each one dressed as a baseball player, like kids from New York. Cousin César's face, identical to a huge grinning mask, looked to left and right, just to make sure everyone was watching him. He was a fat man in his forties, cheerful, freckled like all redheads, and he knew how to ride. He was escorted by an immaculate Chevrolet, ten feet behind him, keeping pace with the mule. The car was being driven by Perla Tobón, César's wife, in the company of her sister Tina. Squirming on the back seat were César Santacruz's three sons: Cesítar, Cesarito, and Cesarín.

The magistrate watched them arrive, attentive; he was a discreet shadow behind his bedroom curtain. All looking radiant, his six daughters waved down from the balcony: no, it wasn't all six of them, he confirmed, Uriela was missing. His wife, still in her bathrobe, had gone down to the front door, laughing with as much apprehension as joy. César was her favorite nephew: "Careful you don't fall off, fatty!" She was accompanied by Juana, Iris, and Zambranito. Iris's voice could be heard, exultant as a little girl's. Marino, the guard, was also witnessing the guest's arrival: no sooner had he heard about the party than he phoned his night relief and told him not to come, he would carry on until the next morning, and now he was spying from the front row, though he had no interest in the mule or its rider, but rather in Iris, who, on madam's orders, had put on a tight, dark skirt that went well with her golden hair. *And that white blouse*, thought Marino, *it looks like crystal, that embroidered apron, those small shoes, she's a tender calf for me.*

The curious neighborhood housewives laughed surreptitiously. They could already tell that the magistrate's family was of low stock. Who would think of riding a mule in Bogotá? And in this residential neighborhood, dear God! This impending party at the magistrate's house promised to be a circus. Busybodies, they pretended to be strolling through their gardens, watering the flowers, counting trees, but they were keeping one eye on the scandal, immovable as crows.

"Where the hell did you get that mule?" Alma asked her nephew.

"From paradise, Auntie, isn't she handsome? Her name is Rosita and she's more beautiful than my wife. Perla is jealous."

The mule nodded her head, kicked softly at the paving stones, and stretched her neck, coming face-to-face with Señora Alma, face-to-face with Iris, face-to-face with Doña Juana, face-to-face with Zambranito, as though acknowledging each of them. Astride Rosita, Cousin César's face could not stop laughing: he laughed soundlessly—an enormous mask.

"Open the garage doors, Iris," ordered Señora Alma. "And you, fatso, take that mule over to the patio. Iris will show you. That's enough screwing around!"

Perla Tobón had already parked the Chevrolet at the curb,

in front of the house. She opened the door and her long bare legs appeared with a graceful momentum; she waved up at the sisters on the balcony. César sank his spurs into Rosita's flanks and went in through the garage. The whole house became filled with the echo of the mule's hooves, as though a gang of men on horseback had just broken in.

This is my wife's family, the magistrate observed, hidden behind the curtains. *All asses like that mule. But that mule must surely cost more than a racehorse.*

For he had been able to appreciate the mule's perfect ears, long and slender, her silky braided mane, and he had heard her voice, which fluctuated between a bray and a neigh—or was it more of a groan? Yet it was the proud rider, above all, who had put him on edge. He had known about César Santacruz's escapades for years, known all about that orphan, that only child, known of his crooked business, his shady dealings with marijuana in La Guajira. César himself had once confessed, jocularly:

"In ten months, I earn what a magistrate makes in ten years, my business is the business of tomorrow."

"Not tomorrow. Today," the magistrate told him. "Tomorrow's business will be different—and even worse."

Recalling this conversation, Nacho Caicedo did something he never allowed himself to do, unless merited by a joyous occasion: he enjoyed a cigarette. But this time the occasion was not joyous. He simply regretted throwing the party, regretted it on Alma's behalf, and smoked out of disquietude.

The magistrate stubbed out his cigarette in the ashtray. *It won't be long before more ghouls arrive,* he told himself, *including the ones from my family; but those on Alma's side take the gold medal, this César, what a freak, what an oaf, they tell me he didn't even finish primary school. And what about his children?*

41

All three dressed as sailors, three redheads like their papá, and almost the same name for each of them, Cesítar, Cesarito, and Cesarín, what a lack of imagination, but what a gorgeous mother, how can women dress like that these days, it's as if they were undressing; as she left the Chevrolet you could see more than half of it, a "minimal" skirt do they call that? Her name may be Perla, but Ike told us César calls her "perra," bitch, and that she likes a drink, a lady drunk, and how could you not drink with that animal in your bed? In any case, she isn't a good example to my daughters; when will this be over? Why did I start it? Too many guests today for my Alma, my sweetheart, or rather, too many guests for my sweet heart.

<h1 style="text-align:center">2</h1>

The patio could be accessed via a large grated gate leading off the garden. It had once been the site of a dilapidated house, behind the Caicedo home, which the magistrate acquired and had demolished. In its place, he had lain this vast cement patio, with a medium-height wall, green with vines, which faced onto the back street. Inside, there were a number of lone trees, an empty swing, houses for the dogs—three old Saint Bernards—sandboxes for the cats—two Persians, their beds beneath a single roof—and the cage for a pair of parrots, a bamboo palace which was only used at night, because during the day the parrots roamed freely through the world, where they were at no risk from the cats, who'd grown up with them and observed them with more tedium than desire. There was also a storage room, another room for tools, a ping-pong table under a gazebo, and a rustic shrine to Our Lady of the Beach, with its Virgin inside, made of faded blue plaster.

From the top of one of the leafless trees, the two parrots witnessed the entrance of the mule and her rider: they flapped their wings for an instant, then went still. The cats climbed on top of the shrine, watching the mule's progress keenly from its summit; Iris needlessly placated the dogs, who barked without getting to their feet. Cousin César rode the mule around the patio, at a trot, so she could build up confidence, then brought her to a halt in the shadow of the leafiest tree, a blossoming magnolia, at the foot of which she would at least find a patch of grass. Then he dismounted and removed the mule's tack, unhurriedly, under the attentive gaze of Iris, who had never seen a mule in the flesh. He removed the spurs from his muddy boots and tossed them onto the saddle, on top of the damp saddle blanket that smelled of leather. Now the cats roamed over the riding gear, pawing at the tether, sniffing the bridles. Cousin César was sweating, his thick neck drenched, in spite of the cold; his shirt, back, and armpits were all damp. His short red hair, sprinkled with sweat, looked blood-soaked to Iris, and it was only then that she noticed he wasn't dressed for the party.

"My suit and shoes are with my wife," said César, as if guessing her thoughts. "Sooner or later, you'll have to tell me where I can change."

And with a single step, he moved closer to Iris.

"Iris," he said, "bring a bucket of clean water for Rosita. Tell them to chop three dozen carrots and serve them to her in a saucepan. If you can, give her a good portion of oats. Look how easy it is to make friends with Rosita, don't be scared, come." He took Iris's hand and brought it near to the mule's lips, placing her open fingers on the seething brow, on the high crown of the head, on top of the mane, guiding her hand back and forth over the throbbing neck. A few carnations dropped off; the mule bowed her head, raised it, and turned to Iris, coming face-to-face with her.

"Stroke her neck, she likes that," said the cousin. "Look, like this." And, for an instant, César's heavy hand brushed over Iris's blonde hair, above her neck, one of his fingers even managing to tickle her nape. She jumped, as though jolted with electricity, and began running to the door.

"I'm going for the water," she said, shocked.

Behind her, César let out a cyclopean laugh, which she experienced like jaws closing around her neck, invisible but real. Iris disappeared, and the cousin made his way to the door, slowly, ponderously, shaking his red head, with a scheming expression on his face, a furrowed brow. He paused for a second at the grated gate.

He hesitated.

There was no need, he thought, to leave the mule tied up.

3

The white mule was left alone on the patio, letting out a neigh-bray, and then something like a groan; her big, restless, watery eyes took in her surroundings, and one of her back hooves scraped the tiles. She let out a more powerful whinny, and the cats again made for the top of the shrine; the dogs again barked halfheartedly. One of the parrots, the one that preferred not to talk, flapped its wings in fright and flew into the cage, where it began eating a banana; the other parrot flew off in a circle, alighting on the magnolia beneath which the mule was taking shelter; this was Roberto, Uriela's parrot; he belonged to Uriela because she had been the one to teach him how to speak, with a year's worth of patience. She'd been able to teach him two phrases, which the parrot unleashed from time to time. In a very shrill voice, like that of a clown, he would say: "Oh this country, this country, this country," which was the chorus to a popular

44

song at the time, and then, in a deep, funereal voice, like a ventriloquist's dummy: "It's the same, it's the same." On this occasion, Roberto kept silent, still attentive to the echo of Rosita's whinny, as though captivated, as though attempting to learn it, and for the benefit of his learning, the mule let out a pure whinny which caused the dogs to bark for real. The parrot intoned a throaty gurgle, bearing no resemblance to what he had just heard. Then he decided to screech, "It's the same, it's the same," which fatally alarmed the white mule, because never in her life had she heard a parrot's voice, and it drove her out of her mind. From the happy mule she had been or appeared to be, she was converted into a battle mule, lashing out at the tree from which that human voice with feathers had come; she gave the magnolia such a kick that it reminded the parrot he could fly: he flew off toward the garden; the waiters setting out the tables heard him go by like a green flash squawking, this country, this country, this country. On the patio, the mule kicked at the trunk of the magnolia for a second time, shaking it; pieces of bark dropped to the ground, among carnations, because by now Rosita had freed herself of all her flowers as if they were but more harnesses, perhaps even more irksome, even crueler. With wild, satanic, bloodshot eyes, she set upon the dogs that had started barking again, this time not from habit but in genuine alarm; they were forced to get up and flee from the mule, who began chasing them in circles; the cats leapt down from the shrine and slunk swiftly into the garden through a hole in the wall. The mule refused to forgive even the Virgin's altar; with a mere brush to the opening of the shrine, the plaster statue toppled over, pedestal and all, and shattered; one of the mule's hooves destroyed the Virgin's head, the others crushed its garlands, hands, and chest. Rosita immediately renewed her charge, her cowbells and small

45

tinkling bells sounding like trumpets of war; the Saint Bernards looped pitifully around the entire patio, with the mule in pursuit, destroying the dog's houses, the cats' sandboxes, and the big bamboo cage, which she smashed open: with that powerful ram, the parrot who preferred not to talk was turned into a paste of feathers and banana. As they raced, the three dogs and the mule changed direction, heading toward the gazebo for the ping-pong table, and this is where the mule slipped and fell; but she sprang up at once, desperate, leaning one flank against the table and crushing it; then the dogs attacked, prompted more by panic than by valor; one managed to bite Rosita on the hindquarters; immediately, a kick caught the dog square on the snout, forcing it to sink to its knees before collapsing onto its back: the kick had cracked the dog's skull. Now the other dogs were no longer barking but howling in legitimate terror; they had taken shelter behind a tree in a corner, and, before them, the white mule pawed at the cement, pacing to and fro, as if inviting them to come out, as if screaming, cowards! During all this time, the swing was squeaking back and forth, as though an invisible person were swinging on it. The mule continued to trot in circles around the enormous yellowish-brown dog, which lay in a large puddle of blood. But then she slowed her gallop, settled down, and began drinking from the clay bowl intended for the dogs, swishing her tail on top of her back, for her wound was also bleeding, and those first buzzing blue flies she knew so well had begun darting around her.

4

Uncle Jesús now deemed a trip to Chía to be inescapable. While it was true that the municipality was less than an hour away, to him it was farther away than China, in the words of Ike, his hapless nephew. And, in addition, Lucio—that insipid gardener, with the one mad eye, that stony face—refused to answer when addressed, even after Jesús apologized for not greeting him in the kitchen; he found himself alongside a buffoon, a laborer from his sister's farm, *a cyclops,* he screamed to himself, *but he's carrying a wad of cash in his pocket, an offering that belongs to me.* He considered taking it by force, but dismissed the idea: the cyclops had carried him over his shoulder as though carrying a feather, and what hands, strong and dexterous, the kind that work the land: more than a gardener, he resembled a gravedigger.

They were still standing by the side of the highway when a rickety bus with a sign for *Chía* finally pulled up in front of them, wreathed in smoke.

"Why don't we go look for a bar?" proposed Jesús hopefully. "We can get a coffee or something."

"We can get coffee in Chía—without the something."

Uncle Jesús's mouth had fallen open, and, to his shame, he was drooling without realizing it. The gardener was already climbing onto the dark bus that was almost empty, with a group of two or three women surrounded by baskets, and a bespectacled young man reading in the Buddha position. Lucio went to sit on the back seat without bothering to check whether Jesús was behind him. It wasn't necessary to drag Uncle Jesús along. The wretch of a man would follow him for all eternity, sulky but docile; it was clear he believed he could persuade Lucio to give up the money. Should he just hand it over, after making him swear not to go to the party? Should he take a cut, in return? Never, he responded. Those had not been madam's orders; she'd sentenced her brother to a hotel in Chía, and for three days.

The gardener's soul was confused, he was blinded by uncertainty, unsure where truth could be found. Amid his suffering, what triumphed was his absolute loyalty to Señora Alma, to Magistrate Caicedo. And, as though the ground were opening up beneath his feet, in a moment like a flash of dark lightning, he believed it very possible that his employers were asking him to return their favor: *Yes,* he cried to himself, *that must be it!*

He had discovered it.

A sharp shiver ran down his spine: the time had come to show his gratitude.

Because, if he remembered correctly, Señora Alma's nephew had always been speaking on her behalf. From the start, he'd said: "Come with us, Lucio, in case we need your help with taking him out." And who gets "taken out" in this country but the dead?; there are those who say, "I'm gonna take that guy out," or "They all got taken out." He delved into his recollections and appeared to see Ike's face, to hear his voice: "There's no turning back, Uncle, it's perfectly simple, my aunt Alma has given us a one-way ticket for you, my dearest Uncle, to the end of the world." A one-way ticket, repeated Lucio, a ticket to the end of the world, what had he meant by that? To go and not come back, what else could that mean but pushing up daisies?

And that same nephew had then said, turning to face the gardener as he handed him the money: "Receive this as an order and take my uncle to a hotel or to the moon." Receive this as an order, Lucio screamed to himself, could anything be more explicit? An order. There was no doubt that Ike had been speaking in the name of Señora Alma. And the recommendation to take him to the moon had been even more explicit: nothing more, nothing less than the moon … Lucio Rosas let out a piercing sigh, not daring to address this wretch of a man who had sat down beside him—taciturn?—his large brow furrowed, his eyes half-closed, his formidable mouth wet with saliva.

That Ike, the gardener repeated to himself, that Ike had been even more explicit with his next instructions: "Take this monstrosity to Chía or to the other side, but take him and make sure he doesn't come back." To the other side, the gardener cried out to himself, rubbing his face with his hands, what else could the other side mean but death? Had that order really come from Señora Alma? Was Magistrate Caicedo a party to this? Was he being trusted to carry out this task, given that he, after all, had killed a man?

But, he yelled to himself, did this Uncle Jesús really deserve that? Had he committed a sin, a serious offense against his sister, Señora Alma, or, even worse, against the magistrate himself? Was the safety of his employers at risk because of this wretch of a man? Why not? He was a sleazebag who talked too much—hadn't he asked him in the kitchen how a man of this Earth loses an eye?

Yes.

Disappear him.

Send him to the other side.

To the moon.

For the first time, he examined Uncle Jesús. Hunched, sitting very close beside him, his head bowed, lips pursed—and what monumental ears, pointy—he bore the mark, the shadow, the demeanor of the belated repentant, the one who begs clemency of his executioner. Did he suspect his fate? The magistrate's fortunes must depend on something only his repellent brother-in-law knew, a terrifying secret. And now, via his nephew, using coded but explicit messages, he was being ordered to liquidate the problem in the way all problems in this country get liquidated, with a bullet. *And how am I going to shoot?* he thought, dejectedly, *I haven't got my shotgun with me*. He shook his head, as if to cast that wild notion far away from him; it was a misunderstanding: he felt he was losing his mind just for thinking it. From Chía, he should call his employer and set the record straight once and for all, because you could tell the nephew was a loon. But the way in which they'd asked him, in madam's name, to get rid of him ... there was a veiled order, but an order nonetheless, a precise order. Taking him to the other side could mean nothing else but killing him.

5

Inside the Ford station wagon, driving at great speed, the Castañedas had already reached the street the magistrate's house was on. That's when they noticed that, eighty or ninety feet ahead of them, Rodolfito Cortés was turning the corner, behind the wheel of his Renault 4. Ike knew about Rodolfito, whom he believed to be simply one of Francia's admirers, a superfluous rival. Without compunction, he revved the station wagon hard and took the corner, overtaking the Renault and nearly scraping it, before easing off, barely six feet ahead. Rodolfito didn't brake; in fright, he turned the steering wheel at random, the Renault riding up onto the curb and colliding headfirst with one of the oaks lining the street. He hadn't been going fast, and the accident could have been worse; the Renault's fender ended up in a C, and the motor fizzled out. "What are you doing?" Ricardo yelled at his brother, "that was a friend of Francia's." Ike didn't reply; he had braked sharply and was watching through the rearview mirror. The kids from the block, the baseball players, looked on in fascination at the accident, sitting along the low wall encircling their neighbor's house. It never occurred to them that, had

Rodolfito turned the other way, he would have crashed not into the tree, but into them. Nor did Rodolfito consider that the incident could have been intentional, it was just an unfortunate miscalculation. He didn't even check to see who was behind the wheel of the magistrate's Ford. He started up the Renault: his faithful friend hadn't broken down. Rodolfito backed gently out of the oak's kiss, and was about to get moving again, behind the Ford, when, to his horror, the enormous station wagon growled into reverse and began heading straight for him. Rodolfito could think of no other option but to open the door and jump: he went staggering in the direction of the kids, his face a death mask, his arms spread. He was met by the clamorous laughter of the baseball players: the Ford had braked an inch away from his Renault.

Ike drove the station wagon up to the magistrate's house and brought it to a sharp halt, facing the garage. He beeped twice, like lord and master. Immediately, the doors opened: Iris appeared, dutifully. Helping her to push open the doors was the unrelenting guard, Ojeda. The two brothers went straight in, laughing uncontrollably; the echo of their laughter could be heard in the garage. Iris and Marino had already begun closing the garage doors when the Renault appeared. Rodolfito parked his car on the curb, behind Perla Tobón's Chevrolet. Neither Iris nor Marino could explain why the young man getting out of the Renault looked so pale, why he was trembling so badly.

"I've come for the party," he said.

"Of course, Don Rodolfito," responded Iris, recognizing him. "Will you come in through the garage?"

And she held the garage door ajar so he could pass through it. There was another explosion of voices and laughter from inside. It was the Castañeda brothers greeting César Santacruz, in the main drawing room. Rodolfito's eyes widened, and he proceeded hesitantly. He was carrying a cardboard box wrapped in gift paper.

Behind him, Marino Ojeda had finally worked up the nerve to give Iris a kiss, and yet he failed; frightened, she had turned her face, meaning the kiss landed on her ear, which was far worse because it prompted even greater shivers. Later, she would say she felt as if she were dying.

6

"Uriela, are you there?"

"I think so."

The little boys opened the door but did not go in. The year before, they had discovered Uriela's room and it was like magic. Now they wanted to see it again.

"Why, if it isn't the three Césars," said Uriela, encouraging them. "Are you going to stand there forever?"

Uriela had just finished getting ready for the party; she was wearing a long dress, like her sisters, and yet it wasn't technically a party gown, but rather a Guajiro Indian robe, like a shimmer of white, embroidered all over with flowers and birds. And, instead of shoes, she was wearing fique sandals; it was an outfit that troubled Señora Alma.

Sitting motionless in her rocking chair, Uriela had been combing her long black hair when the boys arrived. She was grateful for the spontaneous visit: she had been refusing to go down to the drawing room, from which the roar of voices and laughter arrived sporadically like an ocean. Talking to the boys would be a way of joining in with the party, as her mother insisted. Furthermore, she had already ensured that the little inflatable swimming pool would be awaiting the boys; pumped up, though still empty of water: its squishy

52

dolphin silhouette was a promise; this would be her contribution to the party. She adored children, just as children adored her; this reciprocal love would be the perfect excuse for enduring that day of cousins and extraordinary aunts and uncles.

The two cats took advantage of the children's entrance to dart in ahead of them, like a pair of lightning bolts: in two leaps, they climbed to the top of a wardrobe by the window, then sat there, indifferent, upon their woolen cushions. The youngest of the Césars made straight for the corner opposite the wardrobe, where Melina the witch hung as if flying; she was a green-faced witch with a black hat and a hooked nose, perched on her broomstick, and if anyone clapped nearby, she would begin to cackle wickedly, her eyes flashing on and off as she shook as though possessed, swinging on her broom, flying. This time, no matter how hard the youngest clapped his hands, the witch remained indifferent.

"She's out of batteries," said Uriela. "You'll have to insert these new ones."

She unhooked the witch, leaving it to him to find the compartment for the batteries and put them in.

The other Césars had stopped in front of Uriela's library and were scanning the bookshelves, eagerly.

"Where's the head?" asked the eldest.

"I had to throw it out," said Uriela.

"But why?"

"Because it was starting to smell."

They were referring to a shrunken head, one of those extraordinary Jivaroan heads, the size of a fist, which Uriela had kept as an adornment on top of her edition of *One Thousand and One Nights*. Her parents had brought the head back from Peru, and Uriela appropriated it as she appropriated everything that interested her, which, fortunately, tended

53

to be the things that least interested everyone else. When Uriela was still a little girl, the magistrate had asked her why she didn't leave the books in their place, in the first-floor library, and why she had started taking them up to her room, one by one, scattering them under the table and around her bed. "They're the books I've read," she said, "so they belong to me." "I think it's great that you read them," said the magistrate, "but if your sisters need them, you'll have to put them back." "I don't think that will happen," Uriela had replied, and she continued to take more books, year after year. The magistrate asked himself whether it could be true that Uriela read so many books, from cover to cover. In any case, he thought, she had the dark circles under her eyes of someone who doesn't sleep: *I'll have to take her to the doctor.* But he didn't pursue the matter any further, opting instead to purchase a wall-to-wall bookcase so that "Uriela's books" could be kept in her room.

Uriela had been forced to get rid of the shrunken head because it was starting to smell: a viscous green film had obscured the wrinkled face, and it stank. She'd thrown it out, begrudgingly, for it had been one of the best surprises in her bedroom. She also had a collection of indigenous masks on the wall, some Beatles posters, a self-portrait of Van Gogh, which she herself had framed with bamboo sticks, a black doll attached to the door like a crucified Christ, its head tilted to one side, bald and eyeless (the first doll she'd been given), two enlarged movie stills (one of Humphrey Bogart in *Casablanca*, the other of Sinbad the Sailor confronting a skeleton with his sword), and a charcoal drawing of Sigmund Freud's face with the caption, "What's on a man's mind": the forehead, eyebrows, eyes, and nose of the thinker surreptitiously formed the brazen nakedness of a woman.

She had fossils from Villa de Leyva spread across the floor

like stone paths, and a great glass tank for her turtle, Penelope, a green turtle with red ears (two red lines behind her eyes) which at that moment was conquering the attentions of the two elder Césars. The youngest, meanwhile, had managed to insert the batteries in the witch; he clapped, and the witch broke into wicked laughter. "I'd prefer to never have to leave here," Uriela confessed to the boys, "I'd prefer to stay with you, rather than going down to the drawing room to say hello and force myself to laugh."

The boys contemplated her from the abyss of their happiness. She blushed. Children really did amaze her; only with them did she rediscover wonders that had been inexorably lost over the years. Her dream was to travel someplace far away in the world, and even far away from the world itself. Not to finish her high school studies, much less begin her university ones, which were imminent. All she needed were her books, why have anything more? But not going to university was a dispensation her father would never allow her. She would need to run away from home. This is why, ever since she turned fifteen, she had been working weekends without her parents' knowledge; she worked as much as possible to earn the money that would allow her to escape. Uriela Caicedo, daughter of a magistrate of the Supreme Court of Justice, would dress up as a clown and entertain children's parties and piñata parties, first communions, birthdays; she told stories and performed plays that she herself devised. But she had met with her share of misfortunes. She found a well-paid job at the Poutyface Daycare, where they had a warm-water swimming pool for the bigger children. It was Uriela's understanding that newborn babies could swim without being taught, that the joy of swimming was something they learned in the womb; as such, she had taken the first baby she came across and slipped it into the swimming pool, a baby that had been entrusted to the daycare that morning. And the baby did swim, to the children's delight. It went back and forth like a fish, without a single tear, in fact, it was laughing. A scream tore through the daycare: it was the baby's mother, who had just arrived. Aghast, she retrieved her baby from the water and pointed to Uriela: "Are you trying to drown my child?" Her outrage bore fruit: Uriela lost her job.

After the daycare, Uriela came across another care facility: the Orchard of Peace, the most prestigious of nursing homes, where the most solvent grandparents in Bogotá enjoyed their final days. Uriela, who could read a music score backwards and forwards, took charge of the Music Room, where there were music sessions for the old-timers; there was a good sound system, with headphones for the hardest of hearing; they listened to Colombian music and also some classical, the waltzes of Strauss, Liszt, and Chopin. Not even Uriela herself can explain how it occurred to her to take her favorite record, the White Album by the Beatles, to the Orchard of Peace and put seven pairs of headphones over the ears of the seven deafest, most melancholic old people—four men and three women with completely vacant gazes, already nearing the end. In addition, she had raised the volume as if for a party. The seven furrowed their brows, unfurrowed them, one old man began tapping the rhythm with the tip of his shoe, the eldest woman burst into irrepressible laughter: excessive laughter, thought Uriela, and was about to change the music when the old woman staggered to her feet and started dancing. Uriela had been a second too late in rescuing her from that untimely dance, because the old woman stumbled: it's true that she didn't fall to the floor, but rather into Uriela's arms, and yet this is how the matron of the nursing home surprised them. Uriela was fired, for it was confirmed the next day that the dancer had died in her sleep. Despite the death being ruled natural (many old people died in their sleep), Uriela was deemed responsible by the world; it was an image that kept her from sleeping, causing her anguish and a regret that would return every night of every year to wake her for the rest of her life: the old woman dancing alone.

"And the inflatable pool?" asked the youngest of the Césars. "Last year we went swimming."

"Zambranito and I already blew it up, but it's empty. We'll fill it later. It isn't in the inside garden, because it won't fit among so many tables; we inflated it in the outside garden, under the balcony."

"They'll be able to see us from the street," said the eldest.

"And what does that matter?"

Uriela led the boys over to the wardrobe, where a chest was hidden like pirate's treasure; from inside it, she took a skull.

"A friend gave this to me."

The pale skull radiated in her hands; it appeared to emit a bluish cold, like ice. The mouths of the three boys hung open; none dared receive the skull. The empty eye sockets were *looking at them.* It was worse than the shrunken head.

"Is that what we're like inside?" asked the youngest.

"Ugly like this."

"Where did your friend get it?" asked the eldest, on the brink of daring to receive it.

"From the cemetery. He stole it."

"He stole it," the Césars gasped.

"It was a risk."

"He stole it," repeated the eldest.

"He wanted to present me with a gift."

"Did he have to steal it at night?"

"Night was made for thieves."

"Wasn't he scared?"

"No. My friend is one of those who sing, *I'm afraid to laugh, I'm afraid to cry, I'm afraid of fear and fear's afraid of me*."

"I *do* get scared, all the time."

"I do too. One time, something made my hair stand on end; from sheer terror, my head ended up looking like a hedgehog."

The three boys blinked. They were imagining Uriela's hair as the tips of a hedgehog's black spines.

"And what shocked you?" continued the eldest.

"My uncle Jesús," said Uriela, "his dentures fell out and … he looked like a different Uncle Jesús … there were lots of people."

"Dentures?" said the youngest.

"False teeth, like eyeglasses, which aren't real eyes."

"What else has shocked you?" asked the eldest.

"One time, I surprised papá in the bathroom. I opened the door and … there was papá, sitting on the toilet bowl, can you imagine?"

"The magistrate?" said the eldest.

"The very same."

"Papá says Aunt Alma is our real aunt, that the magistrate is just an old mummy."

"He says that? Please, but then this whole family are a bunch of mummies, you and I included."

Uriela made as if to put the skull back in the chest, but the eldest César stopped her. As though mesmerized, he said:

"Are you really not frightened of that skull?"

"No, why? At night I talk to it, it likes me to tell it stories."

"What stories?" asked the youngest.

"I'll tell you some other day. When you become like this skull."

The youngest leapt back.

Then Uriela performed some sort of conjuring motions with her hand and the skull split down the middle; it was actually a container for candies, a gift Uriela had been given for Halloween.

"And there are three candies left inside," said Uriela. "What a coincidence, what magic, what fate, there are also three of you, aren't there? One, two, three. I'm going to give three candies to the three Césars: one for Cesítar, another for Cesarito, and another for Cesarín, my God, what horrible names, they're worse than mine, but better than my sisters'. You can eat them now. Though I won't be held responsible for what happens to you."

"What's going to happen to us?" asked Cesarito.

"I'm not permitted to say."

"I know," said the eldest, "they'll make us small and people will be able to step on us; it'll be hard for us to study—how're you supposed to read a book when the pages are bigger than this house? Any bee will be the same size as us, it'll kill us with its stinger; someone will have to carry us in their pocket, and risk us falling out; any shoe on the street will be like a battle tank, crushing us."

Uriela looked at him with admiration:

"It'll be worse than that."

"I don't believe you," said the eldest.

"No? Try one. But I won't be held responsible."

"It's like the story of Tom Thumb."

"Just wait and see, Tom Thumb."

Before the eyes of the eldest, Uriela set down the luminous candy. And, though hesitant, the eldest took it, bravely raised it to his mouth, and began chewing—then he instantly spat it out as if he were choking. It was bitter and spicy at the same time, a Day of the Innocents prank.

The other Césars laughed loudly. Uriela reassembled the skull, but decided to leave it on top of her nightstand this time, on public display.

"Uriela," said the eldest, resolutely, "is it true that you won the *Know-it-all Bunny* competition when you were only seven years old?"

"Yes," said Uriela. "It was ten years ago, when you had only just been born."

"Tell us how you won. Papá always says we should be intelligent like Uriela, he calls you the clever bunny of the family."

"He says that?" replied Uriela, blushing, "the clever bunny? Not the know-it-all?"

"The clever bunny."

"There are many clever bunnies in this family. Your papá, first and foremost."

"Tell us how you managed to win."

And Uriela began to reminisce out loud.

7

When Rodolfito Cortés reached the drawing room, he faltered: with one glance, he understood that Francia wasn't there; nor were the magistrate and Doña Alma, the only people capable of bringing order to that ruckus; the horrible Castañedas were perched on either side of a giant armchair in which César Santacruz sat like a king and could not stop laughing mutely, his mouth stretched for all eternity. The Castañedas were holding court for him, genuinely entranced. One of them was asking his sovereign cousin how many millions he had earned that month at the exact moment when Rodolfito made his entrance.

The drawing room went silent.

In another armchair sat Perla Tobón, César's merry wife, and in another, Tina, her younger sister, subtle as an apparition: unlike Perla, Tina Tobón tended to go unnoticed; she was short and skinny, a runt. Reserved, her eyes half-closed as though drifting off to sleep, she wore a checked skirt that reached below her knees, a lace blouse buttoned up to the neck, adorned with a white silk tie, and she was covering her mouth with her hand in order to yawn discreetly.

And sitting on a single sofa, as though glowing, were three of the Caicedo sisters: Armenia, Palmira, and Lisboa; three flames. Armenia immediately stood up and greeted Rodolfito, pointing him toward a distant armchair.

"Rodolfito," she said, "we never dreamed you were coming. You can sit over there."

"So far away from everyone?" said Perla, who was smoking.

Armenia had turned red. With a step like a panther's leap, she approached Rodolfito, facing him:

"What have you got there?" She was leaning forward, her mocking red mouth half open. "My God, it's a gift." And for a moment she turned back to look at everyone, bemused. "A gift for papá and mamá, is that it?" She turned back to face Rodolfito, who had gone pale. "It's for their anniversary, right? Would you look at that: he's the only guest who brought a gift, how sweet, how polite, how thoughtful, show me, Rodolfito!"

Rodolfito hesitated, standing there, embracing his box. He didn't understand. Armenia's flushed face filled him with doubt. Since he'd arrived in the drawing room, he felt that the three sisters had been observing him frostily—sphinxes of ice, but amid flames—and that their six eyes looked him over like daggers, from head to toe.

"Why don't we take a look at that gift?" proposed Lisboa from where she sat.

The Castañedas applauded and César laughed out loud.

"It wouldn't be fair to open a present that's not for us," ruled Perla.

"We'll wrap it up again," said Armenia, reaching her slender arms toward the box. "I'm dying of curiosity."

She brought her fingers down upon the gold bow that sealed the box, still safe in Rodolfito's hands.

"I don't think this is the best idea," he said, trying to take a step backward. This gesture prompted general laughter. Even Perla and Tina Tobón, who seemed the most reluctant, were laughing.

In a flash, Armenia undid the bow and peered inside the box.

"There are two presents!" she cried. "How wonderful!"

"Yes," conceded Rodolfito, reaching his own hand inside and taking out a small marble sculpture, a replica of Michelangelo's *Moses*. "It's Carrara marble," he said, as though reciting the information.

Turning even redder, Armenia reached her hand inside and held up the second gift: it was an item of clothing, shiny, with black and gray overtones.

"What is it?" asked Perla.

"A waistcoat for the magistrate," stammered Rodolfito. "Made of ostrich leather."

"God, poor ostrich!" cried Armenia, and threw the waistcoat over her shoulder, where it landed on the seat from which César Santacruz presided, his enormous face in the midst of another mute guffaw.

"Shit," said César, "you'd have been better off bringing him a bulletproof vest, Rodolfito!"

The Castañedas endorsed this proposal with more genuine laughter, and the three cousins huddled to examine the waistcoat.

"So then that *Moses* is for mamá," said Armenia. "I've never seen anything more beautiful in my life." She snatched rather than took the *Moses* from Rodolfito's hands, allowing it to fall so naturally that it looked like an accident. "Oh, it slipped out of my hands. I think the head has broken off."

"It's alright," said Lisboa, "we can reattach it with a bandage, we'll mend it like they do at the hospital." She had knelt down to look on the floor and was now holding Moses's head, showing it to everyone, but she too let it slip through her hands. The head rolled along like a ball and then came to a stop, frowning, not looking at anyone.

Armenia picked it up, inspecting it.

"Oh no," she said, "it looks like he's lost his nose, what a shame."

Rodolfito was observing the sisters in shock.

"What's going on here?" said Perla. She tossed her cigarette into the ashtray, got up from her armchair and took hold of Moses's head, swiping it out of Armenia's hands, then looked for Moses's body and nose on the floor, and, with a righteous gesture, she set everything down on a little gold table. "It's almost as if you were trying to smash Señora Alma's *Moses*. She's going to lose it for real."

A waiter came in with a tray of wine glasses. He was followed by an elegant young woman in an apron who aroused Cousin César's interest: his pupils shone, looking her up and down. The young woman was carrying a tray with a selection of cheese and crackers. The arrival of the servants calmed everyone down. Rodolfito collapsed as if fainting into an armchair beside Perla, whom he understood to be his one true defender. Cousin César was squeezing himself into the magistrate's waistcoat.

"How do I look?" he asked.

"Like an ostrich," said Ike. "All that's missing is for you to lay an egg."

To Rodolfito's dismay, Perla abandoned him, going off in search of the exiting waiter; she caught up with him, and, placing one of her ring-decked hands on his shoulder, said: "Bring me something stronger, okay? I'm no fan of these colorful refreshments." "It's red or white wine," said the ingenuous waiter. Perla glared at him, and the waiter rescued the situation: "We also have vodka, gin, and rum," he offered. "I said bring me whatever you want, honey," Perla emphasized, "it's all the same to me." She whispered this to him swiftly and returned to her seat beside Rodolfito, as the waiter fled, blushing, in search of more drinks. Now the cousins were clinking their glasses, toasting each other. Tina observed her sister closely: it seemed extraordinary that Perla hadn't accepted a glass of wine.

"Where is Francia?" Rodolfito asked of nobody, downcast.

"In Europe," said cruel Armenia, who was unforgiving.

"She's in her room," said prudent Palmira, in an act of conciliation. She felt sorry for Rodolfito. She still believed the newspaper announcement could have been a lie. Why not? And, what's more, people were right: this poor Rodolfito really did have such a toad-like face, the only thing missing was for him to croak. God only knew what Francia saw in him. Rodolfito inspired genuine sympathy, he really did have the face of a toad, he was a biologist with the face of an amphibian, who, to top it all off, had done his degree thesis on toads, and, according to Francia, was writing a book, *Toad Species of Bogotá*, and slept surrounded by toads of every color. Surely living with toads for so long had caused him to resemble them, with that damp, greenish hair, pressed to his skull, that face with stripe-thin lips, that gesture of his hands like a pair of dangling legs ... *Perhaps*, thought prudent Palmira, *if Francia kisses him in the right spot, Rodolfito will turn into a prince.*

And she burst into silent laughter.

"I'll wait another minute for her," said Rodolfito, mortified, sinking even deeper into his armchair.

"Why don't you go up to her room?" Palmira prompted him, sympathetic.

Rodolfito brightened as though infused with light:

"I'll go fetch her."

And he sprang out of the drawing room—exactly, thought Palmira, like a toad on the perilous banks of a swamp that flings itself straight into the mouth of a greedy duck.

Ike Castañeda, who had been listening closely, couldn't tolerate such an excess of familiarity—*since when does the amphibian visit Francia in her bedroom?* He was about to say something, but decided to stay quiet. He'd made up his mind. It would be better to follow Rodolfito all the way to Francia's room.

So he went out after him.

8

The memory of the *Know-it-all Bunny* wasn't a particularly happy one. As if by agreement, the entire family had been listening to the radio on that decisive Sunday, when the three child finalists went head-to-head. It was a general knowledge competition for children between the ages of nine and twelve years old. Although it's true that Uriela was seven,

Uncle Jesús, her representative, found a way to get her accepted: he revealed that Uriela had been reading books since she was four years old. The organizers tested her and were surprised. What if she won? Such a clever young girl would be the darling of the competition.

The winner would be the child with the most correct answers, but, to claim the grand prize, that child would need to answer the Golden Question, a question set for children by experts that would decide the total sum of the prize money: nine thousand pesos if the child could answer it—an exorbitant sum of money in 1960, which ensured the program was listened to in every corner of the country—and a thousand pesos if they couldn't. In the three years the program had been on the air, no child had ever managed to answer the Golden Question. However, Uriela not only answered it, but from the very start, she easily outmatched the other children she was competing against.

"There was a blond boy, a twelve-year-old," Uriela told the Césars, "and also a black boy, eleven, and me, a seven-year-old mestiza; in other words, all the races."

"Mestiza?" said the youngest. "What does mestiza mean?"

"Black mixed with white, like café con leche."

In the recording studio, Uriela had noticed the black boy's family behind the barrier: his parents, his siblings, and a grandmother who crumpled with sadness, her deep eyes tearful, her lip trembling; her grandson had lost the competition. To one side of Uriela, the black boy was crying, his face buried in his arms, and so too was the blond boy, pale as wax, looking as if he were about to faint.

"Only then did I realize that the blond boy was actually an albino," Uriela told the Césars.

"Albino?" said the youngest. "What does albino mean?"

"It's like the foam on the café con leche."

The panel announced that the girl had won, and that it was only fair for everyone to keep quiet and allow her to answer the Golden Question. Uncle Jesús craned his neck out and yelled for Uriela to offer up prayers to St. Anthony of Miracles: it was then that Uriela became terrified, watching her uncle's dentures detach from his open mouth and go flying through the air. Uncle Jesús looked like someone else; he was horrible: fright-inducing, a kind of broken-down Frankenstein, Uriela told the Césars. But a sympathetic hand returned his false teeth. It was the hand of the grandmother.

The boys crying on either side of Uriela stopped blubbering to listen to the Golden Question. And Uriela answered it without any hesitation. An incredible silence followed her answer. The cash prize, in clean bills—as though freshly printed—was inside a glass case, in view of the audience. Uriela Caicedo answered the Golden Question, and, afterwards, without backing away from the microphone, to everyone's surprise, she was Solomonic: she asked that the nine-thousand-peso prize money be shared equally between her and the male competitors. "That is to say," she said, lowering her eyelids, "three thousand pesos each." Timidly, she added: "On the condition that no one cries."

Alma Santacruz and Nacho Caicedo were choked with pride; they cheered to the heavens, such was the joyful shock caused by the youngest of their daughters, her generous distribution.

"Hold on to your prize money," Señora Alma had told Uriela, "one day you may have a use for it."

"And it would have come in very useful right now," Uriela told the Césars.

Because she no longer had that money. She never did. She never divulged to her parents, and nor did she now to the Césars, how on that Sunday, after paying for a taxi to the neighborhood where she lived, Uncle Jesús had bought her an ice cream on the corner and left with the three thousand gold pesos.

"You shouldn't have shared our prize money," Uncle Jesús had told her. "I needed all of it, it was more use to me than to that blackie or that tomb face, but what can we do now, Uriela, it'll be our little secret, it's a matter of life and death, you're a smart girl, tell me, what do you prefer? Seeing your Uncle Jesús alive and well, or seeing him dead in a casket, stiff as a chicken?"

"Alive and well," said Uriela.

And her uncle:

"I'll return the money to you one day, dead or alive."

And he took the three thousand pesos and left seven-year-old Uriela alone on that corner on a Sunday, eating an ice cream.

"But what was the Golden Question?" asked the eldest César.

Uriela shuddered at the memory. Was she going to cry? Of course not. *Why do these things always happen to me?*

"I don't remember," she told Cesítar. "It's been ten years: your whole lifetime."

"What did they ask you, Uriela? Tell us, you *do* remember."

The three Césars listened to her without drawing a breath.

The Question was: "where in the world was the number zero invented?"

The three Césars exchanged a desperate look.

They didn't know.

"Where?" they asked.

"Look it up," said Uriela, and she left the bedroom, pursued by the outwitted Césars' outcry. Only a minute later, as they were coming down the spiral staircase, she revealed that it was India.

And she felt a great sadness for herself, for that recollection, which grew less auspicious by the day: on that corner, on that Sunday, she had understood at the age of seven that knowledge of anything, pure knowledge, wasn't happiness.

9

They had been wandering through Chía for fifteen minutes, on the lookout for a hotel. Lucio Rosas wanted to get the wretch of a man put up somewhere and return to Bogotá as soon as possible, and not tempt himself any longer with crazy notions of taking him out or sending him to the other side. When they reached Parque de la Luna, outside the church doors, Uncle Jesús couldn't carry on any longer and sat down on one of the rotten wooden benches that were strewn around like a joke.

"I need a breather. To get the ideas flowing."

The impassive gardener sat down beside him.

"It's just that things in life," continued Uncle Jesús, wrapping his hands around one of his knees, "they make you laugh—or cry? I've had five women in my life: I defrauded them all."

He went silent, shocked at himself, as if regretting having said this, as if it caused him suffering.

He redirected the conversation:

"Did you hear Ike, my nephew, when I told him he was an ingrate? He answered that I was the last person in the world he should be grateful to. See, Lucio, how the young are dull-witted, slow, moronic, and rash? When Ike was just a little boy, his mother, Adelfa, my sister, was left a widow. Beto Castañeda, her husband, decided to go and die of heart failure, leaving poor Adelfa more lonesome than the Anima

Sola, with five children: Ike and Ricardo, and those three girls whose names I can't even remember. Poor Adelfa, widowed, out of work, what else could she do? Enter Jesús, her savior. I was the owner of a trucking company, had more gold than you can imagine, lit my cigarettes with paper money, dressed in monochrome. I went to Adelfa and told her: 'You can go live in the house I bought you.' I also gifted her a sewing machine, and Adelfa sewed. She sewed for miles. She was brought back to life. She put her kids in school. As for me, she sometimes made me lunch—until she forgot. And she also forgot that I'd given her that house, title deeds and all, me! It was a simple house, sure, plagued by leaks, but it was a house after all, a place to die, a place to cry without anyone seeing."

Here Uncle Jesús began to weep. He wept silently, but weep he did, for half a minute.

"Because now I'm the one without a house, and I'm forced to cry in public, how embarrassing, Lucio, forgive me this moment of weakness."

With a handkerchief resembling an old rag, he wiped his swollen eyelids:

"I rent a room in a neighborhood I won't name because it has no name, a filthy hole … worthy of me?"

He seemed surprised by his own question, and started weeping again. Then he made an effort to pull himself together:

"In that nameless neighborhood, if the thieves see me go past, they die from laughter—what can they steal from me except my life? Ah, let them take it, and quickly, by God, here is my life, steal my life, thieves, take it now, sink your blades into a poor heart; Holy Virgin, such disdain is hard to bear, how can Alma not invite me into her home? Me, Jesús

Dolores Santacruz, who lent the magistrate a helping hand, assisted him when he was nothing but a pen pusher, who introduced him to councilman Asdrúbal Ortiz, a public official who would go on to define the magistrate's life, councilman Ortiz, may he rest in peace, the good friend I met by chance in the Marujita, the best brothel in Bogotá: that's where I made friends with the councilman, where I presented Nacho Caicedo, and Nacho Caicedo never thanked me, never."

At the mere mention of the magistrate's name, Lucio Rosas became impatient, and he grew even more annoyed at the suggestion that the magistrate frequented the Marujita, the brothel of most ignoble lineage in Bogotá. The gardener's suppressed rage did not go unnoticed by Jesús, who realized his mistake.

"I know you respect the magistrate," he said, as if sharing a secret. "I do too."

And he raised his voice, declaiming:

"Men like him aren't born every day. They make history. What would become of this country without magistrates of the stature of Nacho Caicedo? And he is my brother-in-law, sir, the husband of my dearest sister, Almita Santacruz, and yet look at me here, I wasn't invited to the celebration, they send me away like a convict to the gallows, force me to come sleep in Chía, this pestilent municipality that is Bogotá's slaughterhouse, far from them, where they can't be infected by foul Jesús; they send me in the custody of a stranger, because that's what you are to me, a complete stranger—or an undercover cop? In any case, an unknown quantity, or a new friend, why not? A friend of whom I beg the assistance that is owed to somebody without hope: the hospital dismissed me as a hopeless cause; I have no gold, don't wear ties, so it's go die in the street, dog."

71

Uncle Jesús became deflated. He bowed his head. Genuine tears stained his patched shirt. His head grazed Lucio's shoulder, his throat quivered, he didn't know what to do with his trembling hands.

"We've rested long enough," said the gardener. And he discovered, anxiously, that he was anxious. "Let's find that hotel, mister: you can eat what you like, watch television, be left alone, have a lie down."

"No," said Jesús, terrified. "That's exactly what I don't want: to be left alone."

And from his coat, he drew a piece of multicolored cardboard, folded in four.

"It's a lottery ticket," he said. "Look. It has twelve lines. This is how I spend the money I earn with the sweat of my brow, on the lottery. Because one day St. Anthony of Miracles will make me win the lottery. I bought this ticket last Monday. The draw is tomorrow, Saturday. Millions. There are millions here. Then those ingrates will see, they'll see what a good soul I have and how I bear no grudges. To you, Lucio, I'll give a couple of million; you'll be able to buy whatever you like, maybe you can get that eye operated on, or put in a new one, it'll be made of glass but look real, and you'll always thank your lucky stars for having helped Jesús Dolores Santacruz, you won't be sorry. In other words, I'm giving it to you, Lucio. Receive this lottery ticket, receive luck. See how big my heart is, see how I trust you. I know that when you win, you'll remember me. And you will win, there's no doubt about that. You're a luckier man than I am. Here."

He blessed the lottery ticket like a pope and placed it in the gardener's hands.

And then something happened which the gardener found impossible to believe: Uncle Jesús, that feeble man, who seemed genuinely without hope, following those few minutes' rest at the Parque de la Luna, following his weeping, bolted like a deer.

Lucio Rosas stood up in shock, the lottery ticket in his hands. He checked the date: it was from two years ago.

And, a second later, the worst thing happened: he felt the pocket in which he'd been carrying the money Ike had given him; it was gone; Uncle Jesús had swiped it, cleanly. However, in the next second, the gardener ceased to be a gardener, and the hunter appeared. He didn't even bother to run after Jesús. He took long strides in pursuit of his trail, imperturbable, swift, cold. A twisted smile even darkened his eye-patched features: *You're going to the bus terminal*, he thought, *that's where I'll find you, No Hope*.

10

"Did you see papá arrive, riding on that mule? The mule is called Rosita. Are we going to see Rosita?"

"I saw the mule riding your papá," said Uriela. "At least, that's how it looked to me. But let's go see Rosita."

They reached the bottom of the spiral staircase and walked straight into Italia, in the corridor, sitting by the little telephone table. She had just put down the receiver, her face glowing with satisfaction, and she wasn't dressed for the party: she was wearing blue overalls with the Eiffel tower stamped on the chest.

"But what handsome boys," her clear voice rang out, "the three redheads, how precious, what a trio of angelic children, all three of you dressed as sailors, I'd like to give you green hats and turn you into little duendes." And, as she said this, she embraced each of the boys and smothered them with kisses, on the head, on the cheeks, turning them red with bliss.

"Italia!" the boys were repeating, admiring her.

How could you not worship Italia? thought Uriela. She was undoubtedly the most beautiful of the sisters.

"We're going with Uriela to the patio, will you come with us?" said Cesítar.

"Later," replied Italia. "You go on ahead, we'll catch up with you. Uriela and I have something to do, isn't that right, Uriela? I need you for something."

"She needs me," Uriela echoed in surprise. "Boys, you know the way: the gate is at the back of the garden, open it, then close it behind you; don't forget to close it, otherwise the mule will join the party. Who would she dance with?"

The three Césars were already running to the patio, laughing incessantly. Then Italia's happiness vanished. Solemnly, she clasped Uriela's hands and said:

"I need you to help me carry my suitcase."

"What?"

"So that nobody notices me leaving."

"You're leaving the house?"

"I left a letter for papá on the desk in the library. Besides, he and mamá are already aware of the main point. They're in their bedroom right now. For a moment, I wanted to warn them I was leaving, but the door was locked, so I decided not to knock. Aren't they celebrating their anniversary after all? Let them celebrate in style, let them carry on with getting dressed or undressed. What do they care what happens to me, to their daughter, to Italia?"

"What are you saying? Suitcase, letter?"

Uriela could only guess.

"I've just spoken to De Francisco," continued Italia, as though thinking aloud, absorbed, delirious. "We're getting married, we're having this child." And she touched her own tummy as if she still didn't believe it.

74

"Are you expecting a child?"

"Sixty days."

"I'm going to be an aunt?"

Uriela embraced Italia, but Italia immediately pulled away.

"I haven't got time. Help me carry that suitcase, I don't have the strength, I get dizzy, what an urge I have to vomit all this up," and she continued to rub her tummy. "Let's go up to my room."

Laughter was still bubbling from the drawing room, the voices of César, Ricardo. There was the sound of a glass breaking: "A drink for the dead," said a woman's voice—Perla Tobón?

"Let's go," urged Italia. "We can't let those people discover us."

They climbed the spiral staircase and reached Italia's room: on top of the bed was the magistrate's leather suitcase, the largest of his suitcases, from his trip to Singapore, stuffed like a hippopotamus, thought Uriela.

"Am I going to have to carry that hippopotamus?"

"Only to the street. De Francisco is waiting for me there. I'm going to go live with him. His parents have agreed. His mamá says she'll teach me how to prepare duck in wine sauce, which is De Francisco's favorite dish … how funny … they've got that chicken factory … and yet he prefers duck, they could save a lot if De Francisco liked chicken, don't you think?"

She laughed for a moment, desperately, looking around as if she no longer recognized her own bedroom, the entire house, as if she despised everything.

"Why don't you call him Porto, Italia? Are you planning to call him De Francisco in front of all the other De Franciscos? Start saying Porto."

"You're right. I hadn't thought about that. Portíco is waiting for me on the corner."

"Portíco makes him sound like a portico. Just call him Porto, period."

"Porto is waiting for me on the corner. Why do you have to be such a pedant?"

Uriela hauled up the suitcase and began descending the stairs.

"They're going to see us," Uriela said. "You can't ignore the passage of a suitcase like this one, it's worse than a coffin, the cousins will ask about it, papá won't let you escape just like that, mamá will scream, and the party hasn't even begun yet, the worst guests still haven't arrived, they'll probably get here just as we're leaving, what a scene, me, Uriela, carrying the suitcase of my fleeing sister, it's enough to drive you mad, how is it that you're the one who's running away? I thought I would be the first, and … are you really expecting a child? Could it be psychological? Remember, that can happen: it stops and then it comes back: there's no child, it was all a dream."

"I'm having a child," said Italia, who was out in front, keeping watch. "I'm going to live with Porto. It's nothing out of this world."

"Having a child and living with someone else *is* out of this world," replied Uriela, overwhelmed by the suitcase. "What have you got in here besides your dresses? All your shoes? Your tricycle, your bicycle? Damn, this is heavy."

"Right. Now we run to the door."

"We run?"

"Nobody's watching."

They passed by the drawing room, but none of the roaring heads turned toward them. They opened the front door, and there it was, parked in the middle of the street: the truck belonging to the De Francisco family, a white hauler with a colossal polystyrene chicken on the roof, adorned with the crown, scepter, and cloak of a king. *Pollo Real, Your Chicken*, read an enormous sign. Uriela froze with the hippopotamus beside her. Italia ran over to the cabin of the truck: standing next to the open door waited Porto, his hair down to his shoulders; he was wearing a leather hat with a feather in the side. They embraced. Porto lifted her up and spun her around several times—*like in a fairy tale*, thought Uriela, lugging the suitcase to the back of the truck, which immediately opened, magically, from inside, as though someone had known Uriela was coming.

Porto's entire family was waiting inside.

In the immensity of that compartment, sitting around a rectangular table, with the table and chairs bolted down to the floor of the hauler, were Porto de Francisco's mother and father, grandmother, aunt, and brothers, each with a bottle of beer in their hand. In a corner at the back was an enormous refrigerator with a glass door: Uriela gaped at the number of raw chickens hanging from meat hooks. She was even more surprised by the enthusiastic collective greeting. The man who was surely Porto's father was raising a grilled chicken drumstick to his mouth. His mother was eating too, a wing; she greeted Uriela as she ate. The aunt was identical to the mother, and was smoking. Porto's two brothers hurried to load the suitcase.

"Aren't you coming with us?" one of the brothers asked Uriela. He was wearing a white turban on his head, and his suit was from India, made of resplendent silk, which amused Uriela and put her in mind of a Brahman. His beard reached down to his navel; he had a clay ring in his ear.

Uriela stared back at him:

"Perhaps in another life," she replied.

"There's a good chance this *is* your other life," he said, gravely.

77

"My name is Tutú, I'm Porto's grandmother," said the old woman, coming over. Since Uriela was down in the street, she was forced to look up, her neck bent entirely backward: that's how high the Pollo Real truck was. The old woman greeted her from up there, like a giant, though she was actually small and wrinkled, but agile: she knelt down and extended her hand to Uriela. "We're not sure if your father knows about this, but tell him not to worry. Tell him he should call us, that's why phones exist."

"He'll probably come see you in person," said Uriela.

"Well, even better," said the owner of Pollo Real, sticking his fat head out. Uriela could see he was an imposing man, with a guttural voice and the eyes of a chicken, small and shiny. "We'll have a proper conversation. Correct. Civilized."

Uriela sensed that her sister was making the worst mistake of her life, but there was no time left for talking, for asking. Porto had climbed into the cabin of the truck—he was driving—and began sounding a horn that was the exact replica of a rooster's morning crow. The rooster's crowing spread up and down the street, and the baseball kids witnessed this event with delight. Before climbing in beside Porto, Italia ran to say goodbye to Uriela, while the rooster crowed.

They embraced for the final time.

11

On the tips of his toes, his hands held out like a blind man, Rodolfito Cortés reached the top of the spiral staircase. Only once before had he been inside Francia's bedroom. He struggled to remember the way, which of the three corridors sinking into the darkness to go down. A house with no rhyme or reason, he thought, how much had the magistrate paid for it?

His heart skipped a beat. In the gloom at the end of the

corridor, he saw the open door to Francia's room; and he saw Francia, as if within a yellow mist; he saw her standing in front of the desk, her long red dress, her bare arms and shoulders, one hand on top of the salvaged newspaper clipping, which he, Rodolfito Cortés, did not see.

"Francia, my love."

Francia gave a start. From within the eternity of her ruminations, she had never imagined the traitor would come up to her room to fetch her believing that they were getting married, *my God, what nerve, what shamelessness*, she screamed to herself, and yet she turned to him with a smile and listened in silence.

"Why haven't you come down to the drawing room, my love?" Rodolfito inquired. "I've come to get you."

He crossed the threshold. Then he froze for a second, before making up his mind and promptly kissing her on the lips, *lightly, very lightly*, thought Francia.

But suddenly he looked at her open-mouthed, genuinely shocked:

"Francia," he said. "Are you crying?"

"Yes," she said, "I'm weeping with happiness."

Then Ike appeared in the doorway, irrepressible.

"Cousin, what a sight for sore eyes, how long have you been cloistered away up here? In the words of that song: *It's been a month since last we met.*"

Another shock for Francia.

A month ago, she had kissed her cousin—she'd forgotten, but suddenly, yes, and not just because he had reminded her, with that malicious face, but also because she had suddenly remembered the kiss in all its splendor, its trembling and its force, why had she? And, quickly, she asked herself, *What's got into this madman? What is he doing here? Why has he come to me?* And, her nerves aflutter, she also asked herself: *as children …*

79

did we … ? I think we did, or perhaps not and so what if we did, it's over, a childhood love; but he insists and insists and insists. A month ago? How stupid, why did I kiss him? He kissed me and I let him, oh I don't know, Ike is kind, Ike suffers, he suffers for me, and I enjoyed that kiss, didn't I? Did I?

All these thoughts came to Francia within a second. It unnerved her that Ike had come up to her room behind Rodolfito, thwarting her plans for revenge. Ike was surely jealous, and in pursuit of the inoffensive Rodolfito. *Inoffensive? What will I do? Why all this rage? Why this desire to explode? I want to scream, my temples ache, I'm going to faint again.*

"Have you met Rodolfito?" it occurred to her to ask.

"Of course," said Ike, holding out his hand, and, once he had Rodolfito's hand within his grasp, he squeezed hard, "I saw you crash into a tree; I reversed to come and help, but you jumped out of your car to go speak to some kids."

Rodolfito felt as if his hand were going to break.

"That's right," he said. "I went to ask them the time."

Cousin Ike let go, delighted by this response.

"What are you talking about?" asked Francia. "Who crashed into a tree?"

But she was no longer paying attention, it didn't matter to her; all she understood was that somehow her moment for revenge had arrived.

And, very tenderly, she took hold of Ike's hands.

"Ike," she said, "my first love. Thank you for thinking of me. It isn't nice to feel forgotten. Did you know, Rodolfito, that as children Ike and I were an item; how innocent, but what happiness, over at the La Vega farm … Do you remember, Ike, when we used to go looking for water lilies? You're very tall, Cousin, you grow taller every day."

And she released Ike's hands as if she had slipped into a dream.

Ike listened to her, transported. This really was extraordinary. Francia was always so reluctant … She must surely want to get rid of the amphibian. Well, he would help her. *And I might just be able to steal another kiss,* he yelled to himself, *my God, what a red little mouth you have, it was made for kissing, and those cheeks, that neck, that back, the way your ass looks under that red dress, those little silver shoes—pantyhose? Francia, you're going to drive me crazier than I already am.*

"Let's not go down to the drawing room just yet," proposed Francia, "I need to take three deep breaths before I can stand César, I really dislike him; didn't you see him arrive on the back of that mule? What a bogeyman, what a beast, he scares me; come over here you two, let's talk for a bit, shall we?"

Bemused, they allowed her to take their hands and lead them over to her own bed, making them sit there, on the same side, one next to the other, both looking at each other nervously, stupefied, in front of her. Francia sat in the chair by the desk, resting her elbow on top of the newspaper clipping:

"We were happy, Cousin Ike. As the song goes: *Remembering the lovely youth …* " and she hummed "On Days like These" for a minute, in a very fine voice that touched Ike, who'd been listening to her sing since they were children and had fallen in love with her because of it; it was a voice that sent shivers down Rodolfito's spine, because he had never heard her sing. They had forgotten to sing together, he thought, and surely that was why … And yet he thought with satisfaction about their encounters at the Scheherazade motel, when they would make love with that fervor of the first time, and this was what he wanted to repeat, at all costs: he was suffocated by a monstrous desire for Francia. Was this a farewell? The final flourish? He knew that during the anniversary party they would find the moment, the place, yes, it was unavoidable, he yearned for Francia as never before, Francia filled his dreams.

But I'm not the one you want to marry, Francia was thinking at that same instant, as though guessing his thoughts.

"Look," she said, taking something from the desk drawer. "This was papá's graduation present to me, don't you think it's incredible?"

She held out a gold fountain pen to Ike, directing her words solely to him as she spoke. She looked solely at him:

"It's so expensive that I'm afraid to use it, someone could steal it. It's made of pure gold."

"Well," said Ike, "things are meant to be used."

"No one would ever rob you, Ike, you wouldn't allow yourself to be robbed, would you? For that alone, I'd be willing to give it to you ... do you want it?"

Rodolfito spluttered. Francia's allusion could not have been more direct: three years earlier, they had been holding hands on Calle 19: Francia had wanted to buy a leather handbag to go with her shoes, but Rodolfito was unable to get it for her, not just because it hadn't occurred to him, but also because he didn't have a peso to his name; Rodolfito's parents sent him money from Cali to cover the basics. Francia would feed Rodolfito in secret, giving him pints of milk from the fridge, making him yucca pie and homemade kumis to take for lunch to the residence hall where he lived, she would iron his shirts, mend them, provide him with everything from his toothbrush to his underpants. But that day, Francia was going to buy something for herself, to the annoyance of Rodolfito, who didn't appreciate the fact that nothing would be purchased for him. They were holding hands in the deserted street when two kids appeared.

"They were two little brats," Francia told Teresita, her best friend, "no more than ten years old, their heads shaved, all skin and bones, two street kids who only came up to my belly button, each carrying a screwdriver in his hand. To me—and only me—they said: 'Cough up!' 'Cough up?' I asked them, 'What do you want me to cough up?' I didn't understand. 'Just cough it all up!' they repeated, 'But I haven't swallowed anything,' I said, and then Rodolfito goes and explains it to me: 'They're telling you to give them all your money,' and I couldn't believe it, Rodolfito, translator of street kids, but then I looked at him, my God, he looked as if he were about to die, pale and trembling like a cloud, and he couldn't stop staring at the screwdrivers as if they were already buried in his heart, poor Rodolfito, he was breathless, deflated, and, worst of all, when one of those little louses pressed the point into his stomach, to hurry him along, Rodolfito snatched the bag from me himself, opened it, took out my money, and handed it to them."

"My God, what a fool you are," lamented Teresita, listening to Francia, "I don't know what you're doing with a guy like that. Tell me, Francia, is Rodolfito really that good in bed? Is he hung like a donkey at least? Or did he give you an Indian love potion? What's the matter with you?" "I don't know how to explain it," replied Francia, "it's just that I really care for Rodolfito, he's so fragile, and yet so endearing, so helpless, like a little orphan." "Shouldn't you see a psychiatrist?" replied Teresita. "Fragile and endearing? To me he looks more like a toad, and the things you tell me would make me die of rage, what a fool you are, if a guy ever let me get pawed at by some kids, I'd kick him." "No," said Francia, hastily, "Rodolfito was suffering, suffering in silence, but suffering, that's why I've always forgiven him."

At that moment, Ike was receiving the gold fountain pen. Would he accept the gift? Absolutely.

Rodolfito felt as if his words were coming up from his

stomach, as if he were hauling them up with his hands, one by one, in order to say something:

"You can't write with gold fountain pens."

"Bullshit," said Ike. "Of course you can." He uncapped the fountain pen and wrote something on the palm of his hand; it must have been a carefully thought-out sentence, because it took him a minute that felt like a year.

"Show me," said Francia. She sprang up from the chair, tossing her hair back, a wave of jasmine perfume floating on the air, and leaned over Ike's hand, reading aloud: *Francia, I still love you.* She let out a short, puerile burst of laughter: "How crazy, what a thought, you're going to kill me, but ours was a childish love!"

And she said this truthfully, though feeling genuinely delighted, not just because she had never imagined that the pen would actually write on a person's skin, but because that person had written the words she had just read aloud, and in front of the traitor, how marvelous, she thought.

"Rodolfito," said Francia, "forgive Ike this declaration of love. You must take into account the love we shared as children, and I repeat, as children, for the avoidance of any doubt."

And she gave Ike a friendly tap on the cheek. Then this same hand landed for an instant on Ike's hard knee, squeezing it for seconds that to Rodolfito proved lethal, just like screwdrivers to the heart. Rodolfito gulped: as he watched Francia sit back down in the chair, smiling, he thought how losing her would be like losing a leg. He must surely have thought of it in these terms because he longed to cut off that leg of Ike's which Francia's hand had caressed, or because losing this girlfriend really would be like losing a leg. Then his eyes moved on to Francia, they took in her face, her neck, the round, rosy line of her shoulders, the golden

84

down of her forearm, the bent elbow resting on top of the newspaper clipping…

He went pale. He knew that clipping all too well, the wedding announcement—and with a photo, too.

He made a great effort to look as if he were listening. If he'd been standing, he would have collapsed. He had never imagined that Francia knew. He realized that she would find out sooner or later, but he'd never considered that she might already know.

She knew.

"What I remember best, Cousin," Ike was saying, his voice altered, bathed in tenderness, having forgotten all about Rodolfito, "is when we used to hide in the chaff, do you remember? The chaff, Francia, that pile of straw, the ears of wheat—yellow—and the blue skies, we would play hide and seek there, we all hid and you and I never came out, do you remember?"

Francia blushed. This she did not remember: it had been there that he touched her intimately, and she touched him, there they'd kissed for the first time; it had been from that place that she had fled, as if slipping away, never getting close to her cousin again, she had panicked and forgotten about it. Why? Or had it all just been a game she'd forgotten? But Ike never forgot: over the years he had pursued her in order to remind her. Right then, Francia looked at Ike and experienced the same panic she had as a child: it was as if Ike were sniffing her.

That's how she felt: sniffed at.

12

To Nacho Caicedo and Alma Santacruz, peering out of the window and yet always behind the curtains, lurking shadows, there was no appeal in going down to the drawing room and entertaining the first guests, who were simply their nephews. They preferred to wait for the arrival of the older relatives; the young could keep each other company. Then they saw the dark Mercedes pull in, facing the garage doors. These were Alma Santacruz's sisters, Adelfa and Emperatriz. The two sisters climbed out of the Mercedes, aided by a very attentive Zambranito, who was sporting the leather-peaked hat of an English chauffeur: "Did you make Zambranito wear that hat?" asked the magistrate, surprised. Adelfa and Emperatriz had donned their best gowns; older than Señora Alma, they tinted their hair to hide the grays. They both retained that charm of certain older women which reminds you they were once beautiful: "How gorgeous they look," teased Alma, intrigued that Adelfa hadn't brought her three young daughters with her.

Nacho Caicedo was also dressed to the nines, in a black suit and pale-blue tie, an impeccable white shirt, and gold cuff links, each containing an emerald. But he was paying no attention to his sisters-in-law; the doors to the garage flew open and the blonde Iris Sarmiento appeared, waiting for Zambranito to bring in the Mercedes. The ever-present Marino Ojeda had come to help her, despite there being no need: "I don't like that watchman," said the magistrate. "Unless my eyes deceive me, he's just put his hand on the girl's backside. You need to stay vigilant, Alma, otherwise Italia won't be the only one coming to us with a little surprise." "Fantasies," said Señora Alma, "Marino is a good kid. Last week he chased a thief out of the Ruggieros' garden." "I'm not talking about thieves, but about the girl's ass," replied the magistrate. Señora Alma was pleased to observe that Lisboa and Palmira had gone out to receive the new arrivals, helping them with the gifts they had brought; you could hear their voices: "And where's Alma," Emperatriz was asking, "why hasn't she come down to greet us?" "She's still getting ready," Lisboa was saying.

"Well, I'd better go down now," said Señora Alma.

Her husband put his hands around her waist, and she looked at him; well, this was unexpected: they'd already had their lovers' encounter, why take things any further? She really did look splendid in her long dress, and, though past her prime and made up like an actress from the last century, her eyes and body also told of a soft, not-too-distant beauty. And, with no trepidation, but rather a studied delicacy, and in a single movement, the magistrate raised her dress up to her waist and began rubbing her satin roundness with his hand. Then he uncovered it completely.

"And what's all this?" Señora Alma protested meekly, "are you trying to imitate the watchman? Enough now, I must go see my sisters."

"It's still perfect," the magistrate was saying, hunched over her. "As round as the first time. It's the finest I've ever known."

Ever since their honeymoon, Alma Santacruz had grown accustomed to the fact that her husband would employ compliments of this sort precisely to let her know when he wished to make love to her. As overwhelmed as she was flattered, she wanted to escape that embrace, but he toppled her onto the bed, face down, mouth against the blanket, and, though they were both dressed, he was able to find a way, patient and experienced: "It must surely be because I'm going to die," he was saying, his face contorted, his mouth glued to his wife's ear, which was flushed, febrile, as known as it was unknown. She let him do it, without masking her displeasure, ill-tempered to begin with, yet helping him, fractious but exalted, and, finally, overcome, satisfied at the same time

87

he was. It had been these transformational encounters, these spontaneous eruptions, first taking place from day to day, then week to week, and, finally, month to month, that had ensured they never grew weary of each other.

"You've creased my dress," said Señora Alma.

One beneath the other, they gazed at each other with admiration. With mutual compassion. Then the voices of their daughters in the street alerted them.

"Why haven't they come in yet?" Alma was asking, standing in front of the dresser mirror, smoothing the creases in her dress, "what are they waiting for?"

The magistrate went back to look out the window. He was no taller than his wife, balding, his stomach protruding, and yet he radiated strength from every pore.

"The others aren't here yet," he lamented. "The notables haven't arrived."

"Once they get here, I'll have lunch served in the garden," said Alma, efficiently. "There are enough small tables for an entire army. We'll eat as a family in the dining room."

"Fine. They'll be here. I'm only coming out once the notables have arrived. Go attend to those nephews God graced you with. I'm taking a nap. There's too much hustle and bustle."

"I'll go see my sisters and tell them you behaved like a horse. They'll envy me."

"Send my greetings to Emperatriz. I've always had a thing for her."

"Why would you tell me that today?"

"You know you're the only star in my firmament," said Nacho Caicedo, and they laughed.

After hesitating for a moment, they embraced for the final time.

PART THREE

1

But who were the worst guests, according to Uriela, and who the notables, according to the magistrate, what did they do, what made them suffer, in what order or disorder would they arrive?

It was now after midday; rain had been forecast but the sun came out, the merciless Altiplano sun that reddened the necks of the baseball kids; they tossed the ball lethargically, preferring instead to sit and spy on the events of that party to which a white mule had arrived, to them the grandest of guests, the most intriguing. Was it possible that, once the dancing started, they might be allowed in to ride on the mule? Why not? They knew Uriela Caicedo.

Their mothers were also dedicating themselves to contemplation; bored young women, that Friday would redeem them from an apathy that was more than routine: it was eternal; that Friday could be absolutely anything except just another day: perhaps they would be invited to the dance, allowing them the pleasure of accepting or declining the invitation. Why not? They knew Magistrate Caicedo.

The arrival of Monsignor Javier Hidalgo and his young secretary, Father Perico Toro, reaffirmed expectations: to begin with, it was assumed that the black limousine they arrived in was a funeral hearse, minus its casket. When the clergymen stepped out, the sun throbbing in the center of the sky convinced them of an infernal heat: walking arm in arm, they decided to stop for a short breather, dark birds in the heat wave. As they called at the door, at that precise instant, the day darkened, clouds swallowed up the sun, an apocalyptic thunderclap rang out over the world, and the rain came down as though some gargantuan being had started pissing. A premonition?

Behind the two drenched shadows, the archiepiscopal limousine was disappearing, long and black, as if for transporting a casket. The neighbors on the verge of fainting (how to explain that sunshine and then the opening of the heavens?), the baseball players, the guard, they all spied on this religious apparition, as funereal as it was illuminated; beneath dizzying clouds, in the blue glare of the lightning, Monsignor Hidalgo gripped his black cassock, rippled by the wind, as the secretary ran to catch the zucchetto that had been swiped by the gale from the monsignor's head. Once the hat had been rescued, the monsignor and his secretary planted themselves in front of the door and waited.

The magistrate came out in person to receive them. He led them inside.

The door closed on the downpour.

A sexagenarian like the magistrate, Monsignor Javier Hidalgo nevertheless perceived himself as being much older: hunched and bloated, with no eyebrows, he appeared not to have eyes but rather two minuscule reddish streaks beneath his lids. Uriela couldn't help likening the monsignor's head to that of her turtle, and she didn't enjoy the comparison, feeling it an insult to her turtle. Of the magistrate's daughters, Uriela was the only one who openly detested the monsignor. She was fully aware of the reason for this: years earlier, she had listened in on an argument between her parents about a "secret" connected to him. However, long before overhearing that argument, ever since she was a little girl, Uriela had loathed the monsignor, out of pure childish instinct, she said.

Monsignor Hidalgo did not suspect that his secret had been shared; he could never have foreseen such a lapse on the part of Nacho Caicedo: the monsignor had baptized the magistrate's daughters, had heard the magistrate's own confession, as well as that of his wife, he *knew about them*, and if he had been unable to bless their union, this was only because he found himself confined to that parish in New York at the time, where the Archbishop of Medellín had sent him in the wake of his "first boy." For Monsignor Hidalgo was a deflowerer of young boys, a profaner of altar servers, a sodomite, an abuser, an abductor, and a rapist, but also a friend of the magistrate. The pair, both natives of Popayán, had attended high school together, and ever since those years, they had looked out for each other.

Uriela had learned the details of the secret one morning, while listening to that argument behind closed doors: Señora Alma was opposing the magistrate's intervention in the monsignor's "situation." For, although the Catholic brotherhood and the Pope himself had absolved the monsignor of all guilt, over the course of the years, life had not: his first boy had grown up. From a rosy little six-year-old, he transformed into a brute with lawyers, his soul disfigured ever since the monsignor's first assault. The monsignor spent millions, but was asked to pay three times more; one Sunday, he saw the brute with the face of an executioner, listening in the front row to mass in the cathedral, the mass he presided over, and, afterwards, during communion, as he distributed the Sacred Host, he watched in horror as the brute joined the back of the line and then received the host when his turn came with his libidinous mouth open, not ceasing to contort his tongue like a serpent, before swallowing the body of Christ whole as though swallowing something else. Between sobs, Monsignor Hidalgo confessed to the magistrate that he had been at the point of collapsing, chalice and all. And what compounded his calvary was the fact that the tormentor's communion would be repeated every Sunday, with the monsignor unable to do anything to prevent it, except request an audience with Nacho Caicedo. Only the magistrate could help him, and help him he did: he believed, or purported to believe, in the monsignor's innocence. Alma Santacruz did not, but she was a wise woman in her own way: she forgot about the incident just as she had forever consigned to oblivion other matters of justice that her husband confided in her, perhaps in order to share his burden. The magistrate had the monsignor and defloweree sign an agreement, persuading the monsignor to make use of funds from the Ave María Catholic School, where he was principal, to pay the remaining millions, the final millions, and the nightmare disappeared, the defloweree vanished from his masses; never again, thanks to Nacho Caicedo, did the monsignor have to deliver Christ's body to that uncoiling serpent, never again, thanks to the magistrate, was he required to bear the fruits of his sin. How could he not attend the anniversary, how could he not bestow his blessing?

And next to arrive was Cecilito's orchestra, though all famished and very much looking forward to lunch—hopefully sooner rather than later.

The squall had now moved on, the sun floated darkly in the sky, but at least it was there. The baseball players and their mothers went silent on witnessing the arrival of the orchestral caravan, a cage wagon from the zoo. The *Los Malaspulgas Band, Tropical Orchestra* alighted one by one with their instruments on their backs. They were all young, but every last one of them had wobbly knees, puffy eyelids, purple mouths; their cobweb-covered clothes made it clear they hadn't bathed in weeks, and, as the name of their orchestra—"the Mean Fleas"—suggested, they didn't seem at all happy, or else they adopted sour faces by general consent, in homage to themselves. Of the nine band members, only one was a woman: the vocalist and dancer, Charrita Luz.

Cecilio Diez, leading man, conga beater, and godson to Alma Santacruz, liked to dress all in black. With a black, wide-brimmed hat, dark sideburns, and a black goatee, he resembled a musical Mephistopheles. The whole world knew he was married with children, but *his* world knew he was a homosexual and in love with Momo Ray, his flautist. Cecilito, son of an ill-fated accordionist, and hailing from the same town as Alma, had been fortunate enough to have Alma Santacruz take charge of his life: she paid for his studies at the conservatory and didn't get upset when Cecilito decided that the conservatory wasn't worth a damn and that he knew better. She became his godmother and helped him assemble his orchestra; then a miracle took place: the Los Malaspulgas Band conquered Colombia; now they were playing in Alma Santacruz's home, because she was the de facto mother not only of their orchestra, but also of its director and conga player, Cecilio Diez.

However, being an orchestra man wasn't Cecilito's only feat. In an outburst of jealousy, prompted by "guy troubles," he had killed his first saxophonist with a conga blow to the head. The first saxophonist had been so handsome, so well-endowed, why couldn't he be faithful too? Nacho Caicedo had prevented Cecilito being sent to liven up piñata dances in prison: he cleared him of all national suspicion, absolved him of punishment, and got him a reprieve. How could Cecilito not play at the magistrate's home?

2

Next to arrive was Uncle Luciano, brother to the magistrate and toyshop owner, with his wife Luz and daughters Sol and Luna, and then Barrunto Santacruz, brother to Alma, with his wife Celmira and son Rigo, followed by José Sansón, the magistrate's cousin, Artemio Aldana, a childhood friend, Sparks, a cousin of Alma's, Pumpkin, another cousin, Batato Armado and Liserio Caja, shadowy protégés of the magistrate—in truth, his most discreet bodyguards—the publicist Roberto Smith, infamous for his bad temper and the magistrate's perpetual client, the university lecturer Manolo Zulú, the banana exporter Cristo María Velasco and his fifteen-year-old daughter Marianita, Conrado Olarte, professional magician, Yupanqui Ortega, mortuary makeup artist, owner of the Ortega Funeral Parlor—he referred to himself as a "thanatologist"—Pepe Sarasti and Lady Mar, dentists, Principal Dalilo Alfaro and Marilú, owners of the Magdelene School for Girls, and the twins Celio and Caveto Hurtado—science teachers at that same school—the art teacher Obdulia Cera, the professional cyclist and P.E. teacher Pedro Pablo Rayo, the primary school teachers Roque San Luis, Rodrigo Moya, and Fernanda Fernández, the two Davides, booksellers, the butcher Cirilo Cerca, who was also an amateur baritone, the fiancés Teo and Esther, Cheo and Bruneta, and Ana and Antón, those nicknamed Ingenuo and Sexilia, Sexenio and Fecunda, the aguardiente exporter Pepa Sol and her husband Salvador Cantante—who was mute and also a trumpet player—the one nicknamed The Hen, owner of a supermarket, the Barney sisters, tango singers, and then entire families known only by their unprecedented surnames: the Florecitos, the Mayonesos, the Púas—with both grandfather and great-grandfather still alive—the Calaveras, the Pambazos, the Carisinos, the Místericos, the Pío del Ríos, a rising tide of incongruous names and faces, guileless and expectant; and, with the introduction of the jurists—the magistrate's clerks and interns, grateful subalterns, all stakeholders in the treasury—the watching housewives proclaimed without bias that never before had they seen such wicked and stupid faces, it seemed to them that all the world's hatred, as well as the most sublime idiocy, had arrived in their neighborhood, evil and boorishness combined, the mean-spirited—they commented in shock—or those lacking spirits, the soulless and the unsouled, the dissolute, the unscrupulous, and they also observed how the highest ranking arrived in vehicles provided by the government, with their chauffeurs and aides, while the inferior arrived in taxis; and, disturbed, they looked on as the entire street filled up with bleary, bloodshot-looking eyes, with one of those subordinates—as a joke, or perhaps because they wouldn't let him into the house—becoming fed up and deciding to slip in through the balcony, with everyone watching as he climbed up the window railings, reached the balcony, threw one leg over, then the other, and vanished, and this was followed by the arrival of Arquímedes Lama, a judge, and, with him, as though protecting him, Blanca Vaca and Celia Fuerte and Dolores Justa, his honorable colleagues, ladies who, though young, already appeared more than a hundred years old, and the throng of people did not stop growing, their long, funereal ties waving in the cigarette smoke, their shiny bald heads vying like battering rams to cross the threshold, and amid all the voices and laughter and complaining, it seemed that even the dead themselves were arriving in a dark herd to greet the magistrate, their shadows could be glimpsed howling within, with no need for doors or windows, simply passing through the walls, and with so many of the dead among so many of the living, it finally became possible to understand the monstrous reason for which Uncle Jesús had not wished to miss this party.

3

"Iris," said Cousin César, "I've been looking for you. My wife left my suit and shoes in the library. Where the hell is the library? Perla told me it was the best place to change, better than the bathroom, is that true? And nobody will see me? I'm worried about alarming my cousins with my belly."

From somewhere in her recollections, Iris unearthed the fact that César Santacruz had already warned her that sooner or later she would need to show him where to change. He had also asked her for a bucket of clean water and a saucepan of carrots for the mule. *How could I forget? My head is all over the place.* Iris Sarmiento blushed, apologetic.

They were in the corridor being used by busy waiters: any of them could have shown him to the library, thought Iris. And again, that same shiver she had experienced on the patio, with César and Rosita, paralyzed her.

"Monsignor Hidalgo has just arrived," César Santacruz was saying. "I can't kiss his ring unless I'm wearing my black suit—like for the Day of the Dead!"

He laughed.

Iris thought she had better laugh too.

"It's raining," she said. "The heavens are coming down."

It was all she could think to say.

Cousin César was glancing in all directions. He knew how to get to the library but was pretending that he didn't. Perla had told him she'd left his suit and shoes in there, since it was out of the way, but that he should go change in the bathroom. "I'll come with you," she offered, but César snorted that he could dress himself. He had spent quite some time looking for

Iris all over the house—in the kitchen, the garage, the parlor and the dining room, in the second-floor sitting room, on the balcony—until finally coming across her after he'd already given up all hope, downstairs, in the corridor, one-to-one.

"It's through here," stammered Iris, "the library isn't far." And she advanced very slowly, as though in pain, along the interminable corridor, in front of César Santacruz, who was scrutinizing her. She could feel his eyes all over her body. They paralyzed her.

"And no one's going to see me?" asked César, from behind.

"It's the best place," said Iris, "no one will see you. But you could also go to the guest bathroom. It's big and has mirrors … this house has six bathrooms."

"No. Someone will need to pee while I'm changing. I don't want to be a pain."

They were coming to the library, a distant chamber beyond the parlor and the dining room.

Cousin César entered, but grabbed hold of Iris's hand:

"Wait," he said. "Stay with me, I want to tell you something."

Again, that shiver paralyzed her. She couldn't say a thing, allowing herself to be dragged along as if by the current of a river: she was drowning.

"But what a lovely girl you are, Iris, you're going to make me cry."

She was genuinely shocked:

"Me, make you cry? Why would I make you cry?"

"Because of your beauty, Iris. How old did you say you were? Why do you live with my aunt Alma? What world did they bring you from?"

"I'm her goddaughter," said Iris, "I mean … I'm practically adopted."

She wasn't sure why, but she believed that if she carried

on with her story, this man would release her, would free her instantly. She continued talking, rapidly:

"I was given to them. I was a roadside offering to Señora Alma. That's what she told me. An old woman handed her a baby by the roadside and said: "Keep her." That was me, and Doña Alma kept me, thank God. I'm the same age as Uriela."

"What a load of damn books," said Cousin César, looking around him. "You could bore your life away in here."

It appeared he'd never even been listening to her.

Both turned their gazes toward a distant chair where the black suit was waiting, folded like a marionette over the backrest; the shoes sat luminously on the floor. A large black desk shone in the middle of the room, and it was toward this that Uncle César proceeded, without releasing Iris's hand.

"I think I should go," she said. "I heard someone calling me."

"Don't be scared, I only want to tell you something, come, Iris."

On top of the black desk was a white envelope. Uncle César picked it up and read it aloud: "Dear Father." He smiled, glancing at the back of the envelope and reading: "From your daughter, Italia."

Without ever ceasing his soundless laughter, his face like a silent mask, Uncle César slid the envelope into the pocket of the ostrich-leather waistcoat, which he had kept on. The desk was left empty, deserted. And on top of its black surface, on the edge, Uncle César forced Iris to sit—after grabbing her by the waist, lifting her. She had placed her hands on his shoulders, in order to push him away, but was unable to move him an inch: there was that ruddy neck and that red hair, up against her, but she couldn't speak, much less scream. César's hand on her neck forced her backward, almost asphyxiating her, lying her flat on her back. Then the mask of mute laughter pressed itself between her legs.

4

The hunter had to admit to himself that his wretch of a man was no easy quarry. Once he finally managed to catch a glimpse of him, he realized that Uncle Jesús wasn't heading to the bus terminal, as he'd assumed, but to the center of town: the turtledove suspected he would look for him at the terminal and had taken flight, as if forewarned. *You almost had me*, he thought. It surprised him that his quarry moved through the streets as if he knew where he was going.

Uncle Jesús walked in short bursts, exhausted from running; every now and then, he would turn and look back: nobody in the street. Nobody? There lurked the hunter, stone-faced, leaning his back against a brick wall, or behind a tree, or inside a doorway. This is how the minutes passed, the pair like slinking shadows, one after the other. Uncle Jesús's trail snaked through streets and alleyways; he paused at flea markets, disappearing and reappearing; he kept trying to shake off his pursuer.

In this manner, they skirted the Chía slaughterhouse, amid the unrestrained squealing of pigs ready to be sacrificed. The air smelled of blood. They traveled all the way around the slaughterhouse, before returning to the center of Chía. Near the Parque de la Luna, on a dusty street, Uncle Jesús paused outside the door of one of those old three-story mansions, funereal, with adobe walls: he scanned left and right one last time, pushed the door open, and disappeared. *He didn't have to knock*, thought the hunter, intrigued, what house was this? The hunter spent a long time observing the second- and third-story windows, all with their blinds pulled down. A nameless hotel? It was possible.

Opposite the house, there was a dive bar. Sullen regulars drank inside the dingy hall, sitting before grimy tablecloths. Stains like tomato splatters glistened on the walls. It smelled of aguardiente. One of the regulars, wearing a sombrero, walked between the tables humming Vallenatos, drunk. A sleepy-looking kid was behind the counter, sitting on a stool. On noticing the hunter, he gave a start: perhaps he had never seen a man with an eye-patch. The hunter ordered a beer, but remained standing in the doorway, bottle in hand, not drinking and not lifting his gaze from the house, in case Jesús peeped out. A brief exchange with any of those regulars would have been enough to learn what sort of a house this was, but the hunter had already guessed: "A whorehouse. And he's carrying all the money with him."

He paid for his beer and left the bottle untouched, on top of the counter. The singing drunk collected it like a trophy.

The hunter crossed the street in two bounds and pushed at the door: it opened onto a shadowy corridor. He advanced along it, in the gloom. He was dazzled by the light coming from an ancient garden, with a stone fountain in the middle, drained of water. Limp flowers bowed down onto the parched earth. It was a covered courtyard. Overhead, on top of a mossy glass canopy, it was possible to make out the shadow of something resembling the corpse of an electrocuted cat. At the edges of the stone floor, following its rectangular contours, the three stories of the mansion rose up, all exhibiting identical rooms, with faded blue doors, each sealed with a big rusty lock; only one of the doors was open, on the ground floor, in a corner of the courtyard, and a bluish light undulated inside it. He thought he could hear a woman's laughter, so he crossed the courtyard and peered in.

"I've been waiting for you, Lucio," came Jesús's voice, dejectedly. "Come on in, sit with me."

It was a large space with empty tables and chairs. Jesús sat waiting. A small skylight half lit the room. As if to encourage him in, Jesús rose to his feet: he was holding out a hand with the wad of cash. The hunter immediately recovered the wad: with a glance, he confirmed it was all there and pocketed it. Only then did he sit down.

"It was the only way to get us here," said Jesús. "Otherwise, you would never have allowed it. I had to make you chase me, and now here we are, sir, to clear things up."

"Clear things up?"

"It's that simple."

The hunter questioned whether this wretch of a man had really let himself be followed. He listened, skeptically, to the raspy voice:

"If Alma doesn't want me leaving Chía, then this is the only place I will stay. Anywhere else and I'll leave, you can count on it, and I'll show up at the party in Bogotá. So, Mister Gardener, give me that money and depart with an easy conscience. Tell my sister where you left me, who you left me with, and you'll see she understands perfectly. Alma knows these houses are like my home."

"Your home?"

"Here I can eat and sleep, and also, God willing, do other things. For me, Mister Gardener, God is a woman, the woman of your dreams. If God is willing, all the better, and, if not, there will be other women to distract me. Rest assured, this isn't the first time I've visited this house. They love me here, they respect me, they've known me for centuries, I could literally come in here and kick the dog, as the saying goes."

A woman's laughter could be heard again.

"Come, Miss Piggy," Uncle Jesús encouraged her.

And, becoming flesh in the shadows, the silhouette of a middle-aged woman appeared, plump, small, her curly hair dyed. She held out a pudgy hand to the hunter, and the hunter shook it.

"But what a powerful grip," she said, placing her other hand on top of the hunter's.

The hunter pulled away.

"Are you the owner of this establishment?"

"I might as well be, mister," she said, taking a seat. "I'm the administrator. Do you want something to drink, something to eat? There's mazamorra chiquita, the good kind, with plenty of meat, and mondongo soup."

"Nothing to eat or drink," said the hunter. "I just need for this gentleman"—and he raised his chin toward Uncle Jesús—"to stay in this house until the day after tomorrow. Tell me the cost of a room and three meals until the day after tomorrow. I'll pay in advance."

"Three meals?" smiled the woman, and more trilling laughter could be heard in the darkness. Three women emerged, in skimpy clothing, in bathing suits, despite the cold, all with thin shawls around their shoulders. One of them set down a bottle of aguardiente and some glasses. "It's impossible to set a price; it all depends on the meals."

Her words were met by more laughter. Uncle Jesús laughed, too, sprawled in his chair, holding an overflowing glass of aguardiente.

"You forgot the cigarettes, Little Indian," he said.

The girl who had served the aguardiente went back for the cigarettes; the other two sat down. A faint smell of disinfectant emanated from their bodies. The one called Miss Piggy offered the hunter a glass, but he declined.

"Madam," he said, "tell me the cost and I'll pay. You can

give me a signed receipt. You see, I need proof I've left this man in your house, with all expenses paid for three days. Then I'll go."

"A receipt? But if I can't even write."

Once again, they all laughed, except for the hunter. One of the girls had got to her feet and was caressing his shoulders. She brought her voice in very close:

"But what a serious man, he hasn't laughed once. Why don't you come with me? You can tell me why you never laugh."

The hunter stood up abruptly. The laughter died on their faces; the hunter's chair rolled across the floor; no one picked it up.

"Take it, mister," the hunter said at last, holding out the wad of cash. Uncle Jesús received it happily. "It's over to you now. I've done my part. But don't even think of turning up at Señora Alma's house. Her nephew said he'd give you a kicking. With me it would be far worse."

Uncle Jesús seemed not to be listening, hunched over the wad of cash, as though counting it: he removed three or six bills and offered them to the hunter, holding his hand out across the table. The hunter slapped his hand, the money fell, and the girl who'd been standing leaned over to collect it, slipping it between her breasts: "It's raining money!" she cried. Uncle Jesús shrugged, and the hunter strode from the room, back to the garden, where he walked into the girl bringing the cigarettes.

"Going already, daddy, so soon?" she asked, and, quickly, before the hunter could prevent it, she placed one of her hands between his legs, with a kind of tender strength, but a strength nonetheless, ferocious, encompassing him completely, squeezing him for an instant. *Christ,* thought Lucio Rosas, *she could have torn them right off.*

103

He staggered from the house, pursued by more laughter. Once back in the street, he swore not to return to Bogotá. Not yet. It was true that he wanted to leave Chía as soon as possible, but he would not allow Jesús to get his way. He'd watch over him until nightfall.

Once again, the boy in the dive bar saw the man with the eye-patch come in. He heard him order another beer, watched him clasp it in his hand, standing there without drinking, without taking his one eye from the house across the street.

5

Francia wavered before the two men. One appeared to be sniffing at her, the other was on the verge of tears. She thought she ought to laugh—or call for help? Things had taken an ugly turn. Suddenly, the two men faced each other; it seemed she no longer existed for either of them, and she heard Ike's low voice, growling:

"I need to speak to Francia alone, understand?"

Rodolfito Cortés did not understand.

Ike's voice expanded, as though suffocating him:

"Get lost."

Rodolfito Cortés did not get lost. He couldn't.

"Get lost, amphibian!" And with a snort he repeated: "I told you to get lost."

But the amphibian was unable to do so, owing to his physical fear. Francia's voice came to his aid, sounding genuinely frightened:

"I'm hungry," she said. "It's time to head down."

"Francia," Rodolfito stammered, "the announcement in the newspaper is a lie, I swear it."

The announcement in the newspaper was true, but, for him, in that instant, it was a lie. He was convinced:

"They're trying to come between us. You must believe me or we're lost. I'll kill myself. I *will* kill myself. I swear it."

"You'll kill yourself?" said Francia.

"What are you talking about?" Ike managed to ask through his passion: he was struggling to understand, desperate.

But neither Francia nor Rodolfito were listening, standing one in front of the other, contemplating each other, transported.

Then Señora Alma entered the room. In one glance, she took stock of the situation.

"Lunch is starting, you little starvelings, what are you doing in here? Do you want me to get the leash and whip you downstairs? You're all my children, darlings, and I'll herd you as I please."

Francia was first to take off. For once in her life, she was grateful for her mother's clout. Behind Francia came Ike and Rodolfito, crestfallen, with Doña Alma bringing up the rear: *If I hadn't arrived in time*, she was thinking, *those two would have been perfectly capable of each grabbing her by an arm and pulling until they tore her in half, what faces, my God, what faces, not even in hell!*

6

"And, to top it all off, she's a little virgin. This is my gift from heaven," César marveled, his voice becoming husky as he entreated: "Now I'll need to use a bit of force, my angel, be patient."

He wheezed, and like a wave of fire, his sweaty cheek drenched Iris's face, smothering her.

"You'd do better to save your strength," came Perla's voice from behind her husband, "or you might burst, you sack of lard, you hog!" And she brought the spine of a book down on the back of his head.

With a grunt César Santacruz lurched backward, covering his head with his hands, his pants still round his ankles; he came very close to falling over.

"You just had to show up, *perra*," he said.

With a sob like a death rattle, Iris Sarmiento sprang from the black desk, readjusting her skirt as she fled the library; it was clear that she was crying.

"Easy, Iris, it's not that big a deal," Perla managed to call after her, "the two of us are going to have a little talk later, don't you worry."

And she even had the nerve to shove her husband in the chest, forcing him to fall back onto his ass, before throwing the book at his face; it was the first weapon to occur to her when she had come across the spectacle of her husband struggling to rape Iris. César used his elbow to prevent the book from catching him full in the face:

"You're drunk already, *perra*."

"Not drunk enough, or I'd kill you, slimeball. Do you want me to report this to your aunt? She's such a big fan of yours, she has no clue what you get up to in her home and with her maid."

They remained like that for a few seconds, him sitting, smiling eternally, her crouched, abominating him with her gaze.

But in the end Perla went back over to the door and slammed it shut.

She seemed to be accustomed to this.

"Get changed at once," she said, "or I'll tell Doña Alma

what I saw, and not only her but the magistrate too: he keeps pistols just like you do, degenerate."

"The magistrate?" smiled César, contemptuously.

"Well, if he doesn't, then his bodyguards surely do, that pair of ogres wandering around out there, now get changed at once."

"Careful what you say, *perra*, you're beginning to annoy me."

And, as if everything had now been settled, as if there were no lingering rancor, Perla began passing her husband his suit, piece by piece, and César focused on changing in silence, piece by piece, until he arrived at his white socks and black shoes.

"What a shame," he lamented, "she was a tasty piece."

Perla gathered up the ostrich-leather waistcoat, folded it, and left it on top of the black desk. There, in the pocket of the waistcoat, remained the goodbye letter Italia had written to her father.

"Lunch is starting, or aren't you going to eat, scumbag? Don't you want to swell that belly even more?"

Perla didn't wait for his answer. She left in search of Iris, to apologize for her husband, to beg her not to speak of what had happened, and to offer any sum of money in return.

It was what she always did.

PART FOUR

1

In spite of the vast garden and abundance of tables, the sheer number of guests exceeded all expectations: Alma Santacruz wondered if she should make use of the patio, without any consideration for the parrots and cats and César's newly arrived mule. But she thought better of it: the children would squabble; better for the animals on the patio to remain on the patio and those in the garden to remain in the garden: she laughed furtively at her own joke as, one by one, she greeted the arriving guests—who never ceased arriving.

Alma was sitting with her husband at the entrance to the garden, urging the guests to look for their tables: "Otherwise you'll have to eat lunch standing up," she told them.

Once the guests were seated, she and the magistrate would say a few words; next they would have the Prayer from Monsignor Hidalgo, followed by lunch. Then the Los Malaspulgas Band would play. To that end, a stage had been erected in the garden, with other smaller platforms scattered around it, for dancing. Many of the guests had gathered in groups, mostly huddled around the main stage, to witness the passage of Nacho Caicedo and Alma Santacruz.

The magistrate was leading her by the arm.

To the older relatives, it seemed he was gazing at her with the same fervor as in the first year of their marriage.

Walking behind them came Adelfa and Emperatriz, along with Lady Mar, Pepa Sol, The Hen, and the Barney sisters—respectable older ladies, all surrounding Monsignor Hidalgo. And, farther back, more ladies accompanied Father

Toro, whose expression was austere and judgmental: these were Luz, wife of Luciano, Celmira, wife of Barrunto, and Marilú, owner of the Magdalene School for Girls.

The butcher Cirilo Cerca, an amateur baritone, preempted the words of welcome. "Just one song!" he cried, advancing toward the stage with his arm raised, through the warm press of bodies. "Wait, Cirilo," someone warned him, "Nacho is about to speak," and someone else said: "It had to be Cirilo Cerca, the Living Voice of the Americas!" The crowd laughed at the expense of the baritone, who continued to move forward resolutely.

"He learned to sing while butchering his animals," a voice rang out, distinctly.

And others warned:

"Just hold on a few minutes, Cirilo."

"Don't push in."

"Our host, Nacho Caicedo, is about to speak."

"Don't be a bore."

"Stand back, Cirilo, don't get so close."

More protests, more laughter, but Cirilo Cerca behaved as if he couldn't hear.

And, finally, the familiar voice of the magistrate rose above them:

"Let him sing. It's not a problem."

With such an endorsement, Cirilo Cerca didn't wait to be asked twice. In defiance of his fifty years, he leapt onto the stage, and, without making use of the microphone, shook the garden with his potent voice, completely silencing the crowd.

His voice imposed itself, otherworldly; with no need for piano or guitar accompaniment, it took possession of the air, transfiguring it.

He was singing a song of fated love.

Cirilo Cerca was a short, stout man, and his ribcage—like that of celebrated Italian soloists—bulged beneath his blue shirt. Using his index finger, he pointed toward a group of young women beside the stage: these were Francia, Palmira and Armenia, the art teacher Obdulia Cera, the primary school teacher Fernanda Fernández, the fiancées Esther, Ana, and Bruneta, and those nicknamed Sexilia and Fecunda.

But, as he sang, the baritone's finger froze in the direction of Lisboa: he pointed toward her for all eternity.

Lisboa, like an island, standing slightly apart from the group of young women, was absorbed by that voice. It seemed the song carried to her ears alone. She blushed and would have preferred to find herself on another planet, or at least sheltered, behind this group of women.

The song swelled toward its climax, the voice soaring above Lisboa:

> *On the day*
> *you crossed my path*
> *I had a sense*
> *of something fateful ...*

Once he had finished, the applause that erupted was like another downpour. Cirilo Cerca leapt down from the stage to embrace the magistrate; he greeted Señora Alma with a kiss and retreated, discreetly, making way for them. But as the feted couple ascended to the stage, some saw Cirilo thread his way through the crowd and approach another guest, one of those who'd cried out, they saw him give the man a hard shove on the shoulder, they heard him say: "What was that about me learning to sing while butchering my animals?"

The magistrate's voice, projected by the microphone, interrupted them: "My dearest friends. Today, it befalls you all to listen."

The antagonists went no further; they crossed their arms and paid attention. The one who'd shouted out and caused offence was Pepe Sarasti, a good friend of the magistrate, a contemporary.

The magistrate tensed his body as though in preparation for a monumental speech. They saw him furrow his brow in concentration. And yet, in the end he capitulated, keeping it brief.

He offered thanks to his dear relatives, explaining that it was difficult for him to speak after a singer of Cirilo Cerca's caliber had just sung like a canary, bringing joy to our hearts with his songs of fateful love. "I want you all to be happy in this house, which belongs to everyone. Please put your hands together for the person who has made it possible for us to have the pleasure of being here today, the most life-affirming day of my life: Alma Rosa de los Ángeles Santacruz, my beloved."

Another sea of applause.

Señora Alma took the microphone, but at that moment something interrupted her, a multicolored scuffle among the crowd: the two who had been facing off earlier, to the annoyance of the other guests, were at it again; they were almost certainly friends, or at least acquaintances, however, once again, Cirilo Cerca had pressed his baritone's chest up against his fat adversary's stomach and was pushing. "Please, Cirilo," came the voice of Alma Santacruz, "and you too, Pepe Sarasti: if you want to smooch, then do it somewhere private." The laughter of the audience intensified, and Alma's voice sidestepped the situation:

"Hunger puts men in foul moods," she said.

More laughter.

"So, before we dance, let's have lunch. I'm hungry, aren't you?"

A great *yes* boomed all around her, a baby started crying, as though in agreement, and the crowd erupted, joyously.

2

"Look, look over there," said Señora Alma, and her voice was changing, becoming thicker, because she was salivating.

She was indicating with her ring-decked hand toward a corner of the garden; installed there was a kind of altar: three long forms, resting on tripods, covered in tablecloths. At a signal from madam, three waiters uncovered the forms in unison; a murmur of admiration shook the garden: they were three roasted hogs like bloated whales, their bellies stuffed with shredded meat, the three heads with ears charred to a crisp. Their open mouths seemed to be crying out to be eaten.

"And they were slow-roasted for days," explained Señora Alma, proudly, "to achieve that … crispy golden color … Those who would like lechona can go over and form a line, with no shoving, because your plates will be handed to you there, don't worry, there will be enough for everybody. Those who won't be having any can begin taking their seats at the tables—there are so many, they're almost like a single large one: it will always be possible to talk from table to table, with no need for shouting. The waiters will come to your tables with the rest of the dishes. You need only sit and wait."

Here, someone tossed a red rose at her feet, and she picked this up.

"I will keep this rose forever," said Alma. She was making a great effort not to cry, or at least, that's how it appeared. "I'm going to read out sections from the menu, which is my greatest inspiration, pure poetry." Her hand trembled as she clasped a piece of blue card. "We have veal in red wine, fresh fish, and pork chops. We also have goat stew, roast lamb, and cream of vegetable soup. I recommend the smoked-salmon-wrapped prawn canapés, the grilled asparagus rolled in ham, the chickpeas with quail eggs, the poached chicken with yogurt and apricot garnish, the ham croquettes, the pork and applesauce. Eat till you're stuffed and drink till you're sloshed, my darlings. To finish, we'll have elderflower cake."

As each dish was called out, the guests whistled, their eyes rolled back, as if suspended in a trance. Their mouths were starting to water.

Like a sibyl, Señora Alma raised her arm, and a battalion of waiters appeared from a corner, in single file, nimbly distributing dishes from table to table. Yet a myriad of diners ignored the menu on offer, sweeping like a wave toward the altar of lechonas; there, they formed a festive line that included the subalterns from the Ministry of Justice, the pen pushers, the shark lawyers: they received their plates, finished them, and took second helpings, before asking for an additional plate and leaving the magistrate's house with that plate under their arm, to polish off at home. Were they predicting a dull party, or were they simply being mindful of the extraordinary number of guests? Whatever the case, it had taken no more than the carving up of the lechonas to make the entire Ministry of Justice disappear.

3

Now the magistrate found himself surrounded by his daughters. But Alma Santacruz, the woman who ruled over them, allowed him no time for fooling around; she pulled him aside and handed over what Juana had just discovered while tidying in the library: the ostrich-leather waistcoat and the goodbye letter from Italia—which the magistrate slipped inside his pocket without reading. "I suppose she's gone off with Porto's family," Señora Alma surmised, "it was to be expected." The magistrate was looking up at the heavens, his own personal gesture of dissatisfaction. "If she leaves this house, it will be by mutual agreement," he said. "Until that happens, she'll have to come back here. I myself will go and collect her tonight." He handed the ostrich-leather waistcoat to one of his subordinates, who was leaving. "A gift from the heavens," he told him. Then Alma laid down the law once again: "I think it would be best for us to go to the dining room. We'll eat as a family, with the monsignor."

And, as a group, they made their way to the dining room: they passed between the tables in the garden, greeting one or other of the guests, taking their time. At the front of this group went the magistrate, Francia, Armenia, and Palmira (Lisboa and Uriela were missing), the art teacher Obdulia Cera, the primary school teacher Fernanda Fernández, the fiancées Esther, Ana, and Bruneta, and those nicknamed Sexilia and Fecunda. They were followed by another small group, for Alma had already taken charge of selecting the guests who would be dining with them: her brother Barrunto Santacruz, his wife Celmira and son Rigo, José Sansón, cousin to the magistrate, Artemio Aldana, a childhood friend, Sparks, Alma's cousin, Pumpkin, another cousin, Uncle Luciano, brother to the magistrate and toyshop owner, with his wife Luz and daughters Sol and Luna. Others joined of their own volition, including the judge Arquímedes Lama and his three honorable colleagues, the Barney sisters, the one nicknamed The Hen, Pepe Sarasti and Lady Mar, Pepa Sol and her husband Salvador Cantante, who was mute and also a trumpet player, and several trusted families: the Florecitos, the Mayonesos, the Mistéricos, and the Púas—with a grandfather and great-grandfather who were still alive, as lucid as they were famished, in need of the spread that awaited them.

Señora Alma went over to invite the monsignor through to the dining room, a privileged space. The monsignor listened to her, dumbstruck; he appeared to want to say something, but in the end he didn't, simply joining the rear of the procession to the dining room with his secretary and accompanied by Adelfa and Emperatriz, who refused to let go of them.

In a corner, the monsignor managed to elude his lady guardians, because he needed to speak to his secretary alone. He felt offended, the victim of an insult that had not only perplexed him, but also caused him great sorrow: they had forgotten to invite him to speak onstage.

Above all else, it was he who ought to have spoken first and offered a prayer in the name of all those present, even before the baritone, a shameless butcher who should never have been allowed to sing. How could they have forgotten the Prayer? What was wrong with this family? He could never have anticipated such a monumental blunder. But it would not be he who protested. If nobody did so in his name, then all was lost. If those pious ladies did not raise a complaint, then nobody would, least of all him. It wouldn't be dignified.

"How times change," the monsignor commented to his secretary. "Now nobody offers thanks to God."

"That," said the secretary, "means that something infernal will take place in this house."

Monsignor Javier Hidalgo shook his head, more from sadness than disappointment: he was fully aware of his own faults and asked God for forgiveness; he may have had a sometimes shady past, but for the rest he was immaculate, a righteous man of the church. He was about to respond to the secretary and reprimand him for his superstition (nothing infernal would take place in the house of the magistrate), when he found himself encircled by Alma, Adelfa, and Emperatriz. To their collective embarrassment, the three had deciphered the clergyman's discomfort: they hadn't let him speak, they'd forgotten about him. The three ladies had gone red, but they remained undaunted: "Did you see the lawyers?" asked Adelfa, "they were so hungry that they even wanted to eat the tables, tablecloth and all"; and Emperatriz: "What hunger there is in this country, my God; the sight of those lechonas was the detonator, the lunch had to be brought forward"; and Alma, with a cushioning sigh: "But you will give us your blessing in the dining room, Monsignor. It's more intimate. If it rains, we won't get wet. We can listen to you with due reflection."

Monsignor Hidalgo stopped in his tracks. He stared at the Santacruz sisters, one by one, his gaze coming to rest on Alma for an instant, but then he said nothing, simply proceeding to the dining room.

He has admonished me with a mere look, thought Alma, humiliated. She believed herself unfairly affronted: she couldn't be the one to think of everything, she didn't have a hundred heads, the monsignor should have come up onstage himself, taken hold of the microphone, and offered thanks to God; she'd been misunderstood, was being subjugated. Then she searched in her memory for the monsignor's true colors: *That perverted little priest,* she thought, savoring every word, bitterly. Publicly, she sighed, as though contrite, but inside she was screaming: *He can go fuck himself!*

The young secretary smiled obliquely. Adelfa and Emperatriz were cringing. How could they have overlooked the monsignor's Prayer? How could they have forgotten? It was a mortal sin.

4

For some time now, the three Césars had been searching for Uriela among the crowd, calling out her name in every corner of the garden. They didn't find Uriela, but they did find Perla, in the farthest corner, sitting at a table with three men—to the Césars, three strangers. These were Conrado Olarte, magician by profession, the university lecturer Manolo Zulú, and the professional cyclist Pedro Pablo Rayo, a P.E. teacher. They were drinking rum. None of them seemed interested in the steaming plates of roast lamb, freshly served.

"Mamá!" said the Césars in unison. And it was a piece of news they wanted to shout out, for it had shaken them: "There's a dead dog on the patio!"

The mouths of the three men dropped open.

"Well," Perla said to her children, "we all die someday."

The three men laughed.

The magician Olarte extended a hand toward the youngest César's ear, grazed it for a second, and a fifty-centavo coin appeared between his pale fingers.

"Magic!" cried the cyclist Rayo.

The magician presented the coin to the boy, who didn't want to take it; he looked underwhelmed.

"The clowns will be along later," said the magician. "If I'm asked to, I'll put on my cape and hat and do some magic."

And he needs a hat, thought the eldest César, *because he's bald*.

Perla began drinking again, indifferent.

The three boys already suspected, could already sense, the worlds their mother soared through when she drank: she wasn't the same person, more like a complete stranger. She looked at them without seeing them, listened without hearing.

Then they abandoned her forever.

"Your response," the lecturer told Perla, after making a slow bow, "was philosophy of the highest order. Rest assured, it will make your children think."

And he could not stop glancing down at Perla's legs, at the long bare thighs which had suddenly uncrossed themselves. For Perla had started to worry about her children. She made an effort to go after them, tried twice to rise to her feet, yet twice she gave up: her body was trembling, it was made of gelatin, she felt she had no more strength than that needed to recross her legs like a knot, as if erecting a fortress. And again she raised a glass with her admirers.

5

Uriela saw that the monsignor was heading toward the dining room in the company of her mother and her aunts, prompting her to abandon the idea of eating as a family; she preferred to look for a table in the crowded garden. The tables were set for four; she found one occupied by two of the Malaspulgas, the vocalist Charrita Luz and Cecilio Diez, who were cracking loud jokes and attacking their plates ravenously. She sat down with them and asked a waiter to exchange her plate of goat stew for one of fish; this was another of Uriela's peculiarities that annoyed her mother: she didn't eat meat, except for fish, and then only reluctantly. Beside Uriela was an empty chair that was suddenly occupied by Iris, much to Cecilito's astonishment—wasn't she the family servant?

Iris hadn't sat down to have lunch. "I'd like to speak to you alone, Uriela," she said urgently. She was worried she might be overheard by Cecilito, who was Alma's godson. "Alright," replied Uriela, "but let's eat lunch first." "I'm not allowed," said Iris, "I have to serve." "Serve?" laughed Uriela, "there are plenty of others to do that, you're my sister, you must eat with me." She held out the cutlery to Iris, a knife and fork, then wielded her own and began cutting up a fillet of fish. Iris had turned pale. With a great effort, she began picking at her veal. "Look," said Uriela, "there's strawberry sorbet, if you're struggling."

The girls were the same age, they had grown up together, attended primary school together, and, though Señora Alma had taken charge of ensuring that each knew her place (she sent Iris to a dressmaking course while Uriela finished high school), they remained close; they would go to the cinema together. Uriela had once asked herself if Iris didn't feel more like a sister than her own flesh and blood did.

"The beet salad is delicious," said Charrita Luz, addressing everyone.

"What did you make of the baritone?" asked Uriela.

"A little stiff and bombastic, but serviceable," decreed Cecilio.

"A voice from paradise," countered Charrita Luz. "You can't block out the sun with a finger." She was a tall and bony mulatta, with wild eyes.

Cecilio Diez looked up at the sky, squinted, searched for the sun; then he raised his finger.

"I've just blocked it out," he said.

Charrita Luz exploded:

"Oh Cecilito, you're like a child!"

They continued to eat in the din of the crowd, in the midst of a jungle of mouths that opened and closed, crunching and swallowing without cessation. It was then that Uriela felt a great warmth beside her, or believed she did, and it was Iris, her face glowing, red as a tomato that's ready to be picked. Uriela stopped eating and was about to ask what the matter was, when she discovered the source of Iris's embarrassment: Cousin César was coming over to them. He was carrying a large plate of lechona in one hand and a fork in the other:

"Iris," he said, "give me your seat, go find one for yourself in the kitchen."

Uriela had no time to intervene. She watched Iris jump up, plate in hand, and disappear into the crowd, her head bowed.

Cousin César sat down, that mute laughter on his face. He greeted Cecilio and Charrita, before intercepting Uriela with his arm, because she had been preparing to pick up her plate and go after Iris.

"My little know-it-all cousin," he said. "I've been thinking about you for years, I've dreamed of setting you a riddle, grant me that gift, humor me." And as he talked, he continued to eat his lechona, unperturbed by the peas and chickpeas that shot from his mouth onto the table. Cecilio and Charrita listened to him with rapt attention.

"A riddle?" asked Charrita.

"Uriela is the family sage," Cousin César informed them, "she's the Know-it-all Bunny, didn't you know? But I've memorized a riddle that she'll never be able to guess."

Cecilio Diez snorted, decisively:

"I'll bet you a thousand pesos she will."

"A thousand," said Cousin César, and leaned his face in close to Uriela's, for a few seconds, observing her while he ate. And finally, like a challenge, he recited:

> *If yesterday wasn't Monday,*
> *and there aren't three days left until the penultimate day of the week,*
> *and if the day after tomorrow isn't Tuesday,*
> *while the day before yesterday isn't the third day of the week*

and there aren't three days left until Thursday,
and tomorrow isn't Sunday,
what day is today?

"Thursday," responded Uriela.

And she finished getting to her feet, saying:

"Don't forget to claim that thousand pesos, Cecilito, or this swine will forget."

And she ran off in search of Iris.

6

Lisboa was moving toward the dining room between tables and bodies, when, suddenly, she couldn't take another step: she sensed that someone was summoning her with their eyes, that a pair of eyes was pulling at her, or was it that she smelled something in the air which beckoned to her? The hint of a bitter aroma that disturbed her? She breathed in those emanations, and—the most extraordinary thing—turned to look back at that jungle of teeming souls, devourers of meat, and there she discovered him, alone and isolated, as if no one else existed. The whole world vanished and everything went silent: the only being in existence was Cirilo Cerca, the baritone who not long before had frozen her with his otherworldly voice, the older man who could have been her grandfather, she thought, browned by the sun—shorter than she was? The same height—that ridiculous old man who not only continued to stare at her and smile, but was coming over.

A bead of sweat slid down from her armpit and made her shiver. When had she started to sweat as though she'd raced up a steep street? She believed she must be the source of the increasing bitter aroma, but then immediately she realized that no, it had to be him. She sensed the overpowering confidence of the baritone, who placed his hands on her shoulders and drew her to him, kissing her on the cheek: it felt like an electric shock, she no longer recognized herself, she appeared stupefied, absorbed in a state of semiconsciousness—was she going to collapse? *How foolish I am*. She could make out nothing but the weathered face of that fifty-year-old man, who still hadn't taken his hands off her; only his voice existed.

Lisboa listened.

"Your father invited me to have lunch in the dining room, with all of you, but then Pepe Sarasti overtook me, you've heard the things he says, about how I learned to sing while killing my animals. I learned to sing while dreaming, Lisboa. That's why I prefer to eat here, in the garden, far from that Pepe. Will you join me? Will you allow me that pleasure? I know where there's an empty table."

Lisboa listened. She was unable to utter a word.

As though in a trance, she walked clumsily behind the baritone, who was also the butcher Cirilio Cerca, she couldn't help repeating to herself.

Lisboa was no longer listening to him, much less to the other guests; she was listening only to herself, to her internal screams and palpitations—her breathing? She was a nurse, and in a year she would be graduating, what was happening to her? There was no doubt that her blood pressure was high, she was boiling—a thousand degrees? *My face and hands are sweating, they keep sweating, they're still sweating*, and she let out a huge sigh as though ridding herself of a burden—the burden of herself.

She sat down at the distant table, the table he had found, a table between flower pots, beneath curly golden ferns; long, fingerlike leaves caressed her hair.

"Such eyes, Lisboa," said the baritone, his gaze resting on her. "They sparkle."

But what sparkled most were the baritone's own hazel

eyes, upon her, against her, inside her, further inside, much further, it seemed. A waiter was serving steaming pork chops, strawberry sorbet; Lisboa couldn't tell if it was due to the food or the stranger that her stomach contracted, her intestine squeezed, the butterflies inside her took flight. *All this is because of his voice,* she reflected, ponderously, and the butterflies inside her fluttered frantically, maddeningly; she was so shocked by them, by what was happening to her, that she let herself be swayed by a giggle like that of a little girl up to no good; the butcher Cirilo Cerca, who was watching her, watching every one of her movements, couldn't help laughing too, or else he'd decided to join in with her laughter: they had both leaned their heads forward and were almost touching. Happy. Without realizing.

Lisboa went back to listening to him.

"Are you the eldest of your sisters?"

"I'm the second," said Lisboa. "I'm twenty-five."

Why had she revealed her age? No one had asked her. He continued:

"I'm fifty, Lisboa. I could be your father, but not your grandfather."

With this, he responded to Lisboa herself when she had concluded that Cirilo could be her grandfather. Or had he perhaps overheard her? Might she have thought this out loud? Again, Lisboa blushed, shook her head, laughed once more, and was grateful that the Los Malaspulgas Band had taken to the stage, the music blaring, grateful that the baritone had risen to his feet and said: "Shall we dance?"

7

Iris Sarmiento felt incapable of telling the world about what had happened with César Santacruz. She only wanted to tell

Uriela. They would share in the desolation. Because a devastating loneliness was taking hold of Iris: if Señora Alma were to disappear, what would become of her? She asked herself this question in the wake of the violence she had suffered. For the first time, she understood who she was—or who she wasn't. What she had endured would never have been endured by the Caicedo sisters, she thought. She was called Iris Sarmiento, but her surname, Sarmiento, was an invention; she had no surname, nor father, mother, or siblings. Aside from Uriela and Señora Alma, nobody would care if she ran out to the middle of nowhere and dove headfirst in front of the morning train.

The ruddy face of Cousin César pressing itself between her legs, his nose sniffing her, his mouth biting her, that whole dripping countenance was a filthy recollection that unsettled her to the point of nausea. And, what's more, there was the shame, the degradation: as if she'd been stomped on by a hog in a pigsty. She felt disgusted with herself; she ought to have taken a shower, ought, at the very least, to have changed her underwear, she thought.

In vain, she tried to reveal to Uriela what had happened, as they finished their lunch in the "kids' corner," a long strip at the edge of the garden where small tables had been set out for the children, beneath balloons and streamers between polystyrene giraffes. It was there that Doña Juana had finally discovered and captured the three little Césars, so that they could go have their lunch at once; the three boys had been hiding inside an enormous American oak barrel with iron bands, which stood with its lid off in another corner of the garden. Afterwards, as soon as they found Uriela, the Césars had made her promise that once lunch was over they would visit the patio together: they wanted to show her a surprise, and then they would fill the pool with water, right? They'd go for a dip. In that moment, as the three boys surrounded Uriela, Iris was already wavering on the brink of tears. She felt she had lost her toehold in life, that the world was shifting beneath her feet, swallowing her. Weren't these César Santacruz's children? How to disclose that, not long ago, César had lain her flat out on the black desk and … and then Perla had arrived? How to explain that, later, Perla had followed her to the kitchen, and, right there, amid maids and cooks, in the steam from the pots, she had apologized to her in secret? And how to reveal that Perla had forced a wad of cash on her, repeating: "It's not that big a deal, Iris, we'll soon forget all about it."

Perla had said this and then left.

Outraged, Iris had rushed over to the corner where the garbage can was kept, under the counter, and tossed the wad of cash inside.

And now, instead of telling Uriela the truth that was killing her, without knowing how or why, perhaps because Uriela was yawning, she began talking about Marino Ojeda. She spoke only about the guard, about how he showed up everywhere, as if following her, about how he smiled at her and had tried to kiss her that very day in the garage.

"I felt I was going to die," said Iris.

"Die," echoed Uriela. "From pleasure?"

And Uriela began to laugh, a far cry from the torment Iris harbored within her heart. Iris laughed too, in despair at not being able to open up to Uriela. Instead of revealing her distress, she explained that Marino had asked if she had a day off, so they could go for a walk together. *A day off*, Uriela repeated to herself, surprised and disconcerted: did Iris really not have a single free day? Of course she did, thought Uriela. Or didn't she?

"Well, I'll speak to mamá about the day off," she said, considering the matter settled.

126

She couldn't imagine what abysses, what infernos, were pounding inside the chest of Iris, who again made an effort to share her secret. But she wasn't able to: Uriela had been abducted by a swarm of children who wanted to take her to the patio, wanted to amaze her with the surprise of the dead dog.

Still, Iris wished to persist with Uriela, wished to call out to her and share the burden of what had happened, but at that moment, Juana arrived: her immediate presence was required in the kitchen.

Iris followed the old cook.

She trudged through the cloud of guests.

Then, suddenly, she forgot about everything.

Suddenly, she could recall nothing but her day off with Marino Ojeda, the free day, the day just for her.

Then she raced over to the kitchen counter, the corner with the garbage can, burying her hand in the filth and recovering her money.

8

Shortly before Francia joined the group of young women, with the baritone yet to sing, Rodolfo Cortés had been able to escape Ike's attentions and slip into the crowd, in search of her; he believed he had recovered her, that she was once more grazing from the palm of his hand. When he had asked her to believe him or he'd kill himself, he had noticed Francia's eyes become watery with joy, her love was unbreakable. And a sharp thrill had pricked him in that moment, he was certain she had felt it too. He wondered if he wasn't making a mistake by marrying Hortensia Burbano Alvarado, daughter of the governor of Valle. Would it not be better to keep his commitment to the daughter of the all-powerful magistrate? *It's too late now*, he repeated to himself, locking his fingers together tightly: the best thing would be to end this love story with a final flourish, for them to go hide in some hole, some dungeon of this crazy castle, even under the staircase, and for him to undress her and love her as never before, to subdue her for the last time.

His desire for Francia bordered on the painful. He felt pain. His passion shocked him. But none of this was revealed by his face, his voice. His attitude was that of a timid toad—he knew this himself, said it to himself—and that was the power Rodolfo Cortés held over the world.

Then he spotted her and went over.

He was able to take Francia by the arm, leading her away for an instant from the world of friends that surrounded her. Under a willow tree, he kissed her as never before. He made her agree to meet him in her bedroom after lunch. Francia would be dining with her family, with the monsignor and the magistrate. Rodolfito understood that Francia's cousin Ike would also be there—your childhood boyfriend, he said bitterly—and therefore he preferred to go unnoticed, have lunch in the garden, and then head up to Francia's chamber, where they would come together. This is what they agreed, regarding each other with a kind of mischievousness, with mutual curiosity, like two conspirators. They didn't notice that, amid the blur of faces, the devious face of Ricardo Castañeda floated, listening in on them. He'd been enlisted by Ike to spy on Rodolfito, and it had worked. Ike wouldn't believe the news: nothing less than Francia and the amphibian making plans for after lunch.

Rodolfito Cortés was over the moon. He even rediscovered his appetite. He'd been revived. He chose a table occupied by two strangers: Batato Armado and Liserio Caja, a pair of giants, shadowy protégés of the magistrate, his most discreet bodyguards. Alongside them, sitting in absolute silence, he listened to the voice of the baritone, was won over by the words of Señora Alma, and resigned himself to drinking the aperitif that paved the way for lunch, while time moved on and the cherished moment drew nearer: to lie down with Francia on her bed, the place where he had sat with Ike, the place where he'd been humiliated, his own Francia reminding him of the mugging on Calle 19. This humiliation fed not only his rancor, but also his desire: he desired Francia with an even greater intensity, *to see and feel her naked, to make her shudder*, he cried out to himself, bristling.

It was then that he struck up a conversation with the two great lumps accompanying him. They truly were huge, square-shaped men. *With the faces of mischievous children*, thought Rodolfito. They told him they worked as chauffeurs for the Ministry of Justice, the magistrate was like a father to them. "And you," they asked him, "are you a lawyer?"

"I'm a biologist," said Rodolfito. "I'm the boyfriend of Francia Caicedo Santacruz, eldest daughter of the magistrate, I'm her fiancé."

The bodyguards listened to him with skepticism—then why wasn't he eating at the magistrate's table? They didn't ask this question, but it resonated clearly in the eyes of the giants, the way their lips twisted as if in disappointment. Rodolfo Cortés had no time to come up with an answer, first because they began serving the meal, and second because the empty seat at their table was filled by Ricardo Castañeda, the horrible brother of that horrible Ike.

A waiter immediately set down a plate for Ricardo, who greeted the bodyguards with a nod and Rodolfito with a slap on the shoulder, like a buddy:

"Relax," he whispered, before even touching his food, "I'm not like my brother."

Rodolfito Cortés froze, his knife and fork halfway to the steaming plate.

"What's more," continued Ricardo, seeming sincere, "I apologize if my brother offended you. I know perfectly well that you're my cousin's boyfriend—and aren't you also her fiancé? No point in hanging around, am I right? Because let me tell you, Ike has been dying for Francia ever since they were little. Some fling they had as kids drove him mad. Everyone in our household worries about him; mamá talks about the need for a specialist. I know what went on between you this morning. Ike told you to get lost, right? Ike has assisted many others in getting lost, let me tell you, but today he feels remorseful. Despite his temperament, he has a tendency to regret his outbursts. Today he felt repentant, I swear. Francia herself called him crazy. Francia herself asked him not to meddle in her affairs, not too long ago, in the dining room. No, don't get up. Let me tell you the rest. I overheard the well-deserved telling-off. The truth is, my brother really is a madman, I agree with that assessment. Get this: after listening to Francia's words, Ike failed to see reason, becoming riled up instead, as usual. He stormed out of the dining room without saying goodbye. He stormed out of the house. Ike stormed out of the party is what I'm telling you. Francia and I went after him, but by the time we reached the front door, he was already tearing away on his Harley, poor Ike. He's my elder brother, but he acts younger than my little sisters, you understand? Ah, but why am I here? Francia didn't return to the dining room; she asked me to find you, asked me to tell you that she's waiting for you in the drawing room."

"The drawing room?"

"She wants to lead you by the arm into the dining room, where you'll take up your rightful place, as her boyfriend, her future. But again, I must apologize for my brother, for how crazy he is. I recommend you pay no attention to him, it's the best thing you can do."

Neither of them had touched their plates. Rodolfo Cortés rose immediately, buttoned up his jacket and left, heading toward the drawing room. Ricardo ran back to the dining room, as the bodyguards seized upon the untouched plates and had seconds.

"I'll bet you anything you like," said Liserio Caja, "that the toad-faced kid has just been lured into a trap."

Batato Armado shrugged.

9

In the drawing room, Francia was nowhere to be seen. There was only cigarette smoke. From the far corners, broad, dark cupboards stood watching over Rodolfo Cortés, silently. Inside these heavy pieces of furniture, under giant napkins, the gold-rimmed plates, cut crystal glasses, and enamel pitchers were stored. There, beside those display cabinets, Rodolfito had made love to Francia one inspired night and asked her to marry him. She had given him a set of Baccarat glasses, to sell at an antiquarian's. Later, additional Murano tumblers, Venetian glass lamps, mirrors, and candelabrum were inherited by Rodolfito to offset the expenses of a student in penury, all this given to him by the generous Francia, just as she had given Ike her gold fountain pen.

The memory of Ike caused Rodolfito to tense up. He had already advanced a good distance into the lavish drawing room, with its colossal armchairs, when he felt the hairs on the back of his neck prickle, from sheer panic, understanding too late that this was his instinct warning him. He started to run, but a dark shadow sprang from behind a cupboard and arrested his flight, just as the jaguar, after a brief spurt, smothers the fawn.

Ike wrapped his arms around Rodolfito from behind, immobilizing him, and dragged him to the farthest corner, where he was awaited by an old embossed leather trunk, the kind used during colonial times for carrying white linen on muleback from the coast up to the tops of the Andes.

There was the sound of wheezing as the two men struggled.

The lid of the trunk was already open, as if by art of war; there wasn't much inside, just a thin bed of linen serviettes. It was here that the furious shadow was finally able to bury Rodolfito, after subduing him with a blow to the jaw—unnecessary, since Rodolfito was already subdued, through pure terror: it had been enough for him to discover Ike's eyes, smoldering in the air, a mix of blood and hatred. The lid of the trunk still had its old key in the lock. Ike slammed this shut on top of the curled-up Rodolfito, before grasping the key and turning it three times to the right as though delivering three mortal blows. He checked the lid to make sure it wasn't going anywhere, just like its occupant, then pocketed the heavy key and left the drawing room.

In the corridor, he stopped to listen. No screaming could be heard from the distant trunk; Rodolfito must still be knocked out after that cross punch to the jaw, or else he was awake and bawling, but you couldn't hear him; nobody would hear him. With the sound of voices, should guests arrive, with the inevitable music from the record player, the commotion all around, it would be impossible for anyone to hear him. He deserved it. Who told him to go meeting with Francia in her bedroom? For God's sake, what did Francia even see in that neutered amphibian? Now Francia would get what she deserved, for it would be Ike who was waiting for her.

And I'll switch out the lights, he thought, frenzied. *By the time she recognizes me, it'll be too late.*

He swallowed, wavering for the first time, wondering if he hadn't gone crazy. "Crazy, but with love!" he yelled, exiting the house. In the outer garden, orange with sunlight, he flung the key with all his might onto the roof of a neighboring house. He heard it clatter, far away. He wasn't bothered by the baseball kids watching on. He smiled at them grimly, before going back inside the house and kicking the front door shut behind him.

10

Night had not yet fallen.

To the hunter, it seemed the brothel door was trembling on the other side of the street. He hadn't taken his eye off the door in over a century. His instinct warned him he wasn't the only one spying: Uncle Jesús knew where he—Lucio—was, and the game consisted in who would tire first, him, from waiting for Jesús to come outside, or Jesús, unable to come outside because he was waiting.

Why don't you stay in there and sleep with your hens? he thought. *Oh rooster, how infuriating you are.*

What the hunter had not been counting on was the carousing of the drunks in the dive bar. They had been intrigued by that man holding a bottle of beer in his hand, but not drinking a drop, paralyzed in the doorway. What was he peeping at? And that eye patch, that tough-guy expression. The drunk in the sombrero was the one going to greatest lengths to offer aguardiente to the outsider, who wouldn't even acknowledge him, attentive to the brothel door.

"What are you peering at so closely?" asked the drunk point-blank. He was swaying, carrying a glass of aguardiente in each hand.

Lucio Rosas kept his eye on the house opposite, as though not listening. For a second, out of the corner of his eye, he took stock of the demeanor of the man in the hat: an outsider, an outcast, a drunk loner.

"Could it be that your wife is in that house?" asked the drunk, and from behind him there came a roar of laughter.

Lucio Rosas wasn't ruffled. Now was no time for wasting his time on drunks. He accepted the glass, downed it in one, placed it on the counter, and immediately turned back to watch the brothel door; in those few seconds, the wretch of a man could have slipped away: he examined the door, which was cracked open an inch; then, in the distance, he was able to glimpse something like a coattail flying through the air: it was Uncle Jesús, turning the corner.

Outside, he smashed the beer bottle against the stone sidewalk and set off after Uncle Jesús, who was fleeing at full gallop in the direction of the avenue; this meant he intended to take a taxi, and if he managed to, Lucio would lose him: Jesús could afford a taxi to Bogotá, but Lucio couldn't. He quickened his pace, because the repulsive figure was maintaining his lead. The first nocturnal shadows were now gathering in the avenue. In the distance, there was a red traffic light. He strained his single eye of a bird of prey: Uncle Jesús was nowhere to be seen; only a dark truck waiting for the lights to change, heading toward the highway, an ancient truck, with no tarp, just a long narrow flatbed stacked with something resembling wire cages full of chickens. He kept running toward it, continuing to glance in all directions. The evening shadows swirled: it was possible Uncle Jesús remained hidden behind a wall, or that he'd already crossed the avenue and was gaining ground, scot-free among the houses opposite.

He saw him as the red traffic light turned amber then

green: Jesús was perched comfortably on the back of the truck, legs dangling in the air, and even appeared to be waving goodbye. Lucio loathed him as never before. He loathed that stranger, that sponger, that piece of human garbage who would make him fall into disfavor— or into disgrace? He loathed the devilish creature who was mocking him. He no longer cared whether or not Jesús Santacruz reached Bogotá, to hell with the magistrate's party; this was personal. Ever since he'd seen him in the kitchen (how is it that in twenty years they'd never met?), ever since he'd been confronted with that phrase, *you had a debt to pay*, Lucio Rosas had loathed him. This loathing bolstered the strength in his legs. He hurled himself toward the truck, which was starting up again. With one lunge, he almost reached it, but now the truck was accelerating. The hunter refused to accept defeat. He kept up his pace, his legs not giving in; these were legs that covered miles when he hunted.

Uncle Jesús was still sitting on the edge of the flatbed, legs swinging. His face was impossible to make out: night had now taken possession of the world, imposing a surrender to what was communicated by the lights of the avenue. Nor could Uncle Jesús clearly discern the face of the running hunter. It seemed preposterous that he was persisting. Jesús threw his arms back and rested his head in his hands, like a man lying on the beach with his face turned toward the sun. But his face merely stared up at the sky, a black sky, devoid of stars. He hoped that, when he lowered his gaze, that halfwit, that stubborn mule, would be gone.

But he wasn't.

There, not too far away, the shadow of the hunter continued to swing his arms in the shadows, tirelessly. And, to make matters worse, the truck braked. Was it going to stop? Uncle Jesús's heart skipped a beat, but no, it wasn't stopping, there was a hole in the avenue the truck needed to circumvent. But as a result of that maneuver, the stubborn shadow had already drawn closer.

Now the hunter shook off his exhaustion; it was an experience of pain he was all too familiar with: you simply had to resist and resist until suddenly the pain wasn't pain anymore, it wasn't real.

More ditch-like holes prevented the truck from making headway. Uncle Jesús opened his mouth, he was drooling. In the light from the yellow bulbs, the hunter discovered that the truck was carrying not chickens but rabbits. He took all this in as he ran. And when he caught sight of the smile on Uncle Jesús's face, it was as if he'd caught sight of his own destiny. It was now or never. He summoned his strength, upping his pace, just as another pothole hindered the truck's progress. He was now running only twenty inches from Uncle Jesús's legs, gaining on him. The two men contemplated each other for a second: it was as though they were sniffing each other out. Uncle Jesús swallowed, horrified. Suddenly, he realized that Lucio Rosas wasn't intending to climb onto the truck and sit there chatting all the way back to Bogotá: he genuinely wanted to stop him from reaching the party, wanted to grab him by the legs and pull him, haul him down once and for all in Chía—was he trying to kill him? Then he decided to seek shelter within, and, using his elbows, he began to drag himself backward, making his way between the cages of sleeping rabbits; but now, at last, the hunter had managed to clamber onto the truck, wheezing like a wounded animal, seemingly on the brink of collapse, he clambered on and grabbed Jesús by the ankles, pulling at him. "For God's sake," Jesús screamed at him, "stop this fooling around at once!" He hoped the truck driver might hear him and slam on the brakes, but the driver accelerated even harder and the truck pulled out onto the highway and drove onto a surfaced road, racing like a comet, the wind intensifying, Lucio Rosas was still kneeling in front of Jesús, not releasing his ankles, and then Uncle Jesús screamed again as he was dragged by those rootlike hands that suddenly embraced him, clinging on to him, pulling him close, and then—still embracing—the pair tumbled out onto the asphalt and bounced two, three, four times, as though made of rubber, their legs and heads flailing, before coming to rest under the night, forever locked in that embrace.

11

Just as they were entering the patio, pushing open the large grated gate, Alma Santacruz stepped out in front of them. The boys froze: they knew all about this great-aunt who was directing the party, always busy and in a foul mood.

"What's the matter with you, Uriela?" began Alma, hands on her hips. She was heavyset, and taller than Uriela, taller than all her daughters. "You didn't eat lunch with us. Now your father is asking for you. It seems he wants to reveal prophecies, he needs you, so let's go join him, as we should. There are lots of people asking for you, Urlielita, not just these whippersnappers." She examined the group of boys with a hint of curiosity: "Leave them to run free; they're exactly like their parents were as children, insufferable; you've probably bored them to death already, isn't that right, boys?"

The boys didn't answer.

"Auntie," said the eldest César, "there's a dead dog on the patio. We want to show Uriela."

"Uriela is coming with me," said Señora Alma.

"A dead dog on the patio?" gasped Uriela.

"If that's true," snapped Señora Alma, without waiting for

the boys' response, "go find Doña Juana and Zambranito, and tell them there's a dead dog on the patio of this house."

Uriela looked at her mother in disbelief. Could this woman really be her mother? But Señora Alma remained unfazed:

"Go find Doña Juana and Zambranito in the kitchen. Tell them I ordered the dog to be buried in the spot where it died, six feet underground. So it doesn't smell. Go right now and tell them what I said."

The boys just stood there, hesitant.

"Are you all damned deaf?"

The little Césars sprang back because Señora Alma had craned her neck out toward them, as though about to bite them. But she didn't bite them, instead adding with a laugh:

"Tell them that, and then go with them to the patio. Help them dig, you lazy so-and-sos. Use the shovels. Even little boys need to learn what we do with the dead, whether dogs or little boys."

"We bury them or burn them," the eldest César managed to call back, for as soon as they heard that they would be participants in the burial, the boys had rushed off to the kitchen like a pack of hounds, in search of Juana and Zambranito.

"That's how these things should be handled" said Señora Alma, with a sigh. "I wonder which of the three dogs has died, whether Femio or Vilma or Lucrecio; what a shame, but we'll soon find out, they're very old dogs, they were given to me by Jorge Bombo ten years ago."

And she took Uriela by the arm, leading her along:

"Why don't you come talk to us for a while? Why are you so impolite? Why do you make me suffer? Of all my daughters, you're the only one who will one day cause me grief, the others will all marry and have children. You, I'm not so sure about."

"Neither am I," said Uriela, and they both laughed. But

138

then Señora Alma stopped and looked at her for a moment. Her eyes welled up:

"Oh, Uriela," she sobbed, and her voice sounded like a hoarse moan: "Should I be found dead one day, with a dagger in my back, it will have been by your hand, Uriela."

They immediately looked at each other, stunned, perplexed by these words. Both Uriela and her mother. But especially her mother, who had just spoken those words, though it was as if she were hearing them from the lips of another. She shrugged and gently forced Uriela to resume walking. Uriela couldn't respond, she didn't know how. And yet she wished she could say something to confront the inexplicable.

Both she and her mother had tears in their eyes.

PART FIVE

1

The dining room table sat twenty-four and was made of solid cedar, with wrought-iron imitation elephant legs; it had been the table of a convent refectory, which the Augustinian monks had gifted to the magistrate in tacit payment for his legal maneuverings, for he had prevented a recreational estate belonging to the friars, known as the House of Spiritual Retreats, from falling into the hands of the indigenous people of El Llanto, who claimed the extensive plot on which the House had been erected as their own, through ancestral right. The elephant-leg table was headed by Nacho Caicedo and Alma Santacruz, sitting at opposite ends from each other, although Alma was conspicuous by her absence, her chair empty: she had just left to go in search of Uriela.

To the magistrate's right sat Uncle Luciano, his wife Luz, and daughters Sol and Luna, while to his left was Monsignor Javier Hidalgo, and, carrying on around the table, there was a good portion of the family: Uncle Barrunto, his wife Celmira, their son Rigo, José Sansón, Sparks, Pumpkin, the aunts Adelfa and Emperatriz, with Father Perico between them, then Francia, Armenia, and Palmira, Obdulia Cera, Fernanda Fernández, the fiancées Esther, Ana, and Bruneta, those nicknamed Sexilia and Fecunda, Artemio Aldana, the judge Arquímedes Lama, the three lady judges, the Barney sisters, the one nicknamed The Hen, Pepe Sarasti and Lady Mar, Pepa Sol and Salvador Cantante, and members of other cherished families, among them the Púas—with a grandfather and great-grandfather who were still alive—the publicist Roberto

Smith, Cristo María Velasco and Marianita, his fifteen-year-old daughter, Yupanqui Ortega, Dalilo Alfaro and Marilú, the teachers Celio and Caveto, Roque San Luis and Rodrigo Moya, the two Davides, the fiancés of the fiancées, and those nicknamed Ingenuo and Sexenio.

In order for everyone to partake in the meal, it became necessary to add a second row of chairs behind the first, because no one had any qualms about eating lunch with their plate in their lap so as to avoid missing out on Nacho Caicedo's conversation. And, as more guests continued to arrive, eager to see what was happening, the aid of Batato Armado and Liserio Caja was enlisted: it occurred to the giants to bring in two of the dance platforms, lay them down around the table, and place extra chairs on top, which immediately became occupied; it all resembled a small Elizabethan theater, with the dining table as stage and Nacho Caicedo the leading actor. Any moment now, the tragedy would get under way.

As ample as it was, the dining room could no longer have admitted even an insect. And, while the select savored the elderflower cake, which Alma considered to be a little slice of heaven, the diligent waiters distributed what the magistrate termed "liquid spirits to honor the recently ingested pig." This was celebrated with a roar of laughter, even more so when he added: "And which make pigs of all who drink them!" Apart from the monsignor and his secretary, who only sampled wine, most guests leaned toward rum and aguardiente, and a very few toward brandy and whiskey; the inoffensive ladies drank inoffensive lady cocktails.

When Alma arrived with Uriela, the table was debating what mankind's most exalted foodstuff had been throughout the ages. All agreed it was the egg.

"The chicken's egg," specified Roque San Luis, primary school teacher, "because it could just as well be the ostrich."

"Or the crocodile's," said the one nicknamed Sexenio.

"Even the pterodactyl's," added Profesora Fernández.

"The egg, in any case, whatever the kind," concluded Obdulia Cera.

"I'm not so sure about snake eggs," said Profesor Moya.

"You can't eat snake eggs like you can turtle eggs," countered Obdulia Cera.

"Do people eat turtle eggs?" came a question to nobody from Uncle Luciano, the toyshop owner, brother to the magistrate.

Uncle Luciano did not seem like the magistrate's brother, though he too was a lawyer, and in full possession of his faculties; he had decided to renounce the law in favor of his toyshop. He invented toys and sold them, and while he shared the magistrate's interest in history and politics, his eyes retained the ingenuousness of angels: minutes before the steaming plates were served, he had pulled from his pocket a toy he'd invented, a little tin horse in the shape and style of that of Troy: he wound it up, placed it on the table, and the little horse began to spin in circles, emitting whinnies like diabolical laughter. How had he managed to create this toy with those cackle-like whinnies? Nobody knew, and nobody cared either: his wife Luz didn't laugh, and his daughters Sol and Luna sighed, pityingly, because by now the whole world had grown weary of Uncle Luciano's toys; they were ridiculous; nobody was impressed.

"People do eat turtle eggs," said the one nicknamed The Hen.

"What a bizarre conversation," said Alma Santacruz, mockingly. "It's quite *egg*sasperating."

She was not in good spirits.

143

She was annoyed about Italia's escape, her capricious decision to bypass paternal consent. If, that morning, when Italia came to tell them she was expecting a child, Juana had not arrived with the story about Jesús being dead in the kitchen, Alma would surely have taken charge, would have put Italia in her place, but she had left the predicament in the hands of her husband, and here were the results: Italia had fled.

Lisboa didn't worry her. Alma hadn't tried to convince her to join them in the dining room for two reasons: first, because she was twenty-five years old (she knew what she was doing, she was no fool), and, second, because she had seen Lisboa deep in conversation with Cirilo Cerca at the most secluded table in the garden, both of them enjoying the elderflower cake. If Alma had arrived a minute earlier and seen her daughter dancing with the baritone like sword and serpent, she might well have changed her mind. But she hadn't seen them, and besides, there was something even more intimate that was mortifying her: many of the guests had been encouraging Nacho Caicedo to make a start on his Premonitions; all that prophecy stuff was a load of nonsense best performed in private; it seemed to her that her husband became the unwitting object of mockery when he began prophesying about the things of this world and the next. "Uriela adores my revelations," he had told her, as though confirming that he would accept the challenge of delving into the future only in the presence of Uriela, the person responsible for interpreting his prophecies and translating his broken Latin, and so Alma had taken advantage of this stipulation to go in search of her and breathe some fresh air.

Fresh air?

The garden smelled of roasted flesh.

The music of the Malaspulgas pounded on her eardrums,

with Charrita's voice sounding like a man's, husky, as though coated in oil—was she singing a song to the devil? She mentioned him at least, "Diablo, diablo" she chanted, "espíritu burlón," and again she roared: "diablo, diablo," Alma couldn't understand, she was incensed, how could Charrita Luz sing those words? And how could they all dance along? Who was that huge gyrating black man? And who was his partner? How shameless, better to have come to the party in no skirt at all, she would look less naked, and the woman was locking legs with the black man as if they were foam and water, the music exploded, *diablo, diablo*, like hammers—*fortunately*, she thought, *the music doesn't reach the dining room.*

And she entered the garden in search of Uriela and found her with the boys.

Uriela had taken up the seat recently vacated by Ike, nervous to discover that she was sitting between Ricardo Castañeda and the women nicknamed Sexilia and Fecunda, and yet there was every chance her father would summon her to his side, rescuing her from such company.

It was true that Ike had left the dining room, though not the house; that was the artifice, the ploy: the Castañedas' trap had been set. Francia had finished her dessert and was preparing to leave the dining room. Her mother shot her an interrogating look: she was attentive to each and every one of her daughters; they weren't getting anything past her.

On the pretext of a headache, Francia said she was going up to her bedroom for a nap. "And then you'll come back," said her mother, from the distant head of the table. "Just fifteen minutes, mamá," protested Francia, suppressing a yawn. "The greatest beauty is leaving us!" cried Pepe Sarasti.

Ricardo Castañeda saw his cousin leave the dining room,

wreathed in light, almost floating. Knocking back his rum like someone toasting to himself, he watched her race hopefully toward catastrophe.

2

"Why didn't you turn on the lights?"

The same hands that had stuffed Rodolfo Cortés into the trunk now encircled Francia's waist and led her over to the bed. Francia let herself be led. She answered her own question, laughing, "It's better with the lights off, is that it?," taking off her shoes and lying down on the bed, with a sigh, while the presumed Rodolfito lay down beside her, in the complete darkness, rigid as a tombstone.

In the distance, they could hear the voice of Charrita Luz and the tam-tam of the congas in the orchestra.

Francia didn't suspect a thing: when it came to lovemaking, Rodolfito adored the darkness. She found it amusing how he made love as though he were fearful: fearful of having someone look into his eyes, fearful of looking into her eyes. When had that adolescent trembling begun, that fervor, those spasms of the first time? But now Rodolfo Cortés wasn't trembling as much, this was new. Now Rodolfito was unbuttoning her dress, and she could hear him moaning—it couldn't be, *it isn't him*, thought Francia. "Mad Ike," she managed to say, "it's mad Ike again." She allowed herself to be swept along by that second kiss in a month, its fiery lurch, but then leapt up and crossed the room, her arms feeling in the blackness, all the way to the light switch.

"Get out, Ike," she growled. "Get out now!"

Ike just looked at her while sitting on the bed, completely naked; if he'd had a cigarette, he would have started smoking as though it were nothing. Ike worshiped her in silence, and

Francia became aware that her unbuttoned dress had slipped down below her waist. She immediately turned out the light while she did up the dress, listening to Ike's laughter. Francia again told him to get out, but, by the looks of things, Ike was never leaving; it would have to be she who left. As she groped in the darkness, searching for her shoes, she heard Cousin Ike jump up and embrace her; again, he kissed her and pressed himself against her, distressed and distressing, as though he were being asphyxiated and asphyxiating her. Only then did she worry about Rodolfito, becoming fearful. "Don't force me!" she bellowed, using all her strength to push him away. However, without knowing how or when, they had groped their way back to the side of the bed, and there they sat, panting, as if by some absurd mutual agreement:

"And Rodolfito," asked Francia, "what have you done with him?"

"I haven't killed him," said Ike.

This was the response of the man she found herself with, thought Francia, because he was no longer her cousin, the Ike of her childhood, but a total stranger—this is what she felt, more than understood.

"What did you do to him?"

"He's gone," came Ike's voice in the darkness. And he waited for her to say something, but to no avail. He felt obliged to explain: "I just told him to leave. I told him if he didn't go, I'd stick him in Grandma's trunk."

"In the trunk?"

"In the trunk."

"And that's where you stuck him," said Francia.

"He chose to leave," said Ike. "I wasn't really going to stick him in the trunk, I'm not that big a brute."

In that second, Ike reflected that he should have just threatened Rodolfito. The mere threat would have been enough to make the amphibian go—why had he stuffed him in that trunk?

"The trunk in the drawing room?" asked Francia.

"Of course, isn't that Grandma Clara's trunk?"

"That trunk is hermetic," said Francia, the architect, "if you locked him in there, he'll have suffocated already."

"That's exactly why I didn't lock him in, Francia, who do you take me for? The threat that I'd stick him in the trunk if he didn't leave was enough to send him running."

This didn't seem preposterous to Francia: Rodolfito ran away from everything. But he'd seemed so determined, had sworn that the announcement in the newspaper was a lie, that if she didn't believe him, he'd kill himself—how could he leave after they'd agreed to meet? And how had Ike known she would come up to her bedroom? How extraordinary, she told herself, caught between laughter and terror, how extraordinary, and then she heard Ike's voice in the blackness:

"If you want, later we can go down to the drawing room and make sure there aren't any Rodolfitos in Grandma's trunk. But now don't leave me flying solo, Francia."

To Francia, these last words sounded like a sob. Was Ike going to cry? It was possible, he was crazy.

That whimpering plea moved her, stealing away what little strength she had left. She was conquered by pity. As she sympathized, Cousin Ike went back to unbuttoning her dress, the two bodies contorting noisily in the bed, one because it wanted to escape, the other because it was imprisoning the first. Ike continued to undress her, infallible, and what seemed most terrible to Francia was that all the talk of Rodolfito in the trunk had profoundly excited her: the certainty of knowing that Rodolfito was almost definitely locked inside the trunk, with her in her bed, in the company of this naked madman, was enough to drive her mad, she thought, and she thought this with a kind of lustful joy. But, at the same time, she was also fearful that something awful really could have happened to Rodolfito, why did Ike have to be so crazy? she thought, and when Ike's nose sniffed between her breasts she rebelled, no, no, she couldn't, not like this, no, she whispered in Ike's ear, not like this.

And, slippery as an eel, she began to slide onto the floor, and then crawl once more toward the light switch, in the dense blackness, and yet he went after her, both of them crawling across the floor, she desperate to escape, he already beside himself, the gritting of his teeth ringing out in the darkness, he whinnied as he pressed Francia face down. They struggled like this for several seconds; Francia's head lay upon a pile of clothing on the floor, they were Ike's clothes, his shirt, his pants, his odor. With a shiver, she felt against her cheek the cold gold of the fountain pen she had given Ike and took hold of it, snapping off the lid and doing her best to twist around to face him as he repositioned himself between her legs, as he drew nearer, then she pressed the nib of the fountain pen against his neck and said, "Stop or I'll bury it in you, I swear to God"; "Bury it in me, Francia," said Ike, "kill me now," and saying this, he was already loving Francia, and she let herself be loved—without removing the weapon from mad Ike's neck.

3

Perla Tobón was fading.

She had danced three times, each in the arms of a re-spective admirer, and, with the last one, if she remembered correctly, she had fallen over, or she had tumbled forward but someone caught her in midair and stopped her falling. Which of the three? What strength, what heroism, which one? She couldn't remember; Perla was succumbing to the drink, I'm drunk, she thought, *good Saint Rock, tie up your dog*, and she burst out laughing at the table, surrounded by her three admirers.

The lecturer Zulú, the magician Olarte, and the cyclist Rayo were all men in their forties, of similar stature, with only the magician's complete baldness differentiating him from the others. *These bald men*, Perla thought, admiring Olarte's round, polished head, *they're like walking penises with eyes*, and again she laughed to herself, as she always did when she was drunk; she would begin talking to herself, begin drifting, drifting.

She liked it when a person's jokes made her laugh, forget about her world-weariness, about her husband, the terror of her sons, who sooner or later would end up identical to their papá, about her boredom with herself; that's why she drank in company, to laugh until her flesh ached, another orgasm, she thought, or something very similar at least, she said out loud.

"What?" the men all asked in unison. She wanted to respond but couldn't: the three men and the world had become centuplicated, spinning inside her head; it only lasted a second, but she was on the point of passing out. The men had refilled their glasses—what were they drinking? They offered her a glass but she turned it away with a trembling hand. Incredulous, she heard her own voice, now on the verge of being sick:

"That's enough for me," it said. Her voice sounded as if it were coming through cotton wool: "I need to lie down." Her voice had to be deciphered, as if arriving from far away, and in another language: "Just one minute, then I'll come back and dance, good as new."

"But of course," said Manolo Zulú. "Lie down for as long

as you need, you can sleep in any of the bedrooms. We'll take you."

"I know the way," said Perla. Her voice came out like a gigantic yawn: she was a yawn incarnate. "There's no need."

"It would allow us the pleasure of your company for another minute, Perla," said the magician.

The three men stood up, all behind Perla, like randy mutts; this is what the magician was telling himself: like randy mutts.

"Be careful," said the magician, running behind Perla, throwing his arms around her shoulders, his teeth like daggers, "there are so many people dancing that you could trip and fall."

"I already fell when I was dancing, and I think it was with you," said Perla, lucid for a moment, "I recognize you by your head."

The magician could offer no response. They were ensnared by the lecturer, who embraced them: "Let's stay friends until we die," he was saying, squeezing them by the necks and bringing them into his chest, before planting a rough kiss on Perla's perfumed head, a lock of her hair, which he chewed for an instant, with relish, while the cyclist Rayo cleared a path through the crowd as though using a machete to open up the jungle. Now the magician clung to Perla's arm, as if fearing she might fall over again, but in reality he was bringing his wide nostrils toward her neck and was planning to kiss her on the lips if she didn't object, but she did object, arching her neck backward, exasperated—repulsed?—the cyclist shook his head, the lecturer halted for a moment, ready to back Perla's protestations, but she was laughing, light years away, and moved through the dancing couples like a sleepwalker. The magician caught up with her in two bounds: now he stretched the fingers of one hand toward Perla's ear, drawing a yellow daisy from inside that she was unable to appreciate. The lecturer and the cyclist shook their heads, while the magician trailed in Perla's wake, happy. Happy to be leaving the garden with such a beauty, the drunk beauty, to shut her away and lock himself in with her, cage her, imprison her inside the best bedroom, where anything could happen, he thought, flinging the daisy up into the air.

4

They were ascending the spiral staircase.

In that moment, none of the three men remembered who Perla's husband was, the bloodthirsty César Santacruz, marijuana trafficker, pioneer, tough guy, nobody picked up on that story; they were all jubilant, only sorry not to be carrying a bottle of rum.

The three admirers climbed the spiral staircase, spiraling behind Perla, behind her generous, faltering legs, stair by stair, her supporting arm sliding along the wall. To her, the world was a dizzying whirl of shouting. To them, the world was under her very short skirt, they were rejoicing in the mystery it held; one of the men—or all three?—had even leaned back to get a better look at the small dark mound Perla had between her legs. "What filth," whispered the lecturer, pausing and shaking his head, "aren't we going to show her even a little bit of respect?" The cyclist Rayo wondered if this "filth" was in reference to their spying or to that dark mystery with the allure of a slab of raw meat held out before a dog. "What are you trying to say?" asked the magician, uneasily, already reaching the top of the stairs, without ceasing to peer at Perla's desirable mystery, her throbbing darkness. "You know very well what I'm saying," said the lecturer, "respect, sir, respect," and, as one, they had continued their ascent behind the woman who was disappearing into the shadows. The cyclist Rayo felt obliged to repeat the word "respect," while the magician grew disenchanted. "Instead of all coming to some kind of agreement," he muttered through gritted teeth. Every woman who'd ever shared his bed had been drunk; he claimed he merely hypnotized them into loving him, as magicians do, enthralling them. And the lecturer would have his way with his guileless students: after the subtle threat, they eventually gave in.

The cyclist wasn't thinking: newly married, his wife was expecting a child.

They reached the summit just in time to see a hesitant Perla go down the right side of the corridor. They immediately sprang after her, all brushing up against each other, to then brush up against her, her back, her legs, her backside. Perla Tobón zigzagged along a foggy stretch of corridor, and, of all the doors, she chose the one to the farthest room, which appeared to be front-facing, adjoining the balcony of the house.

She opened the door, entered, and *felt* the men enter with her.

Inside, the open curtains of the window let in a blue half light.

There they stood, balancing against each other, for they'd all been drinking, though none as much as Perla. The lecturer Zulú thought he felt tipsy: *Or is it that I'm* possessed? He was coughing, overexcited, and wondered if it wouldn't be best to depart with a bow and flee as quickly as he could. But the mere sight of Perla's glowing face, her provocative defenselessness, pricked him. No, he would not go: he wanted her all to himself, right away. And he would need to ready himself for a tournament of the champions of the Round Table, he thought. He worried about the magician: downstairs, in the garden, he'd noticed Perla make the mistake of leaning toward Olarte, of selecting him, what irony, that sicko, that wretch, that pervert. He felt humiliated. The cyclist Rayo was simply a happy newlywed, for the first time witnessing the miracle of a woman as beautiful as she was drunk, an angelic creature, all tenderness, he thought, who had got herself as drunk as a sailor, more plastered than all three of the men, poor thing, *tomorrow her head will hurt, her heart will protest, she won't last ten years*. But that was precisely why Rayo idolized her, he who was all discipline, all restraint.

Perla turned to them, and, in a sudden flash of lucidity, was able to make out their faces, becoming frightened for the first time, not just of them but of herself; but of them, most of all, those arms that sought to embrace her, those hands looking to paw her, those mouths to kiss her, those teeth to grind her. She was about to tell them to leave, but decided instead to ask them to bring her a glass of something to revive her, yet she could only mumble, nobody understood her voice, the world was spinning. A supporting hand helped her to walk. She discovered it was the magician's hand, leading her over to the bed and laying her down, putting the pillow under her head, half covering her with half a blanket. Meanwhile, the voice of the crouching lecturer dampened her ear: "Sleep, gorgeous, later you'll come join us, you'll dance with us." *None of us have eaten*, recalled Perla, *that must be why I'm dying, I should have eaten, our plates have been left untouched, is it possible I might wake up sorry tomorrow and be thankful nothing happened? No, no!, s*he yelled to herself, *let it happen, let it happen, let it happen before I die!*

The three shadows stood motionless before her; they looked to her as if made of smoke, of fog. She heard a voice say: "Careful with her: she's a pearl called Perla." *What nonsense*, thought Perla. And she heard a strange noise in the air, like sparks: "It's the electricity from our bodies," someone marveled, "it's blue, look at it, it's the color blue, can't you see it?" *Blue*, Perla said to herself, she could see only the smoky shadows, black, black. "The ship is sailing," she wanted to tell them, absurdly, and in the end she said it, repeated it, "The ship is sailing, it's moving, don't you think?," she'd finally been able to speak, almost inaudibly. "Of course," said the cyclist Rayo, and, to everyone's astonishment, he let out a groan like a ship's horn: it was as if they'd found themselves at a port, the ship setting sail. "You do a good ship impression," said Perla, but now no one was able to decipher her words, though they were only an inch away from her, hunched over, three faces looming over her face. A hand under the blanket had scurried like a rodent and settled on one of her breasts, for just a moment, who was it? *The magician*, Perla told herself, *the roamer*. "She's a female fox," someone posited, "a vixen." "Don't talk garbage," replied another voice, and another: "Respect, gentlemen, respect," and the last: "We're leaving for a bit, beautiful, sleep tight," and then all together, in whispers: goodbye, goodbye, goodbye.

But they didn't leave.

Sprawled face up in the bed, legs crossed like a fortress, arms dead, Perla realized that if she kept still, she could distinguish things, but she was unable to talk, and the fact that the three men were all talking hurriedly—simply because they'd just heard her sigh—and saying so many things to her, asking her, answering for her, annihilated Perla, made her wish right then and there for a huge bucket next to her, a blue bucket into which she could vomit precisely all the miles of words they discharged and that she was forced to swallow.

They realized she was dying of nausea.

"Don't move," said the lecturer, "close your eyes."

The cyclist was running a hand over her damp hair. The magician, who was something else, had placed his hand on her breast again, a gesture that did not go unnoticed by the other two; another hand immediately removed the first from her breast, and a peremptory voice was heard. It was the lecturer:

"Don't push it, Mr. Magician, take things step by step, step by step, don't rush ahead of us. It is for such passions that this lady has her champions with her."

"Yes," said the cyclist, who was thinking not of the champions of the Round Table but those of the Vuelta a Colombia, "she has her champions with her."

The magician was shocked by how they seized his arms, how they restrained him, *what turkeys*, he thought, *they don't realize*. But he put up no opposition and left the bedroom with the champions. As a precaution, one of them pushed the button in the door handle, locking it behind them.

Perla Tobón wanted to scream for them to come back, she was screaming on the inside, *I don't want to be left alone*, she didn't want to be on her own again, but she couldn't speak, it wasn't possible to speak, only to look and listen, only to breathe—or else she'd die.

5

The open-curtained window faced onto the street; night was falling. Perla Tobón surveyed the space in which she found herself, believing she could hear noises very nearby, on the floor, around the edges, she made an effort to peer closer: it was two cats. Or was it? It was two cats and a sort of fish tank, inside which a turtle was chewing a cabbage leaf. *Is it a turtle?* she asked herself, straining her eyes in the yellow gloom, answering in disbelief that it was. *And those cats?*

What are they doing scampering around over there? Are they going to eat the turtle? No: they seem to be friends.

And she lay still in the bed again.

She believed the nausea was finally subsiding, or this is what she wanted to believe. Now her eyes were exploring the ceiling, the shadows, and she made out the spectral effigy of Melina the witch, perched on her broomstick, the hooked nose, the satanic eyes, motionless or flying far away in the yellow sky, distant but incoming. *Is that flying thing really a witch?* she asked herself in amazement, and again the nausea; she decided to close her eyes. Then she heard something like the sound of a key in the lock, the door opening; her eyes widened in terror. She was grateful to discover it was the magician, bathed in that cloud of yellow light, advancing toward her, his voice a murmur: "Perla," he said, "I've just come to check that you're okay," and he continued to move toward her, a smile on his face.

She heard him very nearby:

"I'd be the happiest magician in the world if you'd allow me to lie down next to you. Only lie down, I'm exhausted. This party is a circus."

Again, Perla wanted to speak but couldn't, she was unable to, it was like being on the brink of death. She was about to stretch out her arms, summon the magician with gestures, encourage him, but that's when, dumbfounded, she noticed other shadows enter the room and spring up on either side of the magician.

"What a persistent fellow," came the voice of the lecturer.

"He was only able to get in because he's a magician," said the voice of the cyclist. "Or because he used a hook, a wire, like any burglar, any thief."

The magician was about to protest, but again the champions seized him by the arms and pulled him toward the door, this time with all their strength. The three men struggled in front of the bed from which Perla watched on, lying face up, unable to move, unable to speak, and yet inside she was laughing, saying: *Come, come, there's cake here for everyone,* and she touched herself as she said this, pointed to herself. But she couldn't speak the words, only blink.

"Go back to sleep, beautiful," advised the lecturer.

And the cyclist:

"You'll thank us tomorrow."

By then, the magician had managed to slip free of the arms that restrained him, and, exasperated, was readying himself for a serious brawl; he pounced. The lecturer broke his momentum, grabbing him by the ears. "Do you want me to yank all the magic out of these ears?" he asked him, pulling the magician's ears downward with such force that they both popped. The magician was dazed, defeated. "Incompetents," was all he could say, his eyes welling up as a result of the punishment. The champions left, dragging the magician and again locking the door behind them; again the silence, again the darkness.

If she lay still, she would fall asleep, thought Perla. Or would she prefer to die? *Yes, yes, right now.*

She endured centuries of waiting.

She assumed the magician would not come back, that none of the champions would return. And she managed to drift off for just a moment, because then she half glimpsed that someone was beside her, and they had been ever since she'd fallen asleep. She sensed that a sinister shadow was pulsing beside her, believing she had been able to make it out before sinking into sleep: it breathed beside her, listened to her. She woke suddenly, her eyes wide, and finally caught sight of the skull on the nightstand next to her, a real skull. "Mother of God!" she cried—a skull was staring back at her.

This scare frightened away her drunkenness; she leapt up in bed; yes, it was somebody's skull, surely a dead man, for God's sake, was this the magistrate's bedroom? Impossible. Who slept in this bed? Which of the Caicedo sisters? Only a madwoman could sleep with a skull.

Then she staggered out of the bedroom. She was swaying, but moved as quickly as she could, to prevent sleep from hunting her down in that room full of witches and cats and turtles, lurching along the corridor, her arms moving like propellers toward the light: it was the balcony, the doors thrown open, seemingly waiting for her with open arms, festooned with roses and tuberoses and streamers, clouds of cellophane cascading from its walls like a fairy castle.

She leaned against the balcony and gulped the cool night air. A mist of fragrant herbs wafted up from the outer garden, lulling her to sleep like a narcotic. She could sense the tree leaves rustling, and thought: *I'm alive.*

The breeze continued to bring more sleep-inducing emanations: she rested her head on her crossed arms and went still; from the street, normal, peaceful sounds arrived: the voices and footsteps of the neighbors, a car's motor being started; behind her, distant but lively, she could hear the sounds of the party in the garden, the tropical orchestra, the soothing congas; she would go back as soon as she'd recovered; a vodka should revive her.

Standing there, leaning entirely against the balcony, Perla Tobón fell asleep.

6

Cousin César had not recovered from his truncated loving of the maidservant. He was searching for her in the crowd like an orphan. He couldn't rid himself of Iris, her body, so, so close. It was a dagger to his liver, an intimate frenzy he needed to indulge, or else it would be worse. He didn't want to go to the dining room and spend a pleasant time with family, he had no interest in his aunt Alma or his own children who—where were they? And what did it matter? Like a man possessed, he wandered that whirlwind of a party, from top to bottom: he needed to find Iris or he'd explode. Why the hell had he toppled her in the library? Now he'd become his own victim.

And Iris was nowhere to be seen, not even in the kitchen.

From there, he returned to the garden, strung out, what a yearning he had to kick some asses. He froze among the bodies. An excruciating hatred passed through him: just one more unrestrained minute and he'd pounce on that cavorting black woman dressed all in white. *What should I do? Cursed Iris-less world!* He imagined some kind of replacement, but who? A waitress? The first one he spotted had potential, but what if she screamed? And why not his wife? After all, she belonged to him. Ah, he remembered: he'd discovered Perla a few hours earlier, without meaning to; he'd spied her drinking with three men, nothing extraordinary there, always very well accosted, darling *perra*, she'd never learn. César had counted the men, identified them, and made a note. For him, doing this was significant. Of course, he hadn't gone over to rescue his wife from the trio of suitors, but he'd made a note of it.

Perla no longer excited him, she was an adversary, he should never have had children with her. Without going any further, had she not prevented the consummation of his business with the maidservant? She'd even called him a sack of lard.

He would need to find his sister-in-law Tina, he resigned himself: for years, he'd had an understanding with Tina

Tobón, she was his shoulder to cry on, but where was she breathing, where was she hiding, *why aren't you there when you should be, dwarf of my life?* He continued to scan the horizon of dancing couples, strangely lit by the garden lights; Alma Santacruz had ordered these to be fitted with multi-colored bulbs: each region of the garden swam in a mist of colors—which all looked black to César. His unsatisfied primal urges darkened everything for him. He would not regain control of himself until he'd bound himself with Iris's love. What he had was an illness, a doctor once told him, so he needed to find the remedy: continence, willpower. *There's only one remedy*, thought César, *a girl down here, under me, sweating from her cunt.*

Tina was the solution, the ever-ready Tina Tobón, who understood him through and through. She resembled a little nun, and yet, what a love vermin, her timid face transformed into a screaming kiss, her body nothing but jaws, opening to swallow him. One time, she had alarmed him while loving him, she had seemed to want to kill herself and kill him. Ultimately, it would have been better to have had children with Tina, trusty, lusty and dependable Tina. Not that bitch of a harpy who would rather see him dead.

Then a finger in the middle of his back surprised him like the barrel of a gun; it was Tina, out of the blue.

"Tina, at last," he said. "Where have you been hiding?"

"I've been following you for hours. Don't tell me it was me you were looking for."

"I was looking for you, who else."

She peered into his eyes:

"For today, I'll believe you," she said.

"Come on, let's go where we must," César urged her.

"Where else would we be going?" she said.

What a transformation, what a voice, no one would have

recognized her, short and scrawny, a runt. With that checked skirt reaching below her knees, that silk tie, who would have thought it? Her straight answer put him at ease. She truly was his salvation.

Their arms around each other, they first raced off to dance, and, in the midst of the flying bodies, they attempted to get up to mischief, becoming entwined while standing, and yet the lights came and went like beams from a maddening lighthouse, revealing them; the risk was enormous. They were on the verge of doing it in a corner of the corridor leading to the kitchen, behind a statue of the Baby Jesus the size of a ten-year-old boy, under shrouds and tinsel like a private temple, but the one nicknamed The Hen poked her merry pink face in to look at them. Tina Tobón, a picture of composure, suggested they go up to one of the bedrooms, it would be better, she said. César obeyed but still wanted to have his way with her in a quiet corner, sitting her on his lap, and they were already behaving shamelessly, believing themselves free from danger, when a waiter appeared, asking if they preferred champagne or rum. They were leaving the garden once and for all, slinking away as quickly as they could, when César's bliss dissipated: he saw three men coming out of the house; two were securing the third by the arms, as if helping him to walk. The three men paused a short distance away, drunk; they were the same men who had been with Perla. Where had they left her? They'd surely taken advantage of her, he would have to go see Perla; just by looking at her he'd be able to tell what they'd been up to, whether they'd done it or not, and then let the birds deal with the consequences: he wouldn't be mocked by anyone, he wasn't a person you dicked around with.

He knew those three.

Hadn't he seen the bald one working as a magician at a bazaar full of whores? What was he doing in the magistrate's home? So this was the company kept by Nacho Caicedo; that magician was an oaf, but also a two-faced soul, a scoundrel. The cyclist Rayo was an idiot, a teacher at the school Nacho Caicedo owned "shares" in, but the lecturer Zulú, that big shot ... that famous brain had been accused of rape by one of his students; the magistrate Caicedo had rescued him from the guillotine; *what birds, I should have taken charge of Perla when I first saw her with them; now I'll have to find her, look at her, determine whether or not they did it.*

And, accompanied by Tina, he entered the house.

His urges had changed.

He forgot about Iris, forgot about Tina, nothing else mattered, except for Perla, who was running wild and needed to be taken in hand like an unbridled mare, she needed to be reined in, shown who the rider was, shown who was on top and who was below, who dealt the lashes and who received them.

7

As they climbed the stairs, Tina Tobón had the temerity to embrace him from behind, clambering on top of him and repeating: "Kiss me." "Wait," César told her, disentangling himself, "let's go up in silence." Nothing could be heard on the second floor, there was nobody behind the row of doors. The sitting room was engulfed in a half light, which brightened down the main corridor leading to the balcony. César immediately recognized the distant figure slouched over the balcony, the halo of that head seemingly lost in contemplation. On tiptoes, he made for the balcony, pausing halfway there.

She's sleeping, he thought: it wasn't the first time he'd seen the bitch asleep on her feet.

César and Tina were in the small area preceding the balcony, next to Uriela's room; there were two armchairs, and a coffee table with fruit. César sat down in one armchair and Tina the other, and there they waited, in absolute silence, watching over the figure on the balcony. Then Tina averted her gaze, as if in terror: something was about to happen. She watched César rise and take three steps in that direction, his arms extended toward Perla, but not going any further. He came back to Tina, sat her on his lap, and began kissing her. Then he froze, his head on Tina's bosom, his ear against her heart, as though listening to it. Both were sweating in the cold. César felt as if he were bursting with anticipation, and said out loud, or merely thought: "If I could be sure that she landed on her head … bye-bye *perra*! I'd need to grab her by the calves, lift her so she turned her face to the void, then let go, shit, she'd snap her damn neck!" At that moment, Tina began kissing him again, but he pushed her away and sat staring into her eyes, licking his lips as he did so, then biting them. Tina flinched; again, César was walking over to Perla, though without stopping this time. His face became a mute laugh; he advanced slowly, every step precise, wrapping his arms around her hips, lifting her up and tossing her over the side, headfirst. At the same time, as if by a miracle, there was a cheer from the guests, celebrating the start of another cumbia. César returned to the armchair, looking at his hands as if they did not belong to him: he stared at his trembling hands, the hands of another: *Doing it to the mother of my kids wasn't like doing it to just anyone,* he thought, as if in justification. And he sat down beside Tina, who'd been turning her face away the whole time, toward the blackness, not wanting to witness anything. César was sweating, dazed: he wasn't capable of leaning over the balcony to confirm the results, instead returning to the chair so Tina could rescue him from the horror. But Tina was looking somewhere else, she hadn't seen a thing. In the long run, thought César, it was better that Tina hadn't been watching him, and better not to lean over the balcony, because someone might well recognize him. "How stupid I've been," he finally whispered, bowing his head like a child on the verge of tears. But then he heard something like a growl, and this was coming from Tina Tobón, who was kissing him, straddling his lap, squeezing him. Where did she get the strength? She began pulling down his fly, searching for it. "Hey," said César, "wasn't she your sister?" "I'm much more than just that," she said, "I'm yours," and she discovered him, convinced him; her checked skirt had risen up to her thighs, the open buttons of her blouse revealing her frenzied breasts, her silk tie turned round the other way like the leash of some strange animal; the pair crashed together furiously, then crashed together again, to the point of screaming, becoming a shared sweat, while continuing to gaze at each other as if on the brink of unleashing the same senseless laughter.

Then César pushed Tina's body aside and leapt to his feet, urging her from above: "Come on. We need to be somewhere people can see us."

8

"Well, run and look, Zambranito, and take care of it! If there really is a dead dog on the patio, do what madam said, I don't have time for burials, I've got enough to do providing food for all the dancers. Bury that dog and you can go to bed."

Juana Colima finished wiping her hands on her apron and turned to Zambranito, who was still looking at her questioningly, irritated. He'd just informed Juana he was going to bed, to sleep, and then the boys had arrived with the news about the dead dog. *Luckily, it's still daytime*, thought Zambranito, *if I really do need to bury a dog.*

The boys swarmed around him, awaiting his decision.

"Go to the patio with the boys," Juana repeated, "madam doesn't play games. If she ordered us to bury the dog, then it must be true, they aren't making it up. Afterwards, you can go to sleep."

"We aren't making it up!" chorused the swarm of boys. "She told us to help you dig!"

Zambranito left the kitchen, surrounded by shouting, by looks of encouragement, by hands all wanting to touch him. He thanked God again that it was still daytime.

"You'll have to use a shovel," the eldest César warned him. "Auntie Alma said six feet underground."

Yes, of course, thought Zambranito, *six feet under cement, you mean.*

And to the boys he said:

"I'll believe it when I see it."

Zambranito wasn't what he'd once been, he knew that himself, was conscious of his increasing idleness, his sore knees, his toes, the aches here and there; every task was carried out reluctantly, he had lost his dedication, his precision. Not long ago, the magistrate had told him: "If you want to retire, Zambranito, just let me know, I'll keep paying you punctually, you can go back to your town, buy a house with two trees and a hammock, sleep when you like, you needn't worry anymore." He had said this after Zambranito fell asleep in the middle of lunch, his head to one side of his plate. Zambranito apologized, grumpily, explaining that he'd slept badly the night before. He never disclosed his true age to anyone: he was already over eighty, though everyone assumed he was in his sixties; he himself proclaimed this every year: I'm in my sixties, I don't want to retire. The truth is, he was exhausted just by waking up. As far as he was concerned, he'd be happy to go on sleeping after he woke up, happy if they'd let him sleep until he died.

He had his own room in that enormous house, in front of a small patio behind the kitchen, to one side of the bedroom where Iris and Juana slept, the two bedrooms ample, independent, almost like two separate apartments with a bathroom and a television. The magistrate had hired him into his service years earlier; he'd been a simple courier for the Ministry of Justice, yet they had forced him to resign, accused of stealing an emerald ring the minister's secretary had left in his office. He was unmarried, with no children. A man with no friends. He was old.

Years ago, he'd stood out for his efficiency. To the magistrate, he was just what the doctor ordered: Zambranito knew about electricity, about plumbing, he'd been a mechanic and a carpenter, he was the perfect handyman, a jack of all trades, he could repair anything that lay in disrepair, the station wagon's motor, the blender, the washer, the dryer, the radio; he weatherproofed the roof, painted the walls, while also polishing the shoes of the entire family, leaving them sparkling like mirrors; his latest shortcoming was that he no longer drove the Mercedes with the competence of old, floundering at the steering wheel, mixing up the gears, braking for every little thing. He was excused from driving at night: the magistrate's eldest daughters would take over; Zambranito had permission to sleep.

Zambranito didn't like little boys.

And, surrounded by those little boys, he crossed the ocean of bodies: the music of the Malaspulgas was infecting everyone with a mad frenzy. Zambranito advanced with his ears covered. On reaching the large grated gate, which separated the garden from the patio, he considered the possibility of going in alone; he pushed open the heavy gate but couldn't prevent the boys from slipping through ahead of him; he followed, slamming the gate shut with such force that the locks and chains rang out; this was the gate separating the house from thieves, because the patio was practically unprotected. Well, the dogs slept there, what more could you need? The patio wall facing onto the street wasn't remarkable for its height: the high wall was the one overlooking the garden. The patio's grated gate resembled that of a church, and was secured every night with two padlocks by Juana, lady and mistress of the keys. Zambranito took this as an affront. They wouldn't grant him the authority of the keys, nor the possibility of ridding himself of these little boys and doing things alone.

In the evening light, the enormous patio resembled an oasis. He'd have liked to be alone and able to lie down in the grass, under the magnolia. But there, in front of the magnolia, head bowed and motionless as stone, stood César's white mule.

Zambranito crossed the patio. On the way, he noticed the smashed dog houses, the destroyed parrots' cage: one of the parrots had been turned into paste. The huge Saint Bernard lay curled up on the ground. Was it dead? Unconscious? The children formed a ring around it; Zambranito pushed past, but not before discovering that the shrine to Our Lady of the Beach lay in ruins, the Virgin in pieces, her sacred head crushed. He crossed himself, open-mouthed, overcome with surprise: he saw the overturned sandboxes, the sand and cat shit strewn everywhere, and, in the distance, the mangled ping-pong table; the extensive surface of the patio looked as if it had been hit by a hurricane, and yet still he didn't understand. He was left standing alone beside the dog's cadaver, because the boys had rushed to the high garden wall: from up above, Roberto the talking parrot was looking down at them, coming and going. "This country, this country!" the boys shouted up at him, fully aware of his antics, calling to him, but the parrot had decided not to talk. Zambranito knelt down to examine the dog. Where were the others? Lying sprawled out but awake in a distant corner, the other dogs watched Zambranito without approaching, without coming over to greet him. "But what could have happened here, boys?" Zambranito called out from where he was kneeling, as if expecting the dogs to tell him, as if expecting them to call back the answer.

And then he noticed the large, dry bloodstain on the cement. He examined the yellowish-brown dog more closely, recognizing the mole on its lip. "It's Femio," he said, scratching his head, distressed. He had loved that dog, loved all those dogs, had cared for them since they were pups, taking them for walks every morning; they were a source of pride; it wasn't easy to walk three Saint Bernards and make them obey you, what had happened? *He was killed by that diabolical mule,* he told himself with a snort; he finally understood, gazing with dread and admiration at the distant mule, with her head bowed, stone-still, as if ashamed, under the magnolia; her ears brushed against the tree trunk; there was no sign of a noose tethered to her long neck. *She's loose,* Zambranito realized, mortified, *that blessed mule is loose. But why would she go kicking Femio?*

By this point, the boys had discovered the tool room, equipped themselves with picks and shovels, and were awaiting orders; other children, less interested in the burial, took turns riding on the squeaky swing, or equipped themselves with stones to throw at Roberto, who was determined not to talk, coming and going above the wall; others decided to take turns chanting at the nervous mule, who spun around on herself and groaned, her eyes wide, her cowbells clacking, along with her desperate hooves. "Quit messing around with that mule!" Zambranito yelled at the children, who immediately stepped back, frightened by that old man scratching his head, because there was a note of horrified alarm in his voice. Zambranito also knew about mules and horses: he had spent a year working in the stables of the Techo hippodrome. "We need to get that mule tied up as soon as possible," he thought out loud, "why didn't they tie her up?" He headed into the mule's vicinity and looked for her tack; finding the rope under the riding saddle, he had already started tying the slipknot when he heard the parrot squawking, shocked; one of the children had managed to hit him; the parrot began flapping in circles and the mule raised her head, her eyes bloodshot. "What are you doing to that parrot, you little bastards," cried Zambranito, having made a mess of the knot, "why are you throwing stones at him?" The children regrouped in silence, waiting for the old man to tell them off: he'd said *bastards*, a bad word. They were boys and girls of all ages, cherubs dressed for a party; at ten years old, Cesítar was the eldest, and, it seemed, the most sensible. "Take your little friends through to the garden," the old man begged him, exasperated, "it won't be long before the clowns arrive, and there'll be marionettes." But the boy wouldn't budge. In his hands, he clasped a shovel that was bigger than he was: "Aren't we going to bury the dog?" he asked.

"First, I'm going to tie up this mule," said the old man.

"It's the same, it's the same," Roberto screeched for the first time, from the top of the magnolia; the children all laughed as one; the mule let out a bray-neigh and went back to spinning around in shock. "Just leave that mule alone!" yelled Zambranito. The children were taken aback by this order; none of them were bothering the mule. Zambranito had now finished tying the slipknot and was approaching the mule, cautiously, with the tact of an expert. The children, tired of listening to orders and counterorders, ran over to the wall facing the street and prepared to climb onto it, using hands and backs as ladders. "If you want to get to the street, use the gate!" Zambranito yelled at them, thinking, *little sons of bitches!* Because a couple of the children had already managed to climb up, and were prancing along the top, balancing. It wasn't a very high wall, about six feet. Zambranito scratched his head. "Get down from there," he yelled, "or I'll call your papís so they can come and warm your hides with their belts!" The two daredevils immediately climbed down. Zambranito approached the mule, holding the back of one hand in front of her nostrils, so she could smell him, and he began scratching her neck, pacifying her. "Whoa there, pretty mule," he said as if crooning, "whoa, easy mamacita, whoa there." He was fully aware that the mule was on the verge of passing out. He could see it in her watery, reddened eyes, and her despair was so great that he could almost hear her gaze exclaiming: *Get me out of here*. She was begging him.

As he ran his expert hand back and forth over her sweaty neck, he was thinking about the dog's burial. "I can't bury that dog," he said out loud, as though talking to the mule, "this is cement; not in six years could I dig a six-foot hole, a foot for every year, this is a job for Lucio. Where is Lucio? What is he doing? Better to bag that dog and throw him in the Río Bogotá, where everyone disposes of their dogs, I'm not about to start burying dogs, not even good old Femio, poor Femio, who told him to go barking at this pretty mule?

What happened, pretty mule? Were you provoked? Aren't you going to tell me?"

The children listened to him, dumbstruck.

Zambranito tried in vain to reconstruct the events of what had occurred, and he was just preparing to slide the noose around the mule's neck, when Roberto once again did his thing, to the delight of the children: "Oh this country, this country, this country," he screeched, and the mule jumped, more nervous than ever, and trotted in the direction of the clapping children. "Get the hell away from there!" Zambranito urged them, trotting alongside the mule. Sprawled in the distance, hemmed in by panic, the surviving Saint Bernards began to howl; they weren't even barking, they were simply letting out ominous, piercing howls, as Zambranito trotted alongside the mule across the patio, whoa, whoa, my pretty. They came to a halt at the very center, next to the pieces of the shrine; there, the old man was able to pacify the mule again, or so it seemed: he lay his hand on her back, his head against her neck, so as to quiet her down and be able to tie her up once and for all. But like fate, like a judgment, Roberto flew past, grazing the mule's ears and squawking, this country, this country. "Oh, you fucking parrot!" cried Zambranito: by then, he had realized who it was that was unsettling Rosita, but it was too late: in his haste to pacify the mule, the hand he caressed her with unwittingly came into contact with the bite dealt by Femio, slapping Rosita there, just as the parrot swooped back toward them, screeching, it's the same, it's the same. The mule instantly spun around, lifting its hind quarters and kicking at the chest of Zambranito, who collapsed into the ruins of the shrine and ended up sitting with his back against the pedestal.

For the children, this event was the beginning of a mortal

game that fascinated them: they started running around the mule, shouting and laughing, with her kicks passing mere inches from several of their heads; they were saved by being children. The parrot escaped the commotion; free in the sky, he flew back into the garden. Now, in the middle of the patio, Rosita scraped her front hooves against the cement floor, as the children formed a ring around her. Suddenly, Rosita gained momentum, and, to their shocked disbelief, set off on a tremendous dash toward the wall facing the street. The children watched her leap, narrowly clearing the wall, and cross to the other side as if she were flying, and then they heard nothing but her hooves disappearing down the street. They listened to her escape the house, as if it were they who were escaping, and they were overcome by a joyful cry: "Did you see her jump? She flew higher than the parrot!" Only then did it occur to them to check on the old man sitting among the ruins, his back against the pedestal. To everyone, it appeared that he was sleeping.

9

A short distance from the edge of the highway, in the middle of a mass of shadows, a single shadow rose to its feet; the night caused it to vanish, bit by bit, before returning it again, under the glow of the street lights. "If nothing else, you made a good mattress," said Uncle Jesús, as if continuing their conversation, brushing off the dust. A sleeve of his coat and one of his pant legs were ruined, but he was still alive, without a scratch on him: he'd had a lucky fall. "Thank you, Lord, for your mercy," he yelled into the emptiness. "Today you have saved the good guy from the bad guy, once again."

In the dim light of the street lights, he looked for the last time upon Lucio Rosas, gardener, hunter. Blood seeped from his open forehead, reddening his face. He no longer had the eye patch, just a wrinkled hole like a purple darn; he looked different, he had the face of someone else, a stranger. There was no one around, no witnesses.

Uncle Jesús went back to the edge of the highway as though tangled in laughter; he had a limp, but he was still alive.

He offered further thanks to God when he realized he might be able to find a taxi. "Or I'll walk to Bogotá," he cried, shaking his clenched fist at the world. "Damn you all, haven't I been walking ever since I was born!"

He turned back to look at Lucio Rosas' corpse. He could no longer see it. The night had swallowed it up.

Lucio Rosas splintered into a million lights and gazed down at himself in the body that lay bleeding, and yet he did not experience any kind of shock, he wasn't distressed; on the contrary, he had been blessed with an extraordinary sense of relief.

And, hovering like a whirlwind, he arrived far sooner than Uncle Jesús at the magistrate's house.

Like a breeze, he passed through the walls and passed through the bodies of the guests, passed through the greenhouse where he kept his work tools, passed through the bunk where he'd lain, passed through the garden of roses and tuberoses, and, with a single step like another gust of wind, he appeared inside his house on the Melgar farm.

There was his wife, sitting at the table.

He became a breath of air behind her, brushing his hands over her head before disappearing: she felt as if someone were sighing next to her. She rose from the table, opened the front door and peered out: a sky full of shining stars.

10

Lisboa listened.

"I have to tell you something that may disturb you, Lisboa, but it's something you need to know.

"I haven't had an easy life.

"My father was a widower from the time I was born, by which I mean … when the delivery became complicated, the midwives asked him to choose a life, your wife or your child? My father chose me. I can swear that I'd have preferred not to have been born, for my mother to still be alive. I grew up with guilt. This guilt was reinforced by my father, a bitter man who never remarried.

"One day, he told me he'd chosen me because, otherwise, my mother would never have forgiven him; I couldn't believe it; to me it seemed he regretted his decision.

"He died in his sleep, having drunk too much and choked on his own vomit.

"As my inheritance, he left me the butcher's, a raw meat outlet, a simple butcher shop in a simple neighborhood. I'd already been trained: my father put me to work when I was seven. There were no games or friends, my only companion was a small battery-powered radio, with its ballads and boleros. I was twelve when my father died. I didn't go to school, but I knew how to read and write and add and subtract and divide, especially how to divide, Lisboa; I divided meat with my cleaver, carving it from sunup to sundown. I dreamed about chopping meat, selling raw meat to an infinite line of buyers, go ahead, laugh at my dream.

"Now I'll tell you another, more intimate dream.

"At that age, with no family or friends, I can't explain to myself how I was able to make a living. I got lucky: I wasn't robbed, I wasn't cheated; my father's meat suppliers would give me credit. By the time I turned twenty, I was already the owner of four meat outlets in different neighborhoods of Bogotá. By the time I was thirty, I was providing jobs and paying taxes, owner of my own farm and my own livestock. I could supply myself.

"I stopped chopping meat and dedicated myself to the thing I most enjoyed: singing. I trained my voice at the Caruso Bogatano academy, where I was a distinguished student. Aside from improving my business, making exponential profits, I thought of nothing else but singing. Singing and only singing, without ever asking myself what or who for. I'd never had a girlfriend, believe me, I didn't take time off, I wouldn't buy myself a shirt, a pair of shoes. Singing was everything. If something else presented itself in my life, I ignored it, believing I would be betraying myself. Then I'd repeat to myself: I need to sing, and I would sing all through the night—like a canary, just as your father said.

"I must surely have sung in my sleep, Lisboa: yes, it's very likely that I sang as I slept, a kind of madness.

"That's when evil knocked at my door.

"Two men showed up at my farm; they assured me they were my father's sons, my elder brothers, and had a right to what my father had left me, that is to say, to half of what I'd earned from the time I was twelve to the time I was thirty, earned with the sweat of my brow, not my father's brow, much less my brothers'. It didn't bother me, Lisboa. I wanted the two men to be my brothers, I believed them, I offered them lunch at the farm, with my employees.

"I sang to them.

"We got drunk.

"I would never be alone again.

"They didn't seem particularly concerned with the human

side of things, there was no attempted embrace when they greeted me, nor did they inquire after my health or ask about our father's final days; they asked only about my money. They wanted to know how many head of cattle I owned.

"They were sons of another woman, of course: we were half brothers. Though there was no family resemblance, not even between them.

"Magistrate Caicedo came to my rescue, Nacho Caicedo, your father, Lisboa, more than a lawyer, a man of integrity. He inserted truth in place of the lie.

"I didn't give those crooks a peso, but I came awfully close. They were neither brothers nor half brothers, simply a pair of scoundrels, as the magistrate demonstrated with a wealth of questions, interrogations, answers, and cross-examinations ...

"Since that time, I've been an indebted friend to Nacho Caicedo. I must surely have met you when you were a little girl, Lisboa, surrounded by your sisters. It's very possible you used to smile at me, I don't remember. Now time has passed. Time passes and life does too. It's true that I could be your father—why lie to myself?—but I couldn't be your grandfather, Lisboa. I'm just a friend who sings. And I discovered you while singing.

"I almost stopped singing when I saw you, but I decided to continue so that you'd continue listening to me ...

"And my dream would come true.

"I dreamed I would meet the love of my life while singing, dreamed that she would listen to me as you listened to me, Lisboa, and in that dream I sang the song I did today, as you listened to me, I ... the words of songs are often prophecies ... my fate came to pass, I never thought I'd finally sing the story of my life to the woman I had dreamed of while singing ...

"Lisboa, I—this is hard for me to say and reveals my innermost secret—I'll tell you, but where to begin? Lisboa, I have never known a woman, ever since I became a man, I haven't known women, can you believe that? Are you laughing? Do you pity me? Yes, yes, Lisboa, I've been a saint, a kind of Saint Cyril by force, your laughter makes you cry, Lisboa, it's beautiful, do you want a handkerchief? Careful, the glass has spilled, it was my fault, forgive me, never mind ...

"I wake up alone in my bed and tell myself: this isn't right, business is going well, but I'm not, I'm not well at all.

"The years have passed and now I'm fifty. And every morning I tell myself: this isn't good, this isn't good at all. Every morning I repeat this, before jumping out of bed.

"Surely singing on my own has aged me.

"But I'm not defeated yet: seeing you has revived me. Lazarus, come forth. I'm your age, I'm younger than you are, Lisboa, see what love is, it has made a child of me!

"I'm going to tell you another truth, and this is no dream: I suffer from fainting spells, I fall over from time to time, it's tiresome. You probably know what a vasovagal syncope is. Sometimes I lose my balance ... If I'm standing, talking to someone, I have to grab hold of their shoulders to keep from falling; they're always surprised when I embrace them for no reason, no one knows about my fainting spells, and while the blackouts last—a matter of seconds—I embrace them tightly, like a shipwrecked sailor who discovers a plank amid the waves; it's an unwarranted embrace, a strange embrace.

"And if I find myself alone, I simply fall, with no one to hold on to.

"But they aren't frequent fainting spells, I understand them now, I see them coming and anticipate them, sit myself down in a chair or kneel and wait for the fainting spell to pass. I laugh at the fainting spell, which is like laughing at myself. I know this is how I will die, Lisboa, but only in a hundred years.

"I don't want to die unless I can be with you first. With you I'll travel the world, though you laugh; we'll go to Kyoto, or wherever, but go we will.

"I don't ever want to see another cow in my life.

"I wasted my life counting cows, but I haven't wasted all of it.

"And these fainting spells are a warning, I need to start living as soon as possible, sing through life, from port to port, and, if I fall, your love will get me back on my feet, Lisboa, I'll be able to embrace you for the rest of my life; let's go see the world, the world awaits."

Lisboa listened.

The baritone took a sip from his glass. Had he had too much to drink? Lisboa stared at him, thunderstruck; she felt like a sheet of paper about to tear down the middle: moments before, he had kissed her as if he were undressing her. Now she looked at him beneath the garden ferns, his eyes were waterlogged: no, he had all his wits about him. What to do, how to respond? Laugh or cry?

In any event, she said:

"First, let's leave this house."

The baritone stood up immediately. Was he weeping in silence? He took Lisboa by the arm.

"My car's outside," he said.

Lisboa listened.

11

Sprawled out, a dead but living doll, Perla Tobón wasn't just sleeping: she was snoring. Under the balcony, in the middle of the inflatable pool, inside its squishy dolphin silhouette,

Perla's long body glistened as though naked, victorious, her arms extended; half-submerged in the blown-up pool, she appeared to be swimming motionlessly.

And, nearby, among the ferns, Iris and Marino were locked in each other's arms. They hadn't heard Perla fall. How could they? They were kissing. Perla snored, and snored, and snored. A nascent moon appeared behind the clouds, the music inside the house intensified, and Iris and Marino held each other even more tightly.

"Where have you got to, Iris?" They heard the front door open and Juana's angry voice ring out. "Are you there, girl?"

Iris was about to reply, she even sprang up, but the guard's arm held her back: "Play deaf."

They could sense the presence of the old woman, alert, scouring the night:

"Just wait till I find you, Iris. It's a sin. You'll be sorry."

It was as if she knew Iris was outside, in the arms of the guard.

"I'm going to leave this door open in case you've lost your keys, Iris. Just say your goodbyes and come inside."

They continued to sense her presence for a few moments. Then, nothing. Iris and Marino laughed. The trees lining the street shielded them from prying eyes; it was dark already, and the baseball kids had forgotten about the party, as had their mothers. Iris had never dreamed that she would one day do what she just had—disobey. If, instead of Juana, it had been Señora Alma summoning her, she would surely have obeyed in an instant, terrified. But with Juana, she could allow herself to disobey. The woman was an old grouch, but also a friend, in spite of the threat, and she had left the door open, even though Iris did have her keys. She took a deep breath, content. Marino's lips began kissing her. Kissing her? They were more like nibbles.

Iris wondered if she should run to the door. Marino's hands were moving farther and farther downward. She objected, but did not push him away. What was this? Her body. This had never happened to her before. Her body did not belong to her, would not obey her, it melted; and, the truth is, she had already done more than her fair share of work: all afternoon, and a good portion of the evening, had been spent by herself, taking care of the children.

The children.

The arrival of the clowns had been the first challenge: sitting the children down, arranging them by size in the "kids' corner," beneath balloons and streamers, between polystyrene giraffes. Iris herself had directed the installation of the platform on which the clowns' stage was erected; after the clowns, she was required to set up the little puppet theater, but first she served lunch to the puppeteers and ...

The big challenge had come when darkness fell and the clowns and puppeteers departed: she was left alone.

She was forced to skip rope, play hide-and-seek, the headless nun, cops and robbers, blind man's bluff, until she'd worn the children out; she was forced to lead them like cattle up to the sitting room set aside for them on the second floor, furnished with toys and cushions and mats; she was forced to herd them exactly like cattle in a cowboy movie, with the smallest then requiring her help with shitting, cleaning themselves, blowing their noses; she was forced to put up with their rows, refereeing fights in which she became the victim, the injured party, whether of a small kick—but a kick nonetheless (some of them wore orthopedic shoes)—or a scratch on the legs, worse than a thousand cats; she was forced also to distribute them among their improvised beds so they could sleep until the end of the party. But when would it end? Surely not until sunrise. And she would have to take care of the children when they awoke, comfort them so they didn't cry, feed them, present them freshly combed to their worn-out mothers, always shamefaced, always grumpy, always at odds with their drunken husbands.

Everything with the children had been a baptism of fire.

In the second-floor sitting room, filled with toys, she had sat them down on cushions and told them stories. She would have liked, at least, for Uriela to have helped her with the storytelling. But where was Uriela? Señora Alma had taken her off to the dining room. How was Uriela able to play with children without ever tiring herself out? How was she so enraptured by them? Iris didn't particularly enjoy playing with children—or rather, she *didn't* enjoy it—but then again, Uriela didn't help with carrying the smallest ones, Uriela didn't clean them, and that toddler's shit made all the difference, she thought, surprising herself: Iris had never thought the way she did in that moment, and she spent the rest of the evening thinking about how Uriela didn't clean the smallest ones, about how their shit made all the difference. She was shocked to find herself loathing Uriela for the first time. If Uriela was just like a sister to her, why did she suddenly loathe her? Iris made a superhuman effort not to cry, not to go in search of Uriela so she could apologize for thinking about the children's shit and the difference it made.

When the children had finally gone to bed, defeated, she tucked them in one by one and switched out the lights. It was a sea of sleeping children. She asked herself if it wouldn't be better for her to sleep there, in the middle of that mattress of kids. They gave off a kind of pinkish warmth, it would be enough to lie down in the light of those bodies and fall asleep, drift off, preferably forever, innocent to the world. No, she yelled to herself. Lying down to sleep with the children would not be looked upon kindly by Señora Alma.

Her legs were shaking.

She closed the door and staggered down the spiral staircase. She felt faint with exhaustion, with bitterness: she really was having a bad time of things. Hadn't that filthy hog who smelled of pig been snuffling at her that morning? *And he came so, so close to putting it in me. Why didn't I change my clothes? My God, I smell of pig too.*

And she headed to the kitchen through the electrifying music, and it was the music itself that reanimated her; the music instilled a warmth inside her, it prompted her, it propelled her. She decided to leave the house, to go to the store and buy salted peanuts; no one in the house had asked for peanuts, no one had sent her, she simply left to buy them with her own money, and the store was closed—as she'd predicted.

But Marino Ojeda had been waiting in the street, and now he had no intention of letting her go.

12

Moments after the mule took flight, the clowns had appeared at the patio gate; they were three clowns in yellow wigs, grinning but silent, beckoning the children with their hands. They appeared and disappeared, with the children abandoning the patio in a herd, running screaming in search of the clowns, passing between the bodies at the party like a deafening river; occasionally, they caught sight of the clowns, and the clowns gestured to them, summoning them, before slipping away again, with the children returning to the chase. These were the clowns Señora Alma had hired for the party. Iris and Juana kept an eye on the proceedings, with Iris taking charge of the smallest ones, the stragglers, those who cried, those who fell over. Amid the tumult of children, Juana Colima inquired about the dog, about the burial, about Zambranito. Faced with so many versions of events, she concluded that the old man had been unable to bury the dog, that he'd stuffed it into a sack to take to the Río Bogotá another day. She also heard that the mule had flown like a parrot, but this she could not believe. She did believe, however, that Zambranito was sleeping, that Zambranito was asleep. *He'll have gone to sleep*, she thought.

Then she secured the padlocks to the large patio gate.

PART SIX

1

And still Nacho Caicedo's prophecies kept everybody waiting. After lunch, he said it would be better to wait until
nightfall to enter into "a covenant" with the premonitions:
daylight isn't a favorable guiding thread, he said, but the
night is, night and prophecies go hand in hand like a pair of
lovers. The women let out a tender *Oh*. Marianita Velasco,
fifteen years old, daughter of the banana exporter Cristo
María, was among the more impatient ones; she was dying
to hear the revelations; she'd been told it was a diabolical
game. Pale as wax, Marianita had a broad, domed forehead
that made her look pensive, fixed gray eyes as expressionless
as icebergs, and long black hair reaching down to her knees.
Her mouth was twisted into a permanent sneer of irritation;
she hadn't wanted to try any of the dishes presented to her,
instead demanding a "Presley Burger," which would have to
be brought from an American restaurant; she appeared not
only disappointed, but also bored. The magistrate offered
her a preview: he told her that, in less than thirty years, water
would be sold in bottles, and a bottle of water would cost
more than a Coca-Cola. "The whole world will go thirsty,"
he said. "Thus starts the beginning of the end." The girl's
stupefaction was sincere, as was that of many others—bot-
tled water? More expensive than Coca-Cola? The revelation
was a letdown. It was assumed the magistrate was fooling
around; now no one would press him for more prophecies.
 Inside the dining room, that small Elizabethan theater,

and in defiance of the dancing in the garden, the afternoon proceeded with singing.

The Barney sisters sang.

Women in their fifties, both thin as a wire, they leapt up onto the stage, where a space had already been cleared for them. Guitar accompaniment was provided by the Davides, booksellers, who had taken responsibility for backing any spontaneous performers. But this time they would be playing for none other than the Barneys: voices of gold. The Davides tended to get invited to events not so much as booksellers, but as guitarists. They could always play what was needed. They were yet more grateful clients of the magistrate: thanks to him, they'd been able to dodge a powerful defamation lawsuit. The two Davides ran their own journal, *El Dolus Bonus*, in which the preeminent law professors in the country honed their craft. Their prestigious bookstore, the *Justiniano I*, spanning six floors, wasn't renowned for its poetry selection; they sold and published only legal texts, containing acts, referendums, legislation, codes, constitutions, laws and loopholes, articles, clauses. Nacho Caicedo was one of their regulars.

The Barney sisters, with black cigarettes dangling from silver cigarette holders, always dressed like men: blazer, tie, and pants; they wore felt hats, à la Gardel, and polished, two-tone shoes. Their eyes looked sad, perhaps an intentional sadness, in line with their act.

They sang a tango, then another.

The sisters had been famous in their youth, when they formed a duo known as the *Pureza* Sisters—named after the prominent soap brand that sponsored them. On radio programs, on the records they released, at their concerts, they were promoted as Las Puras, "the pure ones," because that's how they were known to their devoted fans. Their detractors, however, had dubbed them Las Putas—"the whores."

They were famous because, in 1935, thirty-five years earlier, at only fifteen years old, they had borne witness to the death of their idol, Carlos Gardel, at Medellín airport. That morning, they had gone to see Gardel off in the company of hundreds of fanatical fans: the singer was touring the country, and who knew when he'd be back. While taking off, the plane he was traveling on to Cali that June 24th collided with another plane that was taxiing on the runway. Both planes, brimming with gasoline, went up in a single ball of flame. The Barney sisters had been among the exalted who wished to immolate themselves so as "to feel what Carlitos felt," "to die that same death," "to rise again with him." They attempted this on the patio of a school in Medellín, and even the principal joined in. The Barneys had been among the youngest and were saved from being roasted to death by a stranger—an angel, they would say years later—who pulled them away from that human conflagration; he set them free and hauled them out of there, when they were already soaked to the bone in gasoline. He rescued them from themselves, from their pain. Other fans did manage to torch themselves, but never achieved their goal. Only one had been able to feel everything Carlitos had, to the very last drop, and this made her glorious. Her name would be repeated at every concert performed by Las Puras, who paid homage to her memory: "This spiritual gathering," they would say in unison, with tearful voices, "is dedicated to Lorencita Campo de Asís, who immolated herself in the fires of love on June 24, 1935, when the Song Thrush died."

They sang "Tomo y obligo," "La cama vacía," capping things off with the classic "Adiós muchachos." The ovation was unsurpassable. Amid its thunderous reverberation, no one heard Marianita Velasco calling out to learn more about that Lorencita, as well as the identity of the burnt

Song Thrush. Only Uriela was listening to her, four or six places away, at the enormous table; only Uriela nodded and smiled at the question. They had chosen each other. They were the same age, and this drove them to sit next to each other—for many of the guests were now swapping places, at their leisure.

2

And there was a trumpet performance by Salvador Cantante, husband of Pepa Sol. Salvador Cantante did not do justice to his surname: far from being a singer, he was mute. But he played the trumpet like a god. Wicked tongues claimed he'd had his tongue cut out as an act of lover's revenge. Others claimed it was an accident: he'd been petting the little dog a friend was holding in her lap, smooching it on the snout, when the little dog lost its temper, and Salvador Cantante lost his tongue. Who to believe? The fact is, before his mishap, he had played the trumpet like a god. An acclaimed soloist, he'd even performed in Cuba. When President Echandía summoned him to the Palacio de San Carlos, he chose not to go: at thirty-four years old, he'd lost his tongue. Now he was sixty, his audience made up of friends, relatives, and ever-present protectors like Nacho Caicedo, legal adviser to Pepa Sol, his wife, a thriving aguardiente exporter.

Like a tempest, a whisper, a bewitching siren, a breath of wind, a sprinkle of rain, a waterfall, the trumpet transported the audience from one paradise to another, before going silent, amid the silence of all who listened. It was supernatural.

The magistrate's eyes misted over.

The twins Celio and Caveto Hurtado, science teachers, hopped onto the stage. It turned out they were animal impersonators. Each squawk, each snort, was identified by cries from the audience. The dining room resembled a farmyard, Noah's ark resurrected. According to the teachers' explanations, the guests were treated to the bray of an ass, the low of a calf, the hoot of an owl, the snort of a horse, the squeal of a pig, the croak of a stork, the call of a swan, the caw of a crow, a snake's hiss, a cicada's song, the bleat of a deer, the chirp of a cricket, the grunt of a wild boar, the roar of a lion, the chatter of a parrot, the howl of a monkey, and the quack of a duck. They also witnessed mewling, howling, clucking, clattering, yapping, growling, squawking, cooing, chirruping, warbling, twittering, screeching, bellowing, and shouting. Uriela and Marianita heard none of it: they were listening only to each other. At one corner of the table, they were conversing almost soundlessly. Each appeared to be marveling at the other. Uriela had never seen a paler girl, with longer, darker hair.

"Do you have a boyfriend?" Marianita asked her, point-blank, following their intimate preamble.

"No," said Uriela, taken aback.

"But you've had one?"

"Yes."

"I have three boyfriends," said the sullen Marianita, her extraordinary brow pensive. "And I make love to them all."

"At the same time?" asked Uriela.

"Of course not," Marianita snapped back, her eyes flaring. But then she seemed to forget about everything, focused on examining the faces around them. She paused for an instant on the brooding face of Ricardo Castañeda, who was drinking alone.

Uriela was perplexed by this conversation. True or not, Marianita's boastful revelation had disappointed her, and yet, she was also disconcerted: Marianita seemed to her like someone set apart from the world, someone who dreamed out loud, and now, out of nowhere, she heard her talking about a trip she'd taken to Manaus, a sensual city, she was saying, bodies were pursuing me, bodies pressed up against me, squeezed me, there were bodies over there, bodies over here, bodies even closer here.

"Flesh," observed Uriela, with affected wonder, but Marianita either didn't hear or didn't understand. She was looking intently at her painted fingernails.

Uriela thought that she had never met anyone who charged into conversation in this way, with such confessions, and those north-pole eyes, she thought, slate-gray eyes. Weren't they just like the monsignor's?

In the distance, the monsignor and his secretary listened contentedly to the hecatomb of animals. The laughter of the diners added to the racket; even the waiters, coming and going with trays full of more liquid spirits, stopped to listen to the babbling, murmuring, gasping, humming, whispering, chattering, stammering, lisping, belching, yammering, crowing, hiccuping, moaning, hissing, shooing, and hollering that emerged from the minuscule throats of the teachers. The room seemed to teem with elephants and bats, with the flapping wings of a tremendous pterodactyl. But then Uriela and Marianita went quiet because the animals had gone quiet: the Hurtado twins had finally reached the end of their repertoire. And they were met with applause. The guests stomped their feet furiously against the platforms, a white dust rising from the boards, like snow.

Next to take to the stage was the art teacher Obdulia Cera, young and carefree. Her special talent for drawing laughter was mimicry: she was a spectacular mime. Her number consisted of demonstrating, by use of hands and facial expressions, that she found herself locked up inside a tower. She would escape by climbing down the never-ending wall and throwing herself into the sea, where she swam and fought with a shark, defeated it, and found salvation on an island, before lying down to sleep under a palm tree.

Uriela and Marianita applauded, truly moved.

There was a reciter of poetry: the one nicknamed The Hen, owner of a supermarket. She was very overweight and heavily made-up, and her voice screeched like rasping knives. She recited "The Poor Old Lady"; "Mambrú"; "Song of the Deep Life"; "One Night, One Night, One Night Full of Perfume, Full of Murmurings and Music of Wings";" The Raven"; "The Ballad of Reading Gaol"; and the words to the National Anthem. The corpulent Hen frightened many away with her recital. Some left the dining room tactfully, others beat a hasty retreat. They preferred to go outside and dance. Even The Hen herself joined the deserters, without any sense of shame; she was followed by several families: the Florecitos, the Mayonesos, the Mistéricos. But the Púas stayed behind: the grandfather and great-grandfather were among those most interested in hearing the prophecies.

They waited open-mouthed.

"Our audience is becoming ever more select," said the magistrate, raising his glass to his listeners.

The night had begun, his condemnation.

3

"What's your ex called?" Marianita Velasco went back on the offensive.

"Roberto."

"Isn't that the name of your parrot?"

"I didn't realize you knew what my parrot was called."

"And why not?" Your parrot is famous. Isn't he the one who squawks, oh this country?

"The very same."

"Didn't you get bored teaching him that?"

"I laughed."

"Why did you give him your boyfriend's name?"

"That's just what parrots get called, generally."

"Your boyfriend can't have liked that."

"I never asked him."

"What would you say if I had a parrot and named her Uriela?"

"I'd say that Uriela would speak like Socrates."

"Socrawho?"

"Soh-cra-tees."

"What does your ex do?"

"He's got it into his head to build a hot air balloon, like Jules Verne, and take Bogotanos up in it. He'd charge by the trip."

"What a guy! He'll be a millionaire. In Bogotá no one goes for balloon rides. I'd be first in line to go up. Would it bother you if I met your ex?"

"Why would it bother me?"

"Because men always fall in love with me."

"Ah."

"And has Roberto—your ex, not your parrot—has he built that balloon yet?"

"Roberto not-my-parrot says he doesn't have a peso for the parts; they're very expensive. He would have to bring them over from another country. He's looking into a way of making the parts himself; it would end up cheaper."

"That really is a problem."

"I suppose it is."

"Are you still in love with your ex?"

"We're good friends."

"But do you love him or not?"

"I love him as a friend."

"What was it like *doing it* with him?"

"What do you want me to say? It wasn't like doing it with someone else."

"Have you really done it with someone else? You don't strike me as the kind of person who'd do it with someone else, Uriela."

Uriela didn't answer. She hadn't even done it with Roberto. Roberto was just a friend from the neighborhood. At seventeen, Uriela had never had a boyfriend, but this Marianita, this strange little monster, she thought, had unsettled her to the point of forcing her to lie.

"You love him, Uriela," Marianita was saying now. "I can see it in your eyes."

"Really? How do my eyes look?"

"Red. You're about to cry."

Uriela burst out laughing.

"No," she said. And then she explained with her customary frankness: "It's just that when I'm about to yawn, my eyes go red."

And she let out a big yawn. Her eyes seemed on the brink of tears. She thought it would be a good idea to go to bed, but her father's impending prophecies obliged her to stay. If they had let her choose, she would have gone to bed in the company of her turtle, as she did every night, beside the fake skull. She missed the solitude of her window, which equated to the street and the sky: she would leave the curtains open to let the morning in, awakening her to the new day.

Then Marianita Velasco observed her closely for the first time.

"Listen," she said. "It's very easy to make Roberto come back to you."

"He hasn't gone anywhere. He lives on the patio of this house."

"You know I'm not talking about the parrot."

"I don't want the other Roberto to come back to me, you can be sure of that."

"Listen to me, I'm going to tell you how. I know exactly what you want."

"You know what I want?"

"These are secrets, Uriela, and they'll make you happier than you can believe. Have faith: I'm the one they call the Woman Who Knows How to Pray."

"Are you really that woman?"

"Really," replied the fifteen-year-old girl.

"Alright then, tell me the secrets," Uriela resigned herself, glancing around in embarrassment. *What hogwash*, she thought.

But what she heard removed her from her doldrums.

"If for nine straight days you count nine stars in the sky, and on the ninth day place a hand mirror under your pillow, you'll dream the name of the person you're going to marry. It could be Roberto."

Uriela laughed loudly.

Marianita continued, resolute—or was it all a joke, thought Uriela.

"There are many ways," said Marianita, "and you can bewitch him with any one of them. On the day you see him, you should attach to your clothes something old, something new, something borrowed, something blue: you'll drive him crazy. Give him some water, then drink from the water he leaves in the glass: you'll learn his deepest secrets. To enchant him with love, it's enough to brush him while you're dancing, your back covered in magic ointments, and I'll tell you later how to prepare these ointments, but, in any case,

I warn you, it relates to your blood. Endeavor to get hold of an item of Roberto's clothing, or any other belonging, and carry it with you, strapped to your left leg, from morning till night: he'll weep to see you. Write his name on a red candle: when the candle burns out, he'll dream of you, he'll marry you. Prepare an infusion of rue and violets, with a dash of your saliva; find a way to add it to the water he bathes in: he'll be left seeing little stars because of you, in other words, he'll die unless you speak to him, he'll actually die, he'll hang himself or something. Take a lock of his hair, or a fingernail clipping, and bury it along with a lock of your own hair or a clipping from your own fingernails: he'll groan with passion beside you, for all eternity. Find a dove's feather, the wings of an insect, a pinch of musk, then crush this all up and put it in a little bag under his pillow: I won't even tell you what happens, he'll be like a dog with its owner, wagging his tail when you want him to—you get what I mean by wagging his tail, right?—he'll be a complete man-dog, and if you want you can kick him. Write his name on a piece of paper and place it under your pillow, then take the pillow and embrace it as if it were him, repeating his name many, many times, until you feel sleepy: inevitably, he'll be yours, not only in your dream but in real life too. You can go out on the riverbank at midnight; you should be barefoot; in the water by the riverbank, you should lay a board, stand on it, then hop up and down saying: 'I shake my body, my body shakes the board, the board shakes the water, the water shakes the devils and the devils shake Roberto, so he comes to me.' With that, he'll run to you, wherever you are; you'll see what he does, hear what he thinks, even if he's a thousand miles away; you'll dream him at will, but be careful: it's possible you'll grow tired of his idolatry. During the new moon, go out onto the patio of your house, naked, and murmur in the direction of the moon: 'Moon, moon, you who hear all, hear me too.' Then the moon will listen to your wishes and bring them about in less than a year. And if you believe your Roberto no longer loves you, you should take a bit of wax from a candle that's been in the hands of a dead person and a sliver of wood from a cross; you should secretly sew the wax and wood into Roberto's shirt; his love will be reborn a hundredfold, he'll fall head over heels for you. To ensure his love is kept alive, you should bury his worn underpants and plant an evergreen succulent on top. You can snip the claws off your cat and boil them in the coffee you serve him: he'll whoop, he'll melt for you. The brains of a magpie, dried and powdered, are good for driving him mad with love, if you put this in his soup."

"Is that true?" spluttered Uriela.

"It's how they all fall in love with me."

"Doesn't it give them a stomach ache, don't they get poisoned?"

"If you step on your cat's tail, you won't get married, and the cat will never hunt mice again."

"Thank you, I don't want my cats to lose the pleasure of mice."

"Uriela," Marianita said then, "aren't you bored of this funeral? Let's go out to the garden, I'm sure we'll be able to dance. Let's escape. Together we can leave the dining room without papá calling me over."

And Marianita began getting to her feet, her long black hair falling like waves all around her. Uriela gazed at her, stunned:

"I can't go with you at the moment. I want to listen to papá."

"Is that man your papá? Mr. Water and Coca-Cola? What a guy. He seems drunk."

"He never gets drunk," said Uriela. "He's with his guests, and later he's going to speak and I want to hear him."

"Is that thing about the premonitions true? I think I'm more of a seer than he is. I'd better go tell my papá we're leaving. I can't stand the boredom, Uriela, goodbye. It was nice meeting you."

And Marianita Velasco stood up. She didn't go tell her father they were leaving, as she'd suggested, but swapped places instead, opting for a seat beside none other than the menacing Ricardo Castañeda.

Uriela sighed.

4

During their centuries of waiting, the magician Conrado Olarte and the champions—the lecturer Zulú and the cyclist Rayo—prayed for Perla Tobón to make her entrance in the garden, to arise from the night like a flame, renewed of blood, revived, ready to hang around their necks, to pinch them, bewitch them, to dance with each of them and resume the games, the games, the formidable games. The three men were drinking beside the door through which the apparition would arrive. They cast suffering glances toward the back of the house, on the second floor of which they believed the belle de jour to be sleeping, soundly, without ever imagining that she was in fact sleeping soundly outside the house, in the inflatable pool, snoring at the moon.

While waiting for her to appear, the magician and champions dedicated their time to recalling grisly love affairs, dramas from which they emerged as triumphant protagonists, unvanquished combatants. There were oriental nights in the brothels of Bogotá, they said, with ebony-skinned women, real women, and yellow-skinned indígenas who looked as if they'd arrived from Tokyo: I remember one who burst into song at the very moment I breached her; another one told me, "You split me in half," they're loquacious, they have plenty to say, those insatiable crannies; in Manizales, a woman on horseback looked at me and I followed her, we ended up in a stable: it was three thrusts on top of horse dung; I remember another who pretended to be asleep, and when her moment came, she wailed like a fire truck; another one was very pale, and yet down there she had something resembling a Santa's beard, only black. My aunt used to show me her inferno when she lay down on the bed, it was an every-morning ache, me, still a young boy. I came across a missionary sister: we got right down to it, and I felt as if I were entering an unfathomable chasm, I went from one side to the other without ever touching the walls, I was convinced I'd be able to climb inside, shoes and all.

They grew tired of waiting and dove headlong into the dining room, where Perla Tobón would be sure to make an appearance sooner or later. It wasn't cold in the dining room, but fresh air was in short supply; there was only cigarette smoke, the scent of food, tightly packed bodies, sweaty armpits, clustering necks, coughs, sighs. Some were already lurching around, drunk. With all those platforms spread around the dining room, with all those faces, cheek by jowl, each keeping abreast of events at the enormous table, the magician and champions believed they were walking into an amphitheater where a fight to the death between gladiators was about to begin. The three men searched for their seats, happy, expectant.

Shortly afterwards, Francia arrived in the dining room, her long red gown looking as though it had never been removed. She almost ran over to Armenia, who was talking to the primary school teacher, Fernanda Fernández. From a distant corner, Francia felt her mother's gaze reprimanding her, but she met that gaze with an innocence so categorical that no further explanations were required.

Armenia Caicedo was bored. Her sister's arrival reinvigorated her, and, without any hesitation, she turned her back on the teacher in order to face Francia, who sat down beside her and clasped her hands.

"Were you sleeping?" asked Armenia. "How I envy you. I wish I could do the same. If papá doesn't start his revelations soon, I'm leaving. Have you heard? Palmira went to bed without saying goodnight, Lisboa hasn't appeared, Italia ran away from home."

Profesora Fernández looked for a seat beside the teachers Roque San Luis and Rodrigo Moya, bruised to the soul by Armenia's slight, turning her back without any warning, without a polite "pardon me." There was no excuse: she'd been snubbed.

Francia's arrival was of no interest to Ricardo Castañeda, unconcerned with checking on his brother's fortunes; he was being dazzled by the extraordinary girl who'd sat down beside him, the Woman Who Knows How to Pray, Marianita Velasco, a cube of poisoned sugar.

"I wasn't exactly sleeping," Francia divulged to her sister, in whispers.

Armenia looked her up and down.

"Who were you with?" she asked.

"Ike."

"Are you crazy?"

"I am."

"And the little toad, what did Ike do with him?"

"If you're referring to Rodolfo Cortés, he left already, a century ago."

199

"He left?"

"Ike ordered him to go."

"He ordered him, just like that?"

"Yes."

"And I assume the little toad fled with his tail between his legs. How wonderful; but also how terrible, Francia, that Ike has a screw loose, how could you bring yourself to be with him?"

Francia wasn't listening to her. She was asking one of the waiters to bring her a passion fruit juice and a plate of cold lamb with French fries, please. She looked hungry—spent? Francia ran her palm across her face as if she were just waking up. Armenia gazed at her in admiration. Suddenly, she gave a start, bringing her eyes in closer.

"Francia," she said in a hurried whisper, "you've got blood on your arm."

And she made a point of glancing down at Francia's arm, which was resting on the table. Francia immediately withdrew her arm and glanced at it herself, half-hidden under the table.

"So I do," she said, perplexed.

She quickly dipped her fingers into a glass of water and set about cleaning off the bloodstains, then looked for a napkin and rubbed her arm, forcefully. The blood disappeared.

"All set," she said.

"All set?" gasped Armenia. "Whose blood is it?"

"It's Ike's," replied Francia. "Relax. I poked him in the neck with the fountain pen ... it wasn't a big nick, I don't think he even noticed."

"Not a big nick, eh? You know, that Ike is one sandwich short of a big nick ... "

"Don't be ridiculous."

"And him? Where is he?"

"Snoring, Armenia, on the floor. We ... went ... six times, you understand? I locked the door when I left so no one would find him. Later you can come with me and we'll rouse him, he can't spend the whole night in my room. Mamá would skin me alive."

"Of course," huffed Armenia, "where's the pleasure in skinning you if you're already dead?" She was no fan of Ike. She pitied the little toad. *It's hard to tell who's worse*, she concluded, *the deceitful toad or the family loon*. Then she discovered yet more blood on Francia's dress. The red blood stood out on her red dress, and also on her shoulders, like stains, like red love bites. But now she said nothing to her sister. She felt nauseated. She realized that her sister smelled of sex, smelled of Ike, smelled of bodies, and, above all, she smelled of blood. *How disgusting*, she thought, *Francia should go take a shower*.

César Santacruz and Tina Tobón walked in. Nobody noticed them except Señora Alma, whose only distraction was observing the guests who were coming and going. She didn't detect anything peculiar in the physiognomy of her favorite nephew, and felt grateful he wasn't drunk, as per usual. She saw that he was cradling a monstrous plate with the remains of the last lechona. *He never stops eating*, she told herself, *the good life will be the death of him*. She noticed that Tina was carrying a bottle of rum, and that her eyes skittered nervously around the dining room, not settling on anything. *Now that Tina does look guilty*, thought Señora Alma, her senses sharpened: *She's surely still in love with the fatso, she's dying for her brother-in-law, that's what girls are like these days, a sister's husband is the juiciest, and when it comes to this fatso who earns like a president, what sister could resist? The safe bet is that the fatso is going along with it, that pair look like they're*

201

up to something, they probably locked themselves in the bathroom to count little stars; this César gives me a headache.

César and Tina had the deference to go and sit beside her, and Alma Santacruz glowed with pride: her nephew was the only one who'd remembered her. "Auntie," she heard him say, "what are you doing all alone, isn't it your anniversary after all? Don't tell me we're going to be listening to prophecies; let's have a drink, then we'll run outside, and dance to a song of your choosing, this rum is exquisite, it's cold, I haven't been able to stop eating this lechona all day, what a party, I must weigh a thousand pounds already!"

But the entrance of Perla disrupted César's loquaciousness. It paralyzed him for the rest of his life—which was nothing more than the rest of the party. To begin with, a sort of fear and stupor, followed by hatred and anguish, asphyxiated him; he withdrew into himself to avoid rushing over and killing Perla for the second time.

Her sister's entrance almost caused Tina to pass out.

The two accomplices, their hearts in their mouths, watched her arrive, drowsy but revived, staggering. She rested one hand on the door, her forehead glistening, and they heard her ask: could some living soul bring me a beer? She was smiling at the world. They watched her sit down with Dalilo Alfaro and Marilú, owners of the Magdalene school. She crossed her long legs in the chair like an imposing queen, and it wasn't long before the champions sat down beside her, dazzled. Perla Tobón had been awakened by the cold. She never learned how or why she found herself outside the house, in the outer garden, immersed in the inflatable pool—this was par for the course when she drank. She would never have suspected that she'd fallen asleep standing on the balcony and then been tossed headfirst into the void by her husband. Numb, stumbling around, Perla had made her way to the front door of the house and found it open; she didn't notice Iris and Marino entwined among the bushes, but simply entered and shut the door. Her thirst was killing her, she clasped the cold beer, reinventing herself, "This is only the start!" she cried, impressively; she was grateful for the relentless attentions of her champions, and yet she didn't want to dance: "I prefer the warmth of the dining room, later we'll see," she told them, overwhelming them with desire. Then she asked for a brandy and raised her glass to them. The brandy burned her throat. Her stomach, her spirit, received it like the devil's word, peerless, a good omen, she thought, now lucid, sharp, a diamond.

The entrance, following Perla, of herds of other families, who came in tired from dancing and wanting to be entertained in the shadow of the magistrate, diverted Señora Alma's attentions: she didn't notice César's pallor, how he chewed his lips, she didn't notice the sudden disappearance of Tina, that lifeless doll. Once again, confusion reigned: the Calaveras, the Pambazos, the Carisinos, and the Pío del Ríos all arrived.

"It's growing, the audience is growing," the magistrate greeted them, spreading his arms.

5

Something must have flown in through the dining room door, a dense but rapid blur, rising through the cigarette smoke. The women nearby started shrieking. Others, at the back, echoed them. The bird or insect crossed the room. It was impossible to make out what it was due to the quantity of smoke that floated like a curtain. The women remained as if possessed—more as a game than from terror. The bird or insect was flapping loudly, an intermittent blur visiting each corner of the room, hitting not only the ceiling but also the floor, from which it would renew its blind flight and disappear: at any moment, it might get under skirts, inside dresses, a fact understood principally by the women: it had happened before.

Sparks, Alma's cousin, along with Pumpkin, another cousin, stood guard. They had a reputation for being hard men who didn't dance. Especially Sparks, who owed his nickname to the quickness with which he unholstered his revolver and "sent sparks flying" in all directions. The shrieking rose to a crescendo, and Sparks didn't hesitate to reach for his belt. The women shrieked even louder. Despite his coarseness, Sparks—an average Joe in his forties who'd never killed a fly, in the car dealing business—retained the affections of his cousin Alma Santacruz: he made her laugh. A troublemaker who was really all talk, Sparks was thanking God for this opportunity to shoot. Now he was aiming tremblingly at a distant corner of the room, causing the women to shriek with even greater enthusiasm. "Now Sparks, we'll have no shooting in my house!" Alma Santacruz yelled at him, but she too was shaking with laughter. The magistrate was looking the other way, circumspect; Batato Armado and Liserio Caja, who were still eating insatiably, kept glancing over at him, in case he instructed them to remove the drunk from their midst.

Someone, it was never established who, cried out that the bird or insect was none other than Uriela's parrot. Immediately, Uriela, who found herself with no other company aside from her chair, rose to her feet. She knew all about her mother's cousin, that goon. The fact that he was pointing his revolver at Roberto distressed her, even if she couldn't make Roberto out in the smoke, couldn't hear him: this was strange, because Roberto usually took advantage of crowds to show off his squawking. *It could be that he's frightened,* Uriela told herself, *or outraged.* Overhead, in the cloudlike smoke, a dark wing appeared and disappeared like a distress signal. Uriela grabbed an apple from the basket, and, barely taking aim, hurled it at Sparks, sending it just over the heads of the guests, just over the bottles, just over the chairs. The apple caught Sparks right on the cheek and knocked him over; it wasn't for nothing that Uriela played baseball with the neighborhood kids: her aim was legendary.

"Uriela, what have you done!" Señora Alma was screaming now, amid the silence of the women, for they had stopped shrieking and were looking at Uriela with reproach: there had been no call for that. Alma ran to the corner where Sparks had collapsed. He was being attended to by Pumpkin, an expert in wounds, a veteran: he'd been a combat medic in the Colombian Battalion during the Korean War. The blow to Sparks's face had not been serious, there was no blood, only a bruise. Sparks sat back down again, still in a stupor, and holstered the revolver without firing—his greatest disappointment. Stunned, he was massaging his cheek. "Who hit me?" he asked. Finally, the thin voice of his cousin Adelfa replied: "It was Uriela, without meaning to."

"She's off the hook," said Sparks. "But if it had been a man, I'd bury him right here."

The crowd let out a laugh like a gunshot.

And inside that smoky gray space, it was discovered that Uriela's parrot was in fact a bat, one of the many that had been shocked into flight by the revelry in the garden. It got out the same way it had come in, and the women were afforded the pleasure of shrieking in terror, one last time.

Dismayed, Uriela went to sit beside the magistrate. And, simply to change the subject, simply to be annoying, she asked her father what "transcendental" reason was keeping him there.

"Admiratio," said the magistrate, in Latin, also to be annoying.

But Uriela was in no mood for broken Latin.

"Papá," she said. "I want to leave."

"It seems that Adam's apple can also be used for felling drunks," her father replied. "What a throw. Did you practice that?"

"Of course not, papá."

"Of course you did: I watched how that apple spun like a heart and smacked the gunslinger right on the snout. I thought you only excelled with words, my dear. That apple whack was biblical."

Uriela sighed; her father laughed.

"You can go," he said, curt this time, inexpressive. "No one's forcing you to stay."

Uriela didn't hear him. At that moment, she had noticed Marianita Velasco leaving the room, hand in hand with Ricardo Castañeda.

The banana exporter Cristo María Velasco had granted his daughter permission to go and dance.

"Cousin Ricardo is leading away the girl who knows how to pray," Uriela told her father. But this time it was he who wasn't listening. He was looking for a cigarette, the second he would smoke that day; he put his hand in the pocket where he kept his cigarette case and came across the letter that Italia, his runaway daughter, had left for him inside an envelope.

"Italia's letter," said the magistrate, as though receiving his own wake-up call.

And he began to read as he smoked.

Uriela's curiosity was aroused by the fact that her father was reading the letter to himself, not worrying one iota about the gathering, he who until that moment had taken great pains to respond to every question, every look. Uriela was waiting for him to finish reading and say something, but the magistrate took his time; the cigarette went out in his hand; Uriela placed an ashtray beneath it and the long tail of ash dropped off, whole. Her father sat there with the butt between his fingers: he read the letter over and over again, as if he couldn't understand it or was trying to learn it by heart. Uriela would have liked to read the letter, but her father stowed it away again, absorbed in who knows what contemplations. Uriela preferred not to interrupt. It was impossible to believe, but her father appeared on the verge of tears, or else he was crying in silence, his eyes watery. She had never seen him cry, or perhaps he wasn't crying, for not a single tear fell from his eyes.

No one in the dining room noticed this development. Sparks and Pumpkin had started telling jokes, one after another, and their audience spurred them on, enthusiastically. From time to time, Uncle Luciano would chime in, as well as Uncle Barrunto, José Sansón, cousin to the magistrate, Artemio Aldana, a childhood friend, the publicist Roberto Smith, and Yupanqui Ortega, mortuary makeup artist, each with a hundred jokes inside their noggins to share. Suddenly, everyone began scouring their memories for the best jokes. It was a huge contrast to the distress being experienced by the magistrate, to which the only witness was his youngest daughter.

"Did you know that Italia is pregnant?" the magistrate whispered, more as though asking himself.

"Yes," said Uriela, remembering how her sister's escape had seemed like a mistake to her, but who was she to judge?

"Well, she doesn't want the child."

Uriela recalled the details of her encounter with Italia.

"It didn't seem that way to me," she said. "She looked happy." The magistrate didn't say a word. Uriela felt obliged to come clean: "I was with her when she ran away. I even carried her suitcase out to the street. Her boyfriend was waiting for her there, inside a truck full of raw chickens. The whole family was there. Even the grandma."

"She doesn't want to have the child," the magistrate repeated.

Uriela strained to recall.

"It seemed she did."

"Well, here she writes the opposite," said the magistrate, moving his hand to his pocket, and yet he gave up on retrieving the letter again, to the dismay of Uriela, a voracious reader: wasn't the letter from a sister with a baby on board even better than *One Hundred Years of Solitude*?

"She doesn't want the child," the magistrate repeated, interlocking his fingers, firmly. As if for the first time, he understood, stunned, that Italia didn't want the child. "Never, not even in my dreams," according to the words written in the handwriting of a kindergartner. And she begged him to help her avoid having it: "I couldn't say it to your face, but in writing I'm capable of anything, rescue me from that house of chickens this very day, papá, and you can teach them a lesson at the same time. Help me or I'll die."

This unexpected truth had shaken the magistrate to his core, not only redeeming him, but also suffocating him. Wasn't Italia the only person in a position to decide? This first question unsettled him: what business was it of his, or the boyfriend's family, vendors of chicken, or even the inept boyfriend himself to decide for Italia?

And as for religion? He knew all too well what his friend the monsignor would say; he'd raise high heaven, tear at his robes.

The magistrate stayed silent, his eyes staring into emptiness, as the dining room filled up with more joking and laughter; the voices emerged from every corner, telling the sauciest of fables, competing to be heard. Even the fiancées, Esther, Ana, and Bruneta, participated with dark and dirty jokes, their fiancés egging them on, indecently.

The magistrate furrowed his brow. His intimate debate appeared to be crushing him: the right to life, the moral obligation, or every woman's free and personal choice about what concerns only her. But did it concern only her? Of that muddled sea in which he appeared to find himself submerged, Uriela was the only witness. Uriela, oracle of her sisters, did not know how to extend a hand to her father, the erstwhile infallible Nacho Caicedo. Suddenly, she heard him speak, staring dumbfounded in the direction of the letter in his pocket: *Optime ais.* And then: *Delectabilissima sunt quae dicis.*

To Uriela, that whole business with the Latin now seemed ridiculous. An inappropriate game. She had started learning Latin as a girl, from a bilingual tome of the fables of Phaedrus. Years later, she would improve it with a volume by Nicholas of Cusa. Her father had learned Latin at school—in his time, it had still been taught in schools—perfecting it at university. It astonished him that the youngest of his daughters had been able to teach it to herself, using books from the family library. A proud father, he would employ Uriela as a translator during his revelations, when he allowed Latin phrases to slip out one after another. To Uriela, this game continued to seem ridiculous, but she recalled how her father also thought in Latin when he was alone, whether solving a problem, or brimming with joy, or unsettled by melancholia, and that, to him, it was not a game but another way of understanding life. Then she pitied him. She believed he had grown older since reading Italia's letter.

"Satis de hoc," she again heard him say, in a firm and determined voice. And, later: "Mirabiliter et planissime."

It was as if the magistrate had finally discovered the solution. His eyes glittered with resolve:

"Non me puto feliciorem diem hactenus hac ista vixisse. Nescio quid eveniet."

Now he was weeping with happiness, and yet he regained his composure, rubbing his eyelids, ashamed.

"Non te turbet istud," he said. But which of his daughters was he telling not to worry? Uriela herself? Italia in the letter? Uriela never knew.

Having said this, the magistrate rose to his feet.

Alma Santacruz was now beside him. Only she, among all the diners, had been able to sense something going on with her husband. And, nevertheless, the married couple looked at each other as if they had never met.

"I'm going for Italia," said the magistrate.

"I thought you'd decided not to go."

"Stay here. Keep a close eye on our guests. Yours in particular: ensure that no one unholsters their revolver in this house again. Order the waiters to serve more roast pig to the pigs. Tell them that, instead of liquor, they should offer mandarin juice, as a symbolic farewell. I'm leaving. I won't be long. I must go for my daughter."

"Our daughter," Señora Alma managed to interject.

She, the law-enforcer, the executor of all matters of the house, the person who ordered and disordered life, understood when she was no longer the one giving the orders. It had happened fewer than three times in the history of their marriage, but when it happened, it was absurd to offer any resistance.

"Let me come with you," she said.

"You are the other head of this family," ruled the magistrate. "It's here you're most needed."

"Then let Uriela go with you."

"I'm going alone."

"You don't know where the De Portos live."

"In El Chicó, on the other side of the bridge. Italia wrote down the exact address. She knows I'm coming. She's waiting for me."

"In any case, it's a long way, in these hours of darkness."

"Woman, I don't care if it's Timbuktu."

"It might as well be."

The magistrate let out a long sigh. Señora Alma shot a meaningful look toward the bodyguards, who immediately stood up and came over, ready for anything.

"You're staying here too," said the magistrate. "I don't need you. Better to keep an eye on the gunslinger. I've said I'm going alone." He felt in his pockets, where he kept the keys to the station wagon and the Mercedes. "I'll take the station wagon. It's not a good idea to drive around Bogotá in a Mercedes at this hour. I won't be long."

"It's late," insisted Señora Alma. "The De Portos must be sleeping. You'll wake them."

"Italia's waiting for me, her father, in case you've forgotten."

Alma Santacruz made a gesture of hopelessness and the magistrate left the room, pursued by the eyes of all the guests. He didn't say goodbye to anyone. Uriela and her mother accompanied him to the garage and opened the doors.

211

News of the magistrate's departure soon became public, and with him went the little necessary order that remained. On her own, Señora Alma was not enough. The waiters assumed the instruction to serve mandarin juice instead of liquor was another joke. No one obeyed anyone. That's how significant the magistrate's absence was.

In the garden, the orchestra redoubled its efforts. The guests sprang up to dance en masse. It was as if they were celebrating Nacho Caicedo's untimely absence. Everything would be permitted.

"He won't be long, will he?" Señora Alma asked her daughter, once they had finished closing the garage doors.

"No, mamá. You can rest easy."

"My God, it felt like the last time I was seeing him alive."

Again with the drama, Uriela told herself, dismayed, embracing her mother as they walked back to the dining room. She listened to her in resignation.

"All because of that capricious girl, why did she have to go and get pregnant? Why didn't she wait until after this party to give us her wonderful news? What a gift, my God, what a gift, what a day she chose, she did it out of pure spite, she did it on purpose, and she's my daughter, Uriela, your sister, more like our enemy, no? I should have had only one daughter, but which one? You're all a cross to bear, none of my daughters will be like me, none will find a husband like your father, I'll suffer for you, what kind of families will you have? Let's hope I die before I see it."

Señora Alma was weeping again, her head bowed, her face hidden, so no one would see. She entered the dining room and burst into feigned laughter at the first gag she heard from Sparks. She took her seat as though nothing was troubling her. But inside she was screaming.

7

It was then that someone, some wandering specter, sat down at the table and grabbed hold of the platter of lechona that the debilitated César had left untouched. He began shoveling down handfuls of lechona, head bowed, a strange guest, or the guest no one had invited. This must surely be why a silence began to weave all around him; as he paused to drink, as he raised his head, the silence was complete.

"Damn, I can almost hear this lechona squeal," he said, continuing to eat, with no further comment.

It was Uncle Jesús.

Though faint, his gruff voice was immediately recognized by his audience.

The general laughter, like another gunshot, another language, uplifted him. Jesús waved his hand in greeting, but did not stop his chewing. Ashamed, Señora Alma took pity on him. She felt guilty about not having invited Jesús from the start. What harm could this creature of God do them? Wasn't he her brother, after all? *It's true that he's a parasite*, she thought, *but what else could he be?*

And she didn't bother to investigate why the "task" entrusted to her nephews had been thwarted, why Jesús had arrived against her orders. She set to celebrating, like all the rest, the unexpected appearance of the youngest of her siblings—who hadn't stopped shoveling down handfuls of food.

"Where have you been, No Hope?" yelled Sparks, from the other side of the table.

"Walking," replied Jesús. "It's the best exercise for reaching the grave."

The diners were captivated by the absurdity of this statement.

"It is one of the most complete forms of exercise," clarified the monsignor, taking charge. "The one most often practiced by Our Lord Jesus Christ."

"Different Jesús," said Uncle Jesús.

The monsignor ignored this clarification. His voice adopted the tone of a sermon:

"Not only did He walk through the desert for forty days; He walked from Egypt to Nazareth, from Nazareth to Jerusalem, was sighted in Capernaum, Gennesaret, Bethsaida, Tyre, Caesarea, Bethany, and Jericho, in infinite comings and goings. He walked, if we calculate His full journey, the entire distance around the world, the world He Himself created, with the Father and the Holy Spirit."

"And he walked carrying the Word on his back," said Uncle Jesús, with the intonations of another sermon, "he walked curing the blind, cursing fig trees, exorcising women, healing the sick and drinking wine, for he was a man of flesh and blood, and later he sat down so they could wash his feet, which were kissed ... by beautiful saints ..."

"Beautiful saints!" gasped Father Perico Toro, as if he couldn't believe it.

Uncle Jesús paid no attention to him. He carried on addressing Monsignor Hidalgo:

"They were tired feet," he said plaintively, "muddy feet, poor feet, neglected feet, the shredded feet of a vagrant, as was only just."

The monsignor offered no comment on these words.

"It's very easy to be an atheist, sir, and very hard to be a true Christian," Father Perico Toro intervened, scandalized by the monsignor's silence.

Uncle Jesús ignored him again, or perhaps he hadn't heard him, or wasn't spoiling for a fight with a young man of the cloth, a mere subordinate.

"I arrived here walking from Chía," Jesús informed the monsignor. And he pushed away the empty plate. Then he raised his head, eyes flooded, his face a picture of tragedy: "I arrived from Chía, many hours from here, if you're coming on foot, with your shoes in tatters. I've come from a hotel in Chía, where I was ordered to stay to avoid attending this party, to avoid dispiriting you with my presence, to avoid my family being sickened by my words—did you think I wouldn't tell them? Well, I just did. I ran, I fled, and here I am, revived. Ingratitude is a sin, but the ingratitude of a sibling is a mortal sin."

"Jesús," interrupted Alma, her voice a loving plea. "You're here now. You've arrived. You've just polished off a healthy plate of lechona, what does it matter about the rest?"

"A plate of lechona is not enough," began Jesús.

"I can send for more if you like."

"I was saying that a plate of lechona is not enough to make a person happy. That plate must be served with love, the same charitable love that we learned from Our Lord Jesus Christ. In any case, thank you, Almita; what I ate will suffice. And forgive me for coming to your party; I'm well aware that I shouldn't have done it. I'm well aware … " And he seemed on the verge of tears, his voice breaking: "Forgive me, everyone. Here is my neck. Take my head if you wish."

A murmur of astonishment shook the room. It was followed by another of reproof, but also of impending laughter. Uncle Jesús's words were unpredictable: anything could happen. Furthermore, and to even greater bewilderment, Uncle Jesús seemed to be offering his neck to an invisible executioner; hunched over, in silence, he waited.

Señora Alma sat down beside Jesús and embraced him.

Another sea of applause.

"Parable of the Prodigal Son," said the monsignor, and

the hordes all raised their glasses as one. Jesús felt within his rights to correct the monsignor:

"Not son. Brother."

More laughter.

Alma Santacruz asked them to bring out a sample of the fish, the veal in red wine, the goat stew, and the roast lamb, so that her prodigal brother would not miss out on anything.

"If you insist, Alma," said Jesús, enraptured. And he shook his head: "Goat stew? I'm sure the kitchen doesn't have the dish I like best of all: my chicken hearts. But there are so many hungry people in the world … it makes a man ashamed to eat all that. I … they say you shouldn't look a gift horse in the mouth … "

For at that moment, the first dish had landed and was steaming under his nose. Uncle Jesús sneezed.

"And a mug of agua de panela," he said. "I've caught a cold. I know somebody who died of a cold, not too long ago, on the highway … as I may also die."

8

This reference to dying of a cold sparked off a conversation. Was it better to die from a cold than from a lightning bolt in a storm? There are deaths and there are *deaths*, among them the most bizarre: I heard about a traveler who was found lifeless in the Putumayo jungle, at a spot known as the End of the World: they ruled out homicide, but it may have been a cold. That's nothing, said another voice among the voices: I don't know if you remember Pipa Hurtadillo, not Fat Pipa but Skinny Pipa, "No-Girlfriend" they called him, well, one dark night on a dark street he fell down a manhole and there he stayed. One night on a street? That's nothing, the children of Yina Ciempiés were playing with pea shooters and one of them choked to death. Young Samuel, son of Old Samuel, got his scarf caught in the side mirror of a passing van and there he stayed, stiff as a chicken. The widow Fabricia, who lived on the corner, arrived home thirsty, uncapped what appeared to be a bottle of Malta, and drank it: it was insecticide, a pest killer, can you believe it? There she stayed, refreshed. That's nothing: María Lafuente was walking along the beach between palm trees and a coconut fell on her head; now she drinks coconut water in paradise. Pablo Sol was killed by a lightning bolt while pissing in the woods. Max Pienso was bitten to death by his own dog one Sunday. I remember those twins, the Pintas, they were playing soccer on the school roof and fell off, now they cry goal in the cemetery, you can hear them at midnight. It isn't clear why the Luceros' father stuck his head through the small bathroom window and hanged himself. Was he trying to kill a cockroach? Was he spying on the hired girl? It was never established. A brick fell on Fito Álvarez's head as he waited for the bus. La Nena Blancura's uncle had just hugged his wife, then he dove into the pool and there he stayed, swimming for the rest of his days. The Candongas, remember them? We now know that they were making love, when it occurred to her to do a headstand and ...

"Please!" interjected the monsignor, "I'm begging you in the name of God: this is not how you deliver news of a death, this is not how you speak of the dead! Death is something that demands respect, reflection. For the believers among us, death is the opening of a door that will lead us to God. For the nonbelievers, it's the same. All men open that door, whether they wish to or not. Deaths that occur arbitrarily, sudden deaths, unforeseen deaths, peaceful deaths, those due to illness, old age, all these deaths are deserving of our respect. There's no need to comment on them more than once, no need to poke fun. Because "how will we die?," this is the question, this is what it is all about, this is why men suffer from the moment they are born, from the smallest to the greatest, may God have mercy, may God help us face that transition, may He grant that, at the final moment, someone is with us, to give us their hand. But if we are alone, if we have been left alone, we will not despair: God is waiting."

At this, a deep sound, like a blow to the bowels of the earth, a sharp blow, a prodigious tremor, with no echo, paralyzed them all for an instant. The momentary swaying was terrifying, several seconds worth of trembling that became embodied in the clinking cups and glasses, in a jar of tomato juice that rocked and fell, leaving the floor bathed in blood. That heavy stomp in the depths underscored the monsignor's exhortation, as though God and the devil were consecrating each and every one of his words.

"It's the pipework," said Jesús. "You need to get it looked at, Alma, or it could burst."

More laughter.

"It's true," continued Jesús. "Bogotá's plumbing isn't just rusty, it's also poisoned. One of these days it's going to explode. It's an open secret."

None of those listening dared to respond.

Monsignor Javier Hidalgo had never looked so uncomfortable. He squirmed in his chair, unable to mask his discontent. He turned to Señora Alma and looked at her, gravely:

"My secretary and I are leaving, my dearest Alma, this has been more than sufficient; we joined you on your anniversary and shall continue to pray for you. Our regards to your husband, when he returns. From this day forward, we shall petition for this marvelous family, and pray that all is a garland of triumphs for you. I'm leaving. But God's shadow will remain in this house."

And he rose and performed a slow and silent blessing.

Father Perico Toro had remained seated. The monsignor glared at him.

"No, don't go, Monsignor!" Adelfa and Emperatriz appealed in unison.

The Barney sisters were also moving toward the chair from which the monsignor presided, near the head of the table, where the magistrate was conspicuous by his absence. It was in this direction that the ladies all hopped, arms extended; they were accompanied by the three honorable judges—who hadn't said a word during the entire feast, but had drunk and eaten like elephants—and, behind them, from their respective corners, came Luz, Celmira, Marilú, Lady Mar, and Pepa Sol.

They didn't merely surround the monsignor, but also looked for a seat beside him.

"On the contrary, Monsignor," Emperatriz was saying, "we would like you to continue speaking to us, we want to listen to you."

"That is why we've gathered here," said Adelfa. "The night is young, Monsignor."

The monsignor sat back down.

"Let's go out to the garden, there's dancing!" Jesús proposed to the monsignor from where he sat.

But now nobody was paying any attention to him.

Nobody except Sparks and Pumpkin, and the bodyguards Liserio Caja and Batato Armado, who were heartily enjoying the arrival of Jesús, as if he were but another dish.

Uncle Jesús had spoken with all the candor he was capable of. His dance proposal was unsurpassable. It's true that he'd been joking, he was aware of this himself, but he'd been joking in the most innocent of ways, for who doesn't enjoy dancing at a dance party? Had he committed a sin by inviting the monsignor to dance? A faux pas? He felt his sister's eyes bearing down on him, fearsome judges. *Alma was absolutely right not to invite me to the party*, he thought, *how hopeless I am, why was I even born?*

Since nobody cared to listen to him, a heavy cloud of disillusionment came down over Jesús's enormous forehead, darkening his eyes and saddening his mouth—which stretched downward from ear to ear. They had forgotten about him. In a matter of minutes, he had become a pariah again. A doormat. But he needed to bounce back, to overcome, to reclaim his hold over the world in the twinkling of an eye.

He was suffering.

9

"Adelfa," Uncle Jesús said then, "where are your girls, my nieces, I don't see them. I saw Ike and Ricardo this morning, and thoroughly mischievous and abusive they were, and I endured them, but the girls? What have they done with themselves? Don't tell me they're dancing in the garden."

"They're at the House of Spiritual Retreats," Adelfa was forced to explain. "And that is where they'll stay this weekend, I couldn't bring them."

"What do you mean you couldn't bring them," asked Alma, "do you have them tied up or something?"

Señora Alma had already been aware of the absence of her nieces since that morning. That the three girls were taking part in those Spiritual Retreats upset her, though she couldn't explain why. The news seemed to unsettle her; it caused her a sharp and bitter nausea, as if she were suffering not only in her stomach, but also in her soul. Why? This hadn't happened to her for a long time; it must somehow relate to her husband's departure, and, in particular, her anger at the flight of the pregnant Italia.

"The girls are in very good hands," the monsignor intervened. "They are in the hands of God Himself. I know that House well. I built it with my own two hands."

The bodyguards exchanged a sly look, as if attempting to imagine the monsignor's delicate hands laying brick upon brick.

Hearing the words "in very good hands" wounded Alma Santacruz to the core. Suddenly, and without meaning to, in spite of herself, she recalled the monsignor's true nature and was no longer mistress of herself. However, she preferred to unleash her rage upon Adelfa, her own sister:

"Your daughters aren't old enough to be left alone," she said, "in *any* house." She attempted to rein in her tongue, but couldn't: "Even if it is the House of God." And then, dumbfounded, she heard herself utter: "What House? What God?"

"What are you saying, madam?" interjected the trembling voice of Father Perico Toro. "The House of Retreats is a refuge where the word of God abides. A haven of peace. The ideal place for young people. Only there can … "

She would never have responded, but this man was insisting:

"And what do you know, you little dung beetle?" asked the irascible Alma Santacruz, as comical as she was terrifying. "Your intellect carries no further than your rancid breath!" And then a whirlwind of rage swept her up and carried her away forever: "What the hell have you come here to talk about? *You* are the devils. Today, I can only regret that at one time my own daughters were left alone with these men of the cloth, in their duplicitous hands. I pray to God that nothing untoward took place. I pray that He protected them once and a thousand times from these devils." Her voice dwindled away, out of breath.

"Mother!" gasped Francia, from her seat.

"Mother!" repeated Armenia.

Both sisters had gone pale; their mother had shocked them—had she been drinking? She didn't tend to. The other ladies maintained their silence around the monsignor, a humiliated silence. Uncle Jesús was the only one whose face lit up, as if he had just received some glorious news. He was examining his sister Alma, wholly satisfied, proud of her. And for this very reason, Alma felt ashamed. The fact that she had made Jesús proud horrified her. Because the presence of her abominable brother had also determined her foul mood, her inner screams. In truth, she had never approved of Jesús's arrival. Oh God, how ashamed she felt at having said what she had, and how she rued having pampered Jesús, having embraced him. *That beast of beasts*, she lamented, *why did I embrace him? Now he's laughing like a demon at what I'm saying, now he's relishing my indiscretion.*

Suddenly, and without knowing why, she recalled the time when Jesús had been involved in an accident, another of the many accidents that pursued him: he was hit by a motorcycle and ended up in the hospital. She'd been forced to go to the tenement house where Jesús lived, in that squalid neighborhood, and she had entered his room: she had needed to collect his citizenship card, which Jesús never carried with him for fear of losing it. Then she discovered the narrow bed, worse than a convict's, a pair of tattered boots to one side, the filthy socks, the shirts and pairs of underpants strewn everywhere, the little nightstand, cracked and hobbled, bearing the ancient Bible with a worn cover in which Jesús kept the citizenship card. She opened the Bible, recalling with tenderness that, as a young man, Jesús had wanted to be a priest, as well as a poet. She found the card, and was leaving the room, when it occurred to her to look under the bed.

Why had this occurred to her? She saw things that revolted her, far more than the awful smell, things that terrified her: inside a cardboard box, in a corner under the bed, there were women's undergarments. This made her skin crawl: why did he keep this underwear   and they were used items, in all sizes, for girls and for women. She would go and ask Jesús himself, she had thought, but then immediately forgot about the discovery, as she did whenever something left her mortified. On that occasion, she'd found herself thinking that it might perhaps be better for Jesús to come and live with her, and she was outraged with herself. Why? Sooner or later, she would fall victim to his ingratitude. And so she hadn't helped him. Until that point, she had always been stirred by a desire to help the black sheep of the family. This same debility had assailed her when she saw Jesús sitting at the table, eating with his hands. *He's as great a beast as these priests*, she thought now, *but these priests are even greater beasts, they are Lucifer himself, my husband and I should have gone away to Cochin-China, or never got out of bed at all, better to be sleeping far from the whole world than at this topsy-turvy party.*

In spite of the rage that was suffocating her, the remorseful Señora Alma avoided the monsignor's gaze. But Monsignor Hidalgo was no longer looking at her; now he was consulting his watch; he needed to leave, needed to flee at any cost.

He suspected, with strong grounds, that the magistrate had shared *his secret* with Alma Santacruz, that viper-tongued woman. He shuddered. *That tyrannical matron, sacrilegious, despotic, what a grave error*, he thought, *this cruel woman is even crueler because she knows about my sin, what humiliation, I have just now glimpsed the form my penance will take until the very end of my days, help me, Lord, help me to face the absence of forgiveness.*

And, almost without realizing, almost on the brink of

tears, he drank from the glass of wine his secretary had proffered to help revive him, downing it in one.

His audience raised their glasses to him, in silence.

But to leave at that moment, the monsignor was able to reflect—for he was struggling to gather his thoughts—to flee from that celebration of wickedness would be to corroborate every one of the blasphemies uttered by that fiend. No. He would need to wait for the magistrate, would need to ask him in private for an explanation, or at least exhort him to silence that Medusa he called a wife, silence her or hang her, he thought, vindictive in spite of himself. And so Monsignor Hidalgo and his secretary did not say their goodbyes, explaining that they would take a turn around the garden until the magistrate arrived.

Uncle Jesús was laughing to himself: *Take a turn around the garden? With all that music they'll be forced to dance!*

Señora Alma, head bowed, dismayed, rueful once again, allowed the priests to leave the dining room, without comment.

And yet not one of the ladies dared to go after the monsignor.

Alma Santacruz still held the power.

10

It wasn't simple pleasure, Monsignor Hidalgo yelled to himself, in protest, *it was pain.*

He suffered eternal nights, in the wake of sinning. But the boys, who to him were like a single boy, called out to him again and again, overpowering him. After days of penance, safe in the refuge of God, he would again hurtle into the red, hungrier than ever, renewed by his pain. His voracity was infinite.

In vain were the cilices he imposed upon himself, day and night. Mortification of the flesh was not enough. Far stronger the ravenous desire that awaited him, sooner or later. He slept wrapped in a bristly goat-hair blanket, with a strap of spikes around his waist. During the day, under his shirt, he wore a stiff vest made of sackcloth. If only he had been able to find a garment made of camel hair like that worn by John the Baptist. He invoked the example of Saint Athanasius, of John of Damascus, of Theodoret, sanctified through flagellation. He had been on the point of abandoning the cilices after reading that Saint Cassian disapproved of their use, because it satisfied the vanity of the one using them. But he needed to punish himself in one way or another, and so he employed the metal belt equipped with spikes; sometimes he would tie it to his thigh, his armpit; the wounds caused by the cilice never bled, but they left visible marks. Naked as a Nazarene, he would contemplate himself, fervently, crisscrossed with wounds.

Newly ordained into the priesthood, at the boys' school where he gave classes in religion, and where his passion strayed for the first time, he had noted that his wickedness wasn't simply familiar, but shared, and not just by the other novices, but by their superior. In fact—and though he refused to acknowledge this—he had chosen to enter the priesthood because he had understood, from surreptitious confessions, from covert testimonies, from gossip, what went on behind the stone walls of the boarding school. Kindly Father Nemesio, headmaster at the same school, had given him a wooden box with a cross carved into the lid. When he opened the box, in the solitude of his cell, he had found that it contained a Spartan whip. If the headmaster never said a word to him, then this was simply because he preferred to offer him that extraordinary symbol, the scourge. With it, he resisted for a year. He would lash himself and pray out loud, and yet he succumbed. As the years went by, he had made himself a crown of thorns, to serve as a pillow, in order to evade sinful sleep. Even so, he was unable to conquer concupiscence, which would wake him and set him planning, excited, savoring in advance the next step, the next boy. He sinned over and over again, which was akin to suffering, but who could understand his suffering? Perhaps through that suffering, which was real, he would more than atone for his sin with the boy. Because the boys sinned, too, thought the monsignor, defending himself, the boys invited him to sin; why did they embrace him, why did they call out to him? Why did they caress him with their little hands? Those weren't rosy little hands. They were the bloodied hands of the devil, which the boys turned against him.

With every boy, he saw a concupiscent smile coming toward him, with the capacity for evil, and concupiscence gives rise to sin, he yelled to himself, and sin, once committed, engenders death.

He was bound to the suffering, to the empire of death. His inclination toward evil was his human nature, and he was no longer able to resist it; he always ended up defeated. Aside from torture, the daily flagellation, he was consoled by his certainty that every one of his equals, whether superior or not, suffered from the same evil. The Church was nothing but the home of that suffering. Its members did not share this openly; it was a secret, but a tacit truth among them. They assisted each other in silence, supported each other, and though suffering reigned, concupiscence brought down all of them, it was master of them all, it governed each and every one of them, affording them a moment of joy only to later make them suffer—though not all were like him, he thought: in fact, the majority took pleasure without suffering.

This certainty shocked him, and he preferred to think no more.

On meeting Father Perico Toro, he had sensed that the young secretary suffered as he did. They were identical in their pain. They never acknowledged this head-on, openly, but from the first instant, they had both known who they were. Identical. Once Father Toro had confessed to him that, as a boy, he had been raped again and again by six priests over a period of three years—from seven to ten years old. They would take him to the "confessional," and there they would "confess him," as they did with so many other boys. Now the young secretary—who taught catechism at the school—did the same to other boys, he "confessed them," and his pleasure was equal to his pain.

For years, ever since that first look between monsignor and secretary, they had belonged to one another.

They were united by the Secret.

The sheer prevalence of the stigma was overwhelming, the monsignor reflected; it yielded a result that seemed impossible: of every ten Catholic priests around the world, at least eight participated in the same sin; the remaining two did not participate simply because they didn't dare, and yet they wanted to. The priests would never attempt to find natural relief in the women dedicated to that purpose. This type of relief did not concern them: their objective was different. They were a brotherhood of shadowy scholars, consolidated over centuries by the same sin. That sin was their distinguishing mark.

"Of the woman came the beginning of sin, and through her we all die," they would recite with the Ecclesiasticus—inexplicably, because in all that suffering there wasn't a woman to be found.

He had not fallen victim to the "elements of this world," the monsignor repeated, justifying himself. In his case, there were no thrones or dominions or principalities or powers. He was humble. Charitable. Yet he lay submitted to his passion, the flesh of boys.

"Kyrios, Kyrios," he would invoke every night, to protect himself and escape, but by that time the latest quarry would have fallen and everything was ready, not the seduction of the boy (for this was impossible, you do not seduce a boy), but rather his fear, his paralyzing terror.

All around him, the other brothers prayed and did penance through mystic chants, seemingly pure, like actors playing their parts. "The ends of the world are come," he repeated to himself. Death, Sin, and the Law were the reality surrounding them. He recited Paul the Apostle—"For we know that the law is spiritual: but I am carnal, sold under sin. Now if I do that I would not, it is no more I that do it, but sin that dwelleth in me"—before concluding: "For the good that I would I do not; but the evil which I would not, that I do." Yet this was not enough. He could not ignore that he was distorting Paul's conclusions, to exonerate himself. He persisted: "The malevolent force unleashed into the world by Adam's transgression is what keeps man imprisoned and enslaved." He paraphrased Saint Paul, while recriminating himself; he echoed his lamentation in screams: "O wretched man that I am! Who shall deliver me from the body of this death?"

He wished to believe that there was no condemnation for those who abided with Jesus Christ, for the *Law of the Spirit of Life in Christ Jesus* had freed them from the laws of sin and death. But he did not believe this. He was unable to believe it. He had lost his faith. And he read: "It is for freedom that Christ has set us free." He was preparing to close the Book when a chance phrase made him shudder: "But do not use your freedom to indulge the flesh." The fleshly desires were immorality, impurity, sensuality, idolatry, sorcery, enmity, strife, jealousy, fits of anger … He closed his eyes, defeated: his situation was worse. He would never inherit the Kingdom of Heaven.

That was his curse.

11

"I need to speak to the magistrate for a moment," the monsignor was saying to his secretary, "but I could also do that tomorrow, don't you think? I'm not sure what to do; how sad it was to hear Alma Santacruz's words, who would believe it; I have blessed her family, I consecrated it, I am the blood of her blood, but today I was victim of her slander, a viper disguised as hummingbird, a Pharisee, how to respond, how to lower myself to her words? She trampled over me in front of the good ladies, managing to cast me out, propel me into this garden of evil."

And, as if in response, a libidinous atmosphere arriving from the dancing bodies enveloped them. A perfumed young woman walked past, swaying her hips. Father Perico gulped, but the monsignor put him at ease:

"Since nobody knows who we are," he said, "they believe we are a part of them." And he sighed, captivated: "We aren't simply another pair of dancers, we do not dance."

He was looking all around, as if newly lost in that jungle of bodies, and yet bursting with curiosity.

"This is a perfidious party. But there is a reason God has subjected us to it. It is His reprimand. Later will come reflection. How are you feeling, Father Perico, are you listening to me?"

"I can hear you, Monsignor."

In spite of this momentary lasciviousness, the pair so recently insulted by Señora Alma had not recovered from their humiliation. They walked arm in arm, ignored by the dancing masses. In the end, speechless with indignation, they sat down at a table and waited in silence. What were they waiting for? By the looks of things, the magistrate would take a thousand years to return.

Providentially, a waiter who recognized them came to their table and offered them a bowl of fruit. They asked for wine. Amid the thundering of the Malaspulgas, they could barely hear each other, and gave up on talking. After knocking back several glasses, they saw the old cook Juana approaching. She was running, red-faced: she had learned that Their Eminences were in the garden and had immediately come to ask what she could offer them. She arrived just as they were preparing to leave the garden and the house. The monsignor blessed her, and she happily bowed her head.

In this old woman, in her primitive humility (far purer than that affected by the ladies), Monsignor Hidalgo found reasons to stay.

And unable to believe it, he heard his own voice.

He listened to the words he uttered, his own words, employing the same argument as his adversary Alma Santacruz, and yet he did so knowingly, although he believed it wasn't he who was talking, but Evil:

"And the children?" he asked the old woman. "It isn't good for children to be on their own, to be wandering around, at this hour, during this ... party of perdition."

"Oh, no, Monsignor. The children are in bed. They're all fast asleep on the second floor, shut in the same room. Well, of course they are! You can't have children roaming the house at this ungodly hour."

The monsignor nodded cheerfully and blessed the old woman again.

He would no longer be leaving the party. Now something more powerful than himself was keeping him there: if he could only sniff, without touching, at least sniff the flesh of those children.

12

He hadn't traveled far from the house when a commotion in the street forced the magistrate to halt the station wagon. He assumed his anniversary party must not be the only celebration on that Viernes Cultural—as Fridays in Bogotá had recently come to be known. He sat there looking through the windshield; there was a house on the corner with open doors and lights on in the windows. *It's another party,* he thought. *Some of them have come outside for a brawl.*

Young faces floated before the windshield: the men, callow grandstanders, adversaries; the women, like medals with glinting eyes. The magistrate honked sharply, twice, so they would make way. Some of the young men cleared a path, others didn't—either because they hadn't realized or else didn't want to; a girl in a miniskirt was tying her shoelace "without an ounce of decency," he thought, marveling at her and marveling at his own audacity for watching. He honked two more times, patiently. He was able to advance slowly down one side. Once he had passed through the densest section of the mob, he turned to look, like any bystander. It wasn't a brawl. A taxi had run someone over. Someone, or something, was lying in the middle of the road: a large white stain. The magistrate braked again, rolled down the window to peer out, and heard: "Poor white horsey." "They killed the little horse." "Poor thing." The taxi driver was leaning cross-armed on the hood of his car: the taxi didn't appear dented so much as exploded in half, its windows shattered; the taxi driver was rubbing a desperate hand across his head: "Poor thing? It was the little horse that screwed *me* over. It came out of the night, I didn't see it, *it* crashed into me, who's going to cover the damages? My passengers ran off, the scamps, I'd brought them a long way, where are they? They should pay me my fare."

The bystanders had begun moving away, and the magistrate was able to look on, unobstructed. It wasn't a horse. It was César Santacruz's white mule.

But what was the mule doing outside the house, at this hour? How had she been able to escape? Had they brought her out for guests to ride? Had they forgotten to take her back inside? Neither Zambranito nor Doña Juana, much less the sprightly Iris, had been able to care for her; oh pretty mule, what had she been called? Florecita? The magistrate sighed.

He was moving slowly through the retreating onlookers; he heard the music start up again, someone shouted something, celebrating guys and girls clapped their hands and returned to the party; *soon the taxi driver and mule will be left alone*, he thought, *one-to-one, the authorities won't arrive until morning, and nor will I, first I must go for my daughter, then we'll see*. Who was to blame for this misfortune? He would need to look into whether the taxi driver had been drunk behind the wheel, otherwise César would have to cover the damages, you can't leave a mule alone in the street. *I'll go for my daughter and then make sure the mule receives a decent burial, I don't think they'll grind her into meat first thing tomorrow morning, half the meat they sell comes from horses, I'll ask Cirilo, he's a butcher; where is Cirilo, he never joined us in the dining room. We missed his voice; he must surely have fled the party in good company.*

As he moved beyond the thinning crowd, he became oppressed by an incipient but deep-seated fear, worse than a presentiment—could the dead mule be a warning to him? What was this about leaving in the middle of the night without Liserio, without Batato? He wasn't a normal citizen, he was a magistrate, he had enemies, how could Alma have let him leave without an escort? *Was it my destiny?* He began to be unsettled by a remote feeling of defenselessness. Nacho Caicedo, man of premonitions, was lamenting too late, he berated himself. The shadow of danger hovered over him like an ax: he sensed it in the air.

The station wagon continued to crawl toward the avenue bridge. What would he do, for example, if he got a flat tire? He wouldn't have finished fitting the spare before the thieves arrived. In Bogotá, it seemed that even the wind was a thief's informant. Thirty years earlier, when he bought his first Studebaker, he'd been putting it in the garage at midnight when he was held up at gunpoint by three thieves. They were very young and seemed more nervous than he was; it was surely their first robbery; and he talked to them, never knowing where he'd drawn the nerve to speak and convince them of the false step they were taking in robbing a fellow citizen: What will your parents say? Why don't you rob the president instead? He was nothing but an indebted civil servant, be wary of the easy life, prison awaits those who steal, justice may limp along but it arrives, and he gave them some money and shook hands with each of them on parting. He would never be able to do that today. Not only would he be incapable of speaking, but the thieves would never let him, gleefully opening fire, then see you later alligator. The magistrate hesitated. Was he heading back? No. On the other side of that bridge lay Italia with her predicament, and she was all alone. He needed to go and bring her back with him, listen to her again, at least listen to her properly; why hadn't he listened to her that morning? What kind of a father was he?

He accelerated. Floods of cold air came in through the open window, reinvigorating him. Then he saw another horde of young people coming toward him from a corner of the street; they appeared to be carrying golf clubs, or baseball bats, or rackets, surely late arrivals heading to another party; and on the way they would come across César's dead mule. What would César say when he found out? Would he shed a tear, was he capable of crying? A girl pushing a baby stroller split from the group and stepped into the middle of the road, gripping the stroller, her head held high, moving toward him. She was wearing a long white bathrobe, with a scarf around her head; both robe and headscarf rippled in the wind. An apparition. The magistrate reduced his speed and made space for the girl pushing the buggy down the middle of the road; it was impossible for a mother to be pushing a stroller at that hour without at least covering it with a blanket, impossible for her to be pushing the stroller so suicidally, down the middle of the road, toward him. A light went on inside the magistrate's head: the stroller must be empty. And he accelerated just as the girl sent the stroller spinning into the fender of the station wagon, under its front wheels: the left wheel must have become tangled up in the stroller; bright white sparks leapt up from beneath the wheel, a screeching white flame rising from the dragging stroller. There was a noise like the sound of a knife grinder.

Through the rearview mirror, the magistrate saw that the group of kids was running after him. As a result of this distraction, his glancing back at them, he lost control of the station wagon and drove up onto the sidewalk. With a jerk of the steering wheel, he avoided a traffic sign and swerved back onto the road; the stroller was still embedded and going off like a Christmas sparkler: the magistrate didn't know whether to laugh or cry. He stepped on the gas, but without managing to put any great distance between himself and the chasing kids. Suddenly, he saw the bridge up ahead. If that stroller had not still been stuck under his wheel, he would have made it to the other side by now, far from that premonition of the mule—the dead mule whose warning had fallen on deaf ears. He floored the accelerator, but, like iron tongs, the stroller gripped onto the tire, curling around it, immobilizing it. Directly on top of the bridge, the magistrate could do nothing to prevent the steering wheel from spinning all the way around, as if the devil himself were driving: the station wagon rammed into the siding of the bridge, which acted as a ramp, and shot over the railing, landing squarely in the crown of a tree that had been planted underneath: the tree began to crack as it eased the station wagon's fall, assisting it like a leafy hand, bending to deposit its load on the ground. With the station wagon delivered, the tree straightened back up again, halfheartedly, split down the middle. Nacho Caicedo couldn't tell if he was alive. As he hit the side of the bridge, as he lifted up, he'd seen first the black sky and then a great number of leaves against the windshield, flying around, above, below; a vertiginous branch had come in through the window and caressed his cheek, merely a caress, and a stiff twig grazed his temple during a second of life or death like a single inhalation. In the dim light from the lamps under the bridge, he discovered he'd landed in the middle of the train tracks, and that, rescued by the tree, he'd fallen a distance of only five feet, when in reality it should have been almost fifty; it was sheer luck: he'd landed in the middle of the tracks but remembered that the first train came past at ten in the morning; it was unlikely he'd be crushed.

He tried to start the station wagon, with no success. He tried three times, and, after the third, opened the door and got out. With him came a pile of leaves. *I'll have to continue on foot,* he thought, *I'll collect Italia and then send for the Ford.* He didn't have even the smallest bruise, the slightest bit of pain. He marveled at this, feeling his neck, his head, his knees, rubbing his hand over his heart: nothing hurt; there were just tons of leaves all around him, leaves and more leaves, even inside his shirt, against his chest, his nape, his back, twigs in the eyelets of his shoes, in his pockets, his ears. His legs were shaking. Through the darkness, he could make out the top of the bridge and the colossal dimensions of the providential tree. *I could have been killed*! he yelled to himself, and, before starting out again, he went over to the tree and hugged it: "Thank you, tree," he repeated, "thank you, thank you."

Only a short while later he would recall how he hadn't offered thanks to God.

He had forgotten all about his pursuers, setting off on foot, happy to still be alive.

Then an arm was hooked around his neck, and a voice: "Old bastard." He felt something like a reptile on his back. Unable to resist, he doubled over. It was a tarantula with long arms, encircling him. Painfully, he turned to look over his shoulder. There was a wretched little man on top of him, a fellow who looked like he belonged in a circus, with very long arms and a small round torso: a tarantula strangling him.

And he heard other voices, from within the night, directing his strangler: "Keep him there, Four Legs. Make sure he doesn't escape." The voices were shadows that came bounding down the side of the bridge, allowing themselves to slide from the top through clumps of flowers.

"How can he?" replied the tarantula. "This dickhead won't move an inch, he's too scared!"

"What's the matter with you? This isn't necessary," the magistrate wheezed. He wasn't sure who exactly he was talking to; he could see only the blurs of human forms that ended up surrounding him. One of them had to be the girl in the white bathrobe: her pale face swirled around him.

He gathered his strength and shook the vermin off, watching the man land with a pirouette in front of him, his enormous eyes bloodshot, riveted. This was Four Legs, who crouched there staring at him, his arms nearly as long as his legs, his mouth open, drooling, as though about to bite him.

The magistrate jangled the keys to the station wagon, holding them out.

"Here," he said. "Take the station wagon. And here's my money." He took the cash from his wallet and offered it to the vermin and the other watching shadows.

No one took a thing.

"What we want is you, Nacho Caicedo," said a voice like the bleating of a goat. "Put away your fucking money!"

Dumbstruck, he felt something akin to a many-armed embrace, lifting him. It was as if they were offering him up to the sky: black, moonless. But they weren't offering him up to the sky; they carried him swiftly, depositing him in a van that had just parked up to one side, under the bridge: it was one of those Volkswagen campers that resemble a huge sausage on four wheels.

He still couldn't believe what was happening. It was impossible for this to be happening to him. He was surely dreaming, this was a nightmare, he would soon wake up.

They shoved him down onto one of the back seats, his captors quickly filling the remaining ones. Beside the driver sat the person who seemed to be in charge, and who, until that moment, had not turned to face him, but must surely be the one who'd spoken and called him by his name. He calculated that, in total, there were twelve shadows holding him captive. He heard the sound of metal settling on the floor of the van, *those must be weapons*, he thought, although he was unable to tell what type: machetes, rifles? The van started moving, the motor spluttering, it seemed it might explode at any moment. The magistrate was sweating. He wanted to check the time. He saw that his gold watch was missing from his wrist: he'd either lost it or they'd stolen it. Only then did he realize that the girl in the white bathrobe had sat down on his lap, as though he might escape; *this is unbelievable*, he thought, and wanted to speak but his dry tongue wouldn't move, it felt made of wood, a piece of wood under his palate. The magistrate closed his eyes.

Suddenly, he understood that it would no longer be possible for him to so much as breathe without permission.

He'd been kidnapped.

PART SEVEN

1

That heavy stomp in the depths, which had made the guests laugh when Jesús assured them it was the plumbing, that first tremor in the bowels of the earth, could also be heard within other houses and by other souls, shocking and tormenting them, a fear which Lisboa, the second of the Caicedo sisters, was unable to escape.

Since arriving at the home of Cirilo Cerca, she had been confronted by nothing but strangeness. The first thing was the house itself, in the mountains above Bogotá, on the road to La Calera. Solitary. From another world. In another world. Leaning over the railing of a small terrace, outside the main entrance, she and Cirilo were able to lose themselves in their contemplation of the metropolis. Focused on the horizon, Lisboa stretched her pale face out into the emptiness: an avenue like a yellow serpent cut across the city through an ocean of red and blue lights. Black mountains encircled the bulk of the city as though cradling it. Lisboa sighed: the baritone's arm was around her waist. She felt imprisoned, but it was a warm prison within the ice. She shivered, astonished by the cold, by the baritone, the butcher Cirilo Cerca, a friend and contemporary of her father's. What would happen? He had proposed a glass of champagne. Good: she would have that glass and then ask him to take her back to the party. This is what Lisboa had decided, just as Cirilo began to speak again. He spoke about his house; he said it was the most beautiful thing he had created in his life, but also the saddest, for the simple reason that she wasn't there.

"And now you are, Lisboa," he said, gazing into her eyes.

She looked away. He opened the front door. His confession had made her regret being there: it was all a misunderstanding. While it's true that this older man had bewitched her with his singing, that didn't mean things should be thought about in the way he was thinking about them, *hopefully it's just a line*, she smiled to herself, *and what a line, like something from a black-and-white movie.*

"Step inside your house, my dream," he said.

Cirilo Cerca's hand drew her forcefully, for just an instant, because then he let go as if repentant. Any of the three boyfriends Lisboa had had in her life, any one of them, would have had her clothes off by now.

They entered a room with soft armchairs; there was a bed-like sofa, a wooden crucifix on the wall, all this around a stone fireplace as deep as the cave in a fairy tale. The baritone hurried over to light the fireplace, crouching down: Lisboa was left staring at his two enormous knees.

"It's cold here," Cirilo smiled at her. "That's why they invented fire."

And he was proficient with it, for it didn't take him long to get the fireplace going. The flames of the dry twigs and branches licked the sides of the crossed logs, knotted like the butcher's knees. The air filled with pine-scented smoke.

"Lisboa, come with me. I want you to get to know the house that has awaited you for a lifetime."

Another line, thought Lisboa, *this is getting tiresome.* Her discomfort did not go unnoticed: Cirilo Cerca looked directly into her eyes, as though interrogating her. He seemed not just worried, but on the brink of tears.

She said nothing. *Better not to speak*, she thought.

And she followed the butcher.

A large staircase like a marble hand led to the second

floor of the house. From up there, from what resembled a stage balcony, Lisboa looked down upon the room she had just left—the soft chairs, the bed-like sofa, the fireplace at the back—in which vigorous flames were already leaping. It looked just like another city, though cozy, warm: the heat was beginning to swirl like a vortex. Lisboa would have liked to run downstairs and lie beside the fire.

But this didn't happen.

They left the balcony and proceeded deeper into the house. Through the doors that stood ajar, Lisboa caught glimpses of the rooms; they didn't enter any of them, and she never would, Lisboa instructed herself, but she looked in passing: there was only one room with a bed, a narrow bed, monastic, not at all suitable, thought Lisboa, shocked to find that she was blushing. A bed, with nothing on the walls. The bed had to belong to him. It must be his.

They arrived at the other end of the house, where another raised terrace awaited them. From there, a large yellow lamp cast its light over a leafy park. Overwhelmed, Lisboa assumed that she would have to go outside again; she stepped out into the cold and was surprised by the covered swimming pool, a long, gray, illuminated strip; she took note of the sinuous lapping of the water beneath the glass bubble. *Someone has just been swimming*, she thought. She noticed the gardens surrounding the pool; there was a stone fountain from which water bubbled, a pond with a rustic wooden bridge across the middle, all lit up by the large yellow lamp.

And then she sensed another presence with them, behind them; it felt as if the temperature had suddenly dropped. It was a man in a ruana, who smiled. He had a horrible scar across his face.

"Luis," said the baritone, "what a way to make an entrance, you'll frighten our guest."

"Forgive me, sir," said the man with the scar, "I heard odd noises in the night, the lights came on but I couldn't see you. So I came to have a look around."

"It's alright." The baritone took Lisboa by the arm. "This is Luis Altamira, he helps me take care of the house. Luis lives next door, with his wife and little boy. Everything's okay, Luis, go get some rest, don't worry."

Luis held out a rough hand to Lisboa, a hand like terror, because, as Lisboa shook it, she couldn't help staring at the scar that loomed toward her. Luis disappeared without a word. This was another thing Lisboa found strange, and still another was finding herself face-to-face with a kind of glass cabinet, in a corner of the roof terrace, where, hanging from a coat hook, a small white apron was kept, displayed like a delicate work of art that was protected from the elements.

"It's my butcher's apron," said the butcher. "The one I used as a child. Think, Lisboa, of a twelve-year-old boy with this apron as his only clothing, but a happy boy, I believe, in spite of everything."

Lisboa looked more closely. She thought she could make out two stains across the apron, red stains.

Blood.

Old blood, but blood nonetheless.

She didn't know what to say.

She thought again that she should leave. *And the sooner the better*, she screamed to herself.

And there was something even stranger, something that enhanced the bittersweet sensation of strangeness: Luis Altamira, that man with a scar who acted as a butler, reappeared, this time with a guitar in his hands—which he then held out to Lisboa.

"Make him sing, niña," he said. "Let's have him serenade us. Let's have him rock us to sleep. No one sings like he does."

And before disappearing from the roof terrace for a second time, he let out a mirthful laugh, complicit: "You finally have someone to sing for, boss."

Lisboa could do nothing but stare at the guitar that shimmered in her hands, flinching when she discovered bloodstains on the sides and soundboard of the instrument, red, dried-out stains, like those on the apron in the cabinet. The baritone noticed Lisboa's discomfort. He took hold of the guitar and raised it to the glare of the lamp, examining it with an irked expression.

"I was at a birthday party for Fermín," he said, "one of my butchers. Right there, in my farm's slaughterhouse, I played guitar and sang, Lisboa. That's how this guitar got stained with blood."

And peering closely at Lisboa's face, he let out a laugh.

"Please, Lisboa, don't go thinking I'm a guitar murderer."

Forcing a smile, Lisboa offered no response. She felt caught in the middle of a trap. She began to back away, unwittingly, but back away she did. Down below, in the gardens surrounding the pool, she believed she could see trembling lanterns, making the shadows tremble all around them. It was as if the shadows were converging on her. "But what an angel you are," she could hear the butcher saying. Lisboa wondered if she should run. Yes. She would take off through that unknown house and the butcher would come after her: he would sing thunderously throughout the pursuit, his voice rising terrifyingly; perhaps she too would feel like singing as she ran, believing it all just a game, but she would be wrong: somewhere in the house the butcher would capture her, he would tear off her dress with his hand, press her against him like another naked guitar, the scarred butler would probably assist him, she would scream hopelessly, and there, beside the fireplace ...

Lisboa felt ridiculous. Now she was laughing to herself, the nervous but gleeful giggle of a little girl caught up to no good.

"I'll have that glass of champagne and then go," she said.

The butcher gazed at her intently.

"Wait for me downstairs, by the fireplace. You can stop worrying, Lisboa. I'll go get the champagne. We'll raise our glasses and then return to your house."

Lisboa almost ran back to the stairs, descending them gratefully. Nothing she had suspected had taken place, and she didn't know whether to feel thankful or sorry. She sat down in an armchair, the nearest to the fireplace. In spite of the roaring fire, the cold overwhelmed her. She felt disappointed, exasperated.

And then she heard the guitar, upstairs, on the second floor.

Arpeggios like cries for help.

It was Cirilo Cerca, sitting on the stage balcony, his legs dangling down, his knees like cannonballs, cradling the guitar: he floated as if on a circus trapeze: this surely couldn't be the first time he'd done this.

"Just one song, Lisboa," he said.

Beside him, on the balcony, the champagne bottle glistened.

And he started to sing, accompanying himself on the blood-stained guitar.

This was as much as Lisboa could remember: she began to feel conquered by his voice again, she was moved to the marrow by the owner of that voice, by those lyrics, that melody. *Am I going to cry? I'm crying,* she had surprised herself, when the tremor in the depths of the earth took place, and the whole world leapt, turning upside down. The butcher looked at her with helplessness in his eyes. On the stage balcony, the champagne bottle came to life: it danced, twirling around, the first thing to fall down before Lisboa's eyes. She didn't hear it smash, but watched as a jet of foam like a gold curtain spurted up from the ground; then, seconds later, the butcher also fell from the second floor, embracing his guitar—as though the guitar could save him. However, halfway through his fall, the butcher released his guitar, and yet he continued to stare at Lisboa with wide eyes, as if he still couldn't believe it.

Ashamed at herself, Lisboa burst out laughing. And she laughed even harder as the world contorted. *I must surely be laughing from nervousness*, she thought. And she only stopped laughing once she heard—and this time she did hear it—the sound of the guitar smashing against the floor: the pure tone of a single string was left vibrating in the air. The butcher had disappeared from sight; he'd landed behind the sofa with a dull thud, like a sack of meat, Lisboa told herself, laughing again on realizing that the butcher hadn't been lucky enough to land on the bed-like sofa. Lisboa covered her mouth with her hand to prevent herself from laughing, to prevent herself from screaming. She ran to the place where the butcher must surely be, finding him lying on his back, eyes closed, legs crossed, his arms spread like Christ.

"Cirilo!" she cried, kneeling down. At that moment, the heavy rumbling in the depths abated. She placed her hands around his head and pressed gently. She was worried: a fall like that could kill a person. And, like a good nurse, she checked that there wasn't any blood, that he hadn't cracked open his head at least. Now she was feeling his neck, his extraordinary baritone's chest, his knees.

Then he opened his eyes and let out his now-familiar laugh.

"Clown!" cried Lisboa. "You were playing dead!"

And she could do nothing else but kiss him. He responded

to her kiss; his strength, his frenzy, elated her. She understood then that she would never wish to leave the house of that man who sang.

2

The magistrate saw that they were heading along the highway toward the south of Bogotá. He wondered why he hadn't been blindfolded; his captors weren't wearing hoods either, seemingly unconcerned about being recognized. The grim reality of kidnappings was barely dawning, yet Nacho Caicedo had already received warning from the future about the abductions that would grip the country like daily bread. He *remembered* that future, he, a victim of his premonitions. There had already been examples of that ominous reality, and the victims would usually end up sacrificed. The magistrate shuddered. Would his luck be the same? Who were his kidnappers? Common criminals? Enemies? In the light cast by the street lamps, he could see the weapons scattered around the van: were they handguns? Grenades? Machine guns, shotguns? The magistrate grew incensed with himself: they could be weapons made of tin and wood and he would never know the difference. And what if he grabbed one, pointed it at them and ran? He could never do that. While it's true that he owned a revolver, which he kept in a drawer of his nightstand, he had never fired it.

He could hear the men exchanging words, in murmurs. He caught more names: the one sitting next to the driver, with a long dark goatee, they called the Comandante. Another one, up in the front seats, with a parrot nose, was Doctor D. Others, further back, had nicknames: Meatstew, Tick, Pork Rind and Mango Face, as well as Four Legs, the insect who had almost strangled him.

The girl he was carrying on his lap shifted as though settling into an armchair; although she was slim, the magistrate's legs suffered, they were going numb. The girl snorted: there hadn't been an empty space for her in the van, which is why she had chosen him as her seat; or else she'd sat there to watch over him; she was as young as his youngest daughter, thought the magistrate, and it was at that precise moment that the stomp shuddered in the depths of the earth: the girl screamed as the van lurched to one side, and she screamed again as, with another bounce, it returned to its original position; then she screamed some more as the van jumped again, tilting onto one side and traveling for a stretch on two wheels, before driving into the ditch full of toads and garbage that lined the highway, crashing there with a burst of shattered glass and splintering tin and iron.

The magistrate blacked out for a few seconds. He came to as a result of the intensifying heat against his shoes, his calves. A bluish fire was spreading, and the girl in the white bathrobe was still on top of him, her head limp against the front seat; the bandanna had disappeared, revealing a buzz cut. She must have fainted. The magistrate noticed flames catching on the girl's bathrobe, from below, and used his hands to pat out the fire on the material, almost consumed, scorching his fingers in the process, then grabbed the girl by the waist and tried to stand with her, but he couldn't; he slid her off him, managing to get to his feet without letting go of her arms; an asphyxiating smoke was permeating everything; beneath the smoke, the men dragged themselves falteringly toward the front of the van, where the windshield had shattered, escaping that way. Earth and garbage were blocking the doors. He heard the Comandante's orders: "Retrieve the weapons, it's about to blow!" Four Legs' shadow crept along the fiery floor and grasped the first weapons.

"They're burning hot!" the magistrate heard him yelp, "Help me, Mango Face!" Another shadow entered the smoke; they grabbed the weapons and fled.

A wave of fire fanned over the magistrate. He hesitated between escaping or staying there and being burned to death, not continuing with his destiny. He felt weary. But inside his mind, the face of Alma Santacruz urged him to escape; this vision of his wife calling to him was the only reason he chose to head toward salvation. Gripping her by the underarms, he dragged the girl who wouldn't wake up and was as heavy as a corpse: it was possible she was already dead, but the magistrate hauled her along and exited the van with her. He dragged the body to safety, several feet away; the men were also moving backwards, and one of them, the driver, started yelling as he gaped at the burning hulk of the van: "And those guys? Why aren't they moving? Why're they sitting so still in there?" Inside the van, the silhouettes of three seated men could be glimpsed, each in their place beside a window, as though sleeping. A rat scrambled across the face of one of them, sniffing at his nose. "Get out of there!" the stunned driver screamed at them: he'd filled up the van's tank that very evening. "It could blow any minute!" And, as if in response, the van exploded, cruelly, intentionally.

The burst of flame propelled them like a great shove, and they collapsed; the magistrate was first to his feet: it was time to get out of there. He leapt over the girl's body and took flight, wild-eyed, his arms like desperate propellers, and yet his own magistrate's paunch was wobbling from side to side like a shameful burden; he managed to jog some thirty feet, and was already crossing the avenue in the direction of a row of lit-up houses, preparing to cry out for help, when the tarantula landed on his back, lethal and slimy, laughing to itself, and the belt-like arm went around his neck and began strangling him, while the tiny wicked face with bloodshot eyes and putrid breath pressed itself against his cheek and continued to laugh. Never had Nacho Caicedo experienced such hatred, such disgust. He wanted to rid himself of Four Legs at any cost, hurl him off now, not so much with the intention of fleeing as of pouncing on top of him with all his weight and suffocating him. The magistrate fell to his knees. It was impossible to rid himself of the tarantula. He believed he would be strangled to death, but the Comandante came to his rescue: "Let go of him, asshole, we want him alive." Still kneeling, the magistrate began to cough, his hands in the dirt. From there, he saw a truck pull up in front of the crash site, saw the driver and his assistant jump out, heard them ask if there were any injured in need of taking to the hospital. In sole response, Tick and Mango Face shot both men in the head. Their bodies crumpled without a whimper. The magistrate closed his eyes and no longer wished to open them again. Without realizing it, he had begun to cry, and he cried like a little boy, all his impotence inside those fingernails digging into the dirt.

He allowed himself to be dragged and lifted and thrown inside the truck, which had a long black bed and a shredded canvas tarp that let you see outside; the magistrate just lay there on the floor: his strength was gone—or was he dead? If only. Why hadn't he died when he fell from the bridge? He had offered thanks to the tree, he thought, why didn't I offer thanks to God? Then one of his captors smacked him. "Play ball," he said "we've been stalking you for months and now you want to go die on us." Behind him, more kidnappers were clambering in like shadows; only the one who'd been driving the van climbed into the cabin, and he immediately got the truck moving. When the magistrate looked around, he discovered that the girl in the white bathrobe was alive, sitting on top of a sack of corncobs. "Hey, Blondie," said one of the men, pointing at her, "your bathrobe burned all the way up to your pussy." She looked down at herself; her bathrobe was nothing but burnt shreds; she was practically naked, but felt obliged to laugh because the men were laughing.

A speeding ambulance passed by them, traveling in the opposite direction, wreathed in lights.

"Just in time," said the Comandante, satisfied. "We managed to get away just in time."

The magistrate thought he'd seen that face before. It wasn't the face of a kid. It was the face of an old man like him. And it seemed the Comandante was waiting to be recognized, because he sat there looking at him happily, as though wishing to be recognized as soon as possible: *Don't you remember me?* The magistrate was doing his best to recall: he needed to remember where he'd met him, who the owner of that face was. He felt them blindfold him: they didn't want him ascertaining which part of the city they were heading for, or where they would end up.

He could no longer see.

Only hear.

And he heard the voice of Four Legs:

"What a pity about those other guys, the ones who got burned up."

"It was Stink Foot, Razor Blade, and Tumble. They fell asleep."

"That's them to a T."

"Now they're martyrs, heroes," came the Comandante's voice.

And the magistrate recognized that voice. He remembered who the Comandante was.

Impossible but true.

3

Alma Santacruz had fallen prey to her wrath. The victims of her anguish were Batato Armado and Liserio Caja: why had they not disobeyed the magistrate? Their duty was to assist him come hell or high water, whether a flat tire or an assault by a band of killers, she told them, like a fortune teller. She had taken it for granted that they would watch over him at a prudent distance, without him realizing. The two giants, groggy, defeated by tiredness and food, shrugged, not knowing how to respond. Señora Alma had Juana "serve" them a saucepan containing the phone directory, that tome the size of a Bible, so they could look for the number and address of this young Porto de Francisco, abductor and abuser of credulous young girls.

Sparks and Pumpkin poked fun at her: "Relax, Cousin, be patient." Alma Santacruz regretted not keeping the details of her daughters' boyfriends in case of crazy escapades like that of the thousand-times ill-begotten Italia.

She forced the giants to hunch down over the telephone bible, in search of a name and surname. A difficult task: she was all too aware that prominent families did not list their members within the pages of the directory for security reasons. But she needed to try: her husband was running late, time was slipping by inexorably; a pain in her heart, not physical but ethereal, and for that reason shocking, had convinced her that something terrible had happened to Nacho Caicedo. To kill time, she focused on speaking to her cousins, doing everything in her power to understand their jokes and laugh: it wouldn't be long before her husband reappeared with their wayward daughter, whom she would of course deal a well-deserved smack, and then she would be happy, bringing the party to a close with a cry, chasing the drunks out with a broom, silencing the musicians, and taking her husband up to bed, a place they never should have left, for God's sake.

She couldn't help feeling terrified for the fate of Nacho Caicedo, and would have liked to be able to pray, but faith no longer nestled within her, she never even went to mass, she didn't *believe*—despite once having dreamed of the Archangel Uriel—and would never again entrust her tribulations to deviants like Monsignor Javier Hidalgo. And where was the monsignor? she asked herself. *He'll surely be dancing now*, she thought, troubled, waiting with heart in mouth to be passed the phone number for the De Francisco family so that she could rant and rave, "Where's my daughter, where's my husband, return them to me, you bastards!"

The ingenuous lady of the house had entrusted the search for a name and surname to two men who might well be good at breaking necks, but didn't know the alphabet and would struggle to spell their own names. She should have assigned the task to one of her daughters, or even taken charge of the matter herself, because the giants, overawed by the phone book, were making a real hash of things. Hunched over, they inspired sympathy. And in the midst of that deafening party—some had even taken to dancing on the platforms in the dining room—no one directed them, no one offered help, no one had fun with them, except for Alma's cousins, Sparks and Pumpkin, who had decided to recite the vowels: "A-E-I-O-U, gentlemen, don't you remember?" The bodyguards went bright red, like publicly chided schoolboys. It didn't take long for them to admit defeat and assure madam, with their hands on the bible, that Porto de Francisco's number did not exist in the directory.

"Then we must leave it to God," said Alma, with tears in her eyes: she longed to believe that God wanted something good for her.

In spite of her daughters, she felt alone. She had disclosed Italia's situation to Barrunto, and her brother's appeasing smile convinced her that she and Nacho Caicedo mattered to nobody. All they had was each other. If one of them was absent, then the other would die; *I'll die if you leave me.* And she put her head in her hands and rubbed her face in desperation. No one else witnessed her fear, only she did, but she would have liked to share it with the entire world, in screams.

Without meaning to, she glanced over at the dining-room door, perhaps again hoping to see her husband appear. She saw nothing but a piece of black sky, and, all of a sudden, a shooting star. She saw the night and the party as being contained within that star, repeating to herself that it was a good sign, a response from God. A good omen.

And yet she was unable to believe, she didn't believe.

4

Uriela recalled Marianita's voice: "Aren't you bored of this funeral?" Yes, she was bored, the party *was* a funeral. She decided to leave the dining room. As she approached the door, heading toward the garden exploding with music, she spotted her cousin César, who looked thunderstruck and was making a beeline for one of the platforms behind the table: this was where Perla had sat to observe the world in comfort and comment on proceedings, to laugh and drink, surrounded by her champions. From the platform, Perla shone—or her legs shone, on display to those admiring them from below. Uncle César didn't look in good spirits, but he restored that eternal smile to his piglet's face—at least, that is how it seemed to Uriela, unnerved by simply witnessing it, and she listened to the conversation without meaning to:

"Perla, my dear," said the piglet, in his most jovial voice, "shall we go out to the garden for a bit?"

From the back of the dining room, Tina Tobón's curious eyes didn't miss a detail.

"And what for?" responded Perla, genuinely surprised. "What is there to do outside?"

The champions swiveled around in their chairs, as ready for battle as they were to beat a disorganized retreat: César Santacruz was a Big Cheese, as well as Consort to the Queen.

"Dance, darling," replied César, irrefutably.

The champions snorted, placated.

From the top of the platform, faces leaned forward to look at César, who smiled. Perla rose from her chair, walked over to the platform's edge, and held out a hand, which César didn't take, instead wrapping an arm around her hips (as he had on the balcony), lifting her precariously, and setting her down on the ground like a delicate flower. Those on the platform stomped their feet in celebration. In the distance, Tina Tobón ran her tongue over her lips: her dream was coming true.

The couple kissed, pulling closer together, right up against each other, without drawing breath. More applause. Now Perla was laughing, entirely supported by her husband's arms. She'd had a lot to drink, but she was trusting and laughed in the hands of César Santacruz.

This is when her fate was sealed.

5

Uriela watched Perla disappear into the crowd, following the dark form of her husband. Perla was swaying.

Under the swirling lights and shadows, Uriela was left as though dazed for an instant. Someone, a young man emerging from the night, grabbed hold of her hand; a stranger had taken her hand as in a fairy tale, she thought.

"Let's dance," he said.

Not much younger than Uriela—who was he? Could it be her cousin Rigo? He was very tall and skinny, had acne on his cheeks: yes, it was him, but he hadn't recognized her.

"Of course," said Uriela. "Can I just go pee?"

He was taken aback, but composed himself:

"I'll wait here."

"I'm coming right back."

It was true that Uriela wanted to use the bathroom, but was it necessary to say "go pee," she reproached herself. And the truth was, she didn't simply want to pee, but also to shut herself away for a minute in a place with no one else. To rid herself of the memory of her father speaking in his broken Latin. But she was unable to do so: she felt the same fear her mother had when she'd said it was the last time she would see him alive.

Uriela moved through the din in the garden. The dancers were singing; it was a festive cumbia. Suddenly, she ceased to be tormented by the memory of her father: ever since that request to dance, she'd had a desire to dance all night long, even in the arms of her cousin, rather than be bored to death, she thought, rather than end up asleep for ever—as in a fairy tale.

She left the garden and made her way to the nearest bathroom, the one reserved for guests, on the first floor of the house, beside the empty drawing room. There, only distant music could be heard, the occasional muffled cry, echoless laughter. Confident of being alone, Uriela pushed the door wide open: Marianita Velasco was practically sitting in the washbasin, one leg raised above the shoulder of Ricardo Castañeda, who was surely deflowering her mercilessly, judging by the pale face of Marianita, who was weeping without

255

daring to scream—or was she happy? Uriela decided to close the door and move away. *Well,* she thought, *she must have fed him the brains of a magpie or the feather of a dove or the wings of an insect,* but she stopped dead when, from behind her, she heard the faint voice of the Woman Who Knows How to Pray: "Uriela, help!" Uriela opened the door and the ruddy, straining face of Ricardo Castañeda craned toward her, spitting: "Wait your turn, bitch, there's a line!" And then the second tremor in the depths occurred, that alarming stomp in the bowels of the earth, and Cousin Ricardo fell back against the wall, with the heavy Goya painting—that *Fight with Cudgels,* which Uriela had hung to make visitors "think" while they peed—coming down and sounding like another cudgel to the back of his head.

Now Marianita was finally able to let out a shriek, leaping from the washbasin and fleeing as Uriela leapt after her, and with them leapt the world, the walls, the air itself, and yet Cousin Ricardo lay still, his eyes wide open, as though stupefied.

6

Sparks and Pumpkin, Alma's overindulged cousins, never suspected what was coming to them. After the jokes they had made about the bodyguards, their bellowed lesson on vowels, they had dedicated themselves to drinking, discreetly, in their corner of the dining room, on the fringes of the crowd, and were now busy recalling their childhood days, when they used to steal chickens. They were laughing heartily, and yet their celebrations were cut short by Batato Armado and Liserio Caja, standing in front of them, their faces sullen, as if regretting in advance the thing they were about to do. Batato was first to speak, after ensuring that nobody was watching them. He addressed Sparks, Alma's favorite cousin:

"We don't want you to take out your thingy again, mister."

"My what?"

"Your killing thingy, mister. Don't point it anywhere inside the house of the magistrate, who's a man of dignity, in case you've forgotten."

"I thought my thingy meant something else," said Sparks, winking at Pumpkin, "The thing you piss with."

"Be grateful for the the kindness of the magistrate," said Batato, "that he hasn't authorized us to send you flying from this dining room, just like the bat that came in without permission."

"And who do you think you're talking to, you fat bastard? Do you think because you're an elephant you can stomp your big foot and flatten the first decent man you come across? You must surely know that we're the cousins of your Señora Alma Santacruz, your boss's boss, degenerate."

Batato's mouth dropped open.

"Goon," continued Sparks, "what are you planning to do, shoot us?"

"If only."

"Well, we kill elephants too," Sparks snapped back at him. "With bullets or knives or kicks, whatever the elephant prefers."

The bodyguards exchanged a look of commiseration: they had to do what they had to do, there was no other option, their hand was being forced; they didn't want to, but these guys insisted.

The bodyguards were far younger and taller than the overindulged cousins, but the cousins—who were in their late forties—though smaller, had broad backs, brawny arms, thick necks, laborer's hands. They could more than hold their own. And they stood up without any hesitation.

"Let's walk out slowly," whispered Batato, like friendly advice, "then we'll find a nice, quiet place to settle this. We don't want to scandalize the magistrate's guests, do we? We could go to the patio, the garage. Where do you want to go?"

"Let's go, let's go," said Pumpkin, ex-medic and Korea vet. And, sounding bored, he said: "Real men don't just talk."

And one by one they left the dining room.

Anyone would have thought they were heading off to dance.

7

The second tremor in the depths succeeded in momentarily silencing the Los Malaspulgas Band, Tropical Orchestra. The crowd went as far as to scream in terror, though afterwards many of them laughed. Others didn't even notice and kept on dancing through the minute of silence. On hearing "everything's trembling" coming from here and there, a current of horror had passed through the bodies like a wave, but only for a few moments, because then the rumbling retreated, and the partygoers went back to winding to the orchestra's danzón.

Inside the dining room, the party had, in fact, settled down; no one was dancing on the platforms, and now the diners conversed in hushed tones about the tremors and earthquakes that had terrorized Bogotá. Leading the learned discussion were Uncle Luciano, brother to the magistrate, and Barrunto Santacruz, brother of Alma. Both believed themselves within their rights to replace the absent wisdom of the magistrate, and only God knows if what they said was true.

"These little dances of the earth are nothing new," Uncle Luciano was saying. "At six thirty-six on the morning of August 31, 1917, there was an earthquake in Santa Fe de Bogotá. It was seen as the fulfillment of a famous prophecy by Father Francisco Margallo who, ninety years earlier, had stated, in elegant verse:

On the 31st of August
of a year I shall not say
wave on wave of earthquakes
will destroy our Santa Fe.

"That's no premonition," interrupted Barrunto, "merely co-incidence. Earthquakes like the ones we've had today are commonplace. It's simply that we pay no attention, either because we don't want to or because we're terrified."

Uncle Luciano ignored him:

"Two days before the 1917 earthquake, there had been a tremor at ten twenty-five in the evening, which caused some damage. The citizens poured out into the street in the middle of prayers to Saint Emygdius, patron saint of earthquakes."

"It wasn't ten twenty-five, it was six minutes to eleven," challenged Barrunto Santacruz.

Luciano Caicedo shrugged.

"In any case, it was a frightening tremor," Uncle Jesús finally chimed in, "women sprang from their beds, fleeing naked … but it was better to save your skin than your reputation, and it wasn't just children howling, but dogs too. It's said that the mad believed it was a celebration."

"We don't know that, it isn't in the accounts," said Uncle Barrunto, going back on the offensive. "We know that churches were damaged. The hermitage on Guadalupe, which was made of adobe, collapsed, as did the Capitol, and the San Juan de Dios and La Misericordia hospitals."

"It's my understanding that the hermitage came down over the heads of some praying nuns and that only one survived," interrupted Jesús, "the collapsing hospitals didn't cause any injuries, but can you imagine the patients fleeing, with their beds and all, and the nurses chasing after them?"

"Why would the patients run away with their beds?" gasped Uncle Luciano, theatrically. "Pay no attention to Jesús: not too long ago he was telling us that tonight's first tremor was a result of Bogotá's plumbing, which, as well as being poisoned, was also going to explode. No one here is telling the truth: concerning the 1917 earthquake, we know that the train stations suffered damage, as well as some country estates in Chapinero, but certainly not the Capitol or the hospitals."

Uncle Jesús remained undaunted. For no apparent reason, he said:

"Mount Monserrate is actually a volcano. A silent but active volcano. A treacherous volcano. It gives no warning. One of these days, it's going to flatten Bogotá, this sinful city, this city worse than Sodom, this city-cum-Babylon, and there won't be a single stone left standing."

"There was an earthquake far earlier than yours," Uncle Barrunto said to Uncle Luciano, as though intending to settle the argument. Then he raised one finger in the air and proclaimed without taking a breath: "It happened in 1785 in Santa Fe de Bogotá at a quarter to eight in the morning of the 12th of July and lasted three to four minutes."

"Please," said Uncle Luciano, spreading his arms, "the oldest was 1743, you can just give up already."

"Bring me an encyclopedia and I'll prove it. The one in 1743 never happened."

"Are you calling me a liar?" asked Uncle Luciano, a cold menace enveloping his every word.

"Where's Uriela?" replied Barrunto Santacruz, "go fetch Uriela so she can settle this for us."

Uriela endured the minute of silence alongside Marianita, in the garden, to which they'd fled. It didn't occur to either of them to check what had happened to Cousin Ricardo; it was possible he was still searching for them, that he was chasing them and would grasp them by the necks, hoisting them through the air to the top of another washbasin. They were fleeing, hand in hand, they were fleeing. *How strange to be holding hands*, thought Uriela. They unclasped when the dancing resumed around them. To Uriela, it seemed this second tremor in the bowels of the earth was like a second warning, the second bell during a theater production—the one that rings out shortly before the beginning of the tragedy: *there's a good chance the third stomp will send us headlong into the abyss*, she told herself, and only then did she glance at the Woman Who Knows How to Pray, only then did she look at her for the first time. Was she still crying? No. What was happening to her? She'd gone red. Suddenly, Marianita tilted her face toward Uriela and kissed her on the mouth, a kiss burning with desperation. Uriela was left gaping, paralyzed, as Marianita raced off between the dancing couples, as if unconsciously following the rules of some improbable game, or as if she were terrified. *Now all that's missing is for us to dance*, thought Uriela, immediately remembering the cousin who had emerged from the night, grabbed hold of her hand, and asked her to dance: she couldn't see Rigo anywhere, the swirling colored lights confused everything. Uriela held her hand out in the air: Rigo didn't grab it, he didn't persist, he didn't exist, and then she recalled the kiss, with her thoughts not returning to her cousin. She recalled the kiss as if she were once more kissing Marianita, again and again, out of sight, immersed in the churning sea of bodies, both of them trembling. And she could think of nothing else but to go looking for Marianita in the dining room. That's where she found her, seated, and sat down beside her to witness the melodrama being played out by the grown-ups. They didn't speak, and yet they were bound by a secret happiness: it seemed they were laughing in silence.

8

As the debates, concessions, and accounts rolled on, Adelfa and Emperatriz attempted to distract troubled Alma, the hostess abandoned by the host: she wasn't listening to anyone, and that second tremor in the depths had seemed to her like the worst of signs. She was a woman surrounded by other women, and yet alone. Suddenly, nobody was paying attention to her, all swept up in the whirlwind of the party. How long had it been? All at once, Alma recalled her husband's instructions: mandarin juice instead of liquor, but she could see waiters pouring rum in all directions; they hadn't obeyed the order because they assumed it was a joke, and now the place was teeming with drunks; she wasn't interested in asserting herself at this point, no one would listen to her, the joking, the dancing, the provocations went back and forth; it would be different if the magistrate were there, but he hadn't returned, and she was the only one suffering. She no longer glanced toward the door in search of another shooting star, her eyes wandered spiritlessly, lost: for a second, they settled on a point beneath the table—who was sleeping there? Unbelievable, it was the judge, Arquímedes Lama, the judge curled up under the table, sleeping like a log, that old friend of Nacho's, his partner in crime, already in his seventies, a venerable old man, what a poor example, how long had he been out? Had she been sleeping too? What to do? Order for the judge to be roused? But what for? Better that he never woke, this is what Alma Santacruz was thinking, seemingly crushed beneath her fear for the fate of her husband, her bitterness at his absence, as if he had broken a promise.

In a corner of the dining room, she spotted the Púas: grandfather and great-grandfather were conversing side by side, leaning their elbows on the table, heads together, their index fingers pointing to the sky: they were asleep and no one had noticed. Farther back, Yupanqui Ortega, mortuary makeup artist, was talking politics with the lady judges. All seemed to be in agreement. "You should be President of the Republic," Yupanqui was telling the youngest of the judges, "only a woman can save this country from its historic assholes," and they followed this with a toast. *They'll all be dancing soon*, thought Alma. Two young men were playing a game of chess, and others had surrounded them, strangers to Señora Alma, *let's hope they aren't thieves, because there have been cases where thieves disguised themselves as guests*—but what is Uriela doing leaping from platform to platform, latched on to the arm of that girl? Wasn't she Cristo María Velasco's daughter, that girl who had seemingly grown up too fast? How could it be that they were carrying glasses of wine in their hands? How could it be that they were toasting and drinking? She tried to call Uriela to attention but was unable to speak: Alma Santacruz no longer had the strength. *Why*, she thought, *why this party?*

Uriela and Marianita wandered around the dining room, moving from platform to platform. They were listening to the teachers Roque San Luis and Rodrigo Moya, who were talking self-confidently about prehistory:

"Those epochs," they were saying, "when men and women didn't wipe their asses."

"It must have stunk like hell."

Later on, they could be heard saying:

"I think he's drunk."

"That's why he said what he did."

"Otherwise, he never would have said it."

"Drunker than a fly in wine."

Other fragments of conversation floated around, arising here and there:

"It was his invitation to the circus. I regretted it too late."

"And our canoe sank, in the middle of the lake, but he couldn't swim."

"Here goes my cry to the world!"

"It was good meat, in its juices."

"I was young, but poor, I couldn't afford a steak. Today I'm old and rich, but I've got no teeth to eat with."

"Every day, I'm more Martian. I can't relate to Earthlings. They feel a repulsion toward me. I feel repulsed by them as well."

"I began to feel afraid. My own wife told me I was crazy."

"How beautifully it rains, after everything."

"What are you doing at this party if you don't like dancing?"

"My God, don't let me die today."

"God isn't just fat, He also has big ears, but they're deaf ears, and He looks the other way, plays the fool. He really does exist, but it's as if He didn't. They say He's the great loner of the universe."

"The Drunkard is the great loner."

"Then God is my neighbor."

"I was a stowaway on that boat. I don't know how far I got, but I never went back."

"The magistrate told us the bees were dying. And he said it in verse: 'Their buzzing wings / will cease to sing. / Poison on flowers / will do them in.'"

"Television, my boy, that's the future. First, television!"

"Bogotá is the only metropolis in the country, the rest are simply larger and smaller towns; Bogotá contains them all; in Bogotá, no one is Bogotano, but from all Colombia; Bogotá *is* the country."

"I always assumed old people were happy."

"They diagnosed him with severe macrocephaly, a cortical irritation."

"In this country, they're incapable of drawing up serious projects. Anyone who comes up with a serious project gets tossed on the pyre."

"At night, when I'm a free man, I sleep."

"If you like, dear, I'll give you that recipe for the orange cake. If you like, dear, I'll come over to your house and we can make it. When would you like me to come, dear?"

"Demons can appear in any form, even as an angel of light."

"Be wary. Be wary of that. Pay no attention. Don't believe it."

"He told us about his experiments with rabbits: he would open up their skulls and subject their brains to electric shocks, stick them with glass rods, cut the flow of blood to their arteries; he was quite the damn neuroscientist."

"Consciousness will last for several minutes after the body ceases to show signs of life, this has been demonstrated."

"I'm not afraid of dying. On the contrary: I'm extremely curious."

"Dinosaurs sang like birds."

"I'll give a thousand pesos to whoever finds the tooth I've just lost. It's pure gold."

"In Río, we were dancing at Carnival and the lights went out. You couldn't see a single face. People started screaming. I was wearing a miniskirt and someone squeezed my ass beneath it, but really squeezed it, as if it were an accordion. I'm sure it wasn't my husband."

"I stopped loving him after he let out the first fart, silent but deadly."

"That's what they call body language, look at him: sitting there, sprawled out, legs apart, hand on his crotch."

"And he went crazy on the day we least expected."

"I started vomiting in the middle of Sunday mass."

"A little birdie just told me."

"Shameless. It's a wonder politicians aren't sickened by themselves."

"What did she smell like? Like the cork from a bottle."

"Is there something wrong with me, mister? Should I call a doctor? Or will an undertaker suffice?"

"*Kedi* is a Turkish word: I don't remember what it means."

"Those were the days of Pedro el Bestia."

"She won a cow in a raffle."

"I know a boy whose parents threw him out because they sensed he was a wizard."

"What he tells us is precisely this: 'If a dead man can transmit his visible or tangible image half across the world, or down the stretch of centuries, how can it be so absurd to suppose that deserted houses are full of queer sentient things, or that old graveyards teem with the terrible, unbodied intelligence of generations?'"

"Are you missing a tooth? We'll put it back in for you."

"Tonight, I will write in my Diary: Dear Diary, I met an imbecile."

"They say that woman hastened his demise."

"And what a woman: a real snake in the grass."

"The cocks were crowing."

"Amanda Pino's funeral wasn't attended by any of her children."

"As the dress was very black, she looked very white."

"Then, let me tell you, and this is the main thing, listen, are you listening? Listen to me, for God's sake!"

"Last Sunday, we visited his House Museum: inside a glass cabinet, the pants and jacket he was wearing when he was shot were on display; at the back, you could see the bullet holes, the singed cloth, and the bloodstains from the wounds."

"No, sir, a sharp knife is no good for spreading butter."

"Gray is gray. Black is solitary."

"A good day to die."

"I don't know why I'm so worried about the Japanese, I still don't know."

"If you don't have God, so be it. But don't mess with other people's God."

"If you aren't anywhere, then you can never disappear."

"I prefer dogs, a thousand times."

"I like cats. They're enchanting."

"It won't be too long before a cat's tail sprouts from your backside."

"Yes, and I'll meow!"

"Cats should be called *dreams*, because they spend their whole time asleep. It isn't true that cats don't dream, they do dream, and they must dream very beautiful dreams, because they prefer to go on sleeping even after they're awake, they dream forever."

"I see them twitch their ears and listen to who knows what birds while they're sleeping."

"They even sleep with their eyes open, and just for this they should be called dreams, that way people could say, I have a dream called Paco, I have a dream called Luna."

"But dogs are superior. There's a reason dogs are man's best friend."

"Of course. Compared to cats, dogs are dopey, groveling, thuggish ass lickers."

Uriela burst out laughing:

"Who said that?"

"Me," said a stranger.

Uriela was stunned.

The stranger appeared to be a man with the face and head of a cat, sitting at the dining room table.

9

Nimio Cadena. This was the extraordinary name of the Co-mandante. Thirty years earlier, Nacho Caicedo had had a run in with him. Nimio was the accused civil servant, and Nacho the public prosecutor representing the Nation. Nimio Cadena had diverted funds destined for the most disadvantaged children in the country—which meant almost every child in the coun-try–for his own personal gain. It was money that originated in handouts from European governments, who in this way offered compensation, in symbolic sums, expecting gratitude, for their plundering of the countries of South America, their natural larder. Into his own bank account, Cadena had deposited this money, money belonging to the children, money destined for charity homes, food, clothing, and medicine.

The night before the trial, a stranger had presented him-self at the magistrate's home, briefcase in hand. He exhibited the briefcase, opened it: it was stuffed with stacks of cash, and not devalued pesos but green American dollars.

"This is enough to last you three lifetimes," he said. "You'll never have to work again."

And, as the magistrate did not respond, the stranger got

down to brass tacks, doing so in a manner that appeared absurd to the magistrate:

"All you need to do is look out for Nimio Cadena, he's another persecuted politician, another vilified champion, another mistreated hero, as Colombian history will attest."

"Get out of my house," said the magistrate.

"You'll see," replied the stranger. And, as he was leaving, as he turned his back, his voice rang out like cannon fire: "You held paradise in your hands, and now you'll have hell."

Nimio Cadena had been sent to prison.

Of the twenty-six-year sentence, he served sixteen days. They hadn't demanded the return of the millions: he shared his booty with important representatives of justice in order to walk free; it is useless to describe the machinations the corrupt employed to exonerate him; to the magistrate, they resembled circus tricks. As for the looted children, they never saw a peso, much less received an apology, as if they did not exist. Nimio Cadena escaped for the good life, he vanished; it seems he lived it up in Paris and Rome, before returning to Bogotá a few years later: on Sundays, he could be found shopping for groceries in Pomona, surrounded by admirers; here was a citizen emeritus who had played his hand perfectly. That was the last Nacho Caicedo had heard, and he forgot about him, with a lingering sense of bitterness, of anticipated defeat. He believed he'd carried out his duty: he had denounced Nimio's crime to the world. "Corruption and stealing from the treasury are commonplace," he had stated before the jury, "but stealing from disadvantaged children is beyond reprehensible; such larceny is inhuman. It can only be carried out by a … a … "

He had left the sentence unfinished, the silence of the audience completing it: a son of a bitch.

This is how Magistrate Nacho Caicedo would close his arguments when he believed himself to be incontrovertible, and even more so when the courtroom contained his wife, his confidante in triumph and defeat. Alma Santacruz had been present during the magistrate's showdown, and the haughty demeanor of the accused had left her filled with bad omens, Nimio Cadena's bloodshot eyes crossing with her own for an instant like a shiver down the spine. Neither of them would ever forget the other.

And now he was seeing Nimio Cadena again, transformed into a comandante and a kidnapper, but a comandante of what? Comandante of whom? In any case, he was seeing him again, the kidnapper, leaning toward him, that hairy goat face stretching wider and wider, the icy smile pulsing like a tenuous bleat; it was due to this same goat's beard that he had not instantly recognized him. They were inside what appeared to be some kind of abandoned factory, in the south of Bogotá.

"Do you remember me, Magistrate?" asked Nimio. "You ended my life. Or didn't you? Yes, yes, Magistrate. But look how things turn out, what a small world, and now I'm going to end yours."

Well then get on with it, thought the magistrate, but he couldn't say this out loud. He knew that Nimio would kill him on the spot, that he'd be unable to withstand this blow to his pride. Nimio ordered his men to leave them, so he could speak to the magistrate in private. That's when the magistrate became aware of the degree of vengeance he was facing. Because Nimio Cadena wept silently as he spoke. He wept. The magistrate believed he was facing not just vengeance, but also an illness. He only came to understand this as he listened to the weeping of Nimio Cadena, who was utterly convinced that he'd been ridiculed, mistreated. The way he wove things together, the way he interpreted them, and without any sense of embarrassment; this was something that horrified the magistrate. Other culprits accepted their guilt. This one was evidently not a culprit, but a victim.

"Because of you my mother died from shame," he heard him say. "She died when she learned that you, an infamous lawyer, had sent me to rot in jail. My madrecita couldn't hold out a week against the attacks launched upon the family, upon me, her honorable son. She died of pure sorrow. Seeing me in the public pillory killed her, and this I will never forgive, I can't. That's why I say to you, Magistrate: you destroyed my life. I say this so you can be aware of what's about to happen to you. You came at me from the worst side, my mother's side, that is to say, you screwed me over from the angle of life, and you know there's no greater offense for a man, am I explaining myself? Have you got something to say? What could you have to say to me?"

The magistrate was unable to respond.

"Besides that, Mister Magistrate Ignacio Caicedo, besides that grievous transgression, you continued to sin. You specialized in screwing over working people, don't deny it, or I'll shoot you right now."

"Give me a specific case," the magistrate finally spluttered. "There's no point in talking about yours."

"What can you tell me about your dealings with César Santacruz, your nephew?"

The magistrate gulped: this really was the land of surprises.

"I don't have any dealings with him. And he isn't my nephew. He's my wife's nephew."

"We know he's inside your house, we know he's eating and dancing at your party, that pig César, that traitor. But ah, we'll soon go for him, make him dance to our tune, him and the rest, understand? The righteous shall pay for the sinners."

On hearing this plan, this project, the magistrate felt a wave of panic—was he going to be sick? He was unable to speak; Nimio watched him closely, relishing the suffering he'd just inflicted.

"We were heading to your party when you did us the honor of coming out to greet us," he continued. "And we'll be going to your party anyway, Mister Magistrate, of course we will. We'll be the final guests, the last to arrive and the first to leave, by which I mean the only ones."

"They've got nothing to do with this," the magistrate protested. "You're mad, Nimio. And as well as mad, you're wrong. You've got no reason to include my family in your vengeance. If you have matters to settle with César Santacruz, find him and bring him here. If you want to deal with me, then do it. But leave my family in peace."

"And what did you do with my madrecita, cabrón?" asked Cadena, his eyes welling up again. "You left her in peace, did you? The peace of Our Lord."

Is he really crying, the magistrate screamed to himself. Never had a man's tears caused him such horror.

"I'm sorry for your mother's death, Nimio. If she died, it's because it was her time. You and I both know I had nothing to do with it. Let's talk. We have to come to an understanding."

"Finally, he speaks like the magistrate he is," said Cadena. "President of the Supreme Court of Justice."

"Not anymore," said the magistrate, with a deranged sense of hope. Was this why they had kidnapped him? "I was president years ago. Now all that's left is my pension. Do you want something? A contribution? If there's anything I can

272

do for you, I swear I'll do it, anything at all. And you'll leave my family in peace."

"Of course. The good peace of Our Lord."

"I'm not the president of the Court!"

"It doesn't matter that you aren't the president of the Court," said Nimio Cadena. "My vengeance will be the same."

The insanity gleamed in his eyes.

"But who are you, Nimio?" asked the magistrate. "Who are you working with? Who are you fighting alongside? Do you really believe I deserve to die? Because I can see it's the only thing you want. Put your hand on your heart. If I had done what you did, and if it had fallen to you to judge me, wouldn't you have convicted me?"

It was as if they were speaking seriously for the first time.

"I would have accepted that briefcase full of cash, asshole!" said Nimio Cadena. "I wouldn't have fucked up the lives of you and your entire family, or haven't you realized? We're both lawyers, firemen don't step on each other's hoses, sometimes great men like us must sacrifice the small ones to achieve our magnum opus, that's just the way it is, it's the law of human selection, the weak are surrendered for the sake of civilization."

"What are you saying? What law of human selection?"

"Survival of the fittest, dickhead."

"You stole. You appropriated funds that weren't yours. That isn't any kind of magnum opus, and it's got nothing to do with any law of human selection."

Nimio Cadena appeared lost for words; his face contorted. He was swallowing air.

"This is what I get for talking to riffraff like you," he said.

Then he called his men back in.

"Take him to the chapel," he squealed. "And knock him down a peg or two!"

273

10

Minutes prior to his conversation with the Comandante, they had removed the blindfold from the magistrate's eyes: he found himself inside what appeared to be a factory. But what kind of factory? The magistrate was unable to guess. It was a warehouse with unrecognizable machinery. But, in the end, it had to be a factory, because between one machine and the next there hung long steel belts like the ones used for transporting luggage at airports. Belts which slithered like snakes, with nothing on top, but which slithered, squeaking, as though bearing invisible loads. They had sat him down on a small stool and removed the blindfold: it was only Nimio Cadena, with Tick and Four Legs by his side. The girl they called Blondie and the rest of the men weren't with them. As his eyes burned in the silence of the factory—in the whirring silence of the slithering belts—Nacho Caicedo glanced around at the dark warehouse with high, uneven walls, covered in grease, and tiny barred windows at the top; dangling light bulbs half lit the space; and, from time to time, the distant barking of dogs could be heard.

Then he saw the goat face loom over his, the face of Nimio Cadena saying what he'd said. He heard his extravagant justification.

My God, he thought, once Nimio had finished, *if this isn't a dream then help me die once and for all.*

Because he felt he would die, from fear, from rage. And yet he did not.

Who were these people? Were they really going to kill him to settle some ridiculous score? But there's no such thing as a ridiculous score, he thought, and, in this case, the avenger was a simpleton, a madman, which made his vengeance all the more terrifying. Or else what were his intentions? Merely to scare him? Why didn't he clear things up? It seemed impossible that he could be preparing to lead those men to his house, to loot and pillage in search of César Santacruz, it was appalling, absurd that the righteous should pay for the sinners, *my God*, he screamed to himself, and again he felt like being sick.

Following Cadena's orders, the two henchmen led him out of the factory. Outside, everything was a vast black wasteland; they walked along a stretch that snaked between wheelless carts, rubble, smashed construction helmets, fossilized rubber boots, cans, lunch boxes, strange rusted contraptions, huge tanks full of black water, black garbage bags; then he saw the sky once more, and then he no longer saw it, he didn't see it again, they'd stuck him inside a chapel, a temple with its saints and all. *Am I really inside a temple?* The men tossed him like a bundle onto one of the wooden pews and left, the closing door ringing out like a gong behind them, followed by sounds like the twisting of long chains and locks.

He was left alone.

In any case, he was still in Bogotá. After the highway, he deduced that they'd taken a byroad, unpaved, with lots of turns. To the south? The outskirts? What did it matter, the cold was the same. And now he found himself inside a chapel. As far as he knew, only hospitals and schools had chapels. He must surely be inside what had once been a hospital or a school, converted into a factory, because factories didn't tend to have chapels. Or did they? No. This chapel was the remnant of some school or hospital, in the colonial style, with those rough wooden pews and the plain altar; there was a simple wooden table with a high-backed chair behind it, a lectern with the Bible, all presided over by a cross: two formidable, intersecting oak beams. The faint light from two bulbs dangling from cables at opposite ends of the temple half illuminated everything. Statues of saints and virgins rose up on either side, as well as golden metal candleholders, where the candles and tapers of mass had once burned. *Now all I can do is pray*, he tried to console himself, *talk to God*. But he sensed that it would not be long before he began to cry, from rage, from fear, or from rage and fear combined. He closed his eyes: *If I could only sleep*, he thought, and he had just managed to drift off, after some time, when he was awakened by a voice.

"Mister." The voice was secretive, urgent; that of someone hidden, covert.

He looked around in shock.

It was the girl with the burned bathrobe, standing before him. An apparition. She was wearing a cracked yellow rubber raincoat that was too big for her. When had she come in? Or had she already been inside the chapel, or else entered through a secret, hidden door?

"Come on," she said.

The magistrate stared at her in disbelief.

"I know where to take you to be free," she continued. And she pressed him: "But you'll have to run."

He didn't respond, overwhelmed with surprise. But hope revived him.

"Follow me, Magistrate."

11

He made a great effort to stand. His extremities had gone numb. His legs refused to obey him, his feet were made of lead and throbbing like two separate animals. It occurred to him that his body was more cowardly than he was. He recalled that he had saved the girl from the fire. Yes, she was returning the favor. He embraced her, feeling for a second that he would cry, but then he composed himself, swallowing, resolved, and listened to her: "It's this way," she was saying, always in whispers, and she led him straight to the chapel altar. He assumed the door to his salvation must be behind the altar, and he let himself be led. They went up two wooden steps; on top of the stained altar table, millions of cockroaches were fleeing in all directions. Suddenly, the girl pushed him against the altar chair, forcing him to sit down, and burst out laughing. She had burst out laughing after forcing him to sit with a shove. That was all.

Just as with the girl's apparition, two more shadows materialized, encircling him: again, it was Tick and Four Legs, looming toward him, as he remained seated in the altar chair, as if bolted down. Tick grabbed him by the arms, as if he'd tried to get to his feet, as if he could even try.

And, in the meantime, they were killing themselves with laughter.

"Poor little shit," said Four Legs, the ominous insect who had ensnared him from the start, who had climbed onto his back, who had captured him over and over again.

The other man nodded. The girl was the one laughing hardest: she had given him hope and then snatched it away. If it was a matter of taking him down a peg, then he was already on the floor. There was no need for any more. But that wasn't where his fate would end that night. Four Legs was staring at him with an extraordinary fixity, a feline fixity, the cat watching the mouse, the lion stalking the zebra. All that was missing, he thought, was for Four Legs to have also known him years ago, for him to have also suffered a story worthy of revenge. Or was he merely a henchman? As the magistrate began listening to him, he was left in no doubt—not just by his words, but also his tone, like a mixture of loathing and rancor—Four Legs was repaying him for something too, but what? Listening to him, the magistrate was flabbergasted:

"You think I'm some poor devil, right, some nobody? You think I'm only slightly smarter than a chicken, that I'm not worthy of the soles of your shoes, that I'm uglier than a rabid monkey, that I entered this world to a chorus of curses, right? Well, you're about to see what I'm capable of, faggot, watch closely as I yank your teeth out one by one, and then it'll be your eyes, Mister Lawyer, that's how I'll take you down a peg."

He gave a signal, and Tick released the magistrate's arms, now grabbing him by the head and pulling him up against the backrest of the chair, by the jaw, ensuring his face was raised. With the fingers of each hand, he opened the magistrate's mouth, gripping it by the lips. Meanwhile, Blondie secured him by the arms; she hadn't stopped laughing, and was leaning toward him, only inches away; the magistrate wondered if this wasn't the laughter of an imbecile, in the clinical sense, a lunatic, for as she laughed, saliva slid from her mouth and dampened his chest; the three furious faces were above him, he could smell them, could see how the three mouths released steam as they laughed, and he felt a deep nausea, he was going to be sick, but fear itself paralyzed the vomit halfway up his throat when he caught sight of the instrument, the tool: a pair of sharp pliers in Four Legs' hand. He wanted to say something, wanted to plead with them, but Tick's fingers had immobilized his lips, his jaw. Without any hesitation, without trembling, Four Legs placed the two open tips of the pliers on the magistrate's upper-left canine, closed the pincers, and gave a firm tug. The magistrate let out a scream from the depths of his throat, as though he were gargling, the blood soaking his neck, but the tooth didn't move, in spite of the efforts of Four Legs, who was turning red, tugging with all his might; the tooth wouldn't budge; what did come flying out was the partial denture the magistrate had worn for years to replace his rotten teeth, a lateral prosthetic in his upper jaw that flew through the air, and which Four Legs caught midflight, not letting it hit the ground. He stood staring at it, fascinated: "False teeth," he said, "everything about you is a lie, dickwit, probably even your prick, well, now you're going to swallow your lying teeth," and he stuffed the denture back into his mouth, shouting, "Swallow your teeth, scumbag, swallow them!" With great effort, on the brink of asphyxia as he wept with pain, the magistrate swallowed the denture, but it got stuck in his throat and he started choking, turning red. "Run and get water," said Four Legs, "I don't want him dying before he suffers." "Water, here?" replied Tick, "there's not even holy water." The two men turned the magistrate upside down, holding him between them, each gripping an ankle, his head almost scraping the floor. Tick was scared: "Smack him on the back, Blondie." Blondie couldn't stop laughing, and Tick told her: "Smack him, dammit, like you're beating a rug." Blondie began smacking him on the back, each smack a peal of laughter, and now the magistrate was no longer weeping, he offered no reaction, until the denture reappeared inside his mouth and he used his last ounce of strength to spit it out.

In that instant, the second tremor in the depths occurred, the chapel altar subsiding and reappearing, the enormous oak cross twisting around and collapsing mere feet from the girl, and then the magistrate fell to the ground, with the girl and men falling on top of him, while all around them the saints and virgins fell, the entire world smashing its head against the brick floor. The magistrate was still gasping for air, his arms spread, face lying on the ground, bathed in blood and sweat, saved from death by a miracle. Suddenly, his torturers were no longer on top of him. Staggering, he half rose to his feet, like a drunk, on one side of the overturned altar and the fallen cross. Still, the trembling of the earth persisted, the walls shaking, the chapel swirling. The magistrate looked around and could not believe what he was seeing: his torturers were praying. His tormentors were kneeling down in the front pew of the chapel, before the fallen cross, before the altar, before the magistrate himself, who stared at them. They were praying piously. *That's how strong their faith is*, he managed to speculate. They felt that they were paying for a transgression, that God was calling them to attention, reprimanding them. Heads bowed, the two men and the girl prayed tearfully, immersed in their penitence. Perhaps this was his chance to escape: the pain in his mouth, the taste of blood, the tooth that wobbled in his gum as though dangling by a nerve, drove the magistrate in his decision. His legs were no longer trembling; again, his anger and fear sustained him like a different form of strength. The door to the chapel must be unlocked. He moved like a shadow past the kneeling shadows and headed for the door on tiptoes, and yet he hadn't managed to open it before the three praying shadows raced after him, again wreathed in laughter, in bitter mockery. They had pretended to be praying so as to give him one more ray of hope that they could snatch away.

PART EIGHT

1

Without saying goodnight, Armenia passed through the group of women. This included the fiancées Esther, Ana, and Bruneta, those nicknamed Sexilia and Fecunda, and the primary school teacher Fernanda Fernández, who cast baleful looks in Armenia's direction; and yet Armenia didn't even notice, her eyes raised to the ceiling. Was she carefree? To the women, she was just plain rude, *the biggest witch of the Caicedos, thinks she's a queen.* And, nevertheless, they made way for her, parting like the Red Sea.

Armenia had been sitting at the dining room table, a statue listening to José Sansón and Artemio Aldana, both more tedious than a lonesome Sunday: they were talking about hunting and fishing, about trout and bait, about dogs and rabbits and a bear and two fleeing capybaras. She decided to go to the kitchen and have a black coffee so as to be able to endure this party that continued to drag on without her father appearing. She also wanted to nose around in the garden, watch the dancing men and women, and, why not, dance with the first man who presented himself—which would probably wake her up more than the coffee.

Profesora Fernanda Fernández followed her out.

In the tumult of cheers and cries, familiar faces greeted Armenia, while other unknown ones stared at her, as though sizing her up. No one dared dance with her. Someone nearby was saying that one of the Malaspulgas had got into a fistfight with a guest, and that they'd been separated just in time. The reason? The Malaspulga asked the guest's girlfriend to dance, and the girlfriend accepted, but they were yet to complete a single twirl when the guest launched himself upon the Mala-spulga, and, next thing you knew, it was Troy. The adversaries each gave as good as they got. It was the waiters who pulled them apart. The girlfriend burst into tears. Now the Mala-spulga had gone back to his music, onstage, and the couple were dancing. *I'll go to the kitchen*, thought Armenia, *a black coffee will do me more good than this boneyard*. She was repulsed by that image of the two men locked in battle. *If my father were here, he'd have them both thrown out*. At that point, she detected the baleful look, following her, very nearby. It was that primary school teacher, what was her name? She remembered that she'd been talking to her when Francia arrived in the dining room. Ineffectually, she tried to smile in greeting. The primary school teacher remained unmoved, icy, accusatory. Armenia shrugged and slipped away to the kitchen.

It must have been due to the bustle of the party that she found almost nobody in the kitchen; not a single one of the waiters or cooks; they were probably out dancing happily with the waitresses. Only two women were there, patiently doling out rice with chicken into interminable bowls. Sitting at one of the far tables, her head in her hand, Doña Juana appeared to be taking a nap. Armenia approached her with a smile on her lips: "A coffee, please, Juana, the kind only you can make, for waking the dead." Juana returned Niña Armenia's smile, going straight over to one of the stoves, where a freshly made pot of coffee already stood. "I'll have a cup too," the old woman was saying, when the voice of the primary school teacher was heard, always behind Armenia.

"What have you been saying about me? I heard you laughing. Do you think I didn't notice? You were making fun of me."

"Excuse me?" Armenia turned to look at her. Never in her

life had she talked or laughed about this teacher. "What's the matter?"

She stared at her for a second, then shrugged again, turned her back, and proceeded through the enormous kitchen, in the direction of Juana, who was pouring the coffee into a bluish mug.

Profesora Fernanda Fernández didn't even come up to the shoulders of the willowy Armenia. Yet she was burly, and, all of a sudden, she grabbed hold of Armenia's hair as if she were hanging off it. Armenia let out a cry, more from surprise than pain. As she fell backward, she turned her head and body, and she was still falling when she managed to grip the teacher's bra and refused to let go. They both collapsed amid a sound of bodies crashing like bundles and the screams of the waitresses and the Holy Mother of God emitted by Doña Juana as she crossed herself.

The two women rolled around on top of each other. The teacher wouldn't stop pulling Armenia's hair, and Armenia continued to hook her fingers into the teacher's bra, eventually tearing her blouse; at this point, Armenia sank her nails into the tender flesh, and both women continued to shriek as if possessed, as did the waitresses, and especially Doña Juana, who had come to watch in disbelief. The teacher's bra had already become visible; a breast emerged, or rather, it popped out, liberated. Armenia trapped the fat nipple between three of her fingers and squeezed, with the pain causing the woman to release her, the teacher left clutching nothing but black tufts of hair. Then an icy shower, a jarful of water, poured over them: it was Doña Juana, wielding a jar of water from the fridge in her hands. Armenia fled to the back of the kitchen, sobbing, while the teacher ran to the door, with the waitresses managing to catch sight of her bloodstained blouse and wobbling breast, the nipple almost yanked clean off.

"Close the door," Juana ordered the waitresses once the teacher had vanished. "Don't let anyone in now."

Sitting in the spot previously occupied by Juana, her face and hair dripping, Armenia hunched over the mug of coffee, lacking the strength to drink it.

Her tears fell into the steaming coffee.

2

A collective scream rocked the party. Those who were eating leapt up. It was the song of the moment, a blend of salsa and cumbia very skillfully performed by the Malaspulgas. The night continued to be lit by flashing, swirling lights. Everything was green and yellow and blood red, Señora Alma's idea for illuminating the dance floor, so that faces, teeth, and eyes would be transformed by color. Each couple did their best to stand out, including César Santacruz and Perla Tobón, who pressed together, pulled apart, came together again, joined by a hand, a finger, before springing back, sweaty, and once again drawing together, trapping and lifting each other with leaps like a single whirlwind of arms and legs. It was not for nothing that they'd first met on the dance floor, only becoming sated once they ended up in bed. From time to time, César remembered to summon the waiter, and they would pause to drink, before carrying on, their bodies perfectly coupled, every step, every twirl learned by heart.

"The more you drink the better you dance," César yelled in her ear. "My darling, I want you to dance with me alone, is it so hard to indulge me? I don't want you disappearing even once; you're my wife, the mother of my children, how could you even think of going up to the second floor with those men? What were you doing, Perla, what were you doing? My jealousy is killing me, and if I die, then you die with me, my love, I know I'm a thug, an animal, but it's all for you and the children, Perla of my soul, now tell me what you did with those men up there."

"Nothing. I just went upstairs to sleep and they left."

"Really? What little angels."

Perla was fooling around, twirling around like a feather, hanging off her husband's shoulder, speaking into his ear, she didn't want to hear any more about the party, she wanted to go to bed.

"They're scared of you, César, how could they get up to anything? Who do you take me for? How ugly they are, darling, it's frightening, there's no reason to even think about them, better to get out of here. I'll fetch the boys, we can go before anyone notices."

"And Rosita? How can we leave my poor mule all alone? Her feeding trough is back at our place."

"Then you take Rosita on ahead of us, like when we arrived. I'll follow in the car, with the boys."

Perla laughed as they spun, head tilted back, her legs parted around César's knee. She pressed up against him.

"Let's make a toast," said Perla, and she tried to stop and call the waiter, but César spun her around again. "Not like that," protested Perla, "I'll get dizzy!"

César pulled her in close and she stopped spinning; he sniffed the back of her neck like a bloodhound and asked, vertiginously: "When did you learn to fly, *perra*? How is it that you didn't break your neck, this beautiful chicken's neck?," and he nibbled gently at her ear.

She wasn't listening to him, or she didn't understand:

"He stopped me falling over twice," she was saying, incongruously. "But he dances very well, that horrible bald man."

"Ah," said César, half closing his eyes. "Right. Right."

He stopped nibbling at her ear, and, bit by bit, began leading her to the far end of the garden, where the couples thinned out, where the multicolored lights faded into the dense blackness of night. They were dancing next to the large patio gate, padlocked shut, a detail César took in with a glance. "What are you doing," said Perla, "do you want to go onto the patio? We'd be better off going to bed. What are you planning to do? There are guests who'd be scandalized, there are children," but César wouldn't stop sniffing her armpits: "Baby doll," he said, "I'm going to suck your titties for a minute, okay?," and he continued to lead her toward the most inhospitable corner, sidestepping an overturned table, the body of a sleeping drunk, a scattered row of bottles, and pushed her into a kind of jungle of ferns around the greenhouse, without ever ceasing to dance and squeeze her. But the door to the greenhouse had also been secured with a padlock like a joke. Then they danced around the glass hut of the greenhouse in the blackness, finally arriving at the darkest region, where you could no longer make out the flowers and bushes. "Follow me, my love, my darling Perlita, I'm dying for you, just a couple of kisses, a small incision."

"A small incision," repeated Perla, melting, thrilled to discover that he'd actually managed to excite her for once, because for years he either hadn't been able to or wasn't trying. "I'm all yours; don't be so mean to me, you'll see how we make it to old age, don't leave me, love me," she said, with all her soul. "I swear I'm sorry if I've been bad, but I also swear that I've never been bad."

"But it's not for want of trying, isn't that right, *perrita*?"

"I don't like all this *perra* and *perrita* instead of Perla and Perlita," said Perla. She wasn't annoyed so much as resigned and ready to indulge him, so that afterwards she could go to sleep.

They became buried in leafy ribbons, ferns akin to monstrous smudges, clumped shadows, bunches of dangling plants like black pennants. It was there that César slid a hand under her skirt and raised her a few inches from the ground, as she slithered with happiness, becoming an ember, and it was also there that he sank her into the grass, ensuring the large bushes were shielding them from view. "It's cold," Perla managed to say, and then she could say no more, for César Santacruz's hands had closed around her neck and were squeezing.

"How stupid," he whispered to himself. "What did I do, what have I done, what have I done again?"

And then:

"I'll need to think this over. But what did I do. What have I done. What have I done again. Perla, you bitch, see how you made me lose my temper."

César backed carefully out of the dry bushes. Then he pressed his chest to the ground and left the jungle, scouring the horizon of the party: no one was looking. There were only cheers, cries. "Tomorrow, my Aunt Alma's going to faint," he whispered like a snigger, before proceeding snakelike in the direction of the lights, where he paused for an instant, rose to his knees, then leapt up and ran in search of the bosom of Tina Tobón, to shed his tears again—but this time for real.

3

Out in the noisy garden, the champions prowled in search of Perla. While they knew full well that Perla must in those moments be dancing with César, her rightful owner, they wished at least to watch her dance. *Adored Perla, who we came so close to being even closer to: inside!,* thought Conrado

Olarte, exploring the sea of faces that cried out as they floundered. They couldn't find her; it was difficult, because amid so many faces the colored lights didn't help, turning everything into a mask.

"The best remedy is another remedy," said the lecturer. "Let's look for other girlfriends. In Colombia there are more women than men, according to statistics, so how can we not find that wise, generous gal who'll make us forget all about peerless Perla? It's true she has no equal, but she's dancing with her consort. I propose we make for the heart of the dance floor and discover the fairies that await us there."

"But let's have something to drink first, I'm thirsty," said the magician, dejectedly.

The cyclist Pedro Pablo Rayo was thinking only of leaving. This searching everywhere for Perla like bloodhounds struck him as the height of depravity. Of course, he would never forget that night, he, the newlywed. Why hadn't his wife been able to join him? *Because she's expecting a child, she's delicate, in case you've forgotten, asshole*, he told himself, dismayed. He really was plagued with remorse.

"I'm leaving the party, my friends," he said. "It's been a pleasure to share in your company."

But a metallic voice stopped him in his tracks:

"Gentlemen, at last I've found you."

It was César Santacruz, emerging from the blackness.

Although searching for Tina Tobón, once he caught sight of his birds, the world had swallowed him up and returned him transformed into an avenger. The fire in his heart redoubled, his muscles slackened as though preparing to strangle once again. And yet his face was far removed from this intention, illuminated by an eternal smile; anyone would think he was inviting them to toast the health of his Aunt Alma.

The champions were floored. And, nevertheless, the mute

smile on César's face enveloped them, the hypnotic warmth of the eyes of a snake who was also talking to them.

"Come with me," he said, "I want to tell you something. Let's find somewhere quiet. It's about my wife, who sends her regards."

The champions all looked at each other, stunned. They couldn't refuse, that went without saying.

They followed César through the roaring garden, entered the house, and filed down the corridor in the direction of the drawing room. It seemed César was making sure that no one saw them. That's when they became genuinely scared. Where were they going? It wasn't that big a deal, they could talk right there in the corridor in which they found themselves. They stopped, panic-stricken, but César smiled mutely at them, waving them on. He was pleased to find no one in the drawing room; apparently, the whole world was out dancing. César advanced to the middle of the drawing room, and the three champions followed, less than three feet behind. Then César turned to them. The three champions were left face-to-face with him: the magician Conrado Olarte in the middle, the lecturer to his left, and the cyclist Rayo to his right. The eternal smile on César's face faded for an instant. He drew closer to them, inches away, his voice a power drill: "Sons of bitches," he said, "if any of you screw around with Perla again, I'll kill you with my own two hands."

And like a flash, he dealt the magician a headbutt to the bridge of his nose, while at the same time grabbing the respective testicles of his two companions, squeezing them, and yanking downwards with demonic strength. The champions passed out onto the floor.

César Santacruz lowered his eyelids, standing in the middle of the defeated bodies, his hands in his pockets, his face raised to the ceiling, as if muttering insults.

He stood there for a moment, eyes narrowed, until the champions recovered with a single groan, got to their knees, and finally managed to stand. They stared at him in horror.

The magician was bleeding from his nose; the lecturer lent him his handkerchief.

"I think we'd better go," said the cyclist Rayo.

And lecturer, magician, and cyclist exited the drawing room. César wasn't sure if they would leave the house or simply flee to the garden. Their choice. He didn't bother checking. Once again, his strength was abandoning him; once again, that last whimper from Perla, mother to his children, crushed him from within. Now he really did have to find Tina Tobón, and the sooner the better, so that he could shed some proper tears. He was shaking his head, seemingly suffering. He kicked the floor, bellowing "Fuck!" so loudly that the drawing room windows rang out. He was holding his head in his hands: now he would have to flee with Tina Tobón to La Guajira, which was the site of his untouchable kingdom, after all. And his children, what would become of his children? Let the devil take them, he repeated to himself, deranged, before wincing and running outside: this is why he didn't hear the faint struggling, the tenuous cries for help coming from the trunk in the drawing room.

4

It had been a century since Rigo Santacruz, son of Barrunto and Celmira, had fled the dining room. Fifteen years old, he claimed that as a small boy he'd been in love with his cousin Italia Caicedo, whom he spied on during family trips. Since Italia wasn't at the party, he focused on forgetting about her, roaming here and there and drinking too much, which, as he understood it, was what men did. Pale and sickly, he also suffered from terrible acne, and had yet to achieve that "first time" vaunted by his closest friends at the Augustinian high school, where he was in the ninth grade. Very tall, gaunt and angular, he had been given a nickname: *The Knitting Needle*. He had stated that he wanted to go *globetrotting*; this was his greatest ambition, after the greatest one of all: to sleep with a woman, as high school norms dictated. The Knitting Needle was still missing that one final rung to crow about, and he hadn't been having much luck: in the past year, he'd declared his love on three occasions, and all three candidates had burst out laughing, responding no, thank you. His greatest hope for the party was to realize his dream of love. Due to his stature, which made him look more grown up, he wasn't dismissed by older women—in their twenties, but in their thirties and forties too—who took turns using him as a way to parade themselves on the dance floor. Yet the moment they were noticed by more solvent suitors, they would leave the trembling Rigo in the hands of his dreamer's destiny.

His spirits were already sinking, he was already tottering on the brink of suicide, when he saw her.

She was a girl his own age. Wasn't that Amalia Piñeros, the "ugly one" in the neighborhood? What was she doing here, in the home of his Aunt Alma?

"Papá is one of the magistrate's business partners," Amalia informed him, once they had exchanged greetings.

They were sitting at one of the small tables in the garden and had to shout to be heard. Neither Rigo nor Amalia wanted to dance.

"I've done enough dancing for the rest of my life," he said. His pale face glistened with sweat; he wore a shirt, the undone buttons of which revealed ribs like those of Don Quixote. Amalia noticed this out of the corner of her eye. Meanwhile, Rigo took stock of the green miniskirt, her thin bare legs, those long gray braids, her horn-rimmed glasses. *And she's got hardly any tits*, he thought, *but what does that matter?*

Amalia had never danced before, not at this party or any other. No one had ever asked her. Today, she didn't care; Rigo Santacruz was more than enough for her. They began making fun of everything, a primitive bond forming between them. Rigo thought it absurd that he'd once considered Amalia to be the ugliest girl in his neighborhood, how had he not seen it? Amalia was pretty; her breasts shone beneath her blouse, those erect nipples drawing him in, she had that infectious laughter, and how perceptive she was, that knack she had for hitting the nail on the head when it came to mocking those around them. He found himself weeping with laughter at every one of Amalia Piñeros's incisive comments about the dancing women, the waiters, the waitresses, the multicolored lights, the color of the wine, the shape of the glasses, the racket made by the Los Malaspulgas Band. When the second tremor in the depths occurred, Amalia Piñeros wasn't scared; she took him by the hand and said: "The earth is drunk."

They were now lifelong friends.

Finally, Rigo asked her to dance and she came clean: "I don't know how to dance, I've never danced to an entire song in my life." "I'll teach you," said Rigo. And they rose from the table and dove straight in among the dancing couples. He led her by the hand. It didn't matter that Amalia was so short that she only came up to just above his navel. She loved that Rigo resembled the giant Gulliver. She was about to tell him so, when Rigo made a confession of his own: "At school they call me The Knitting Needle."

"What a lovely nickname," she said.

They were still holding hands, not dancing, merely contemplating each other. Suddenly, the dancing couples forced them together. They fell into each other's arms, not dancing, and kissed for the first time. This was the first time either of them had kissed. And, by the looks of things, they never planned to stop.

"It's better than dancing," Amalia said afterwards, licking her plump lips; she said this in a different voice, a voice husky with fire, the same fire that was consuming The Knitting Needle. They set to practicing. Both had been awaiting that opportunity for all fifteen years of their lives; both wanted the same thing: to dive wholeheartedly into the turbulent waters of the first time. And, after further kisses and explorations, without a care for anything else, they could think of nothing but finding the right spot inside the house, the one most suitable, at any cost. Surrendering themselves.

They left the garden and went up to the second floor: on the balcony, the guests offered them drinks. Other guests were playing cards. A drunk slept in his chair, his face inside a bowl of fruit. The face of another had been painted with lipstick. They didn't dare enter any of the bedrooms, Rigo Santacruz knew all about his irascible Aunt Alma. They went down to the drawing room, full of young people like them. They inspected the library, the parlor, finding only guests and the occasional debilitated drunk. It was as if the entire world had made a pact to deny them their love nest. They kissed each other with as much longing as anguish: they would die from love unless they could undress in those turbulent waters of the first time.

That's how they arrived at the garage, the last place that occurred to them.

To all appearances, there was no one in there. They could hear music coming from the drawing room, the Rolling Stones, the backdrop to their love. A single bulb only emphasized the gloom in the garage; the black family Mercedes, parked lengthwise, resembled a strange beast, resplendent and dormant.

"Well," said Rigo, "this place is full of drunks too."

For in the space reserved for the Ford station wagon, conspicuous by its absence, a group of stretched and huddled shadows contorted motionlessly, just like bundles, just like the ruins of men who had been celebrating heartily. These were the forms of the bodyguards Batato Armado and Liserio Caja, and of Sparks and Pumpkin, Alma's cousins.

"Don't wake them," said Amalia: "This is the only place in the world where no one can see us."

"Let's get inside the Mercedes," said Rigo, turning to her and kissing her forcefully. He couldn't take it any longer.

They stepped over the bodies as if through a swamp of crocodiles. The doors of the Mercedes were locked. They leaned against the hood—were they planning to do it standing up? They didn't want to. In a whirlwind of hands and kisses, they gradually slid down among the bodies of the drunks. They were excited about their first time, and determined. With no qualms, once settled on the cold garage floor, they began pushing the bodies of the drunks aside with the tips of their shoes, with their knees, unconcerned about the risk of waking them. They became consumed by an unknown rage, particularly Amalia, who was wearing high heels and wielded them dexterously on the attack, while Rigo used the enormous soles of his shoes; both shoved furiously, pricking, poking, pushing, and kicking—while exchanging giggles—at the sleeping bodies of the drunks. They dug their shoes into those necks and pushed, spearing them in the armpits, the backsides: "How heavy these drunks are." Finally, they had cleared a space, brazenly, and then everything was a hurricane. They were in such a rush that neither of them noticed the blood they had trodden in as they stepped over the drunks, the blood in which they now soaked themselves, one on top of the other, rolling around as naked as they were clothed, nor did they spot the star-shaped bullet holes in the foreheads of the drunks. How had they all managed to kill each other? Had they been playing Russian roulette? One of the corpses, its silhouette, was positioned as though attempting to drag itself away, yellow and rigid, its stiff fingers clawing at the brickwork as though still hoping to escape the party. This was Alma's cousin Pumpkin, war veteran, and the last to die.

5

Francia couldn't bear it any longer. Sleep was a cobweb across her eyes. Rather than succumb like Judge Arquímedes Lama, who snored under the dining room table, she preferred to propel her own body up to the bedroom where she was awaited by Ike, her madman. This is what she thought: *Ike, my madman.* From the head of the table, her mother had glanced at her with infinite sadness and nodded. Mother and daughter had said their good nights, wordlessly. Francia left, and Señora Alma continued to watch over events in the dining room, where servers were coming and going with trays. None of them arrived with the news she was hoping for: the return of Nacho Caicedo. But she remained attentive. She would have liked to be able to pray. Around her, the voices and laughter of men and women rose and fell like the crests of waves on a desolate sea.

Francia opened the door to her room and pushed it closed behind her. On the way to the bed, she began undressing without any shame. What for? If he claimed her again, she would again give herself willingly, she thought. Her cousin was asleep on the floor, as naked as she'd left him. "Ike," she said, "don't you want to come up onto the bed?" Ike didn't respond. A huge yawn took possession of the naked Francia. She couldn't bear it any longer. With some effort, she tugged off one of the blankets and threw it over Ike's body on the floor. "Well," she told him, "it's up to you. Tomorrow we'll know just how to explain this. I won't be lying if I say I never slept with you, because you're on the floor and I'm in bed." And, in the meantime, she slipped under the covers and was shocked by the cold, that terrible cold as she began to drift off to sleep, as if, from down below, from the floor, and in spite of everything, the sprawled-out body of Ike, her blanket-covered madman, were emitting an icy stench.

The one nicknamed The Hen entered the bathroom.

A proud orator, she wondered if there would be time for another poetry session in the dining room. *And this time I'll recite Shakespeare, I'll captivate them. To be or not to be.*

The mountainous woman rolled up her skirt, slid her generous yellow knickers down to her knees, and readied herself for a pleasurable pee. She had been holding it in for a long time in the dining room while she chatted to the Bats—this is how she referred to the Barney sisters, whom the audience had already asked to sing another Gardel. *They should burn themselves for real, the pair of them. What are they playing at? The artistry isn't in the singing but the invention of the song. Even I sing better than they do. And I'm also an interpreter of immortals, and I write poems from my own inspiration, except I'm humble and don't dare perform them in public.*

And she was already peeing forcefully, immersed in her own vapors, finally releasing her liquids, when she discovered the drunk sleeping on one side of the bathroom, in front of her, a gold picture frame covering him like a blanket. *And who is this surprise?* The Hen opened her mouth, dumbfounded.

He's young, that's clear, one of Alma's nephews? Yes, he was in the dining room, perhaps he's pretending to be asleep so he can watch me pee, why not? Kids these days are all a bunch of perverts.

She was unable to see the young man's eyes because they were concealed by part of the frame, but she took it for granted that he'd hidden his face after realizing that she'd spotted him, a certainty that filled her with an unknown pleasure. She took her time over peeing, humming to herself, before getting to her feet and sitting back down again. "I display before you my pale and corpulent body, but the delectable body of a woman in her fifties, unmarried and unattached, a successful businesswoman, prepared to pay for a lover, why not?" She craned her neck out to get a better look at him: this guy was either playing at being drunk or at being asleep, one of the two. *If this young man is straight with me, then I'll be straight with him, and we can take things from there.* Very slowly, she rose, exhibiting herself again, gently running her fingers back and forth over the clump of black hair, enough to prick alive even a dead man, she told herself, pulling up her knickers with a wiggle from left to right and right to left that would arouse even a retarded horse, she thought, becoming disillusioned, for she understood now that the drunk was truly drunk. *What a place to fall asleep, poor thing, he'll surely catch a cold if he spends the night in here.*

And with a mother's diligence, she looked inside the bathroom cupboard and found some blue and white towels, extra-large, which she used to cover the absurd drunk who had chosen a painting for his blanket. However, before covering the drunk, she glanced at the scene in the painting and was disgusted by it: those two men beating each other with cudgels, who would think to paint a thing like that?

* * *

Italia had just finished making love against her wishes. She had told extravagant lies, one after another, and was unsure which of these lies to turn into truth: she had told Porto de Francisco she would marry him, that she'd have their child, that she loved him to death, and she had written to her father to say that she didn't want a child, and to come rescue her from that house of grilled chickens. Porto was snoring beside her. She had never imagined that Porto would snore like that. The truth is, they had never spent a whole night together. Their encounters had always been the same: sex and more sex, until she got pregnant. Now it was different: Porto snored grotesquely and her father wasn't coming for her. In that moment, it seemed to her that the floor was sinking, the bedroom walls leaning in to observe her with great attentiveness: it was as if they were warning her of something. *What a nightmare*, she screamed to herself, *the world seems made of plasticine, papá won't ever come, I'm never getting out of here.*

Prudent Palmira, the first sister to have escaped to bed, had been lying there for hours, when a spongy dream, which burned, began returning her to reality. She resisted, not wanting to wake up. In the dream, a man caressed her in a way her most daring boyfriend never had; she'd even allowed herself a long, deep kiss, which, according to her lessons in morality, was a grievous sin. Stretching even more, uninhibited, prudent Palmira extended her arms and refused to wake up. A famous family story told how, as a girl, when left alone one afternoon, she had heard a knock at the door and gone downstairs to open it to an old beggar woman requesting alms: the old beggar woman told her she was cold and hungry, and, without any hesitation, Palmira led her to the kitchen and showed her to the larder so that she could fill her bag with whatever she wished, and then took her up to her mother's bedroom where she made her put on a dress and a cashmere coat and a pair of shoes that fit her perfectly, before finally saying goodbye. This was prudent Palmira, who now dreamed a man was continuing to kiss her, before suddenly trying to flip her onto her stomach, which is when she woke up and saw that her dream was no dream, but real life; she had woken up lying on her back, with no sheets or blankets covering her, arms spread, and a man kneeling between her legs.

Motionless, and without recoiling or fleeing or screaming, prudent Palmira stared back into his eyes, at his chest, his navel, with every ounce of her curiosity. He was as naked as she was.

"Who are you?" she asked him. "What are you doing in here?"

"Forgive me, Palmira, all I know is that I love you. If you want, I'll go."

She didn't recognize him, and yet something like an ancestral trait, the helplessness on his face, told her that yes, she knew him.

"Who are you?"

"Mateo Rey, Pacho's brother."

"Ah."

Pacho Rey had been a friend from the neighborhood, her first boyfriend, but that had been a century ago, when they were children. And this Mateo had been a little baby with a bottle. He resembled Pacho, who had gone off to study physics in Canada, he resembled him, she thought, but he was actually better looking. Prudent Palmira blushed. They continued to stare at each other in silence. She was still burning, and he knelt down between her legs.

"Then enter, Mateo," she whispered. "But afterwards, you're leaving."

6

Inside the dining room, things were far less jocular than in the garden. They were desolate. The Barney sisters assumed this must be a result of the Day-of-the-Dead expression worn by Alma Santacruz, who wouldn't listen or speak or laugh or allow anyone else to laugh. The audience was dwindling, saddening the Barney sisters; the only thing that could save the party now was a miracle: the return of Nacho Caicedo.

Uncle Barrunto and Uncle Luciano were angling for another head-to-head, to kill time. Sitting at the elephant-leg table, they boasted equal authority: one, the brother of Alma, the other, brother to the magistrate. Both had attended Nacho and Alma's wedding, the baptisms of their daughters, both meddled in all the family affairs. From the beginning, they had been unable to stand each other, but would never acknowledge their discontent. The dispute about Bogotá's earthquakes had only added to this bitterness. Luciano was a toyshop owner, a toymaker, an inventor, and Barrunto, a tailor in the service of Bogotá's elite, owner of an exclusive hat store, the *El Gentleman de Santa Fe*. Both were avid readers of *Reader's Digest*, *Life*, the *El Tiempo* and *El Espectador* broadsheets, of certain school encyclopedias, of the uncountable Tears and Sorrows of the Hero Who Tilled the Sea and Sowed the Wind, of tomes on Vatican history, the history of the Second World War, the history of Capitals, general History and Prehistory, and any other form of history that might present itself.

This time, it was Barrunto Santacruz who kicked things off. And he did so in relation to toys and toy making, Luciano Caicedo's area of expertise and means of subsistence.

"Luciano," began Barrunto, his lips wet with aguardiente, "that little horse you took from your pocket during lunch and made whinny, is that an educational toy?"

"Yes. It teaches children that horses neigh."

"But that can't be educational. Every child already knows that horses neigh. It's a useless toy."

"Don't you think a neighing horse is wonderful?

"It seems a little silly."

"Any person who sees it that way is a little silly."

"Are you calling me silly?"

"Just a little."

"Very funny."

"Well, you called me a liar.

"If the glove fits … "

"The same to you!" snapped Luciano, noting disconsolately that his wife Luz and daughters Sol and Luna were leaving the dining room, and they weren't the only ones: with them went Celmira, the wife of his foe.

The two men turned gloomy.

Barrunto went back on the offensive after raising a glass with his opponent; both men were drinking aguardiente. The wary guests glanced toward the person presiding over the table, Alma Santacruz: it seemed she was no longer paying attention, lost in the clouds.

"It isn't easy for any human being," said Barrunto, raising his index finger, "to admit when he is wrong. But it is indispensable to recognize one's error, one's mistake, one's goof, one's blunder, one's aberration, one's folly, one's outrage, when the life and honor of the entire country are implicated in this very recognition. We don't recognize when we are wrong, we don't recognize—to put it bluntly—when we screw things up: that is this country's principal ailment."

"Of which you are the greatest exponent, sir," completed Luciano.

Uncle Barrunto ignored this barb, a kind of silent laughter on his lips.

"I will show who is the greatest exponent of this national ailment with a single question: which party do you support?"

Luciano's expression turned to one of despair.

"I'm a Conservative, like my brother Nacho and my parents and grandparents. Conservative, like a significant portion of your clientele. And you are a Liberal, as we already know. We've had ample opportunity to discuss the two parties since we met. Today it would be preferable to talk of horticulture, don't you think?"

A collective smile spread through the dining room.

"We have, it's true, had countless discussions," said Barrunto. "Only I forgot to add, out of decency, that it is precisely *your* party that is the symbol of those in this country who have never wished to admit when they screwed things up."

Barrunto raised his glass. Luciano did the same. Their audience toasted with them, truly captivated by this crossing of swords. Some smiled disapprovingly, to defuse the tension.

"And now let's speak of horticulture," Barrunto plunged in at the deep end. "I suppose that you, when not imagining toys, have never in your life planted a flower, much less a tree."

"I have not, I confess, though I don't know why a flower should be considered less than a tree. And I haven't written a book either, and I only have a daughter. I suppose that you, sir, have written a book and planted a tree and have a son, that's what you're getting at, isn't it?"

"I have indeed written a book, yes. It contains over four hundred pages and is entitled: *Why Nobody Tells the Truth in Colombia.*"

"Golly!" exclaimed Uncle Luciano, in surprise. "What can we say about this book? We've yet to even see it. And what trees have you planted?"

"Plenty of guayacans on my farm. And I have a son, Rigo, who will be a Liberal like his father."

"Then it's settled, sir. According to the great magus of the East, you are a real man. You've planted a tree, have a son, and you have written a book we've never seen. You may as well die now."

A brief guffaw from the audience acknowledged the toy-maker's words. Barrunto Santacruz looked up at the ceiling as though summoning patience from the heavens, and drank without raising his glass. Then, to everyone's surprise, Señora Alma spoke. But her sharp, sibilant voice caused more alarm than relief:

"If you two don't stop screwing around, I'm going to pick up this chair and chase you both out of this house myself. I don't care if you're my brother and brother-in-law, I need only summon Batato and Liserio and I can sic them on your asses like dogs, you pair of jerks!"

"Alma," said Barrunto, who had already been informed of Italia's flight. "Almita. Come." And he reasoned in whispers: "Enough. There's no cause for you to speak like that. We know you're worried about Nacho's absence. Don't agonize. The parents of that young man … Oporto … they'll have served him drinks, and so he has remained there, content. That's it: the magistrate is resolving your daughter's situation."

"Then why doesn't he call me on the telephone?" Alma asked of no one, grief-stricken. "Nacho would have called by now. He would have set my mind at ease. You all stay here then, enjoy your politics, I'm going to the kitchen for a while, I want to ask Juana something. I have a question for her. Just one."

Señora Alma rose from the table. She was a human tornado

303

dressed as a woman. None of the other women accompanied her. None of them wanted to.

<h2 style="text-align:center">7</h2>

Uncle Jesús was no longer listening in on conversations.

Hours before, Señora Alma had ordered Juana to see if she could rustle up some chicken hearts in the kitchen and have them served in sauce for "her prodigal little brother." All of a sudden, one of the waitresses, very young and bright of face, wearing a tiny dress on that freezing night, arrived in the dining room and leaned before him with a silver platter in her hands: these were his steaming chicken hearts, a dish to die for. *They smell nicely seasoned,* thought Jesús. *This must be Juana's doing. Juana always smelled to me like chicken hearts.*

And he remembered Juana, the old woman who had once been young, the old woman who had been in Alma's service since before her wedding, and he remembered himself, much younger, forcing her into loving him at the most unexpected moments, now in the kitchen, now in the laundry room, behind a door or under the staircase, he would go to her and, without any prelude, bend her over in front of him and mount her as swiftly as a rooster, with Juana remaining as still as a hen, this is what he remembered, licking at the scent of the hearts. *Juana never ratted me out. Why? Because I'm madam's brother—or maybe because she liked it.*

Juana had grown old, but he never stopped greeting her with a coarse snigger, half insult, half pleasantry, and a look that genuinely made Juana feel sick, because that man, she would explain in three words, gave her indigestion.

"I don't like silver platters," Uncle Jesús told the waitress, continuing to lick his lips. "Since I'm sure you're a nice serving girl, real nice, in your prime, I want to ask you a favor:

bring me an earthen bowl for these chicken hearts. No. Don't take away my hearts, gorgeous. Bring me the bowl and I'll transfer them myself."

A minute later, she presented him with a black earthen bowl. Uncle Jesús carefully tipped his chicken hearts into the black bowl before returning the silver platter into those pink, solicitous hands.

"You can go now," he told her, in the meantime using a hand to rummage for an instant between the legs of the girl, who let out a sob, sprang forward as though pinched by the devil, and disappeared.

Uncle Jesús laughed. His assault had gone unnoticed. He was glowing: he hadn't been expecting this miracle of the chicken hearts. If it had once been aguardiente that would push him toward irrepressible sensuality, now, with the onset of old age, it was his enormous appetite that had been awakened, and even more so when the matter concerned the delicacy that was chicken hearts. He gulped, restraining himself; he wouldn't get carried away; he would proceed with care, savoring it, heart by heart. Amid the steaming scent, amid that air thick with viscera, Uncle Jesús dilated his nostrils so as to be able to smell even more, to become even more excited, *my God, thank you for these hearts, You know that I would give my life for a chicken heart*. His enormous mouth, stretching from ear to ear, yawned open. The fork in his hand skewered the first heart, a heart moistened with sauce as dark as blood. He tilted his head back, like birds do when they drink, and readied himself.

Then he saw him, sitting opposite, just like that morning in the kitchen, and yet he wasn't wearing the eye patch: he revealed the shocking scar, that wrinkle like a purple darn, from which there emerged a kind of shimmering greenish light, an eye of flame. And he seemed just as well-mannered as he had been that morning, waiting on him, a slave. It was Lucio Rosas, gardener, hunter. As if he were there with him, as if he were studying him in his enjoyment. As if Lucio were celebrating him.

Jesús closed his eyes, trying to ignore him. He bowed his head and chewed, but he felt as if he were chewing himself. He squeezed his eyes more tightly shut. Yes. He was chewing his own neck. He would reach his eyes. Now he felt as if he were biting his own heart. He cried out, not a cry to the masses, it was a belch, nothing more. *This is nonsense,* he thought, *look, Lucio, will you leave me alone, will you let me eat my chicken hearts in peace, will you just leave me and go, this isn't fair, you're dead, I'm alive, what more can we do?*

He opened his eyes and could still see him, sitting opposite. He even appeared to be beckoning with his hand, as if wanting to tell him a secret, and he was beckoning with his head too, the flaming eye summoning him, taking possession of him, of his mind. He recalled the gardener lying in the road. "Forgive me," he said, and poured out another glass of aguardiente, toasted, and drank, and the gardener disappeared, and yet his flaming eye remained in the air.

Floating in the air.

Jesús no longer wished to look, shrugging his shoulders, stubbornly. He began to chew the chicken hearts, sensing that they were exquisite, heavenly, and this time he swallowed whole mouthfuls, and yet a twinge deep in his throat informed him he was going to die, that he'd swallowed death, death is all he was missing, he thought. His heaving doubled him over the earthen bowl, and he began vomiting up chicken hearts, with his own chewed-up heart trembling among the rest. The world was spinning.

He was rescued by his elder brother, Barrunto Santacruz. With much tact and stealth, Barrunto helped him to his feet. He was joined by Uriela and Marianita, who were both stunned.

"Take Jesús to the sofa in the drawing room," said Barrunto. "I think he can walk. Can you walk, Jesús?"

Uncle Jesús nodded, disconcerted. He wasn't drunk, but it seemed that way: he felt worse than the worst drunk, *my God*, he screamed to himself, *what is this?*

"Lie him down on the sofa, Uriela," ordered Barrunto. "Find him a blanket for the cold and leave him there. He needs to rest."

Uriela and Marianita took Uncle Jesús by the arms, and he looked back one last time before leaving the dining room. There, the flaming eye remained, watching him. There it remained.

This is Juana's doing, he was thinking, more and more debilitated, *that whore poisoned me, wait till I come for you, I'll use a rope to make you dance my name, I'll hang you, you'll have to confess to your mistress what poison you gave me, oh Juana, it's as if I didn't know you, I never thought you'd dare, if I die poisoned you'll have earned yourself a trip to hell.*

He was sweating.

"Vengeance will be sweet," he said out loud, but neither Uriela nor Marianita could understand him. The drawing room was empty. Inside, he stretched out on the sofa, defeated. Uriela turned out the lights:

"I'm going to fetch a blanket."

Uncle Jesús did not reply.

Was he asleep? No, for he asked them:

"You two, are you a pair of squirrels?"

Surprised, Uriela and Marianita laughed. And, like a pair of squirrels, they took each other by the hand. It was dark, they could barely see, they kissed again, and, when they moved their faces apart, they laughed even more, little squirrels, they repeated, and laughed, eager to kiss again and discover each other in the darkness. Were they going to topple over with their arms around each other? Uncle Jesús shifted around on the sofa, as if making himself comfortable. He said something, but now neither of them could understand. They were laughing loudly, and the music from the garden called to them, let's dance, said one of them, let's dance for all eternity, and they ran off.

Motionless, his hands on his abdomen, he said, "What did you give me, damned Juana, what did you give me, what did you make that sauce with: your blood? Just wait till I recover." Uncle Jesús was fading, he felt as if something or someone was kicking him in the guts, he wept, "I'll never be able to take my revenge, maybe it's true, I have been poisoned," and in the darkness, in the dreadful silence, he heard that voice calling out for help, "Help me," it screamed, real, physical, that voice coming from the trunk in the drawing room. "Help me for the love of God"; Uncle Jesús opened his enormous mouth to take in air, but before him, above him, floated only the shimmering eye of flame. He believed it was the voice of the eye that screamed, suffocating him.

8

Just as Señora Alma was crossing the garden, the Los Malaspulgas Band took a drinks break. The music was replaced by endless murmurs. The cries and laughter continued to spread along Alma's path, as though persecuting her. She paused, overwhelmed, and looked around her, blinking: Alma was offended by the color-changing lights, her own invention. She intercepted a passing waiter:

"What's your name?"

"I'm Manuel."

"And I'm the lady of this house, Manuel. Now listen carefully: go and find Cecilito, do you know who Cecilito is? The leader of the musicians. He has a black hat and goatee and he dresses all in black. Well, go and tell him not to play again. The party's over. Tell him the order comes from Alma Santacruz, his godmother. If he doesn't believe you, tell him to come find me and I'll bash it into his head. Simply tell him that and he'll believe you."

The waiter, who was carrying a tray of glasses brimming with aguardiente, stood staring at her as if he didn't understand. Was this a joke? He'd already endured countless drunken ladies.

Alma Santacruz continued on her way, walking straight into the youngest of her daughters, accompanied by that girl grown up too fast who already looked cross-eyed from so much drinking. Both were holding huge glasses of wine.

"Uriela, you stay here," said her mother. "Or rather, follow me. And you," she said, looking Marianita up and down, "you're Cristo María Velasco's daughter, aren't you? Well, it doesn't look like it. You can see the wine in each of your eyes and even in your nose, dear, what will your father say? Or what will Christ say, which is much the same thing? Hand me that glass. You won't? Hand it to me. There, like that; obedient. I thought I heard your father calling for you all over the house. He wants to leave. And he has the right idea, because the party's over, not just for you: for the whole world. Good night."

Alma Santacruz grabbed Uriela's glass as well, tossing both into a pot of roses, where they could be heard smashing.

"I don't care if these roses die," said Alma, "as long as you don't drink. What are you thinking? Any lowlife could take advantage of you."

Marianita fled to the dining room like a wounded deer. She didn't dare say a proper goodbye to Uriela.

"Come, U," said Alma, impatiently. "We need to find Cecilito and tell him the party's over. I've already sent a messenger, but I don't trust him: he had the face of a clueless moron. You must tell Cecilito to stop messing around with cumbias, that cumbia is what turns the whole world upside down. But no, not now. I'd rather you come with me. We're going to the kitchen. Then you'll pick up the phone and call the police."

"The police?"

"And why not? Your father isn't back, has no one noticed? Damn it, something's happened to him."

"Then I'll go make the call," said Uriela, hopefully: in reality, she wanted to say goodbye to Marianita.

"No. First come with me to the kitchen, I may need you."

Only then did Uriela become aware of the extraordinary agitation that had come over her mother. She had seen her worked up on countless occasions, but never like this.

"The police, the police" she heard her mother repeating to herself, with genuine rage. "Those sons of bitches never show up when you need them most. And it's almost morning. Those same police are probably drunk, sleeping off their daily binge. But we must call them, because who else can we call? My God. Something has happened to Nacho, someone wants to kill him, Our Lady of Perpetual Help, watch over him!"

This last part was uttered in a scream.

"Mamá!" protested Uriela.

"You be quiet," her mother admonished her, "what's all this about getting drunk as a sailor with that brat? What's the matter with you, Uriela? Have you gone prematurely mad? Leave the madness to the grown-ups, you're still a girl, only yesterday I was giving you my breast, now you want nothing more than to drink like a sponge? What misery, where are those other daughters God gave me? Someone probably has them spread-legged under one of the tables, no, no, I don't even want to imagine it, no, not now."

And she continued to advance like a sleepwalker through the crowd.

This is how they reached the kitchen, where only Juana remained, sitting at one of the tables, head in hand, sound asleep. Señora Alma grabbed a plate from the table and smashed it on the floor. Doña Juana leapt up, hands in the air. Uriela shook her head in disapproval.

"What are you doing sleeping when you should be more than wide awake?" said Señora Alma. "You can go to bed once the party's over, you flea-ridden old hag, I've come to ask you just one question, but what question have I come to ask? My God, I've forgotten."

She slumped into a chair, the same chair where, earlier, her daughter Armenia had sat down to cry, and she too began crying.

Juana and Uriela went over to her.

"I'll go prepare some valerian water so you can get some sleep," said Juana.

"No water," spluttered the desperate Señora Alma, her head in her arms. "Wait for me to remember the question, my God, what did I want to ask you? All night with this question in my chest and now I can't remember."

In the vastness of the kitchen, Juana and Uriela kept silent.

And at that moment, the Los Malaspulgas Band started up again.

9

"Where is the monsignor?"

Juana opened her mouth, bewildered.

"Where are those fucking priests?" screamed Alma.

311

"Madam, when everything shook for the second time, they went up to the children, to pray."

"And where the hell have you put the children?"

"They're sleeping on the second floor, remember, in the sitting room?"

"Come, Uriela, I may need you to help me scream."

That's when Uriela realized that her mother was suffering because of the monsignor's *secret*. And she became petrified, following her through the shadows, for her mother was the embodiment of lunacy.

"Where are the children sleeping?" Alma asked. "From sheer nerves I've forgotten."

"Upstairs, in the sitting room."

Her mother was already advancing resolutely through the garden, entering the house, and charging up the bottom of the spiral staircase.

"Come with me, Uriela, I may need you to help me scream."

They stumbled up the spiral staircase. Uriela was surprised her mother didn't open the door to the sitting room where the children were sleeping, instead putting her ear to the crack and stating "they're praying" in a sharp whisper, before silently inviting Uriela to follow her to her bedroom. Her mother hurried inside, and Uriela watched from the doorway as she took from the night table the revolver her father had never used for scaring off thieves or for firing celebratory shots at Christmas—as other heads of family did.

"But mamá," said Uriela, "what are you doing? That isn't necessary."

Her mother didn't answer. She was making sure the revolver was loaded. It was a Smith & Wesson, .32 caliber, an antique, with a pearl handle and floral motifs engraved on the barrel. The chambers were empty. Señora Alma took the bullets from a cloth pouch and began loading the revolver with a steady hand, before slipping the pouch with the rest of the bullets into her bra, between her breasts, Uriela noted, genuinely afraid. She wondered if it wouldn't be a good idea to run and get Francia, or all her sisters, to stop their mother. Would she have time to gather them all before tragedy struck?

In contrast to her husband, Señora Alma did know something about guns. Since she was very small, she had accompanied her brothers into the mountains of San Lorenzo, on days when they went hunting. One day, when Alma was already a young woman, Barrunto hadn't wanted her to join them, making fun of her, clowning around, because it bothered him that Alma could shoot and wore pants: "You don't seem like a woman," he told her.

"Well, I am a woman," responded Alma; such a woman, in fact, that she punched Barrunto right in the face, and they never made fun of her again. On the same day as that knuckle sandwich, intrepid Alma managed to hunt down a jaguar that had been roaming the farmyards of San Lorenzo for months. She planted a bullet in its forehead. It was her momentous day.

It was precisely because her mother knew about guns that Uriela wanted to get help at all costs. But it was too late: her mother was already running to the sitting room where the children were. Uriela raced after her; she had been planning to wrap her arms around Alma and restrain her, but apparently her mother was far quicker: she crossed the dark corridor like an arrow in the direction of the sitting room, brandishing the shining revolver. Then she opened the door and switched on the light. There, amid the sea of sleeping children, Monsignor Hidalgo and his young secretary were kneeling as if praying, hands pressed together, their eyes seemingly levitating.

"Alma!" gasped the monsignor, his voice sounding like a plea: "We're only praying."

"Right," she said. "Praying in the dark."

And she started shooting.

She was firing in all directions, though toward the ceiling and the walls, noted Uriela, relieved: so her mother hadn't completely lost her mind after all. And she was firing with no concern for the children's screams, or were the children not screaming, wondered Uriela, *it's like a dream, quite possibly the only person screaming here is me*. In reality, the only people screaming were the monsignor and his secretary, who leapt up like springs, their hands covering their heads, calling out to God. Not one child awoke, so sound is the sleep of children.

"Mamá," Uriela was pleading, "what are you doing!"

The two black figures of the priests sped past her like arrows. They were fleeing, shamefaced.

The party's over, thought Uriela. She would have liked to have had Marianita by her side, if only to laugh and cry, if only to be beside her.

PART NINE

1

Once Nacho Caicedo had been cornered against the chapel door, the voice of Four Legs rang out, as if commiserating:

"Fine, mister. You wouldn't let us knock you down a peg the easy way, so we'll do it the hard way." And he began examining the chapel door, scratching his head as if resolving a difficult problem.

"Call the Comandante," the magistrate pleaded, struggling to speak. "I can't be taken down any lower." He brought his hand up to his bleeding mouth, touching the wobbly tooth with the tip of his tongue.

It seemed that Tick and the woman had been moved. They stood there watching him, as if on the point of asking, "Does it hurt?" Finally, the magistrate felt his tooth come loose. He had always believed the spitting teeth thing only happened in movies. As he spat out the tooth, he didn't notice Four Legs grab one of the bolts from the door, long and heavy, raise it up, and bring it down on the back of his head. The magistrate crumpled to the floor.

"Careful, cabrón!" yelled Tick. "We're trying to take him down a peg, not decapitate him."

Despite this reproach, Four Legs began savaging the magistrate with kicks. He kicked him hard and meticulously, in the ribs, the crotch, the ankles. The magistrate had already lost consciousness.

Blondie and Tick looked on, spellbound.

"Wait until he comes to," advised Tick. "I swear this isn't the way to take him down a peg. It's the way to kill him."

Because now Four Legs was kicking him in the face. The magistrate was bleeding from the ears. His cheeks had turned purple, and the muffled kicks could be heard in the silence of the chapel. They sounded strange, like grunts.

Blondie interrupted the kicking, giving Four Legs a shove:

"I'm calling the Comandante. You're going to kill our charge."

Four Legs was still holding the bolt in his hand, and he launched it like a spear into the pile of fallen saints. It caught the Virgin on the cheek, but the statue didn't flinch. They heard the sound of the heavy bolt landing, its reverberating echo. Four Legs shoved his face half an inch away from Blondie's.

"Don't you push me again. I'm the boss here."

His eyes were bloodshot, his breath like raw meat. Blondie took a step back. Four Legs opened the chapel door, preparing to leave, but first he cast a look back at the magistrate, at his inanimate body, curled into a ball.

"That one's going to cry when he wakes up," he said. "He'll feel sick to his nuts. I've taken him down a peg, I'm going to check on the Comandante's next orders."

And he began whistling a tune as he left.

Tick planted a knee on the ground and leaned over the magistrate's face.

"I don't think this one's waking up again," he said.

"Really?" said Blondie, and she knelt down very close to the bloodied face. "No," she said, confidently. "He's alive. You can see he's breathing. Should we lie him down on the bench, get him some water?"

"Forget it. That's Four Legs's responsibility. As far as I'm concerned, our little lawyer's already toast. If he's alive, then he's dying. It won't be long."

Blondie had discovered the magistrate's tooth on the brick

floor. She picked it up with her fingertips and examined it under the light from the bulb.

"Look, it's got these sort of little roots. It was a good tooth, hard and white as pearl."

"You were right to defend him from that horse," replied Tick. "Later, the Comandante will take it out on us." He was running his fingers through his hair, looking thoughtful. "And, you know what? This old man saved you from the fire in the van, he carried you out on his back, Blondie. Stink Foot, Razor Blade, and Tumble stayed inside because they'd passed out. It didn't occur to any of us to rescue them. There was no time. And it's not like they made any effort to wake up, they didn't help themselves. The same would have happened to you, it was the magistrate who got you out, Blondie. That knock would have been the end of you."

As he spoke, he went to sit on one of the chapel pews, taking out a pack of cigarettes.

"Want one, Blondie?"

Blondie wasn't listening to him. She was contemplating the magistrate's body with wide eyes, her mouth open like a twisted grimace. She was drooling.

Then she dealt the magistrate's body another kick, and another. And yet another. She shot Tick a triumphant look:

"And what do I care!" she hollered.

And she carried on kicking the magistrate's face:

"What do I care that this son of a bitch saved me!"

Tick shook his head as he smoked.

2

Before Nimio Cadena made his appearance in the chapel, some men filed in, one by one, wearing bandanna masks and sombreros, as though newly arrived from warmer climes, all

317

strangers to Blondie and Tick—who withdrew into a corner to smoke. The twelve or fifteen men passed over the defeated body of Nacho Caicedo, without noticing it, and took their seats on the chapel pews, as if preparing to pray. A bluish cold emanated from their foreheads, their inhospitable eyes, their tight mouths. They were united by a kind of general impatience. Motionless, without exchanging a word, without smoking a cigarette or crossing and uncrossing their legs, they waited. The men only seemed to come to life when their Comandante Nimo Cadena made his entrance, followed by Doctor D and Four Legs. At that point, they rose, stretching.

"And this one? Did you take him down a peg?" asked Nimio Cadena of nobody, hands on hips, the tip of his shoe standing on the magistrate's bloodied tie.

Nobody answered.

"What's he doing sprawled out down there?" asked Nimio, turning to Four Legs. "I hope you didn't get carried away."

None of those who'd been watching over the magistrate responded to the question: Blondie bit her lip, Tick stubbed out a cigarette, Four Legs scratched his head. The Comandante didn't notice Doctor D bend down over the magistrate, and, with a mute smile, confirm that he no longer existed.

"I'm very conscious of how I land my kicks," said Four Legs. "Where I place them. I left him alive. I tortured a tooth, nothing more. He had no reason to die. It wasn't that big a deal."

"Here's the tooth," said Blondie, stepping forward, her hand extended. Nimio Cadena was still facing Four Legs.

"Did you torture it or extract it?" he asked sarcastically. Then he turned to Blondie, ignoring the tooth in the palm of her hand: "Tell me what Nacho Caicedo said."

"He said he couldn't be taken down any lower."

"He said that?" Nimio Cadena narrowed his eyes. "What a hero."

"He asked us to call you, Comandante."

"Of course he did. He'd decided to play ball. Then you come along, Four Legs, and kick him to death in a heartbeat, but what a motherfucker you are; I needed this corpse alive, why did you screw everything up? Why did you have to shit all over my plans?"

And he leaned over the magistrate, knelt down, and shook him by the shoulders:

"Wake up, Nacho Caicedo," he said. "Or at least listen to me before you die. Or listen to me even if you're already dead. Can you hear me?"

His men looked at each other. They hadn't expected this kind of madness.

"Can you hear me?"

He was met with the most absolute silence.

"If you'd like, I can yell in your ear. There's no way you won't hear me."

And he yelled, his mouth pressed to the magistrate's ear, he yelled in a gruff voice, as snide as it was desperate:

"Listen to me, dickhead, wherever you are!"

The men shook their heads.

"We're heading to your house," the Comandante finally bleated. "A promise is a promise. We're going to fuck up your family. And your nephew, that treacherous swine, that lying lard ass, we're going to string him up by the balls, as a thief. Suffer, Nacho Caicedo, suffer though you're already dead. I'm going to castrate your nearest and dearest, and in this way I'll kill you another thousand times, cabrón, you'll have to watch the things I do to your women, you'll be forced to watch, even if you are already dead, you hear me, Nacho

319

Caicedo? I know you can hear me, are you listening to me? Shameless bastard, you killed my mamá!"

His voice broke with a whimper.

Suddenly, he sprang up, and, retrieving a pistol from behind his waist, he pointed it at Four Legs' head and pulled the trigger. There was no gunshot, the pistol had jammed, they could hear the sound of the mechanism sticking. Four Legs looked as if he were about to cry, incredulous, but then he cracked a half smile, imagining the jammed gunshot to be a simulation, a punishment: a mere scare. But a second later the Comandante dropped the pistol, took a knife from his overcoat and plunged it into Four Legs, below the navel, burying it up to the hilt and slicing upwards to the middle of his chest, with the blade and handle disappearing into Four Legs' flesh, his intestines spilling out onto the floor. Four Legs contemplated his own guts as he collapsed behind them, the fingerlike innards pulling him downwards, amid a sound like slurping water.

"To the truck!" the Comandante bellowed then.

No one moved.

Either nobody had heard or nobody obeyed his words.

Doctor D handed him back the pistol he'd dropped:

"I've adjusted the clip. We won't be having any more jammed bullets."

"This has got me thinking," responded Cadena, "knives will be better for the party. They don't make any sound."

The heavy laughter of his men arrived like the deathblow to Four Legs, one of their own.

"To the truck!" Nimio Cadena bellowed again.

The shadows exited one by one, floating soundlessly, as if they didn't exist.

"To the truck!" Cadena continued to bellow.

He was the last to leave the chapel, the last to look upon Nacho Caicedo. He departed with a valedictory gob of spit.

3

There came a moment when pain was no longer possible. In that sort of enforced trance, the magistrate bore witness to things other than pain, as if his pain no longer concerned him, or as if this were a new form of pain. If it were possible, he believed that he would have laughed at himself and the cause of his pain. When Four Legs hit him with the bolt from the door, when he lost consciousness, he felt as if another consciousness were watching over him: *Only Nimio Cadena can save me from death*, he told himself, *the same Nimio who wants to see me dead.*

And he recalled Nimio's face in painstaking detail: it was the exact face of a goat: he had the head of an adult goat, the identical shape and size, as if he'd put on a mask, but it was no mask, and this is precisely what frightened him: there was nothing human in those eyes, and his voice was that of a goat; when he heard it for the first time, he was shocked. It seemed Nimio purposefully intensified the bleating in order to scare people, and yet there was a chance that this bleating could save him from death. It's true that afterwards he would suffer the tragedy of his family who were at the mercy of these monsters, but he wanted to live so he could be there with his nearest and dearest until the sacrifice.

He wanted to scream, Go get Nimio Cadena, I'll absolve him of all blame, Nimio is this country, you can't condemn the country, Nimio is innocent, he deserves the world's apology and a whole life's pension! But he could no longer scream, he felt no pain, he floated far from it, his mind drifted separately, and now he was surrounded by voices and books and visions like memories of himself, the goat face of Nimio Cadena—who was it that wrote of the vilest of all monsters? The sun shall be turned into darkness, and the moon into blood, and the stars withdraw their shining, the heavens shall be rolled together as a scroll, these beings speak no language, but bark like dogs, Augustine wrote that monsters were beautiful because they were God's creatures, monsters, too, are the children of God, no wonder those versed in divine fiascoes tell us that God took the form of a worm: God is fate.

Nacho Caicedo was retreating from the world, and he had yet to recover from the first beating when still more kicks erupted inside his head, a pair of sharp shoes, tips like daggers. The magistrate smelled rather than witnessed the proximity of Blondie or of death—who was it that wrote of filth oozing from their bellies? He began envisioning absurdities, laughing at himself, for he had already begun to die.

He was hallucinating like when he'd drunk yagé in Putumayo, like when his first students gave him LSD without his knowledge: he'd arrived home full of otherworldly visions, it had been the start of his premonitions and dalliances with the future, and he'd carried these on throughout his life, with the horrible certainty, now, that the suffering predicted for the country would first be satisfied within the very flesh of his family, it would be worse than the worst prophecies; now he was raving, the devil and the unicorn loom before you, every rare animal enriches its owner, millions of tongues lick through the garbage, everyone's sorrow, the bones of the illustrious bandido will be exhumed, butchery, children recruited to be devoured, a donkey is worth more than a child, cannon-fodder kids, the incessant murders, the guilty leaders, impunity festers like a dark sore, here rests another,

I kill, you kill, anyone who raises their voice is crushed, a worthy among unworthy millions, in less than a month three luminaries are killed, young and old gather for a shadowy assembly, ill omens, putrefaction, earthquakes—don't forget the earth, says the earth—a soulless country, nothing but sex and full bellies, the warmongers want more war, the idiocy is terrifying, the corrupt thrive and fornicate on top of the Sacred Heart, the whole country is a cemetery, no one dies of old age, torture, the gunned-down, ghosts of victims fill the air, three seize the land of three thousand, the black beast plants its cloven hoof, living and dead are abducted, decapitations, the universe is the victim, it will be impossible to tread the earth without fear, terror on faces, river tombs, no one is guilty, the killer is master, no president can avoid becoming a criminal by action or omission, a nation of a sickly bonanza, the corrupt general is named ambassador, defiled freaks spring from law degrees, macabre messages, schools of barbarity, repugnant politicians will board their planes for Katmandu to celebrate, flaunting priestly robes, pestiferous fungi will sprout in antibiotics, death in the air, no one will talk to anyone, the black night of every day, floating cities will be no use, as the planet dies, enormous spaceships will leave to populate other planets, this country is banished, the rotten earth left at the mercy of this rotten country, this rotten country and the rotten earth dissolving into the rotten depths of the universe, was it getting light? He felt that, if he wished to, he could fade into the bloody line of the horizon; he had heard Nimio Cadena yell "Can you hear me?," but did not or could not answer him, it didn't matter, he felt that he should leave and wanted to leave, to disintegrate, but for some reason he didn't leave, for some reason he remained among men.

4

Nimio Cadena's men clambered onto the long black truck, amid joking and cries like sighs of impatience, and looked for their places beneath the shredded tarp, their eyes watery, pupils reddened, tongues licking, teeth blackened. Some sat on the wooden floor, others preferred to remain standing, all armed like their leader with revolvers or pistols, with knives or machetes, the weapons buried under their armpits, near the warmth of their hearts. All this gear was the result of the Comandante's certainty that César Santacruz would be at the party alongside his best men, and that the magistrate would also have bodyguards. It was a tactical certainty, but also his madness.

Morning had not yet arrived; it was just before dawn, when night is at its darkest. Gusts of icy wind rippled the canvas tarp, inflating it, making it flutter like a flag. Nimio Cadena was surrounded by Doctor D, Tick, and Mango Face, while Blondie, Meat Stew, and Pork Rind had taken seats in the cabin of the truck, beside the driver of the wrecked van, who knew exactly which neighborhood and house they were heading for. The new arrivals, masked and hatted, would only acknowledge Nimio Cadena, would only deal with him. There must have been twelve or fifteen of them; some sat and smoked during the journey; others were lying down, hands clasped behind their heads, trying to make up for lost sleep. A group of them were talking, but ultimately Nimio Cadena's goat voice prevailed, his whine; his bleating was audible above the sound of the truck, proceeding noisily along the byroad, in search of the highway.

"This brings back memories of San Martín," Nimio reminisced. "There were seven beds and seven girls lying on their backs, with no blankets." Here, incipient laughter rose to the teeth of his listeners. "Frightened, poor things, and with good reason; two were the mayor's daughters, three whores, another the schoolteacher, and the seventh a nun"—the laughter erupted, collectively, like a boiling geyser—"she was the only delectable nun we came across from that convent of centenarians. Those seven, before seven lines of fighters ready to greet them, gentlemen." More bitter laughter. "There were around ninety of us!" The laughter rose to an imperious climax. "We were restless guys, awaiting our turn. And, in the meantime, we gave ourselves a helping hand." The Comandante moved his fist slowly back and forth, his mouth open, his tongue lolling out. "Of the seven scaled, six broke down, by which I mean fainted, long before the lines cleared. Only the nun withstood the convulsions. She was sweating, her white habit dripping, her eyes raised to the ceiling: anyone would think she was praying to God in the meantime; but no, she'd gone mad." Now the laughter flowed like a river. Nimio himself was in stitches. "It all took place on a farm," he brooded. "The landowner was some kind of asshole: at the entrance to his home, he'd had two pink marble columns installed, like a Roman. On one column, there was an old Spanish suit of armor, like that of a knight, with a helmet or helm or sallet, a chain-mail shirt, pauldrons, breastplate, gauntlets, poleyns, all rusted, and on the other column, a mummified corpse, still in possession of its archbishop's cassock, its miter, its pallium, its pectoral cross, its ring of purest gold, its crozier—a miraculous Peruvian archbishop, a saint, according to the sign held between its bony hands. Well, we set that archbishop and knight dancing the mapalé until they exploded, we used them for target practice."

"And the nun," cried Mango Face in the midst of the laughter, "what happened to the nun?"

"She could no longer be rescued from her prostration. A body without a soul."

Many of the men booed. The Comandante called for silence; becoming serious, he raised his bleating voice and placed his hands on his hips:

"You all know César Santacruz," he yelled. "That swine is the objective. The rest come as a bonus. Once we've carved him up, we can get some sleep. I want no delays, look for him, find him, and get down to business. If any entertainment presents itself as you search, entertain yourselves, but make sure it takes no longer than a rooster with his hen. César is non-negotiable, keep him in your minds; make it quick. He's already screwed up our business, stolen millions, and slipped through our fingers. But beware! He's not alone. He may be fat, but he hops like a bunny. Now he'll have to pay, along with his family. And we were partners, too, but that's life. I'm only sorry the magistrate won't be sharing this dance with me, he would have loved it. Oh Nachito Caicedo, why did you have to mess with me?"

5

Monsignor Javier Hidalgo and his secretary were spared from the end of the party (may God always protect His flock); the clergymen fled one minute before the arrival of the death wagon, climbing into the black limousine that awaited them, still worried that the deranged Alma Santacruz would be coming after them, firing shots. Also spared were the banana exporter Cristo María Velasco and his daughter Marianita, who left the house at the same time as the priests. They hadn't even turned the corner, each pair in their respective car, when the long black truck burst onto the street with a clamor of smoke and springs, a screeching of brakes.

The men in hats began clambering out, and it occurred to Iris Sarmiento that they must be mariachis. To Marino, she said:

"I didn't realize they were hiring mariachis for the party."

"They always leave them for last."

They were still sitting in a corner of the outer garden, on the small stone wall, under a great clump of ferns that shielded them from view, not far from the inflatable pool, the squishy dolphin shining in the moonlight. It was so cozy in that corner, their love nest, that they hadn't even risen to say goodnight to the monsignor. The pair had been embracing there for much of the celebration, and as the night turned starry, they promised each other the sky and the earth and made life plans: "For the first time, I want to have a child," Marino Ojeda said, "I mean a real child." His words were imbued with clarity, he was a stranger to himself: "A child with the woman I love." Iris had responded immediately: "A child? At once. Whenever you want." She too felt like a stranger as she said this.

Now the mariachis were crowding outside the front door. *How odd,* thought Marino, *none of those mariachis is carrying a guitar.* And he stood up in alarm. He was the watchman, the guardian of the street:

"You'll have to go ask them who they are and what they want, who they're looking for, Iris. It must surely be a mistake, they might be going to another house. I'll come with you."

He was a long way from feeling at ease, as his voice suggested. Deep down, he was sorry not to be carrying his gun with him, the "pathetic rifle" mocked by Uncle Jesús. Too late, he regretted his lack of foresight, placing the blame squarely on his "dick brain," that's how he thought of it, cursing himself: *The fault of my dick brain.* Because, hours earlier, when he'd discovered Iris alone in the night, en route to the store, he had felt the worst thing he could do would be to bring along a rifle that would prevent him loving her as he should, and so he'd left it hidden in the guard's booth, but that booth was on the corner and he didn't want to abandon Iris while going back for it. *The fault of my dick brain,* he repeated, sensing that his hands were trembling. His instinct warned him of the danger: the furrowed brows like melted wax, the twisted mouths, the battered hats of the supposed mariachis all reminded him of only one thing: prison.

Iris, on the other hand, was amused at seeing so many mariachis in the street, outside the house. She went straight over to them, with Marino in tow, weaponless, helpless, with no other alternative.

"We're here on behalf of Nacho Caicedo," said the one who appeared to be leading the band. "We've brought an explanation for his wife. Can you open the door, or should we knock?"

"I've got the key," said wide-eyed Iris. "I'll go find madam and tell her. I'll fetch her right away. Wait here, I won't be long."

She put her hand in her pocket and was retrieving the key as she walked diligently up the little stone path lined with flowers, and then, under the yellow half light of the bulbs, a shadow wrapped its arms around her and toppled her to the ground, one hand clamped over her mouth, the other snatching the key and passing it to another ruddy hand waiting in the air. Marino Ojeda never had a chance: he believed someone was punching him repeatedly in the chest; these weren't punches, but plunging knives; his instant death afforded him no time for surprise. Iris was dragged off by the shadows. One of them let out a muffled laugh on coming face-to-face with the inflatable pool, that blown-up dolphin, where the other shadows held Iris down, tore off her clothes, and bit into her as they asphyxiated her.

With the stealth of centuries of training, the assassins hid Marino's corpse under Perla Tobón's Chevrolet, and Iris's beneath the inflatable pool, all within seconds. There was no one in the dark road, no peering witnesses, no moonlight: like a conjuration, the mist and black clouds had once again taken possession of the street. By this point, Blondie had managed to get the door open, and the men burst in one after another—at the exact same moment, the orchestra flared up as if in welcome, for it seemed the party would be going on for more than just a day, as often happened, and the final guests were arriving.

6

They found no one inside the large entrance hall, which split into three, leading to the drawing room, garage, and interior of the house. Without raising his goat whine, and adopting a very cordial tone as he inspected his men for the last time, Nimio asked those still wearing masks to uncover themselves. "If we're guests," he reminded them, "then what's with all the covering up our mugs?" He was a lawyer of Nacho Caicedo's ilk, as he himself professed, and knew about Cicero, the muses, Vivaldi and Botticelli, but he also spoke the man speak of the quadrupeds he was leading. He often boasted: I know about their instincts, their twisted pleasures, their contrary lives. Yet he finally became exasperated and cracked his bleating whip over them: "This is a big house, you can tell, and it sounds like there are a lot of people here, so ask about César Santacruz surreptitiously, without frightening anyone, we don't want them scattering like lambs, rearing up, knocking us over and stomping on our balls." This is what he said as they walked along the corridor leading to the interior of the house. From there, he scanned the horizon and noticed the door to the guest bathroom, ajar. "You," he ordered half the shadows, "check the drawing room." And, turning to the other half, militarily: "You check the garage, see what you can find. I'll go visit that spotless bathroom, to take a dump. I feel that urge inside the home of my brother Caicedo. I never dreamed of such happiness." The men all cheered as one. And they resembled genuine guests, welcome at the magistrate's party, the final guests.

Tick headed up one small group and led them toward the garage. Blondie made for the drawing room with those who were left. With her went Mango Face and Meatstew, already behaving like leaders because of their closeness to Nimio Cadena, and because Doctor D had gone over to sit at the little telephone table at the bottom of the spiral staircase, where he sprawled out, contentedly, beside large empty glasses, cigarettes and ashtrays, and a bottle of rum. The men observed him enviously. Doctor D poured himself a glass of rum and lit a cigarette, while Nimio Cadena shut himself inside the bathroom. The line of henchmen slithered into the drawing room and garage like a bifurcating serpent.

Inside the garage, one of the men in hats was already kneeling down, examining the collection of sprawled out bodies. Despite his familiarity with blood, he was shocked, his mouth hanging open, as if he were about to cry: Christ almighty, he said, these guys must have had a real good time of it, they're all partied out. The already fetid faces of Sparks and Pumpkin, of the bodyguards Batato and Liserio, appeared to nod in rapt agreement.

Then they heard something like the trilling of a bird. It was Amalia Piñeros, waking from that sweet but furious first time. Behind her rose a face seemingly wreathed in imbecility: it was Rigo, son of Barrunto Santacruz.

A stunned shadow was already contemplating the girlish features of Amalia Piñeros, wandering over them, as though licking them:

"All that beauty just for me. I almost feel bad."

The lovers never got to ask a question, never got to scream. Last to leave this world was Amalia Piñeros.

7

Inside the drawing room, the executioners had become fascinated by the mere sight of Uncle Jesús's face: who the hell is this big-eared guy? What a bat-like face, what a fart, how about that snout from north to south? And that stench of shoes? Stink-footed devil! Uncle Jesús was asleep on the sofa, or so it appeared to his audience, his face whiter than the walls. One of the shadows checked his pulse: this guy's dead of his own accord, he hasn't got a bullet wound, but he belongs to the past.

"Just like everyone in this house," said Tick, sniffing the palms of his hands: he was the one who had terminated the lives in the garage, the one who had taken Amalia Piñeros as his trophy.

The little tables in the drawing room were also loaded with bottles, and the men in hats didn't hesitate. They weren't looking at each other, or even at themselves in the hanging mirrors: they sat like wide-eyed kings in the soft armchairs, their cutthroat gazes focused on the boots muddying the carpet. They were going to drink, their tongues clicked, some placed bets, asking if the crucifix hanging in the corner was made of gold, others pissed in the large vase of lilies by the drawing room door, while still others looked around and grew bored: they just wanted to get this over with and go; those peering up at Christ craned their avid necks, no one daring to scratch the crucifix with a fingernail. "It's just painted tin," said one, giving up and going over to drink with the rest; the last man unhooked the crucifix and slid it under his belt like a sword. They were raising their glasses over and over again while waiting for the Comandante, and it was then that the cries for help coming from the man in the trunk were heard, the soft knocking, the muffled nails against wood, the now distant voice, that voice now forever faint: "Get me out of here."

"My ears are never wrong," said Mango Face, as if boasting. He set off as though following a scent, going round and round, before finally arriving at the trunk in the farthest corner, putting his village-musician's ear to the lid, and hearing, for a few seconds, what no one else could. With a glance, he ascertained the position of the lock, drew his revolver, and fired upwards, point-blank, sending it flying. The gunshot coincided with the distant eruption of a currulao, the unanimous cheer from the partygoers in the garden louder than the blasting shot. Mango Face lifted the lid of the trunk: there were gasping sounds, like someone finally able to breathe. Then several seconds of silence. With quiet satisfaction, Mango Face took two steps back so that all could share in his surprise: during those moments, Rodolfo Cortés was shaking himself free, stretching his arms, testing his legs, and emerging, inch by inch, with the eyes of a frightened corpse. He was met by laughter in the drawing room. The men all drank as though celebrating a circus act. By this point, the man in the trunk had managed to stand, but not to leave the box: the leg he was attempting to raise refused to obey, gulps of air revived him, he regained control of himself, remembered everything, but the faces before him made him question if he had woken up in this world or the next, on Mother Earth or in hell, if he'd been saved by beings of flesh and blood or by tormented souls, if he were alive or dead—at least there was no sign of Ike Santacruz, his executioner. He summoned his strength, and, like a well-mannered child, asked: "Are you guests?" He was met with another volley of laughter. Rodolfito took encouragement: "Are you guests of the magistrate? I'm Francia Santacruz's future husband, Rodolfo Cortés Mejía, and I thank you for lifting the lid of this trunk, you see, it was a game and I lost, I had to let myself be put in this box, that was the punishment."

"Get out of there at once!"

This was the voice of Blondie: sharp, fiery, distinctive, mischievous, the voice of the only woman there. The men in hats, who had only met her earlier that evening, were entranced by her, and this in turn fired up Blondie, who wasn't intimidated by the universal reverence she provoked:

"Get out, moron."

Rodolfito managed to climb out of the trunk, as though raised by the arms of that voice.

He ended up half-seated on the edge, facing Blondie, arms spread, his hands on the sides of the trunk. His knees were trembling. Blondie walked right up to him, leaning her girlish face toward Rodolfito's—she can't be older than Uriela, the magistrate had thought—a girl astonished by herself, and for that reason ready for anything:

"You're out, animal."

The men took another drink. They listened to her, rapt:

"You'd have done better to stay locked inside."

8

Blondie ran her cold hand across his cheek, as though intending to lift his spirits. Rodolfito had his mouth open. In the throbbing silence, he heard the woman's voice:

"*I'm* your punishment, my lovely. Oh yes."

Her words were met with bigger laughs than those the Comandante had provoked with his war gags. The drawing room shook with the noise, though it wasn't happy laughter, but rather funereal, and yet it matched perfectly with the great party that could be heard coming from the garden.

Blondie glowed. For a second, she didn't know who this man was, but in the next second, she didn't know who she was either. This is how she thought, as though justifying herself.

And she seized him by the neck, pressing right up against him, before lifting him into the air; it seemed incredible to her that a man could weigh so little, but even more incredible that he could be so terrified before she had even touched a hair on his head. She allowed him to slide down, almost embracing her, and licked his nose, on the nostrils, as though sampling his snot, then looked back at her audience, challenging them: "Who of you could do what I am doing?" From between her breasts, she drew a sort of copper wire, about six inches long with a hook on the end, a sharp hook which she held up to the light of the spidery drawing room chandeliers, covered in bulbs like cobwebs. Rodolfito slumped forward into Blondie's arms, as if his soul had departed: his legendary cowardice had prevented him from making any bid for salvation, he'd used up all his strength; he placed his hands on Blondie's arms, but inertly, more as though stroking them or encouraging them to proceed with the sacrifice, and what a sacrifice. "It's simple," said Blondie, lying Rodolfito's broken body across one of her knees, hunching over him and shoving the hook up his nostril—all while Rodolfito was fainting from panic—and twisting it for a minute, during which no man dared to drink or crack a joke, twisting it even harder as the carpet began to become

334

soaked in blood, and then, raising her radiant eyes to the eyes watching her, she said: "This is how the Egyptians did it, I heard it on *La Escuelita de Doña Rita*, this is how I extract the brain through the nose, how I can slice the brain up and turn it into this sticky substance that comes out through the nose, right? Yes, yes."

And a kind of emulsion—a thick, multicolored, buttery substance—poured out over the blood.

Holy shit, said one of the men—or rather, screamed it.

Blondie released Rodolfito's body: "All set, now we can mummify him."

The body dropped, and an intake of admiration could be heard in the drawing room, joyful, searing. The men raised their glasses, what a gal! Now no one was looking at the remains of Rodolfito Cortés; their eyes were captivated by the only woman in the drawing room, asphyxiated with glee: years later, she would lose an arm in the Colombian mountains and become a legend, possessor of the nine lives of a cat, famous for what her own captains, perplexed leaders, celebrated as her exquisite cruelty. They would dub her Strategist of Liberty, Mirror of Females, Rebellion, Fairy Godmother, Architect of War—in truth, the tireless architect of massacres, extortion and kidnappings, of refined murders. The very men who fought beside her used to fantasize, swearing that she had continued with the practice of the Egyptian hook, that she ate her enemies' testicles raw, that she made love not to men but to donkeys. Extensive coca plantations would grow under her care, infamy after infamy sanctifying her among her men, her chiefs exalting her with affected titles, à la Simón Bolívar: Liberator of Liberators, Avenging Falcon, Incan Warrioress, Aztec Warrioress, Muisca Warrioress, Illustrious Soldier, Glory of the Plains, Eagle Girl of the Andes, Queen of the Insurrectionists, Rebellious Breast,

Dancing Dynamite, Devil's Din. They would take memorable photos of her, one with Black Pantoja, another with the two Martíns—Little Martín and Big Martín—several with Rooster Gúzman, with the Dwarf King, and a quasiromantic one as she danced with the student Magallanes, both in camouflage, armed to the teeth. She would lead a battle front all by herself, the first woman to hold command, mistress of her jungle, but was later found culpable for the death of one of her chiefs, leaving her no choice but to turn herself over to the authorities so that she could be integrated into the quotidian life of the country, becoming a religion, giving interviews and partaking in lunches with bishops and beauty queens, and yet those same men who had once fought by her side would begin searching for her day and night, in the hope of bringing her to justice, and her destiny would be to spend the rest of her life on the run.

9

"In the bathroom there's a drunk sleeping under a painting that shows two men beating the hell out of each other; the drunk carries on sleeping, or he's dead; let him remain dead or asleep, we're only looking for the hog, that's why we're here."

It was Nimio Cadena, at the drawing room door: he was calmly narrating his parable of the bathroom, still pulling up his pants, adjusting his belt, doing up the zipper.

Doctor D walked up behind him, his pale parrot nose appearing over Cadena's shoulder.

"And all of you," continued the Comandante, "what are you doing?" In the distance he could see Rodolfo Cortés's corpse, lying in a bubbling pool. "I didn't bring you here for that, goofballs. First things first, then we'll see. What, am I speaking Martian? It's all about crushing César Santacruz;

336

until you crush him, we'll have no singing, understand?"
Again he regarded the twisted face in the distance, which
appeared to have no nose: "For today, I'm not even going to
ask which of you dispatched that guy, who might very well
have provided us with information, didn't that occur to you?
Let's get on with this, shall we? To the party, my simple souls!
Find César, then that's it, we retreat."

Was he regretting his plans? Did he require a stimulant,
a bottle or two or three? The men tried to guess. Earlier, he
had proposed certain liberties, but now he was insulting
them. They were grateful he didn't ask what they'd found in
the garage. Neither Tick nor any of the others endeavored
to enlighten him.

Now the Comandante stepped into the drawing room. He
was carefully observing Uncle Jesús, who was lying with his
back on the sofa, hands clasped over his chest like a solemn
corpse, his face a stony blue.

"And this one, what's his deal?"

Doctor D came in behind him:

"Ugly as sin," he said.

Doctor D was dressed all in black and looked exactly like
what he was—a doctor or a cleric or an undertaker. He was
carrying one of Uriela's cats in his arms, a little puss which
the men now noticed for the first time; they were amazed
that it had allowed itself to be apprehended by none other
than Doctor D, and even more stunned by the fact that Doctor D was stroking it tenderly, scratching it under the chin,
scratching its cheeks, and that the cat was letting him do
this. "Look at me, little puss," said Doctor D, "will you look
at me?" His voice, in contrast to the Comandante's, was a
low, resonant bass, like a drawn-out belch: "Do you know
why they call me Doctor D, little puss? You really should
know," and, grabbing the animal's neck, he wrung it like a

337

turkey in front of his audience, before hurling the dead cat into Jesús's pale face. The warm blow to the middle of his face woke Jesús: he blinked, breathed hungrily, as though emerging from the depths of the Acheron, revived. For not even the ghost of Lucio Rosas had been able to annihilate Uncle Jesús.

"Ol' big-ears is very much alive," said the behatted man who had taken him for dead. "I was wrong. No wonder they say freaks like this one never die."

"Who are you?" Jesús managed to stammer. "More lawyers?"

The men found themselves unable to respond, stupefied.

"Where's the magistrate?" he asked.

Though his guts still ached, and an aftertaste of poison was murdering his tongue, Uncle Jesús sat up fully on the sofa and adopted the expression of master of the house, looking around as if demanding a glass of something or other. He didn't notice Rodolfito, his crumpled body in the distance: there were too many faces around him. And he didn't bother to investigate how they had managed to wake him, nor did he notice the cat that appeared to be sleeping next to him.

"Isn't anyone going to offer me a drink?" he asked.

One of the men in hats had already started moving toward him, to put him in his place, but Nimio Cadena paralyzed the henchman with a gesture of his hand:

"Who are you?"

"I'm Jesús Dolores Santacruz, brother to Alma Rosa de los Ángeles, wife of Magistrate Nacho Caicedo. I'm the youngest of my siblings. Who's getting me that drink? I don't have the strength to move right now. Oncc I can move, we'll go dance. Who are you all? I don't recognize you, but just hold on a sec and we'll get to know each other properly."

338

To everyone's surprise, it was Nimio Cadena himself, their Comandante, who held out a full glass to him.

"Don't worry, we're friends," he said. And then, in one of his bleats: "We're just looking for César Santacruz, do you know him?"

That whine alone electrified Jesús, it shook him.

"César? But if I was there when he was born, I held him in my arms. I was speaking to him not long ago. I'm his uncle. He's the son of my brother Rito, may he rest in peace."

He downed the glass in one and would have liked to ask for more, but contained himself. Now he'd fully woken up, now that ring of faces unsettled him. These weren't normal guests, who were they? God only knew. He shuddered. Things weren't going the way he'd imagined. These weren't the magistrate's day laborers, they weren't gardeners, where the hell had he woken up? *I'm in the drawing room, you can hear the party, I'm no longer asleep, but these guys are frightening just to look at, they could tear me to pieces.*

A shiver ran up his spine, a deathly vertigo overwhelming him. To his surprise, Nimio Cadena offered him another overflowing glass.

"We want César Santacruz, that's all, then we'll go. Help us find him."

"I'll find him for you. I've known him since he was a kid, since he was born. Do you want to say hello?"

"A very warm hello," interjected Doctor D.

"You go with him," said the Comandante, pointing to Blondie, Tick, and Pork Rind.

Doctor D winked at them:

"We'll follow just behind, like a train, so as not to scare the dancers, alright?"

And he proposed a toast to the Comandante, as a ruffled

Uncle Jesús left the drawing room, Blondie very close beside him, Tick and Pork Rind bringing up the rear.

10

The publicist Roberto Smith had decided not to say goodbye to anyone. From the dining room, he had gone out to the garden to watch the women dancing. He finished his last drink and then headed down the central corridor of the house, toward the front door. He spotted one of Alma's siblings, the most loathsome one, coming in his direction, in the company of what appeared to be musicians: a shaven-headed girl and two haggard-looking men. He was surprised when Jesús didn't greet him: Alma's brother advanced pompously, his head scanning to left and right, like a prince—or did he look stunned? Yes: as if he were witnessing a procession of apparitions. He saw that the girl was hanging off Jesús's arm; he was distracted by that girl with dazed eyes, the eyes of an idiot or an angel, he thought, and that was when, fatefully, the publicist Roberto Smith, famous for his bad temper, walked into one of those he believed to be musicians. They bumped into each other. "Be more careful, cretin!" said Roberto Smith.

The other man stopped dead. "I'll catch up with you, this won't take long," he told his companions.

They called him Pork Rind, for that is what he looked like, a short, fat pork rind. He turned to the publicist: "What did you call me? I don't think I heard you."

He was forced to address this question to the sky, because the publicist was the tallest person at the party, as well as the stoutest, the only one who had arrived at the magistrate's house with the sole aim of savoring Alma Santacruz's exquisite cuisine. Roberto Smith had come to the party for no other reason than to gorge to his heart's content and meet his fate.

His bad temper was legendary. His wife had suffered it on their honeymoon, during an overland trip from Bogotá to Cartagena. They had been traveling at fifty-five miles an hour when she told him she needed to pee, continuing to repeat it until she could hold it no longer, peeing as she wept. The publicist would never forget this wife who'd wept as she peed. At the advertising agency, Smith had been known to stomp the phone to pieces and chew on the cable because someone didn't pick up; he bit his tongue when he talked, continuing to bite it even once he'd stopped talking; his children were petrified of him; one day he'd crashed a pot of freshly cooked spaghetti against the ceiling and gone after the dog that was barking on his patio, his own dog, beating it to death with the pot. These were the indiscretions of the publicist Roberto Smith. Did he deserve to die with his tongue in his pants pocket?

Some of the guests going past noticed that the publicist Roberto Smith had overdone it on the booze and was being assisted by a musician-Samaritan who sat him carefully in a soft armchair in the corridor, near the guest bathroom, leaving him there like just another sleeping drunk.

11

Pork Rind soon tracked down his colleagues, on either side of Jesús, at the edge of the garden, facing the dance floor, each with a glass of rum in their hand.

"I don't think César likes dancing," Blondie was saying. "Can a hunk of junk like him even move?"

"He's a great dancer," said Jesús. "But I don't see him. We aren't going to find him just like that."

"Well, you'd better find him. First, we'll look in the more remote places around the edges, then we'll tighten the net. Come on. You can find anything, if you go looking for it—even a fight."

They handed their glasses back to a waiter: Blondie's was still full. Then, as if entering a jungle, they penetrated the party, though keeping to the edges, attentive, not overlooking a single male face. They were heading for the farthest part of the garden, the darkest part, the area of the greenhouse.

A short while earlier, at the heart of the dance floor, Tina Tobón was determined to discover exactly where her sister had been *left*. She appealed to César over and over again, pleading with him, she wanted to see her, to only see, promising that afterwards she would follow him to the ends of the Earth.

They both knew this wasn't true.

For after César's revelation about Perla Tobón's fortunes, Tina had cracked. To César's astonishment, the certainty of her sister's death had isolated Tina from him forever. Though it was also possible, César wanted to believe, that Tina was actually interested in verifying her sister's death, in seeing her dead for real. Hopefully, this was all that mattered to her: the sisters had always loathed each other.

César said nothing and led Tina to the blackest corner, behind the greenhouse.

He pointed to the spot, and she pushed the bushes aside to look, before turning her face aside to cry.

César made no attempt to console her, he couldn't: he, too, was stricken with remorse. Through her tears, Tina told him she was going to the bathroom, but that she would be right back. César knew she was never coming back.

In any case, he was still waiting for her when his Uncle Jesús emerged from the blackness: *None other than my Uncle Jesús, here,* he thought. He could see only his uncle, that ghostly apparition, and Jesús stood there staring at him, as if wanting to chat, and yet he didn't say a word.

"What's new, Uncle?"

"Nothing," responded Jesús, as though wishing to scream. "Except that these friends of yours wanted to say hello."

And he motioned behind him with a sweeping gesture.

With one glance, César realized who they were. He didn't take a step back. In fact, he smiled. He regretted not carrying his gun with him, so unsuspecting had he been on arriving at his aunt's party. Jesús didn't wait around to hear the conversation. He scurried off like a mouse toward the swirling lights of the party. Pork Rind made as if to go after him, but Blondie stopped him.

"And Nimio?" César spoke first. "Is he here?"

"Yes," said Blondie. "Comandante Cadena is here."

"Well, then take me to him, Blondie. That's what we all want. It's been ages since we've seen each other. That way, we can get things settled once and for all."

"I'll be the one settling things," said Blondie.

Tick and Pork Rind had now seized César Santacruz by the arms: César felt ashamed, what an ignominious way to die, so suddenly, without at least taking a dozen of them with him. This is where his mind went, disenchanted with himself, but then he fought back, lifting both men into the air and throwing them to the ground, before being felled by a bullet to the head. Satisfied, Blondie stowed her smoking pistol and looked around. She had completed her mission sooner than expected.

And with greater ease.

She could think of no better place to hide César Santa-

343

cruz's corpse than behind the greenhouse, the blackest corner. That's where they stuck him, among the dense bushes.

César and Perla's bodies had ended up together, one on top of the other.

12

Back in the din of the party, Blondie and her two minions discovered that a number of the men in hats were already scattered among the crowd. Some were sitting at the tables, busy devouring whatever was presented to them, and with good reason, for they had endured hours of travel without a bite to eat. One of the men in hats held a hog's snout in his hands and was wolfing it down. Another, in the distance, who'd surely had his fill already, leapt onto the dance floor with the first woman he came across, and, without any preamble, began sending her flying with paso doble twirls in the middle of a currulao. Everyone was drinking with abandon. Blondie marched over to them, this was known as indiscipline, no matter how hungry they were: "Mission accomplished, we're leaving," she told them, half order, half news flash, "move your asses."

None of the men in hats moved a muscle. They carried on eating. Occasionally, enraptured, they would scour the horizon of singing girls, swaying drunks, entwined couples everywhere. The obliging waiters were still milling around, and, egged on, they too had started drinking rum and toasting.

"To the truck," said Blondie. "Those were Comandante Cadena's orders."

"We're going to eat something and entertain ourselves," said a voice not far from her. It was Doctor D, dressed all in black, sitting at a table. "You're efficient, Blondie, you have a bright future, we're grateful to you, but sit down and eat something, sit or dance. Your Comandante has gone to say hello to the lady of the house. Once they've had their chat, we'll scram."

Pork Rind and Tick didn't need to be told twice. They collared a waiter. Blondie's disappointment was visible on her face.

"I'm going to the drawing room," she said.

"You won't find him," said Doctor D. "There's no one in the drawing room. We all want to dance."

The men nodded as they ate. Before Tick, they set down a pork chop glistening with grease, which he began to tear at with his fingers: "Eat something, Blondie, don't be a fool," he said with a wink, his mouth full.

Blondie shook her head.

It all seemed hopelessly wrong to her. The deployment of so many men for something she had been able to accomplish backed by only two struck her as Nimio Cadena's madness—or was it her own madness? Or the madness of everyone? She was mortified by the fact that César Santacruz's uncle, that big-eared wretch, that stinking goblin, had slipped through her fingers; it's true that he hadn't witnessed anything, but he might suspect; she would have to track him down and silence him, if it wasn't already too late, if the police and army didn't descend upon them—weren't they raiding the home of a magistrate after all? Things were being implemented badly, pure madness; impotent, Blondie observed that Doctor D was thoroughly enjoying the minutiae of the dance: in full mourning dress, like an undertaker, he was sitting at a table, smoking. Alone? At that moment, Blondie noticed that Doctor D had another cat on his belly and was stroking it.

FINALE

1

No one knows when the crowd first became aware of their approaching destiny. Too late, they noticed fate hovering over them. The first victims followed one another without raising suspicions. If strange goings-on were observed, they were immediately interpreted as the stuff of parties, domestic stuff, sleeping drunks, arguing couples, hidden women, fleeing women, absent women—either because they were in the bathroom, peeing and chatting to each other, or re-touching their faces in the mirror, purposely delayed, or searching for more rooms in which to carry on the party, or else they had simply grown tired of dancing and gone home.

The vocalist Charrita Luz was the first.

A tall, bony mulatta, life and soul of the party, her large, wild eyes were closing with tiredness. She was taking a break from singing, not far from the stage, her long bare back bathed in sweat, squeezed into a sequin dress. Charrita sweated when she sang, she sweated too much; she sweated so much, in fact, that if the world had let her, she would have performed naked. Now she would need to find the bathroom and dry the sweat from every nook and cranny of her body, as though returning from a dip in the sea. Fatigue waylaid her: she didn't run to the bathroom, simply resting her head on one side of the stage on which her Los Malaspulgas Band continued to play. She had been singing since the afternoon, singing all night long, she needed a breather, or, in other words, to wet her whistle with rum and lemon, for this was her secret. She dozed upright, not far from the stage, her arm leaning on the edge of the black platform where the Malaspulgas had resumed playing. It was the busiest stage; partygoers crammed around it, demanding dance numbers.

The raucous jubilation prevented anyone being able to distinguish a joyful cry from a mortal one.

Charrita Luz drank thirstily. She was wondering about the time and how long festivities would go on for, when a shadow made as if to embrace her, in reality pushing her to the ground and shoving her under the stage, face up, in that ample space between the ground and the bottom of the platform; from there, with her mouth covered by a clawlike hand, Charrita Luz could only look on impotently as the tightly packed sea of shoes danced around her. It was there that the shadow finished subduing her. Charrita managed to free her face, attempting to bite and protest, but the shadow—a voracious maw closing on her neck—snuffed out her voice, snuffing out the song of Charrita Luz forever.

Luz, wife of Uncle Luciano, with her daughters Sol and Luna, and Celmira, wife of Uncle Barrunto, had left the dining room and were wandering disinterestedly through the pavilions of the garden. Too late; the pair of matrons had agreed to find their husbands and demand to leave the party. They were heading back to look for them in the dining room, along the first-floor corridors, when all four women, mothers and daughters, were unceremoniously locked inside the parlor by shadows emerging from the gloom. Inside the parlor, Celmira rebuked a shadow who had put his arms around her, saying: "Don't touch me, filthy rat!" It would have been better to have said nothing, though it would have made no difference: before the incredulous eyes of Luz and her daughters, the filthy rat grabbed hold of Celmira's neck, leaving her head as if facing backwards. Then he tore open her dress, leaning her up against a cabinet, and everyone was shocked: the naked corpse revealed a tattoo. But it wasn't a tattoo: one of her buttocks had been branded like cattle. With a shriek, Luz tried to run. Yet she lost her mind on witnessing them tearing off her daughters' clothes with their teeth; she fainted, or else her heart exploded, none of the shadows bothered to check: they were all now captivated by Sol and Luna. The same thing would happen to the girls as to Amalia Piñeros and so many others.

Profesora Fernanda Fernández disappeared while walking through the garden with the fiancées Esther, Ana, and Bruneta. They all disappeared, just like other women the shadows dragged off into the darkness. Fernanda Fernández had wanted to leave the party in the aftermath of her fight with Armenia, but, to her misfortune, she hadn't left. Offended to the soul by the pitiless shadows, she felt tormented by her indecision: that morning, she had resolved not to come to the party, but during a phone call with Dalilo Alfaro, principal of the school where she worked, he had ordered her to attend. Fernanda Fernández had dressed for the party, presented herself, and then what happened happened.

And the fiancés Teo, Cheo, and Antón, who searched all over the house for their fiancées, met with similar fortunes: their throats were slit in front of their women. Then the fiancées throats were slit. In this manner, death was being apportioned all over the house, transforming it into a house of fury.

2

Out in the garden, which was the heart of the party, the Malaspulgas proceeded undaunted with their music. All at once, from up on stage, they began to notice strange movements in the crowd—as at sea, when calm waters are broken here and there by circles of foam or the splashing of fish devouring each other.

"There are strangers here, people who don't belong at the party," Cecilio Diez told Momo Ray, his flautist, "and I need Charrita with us." The two of them left the rest of the band grooving and jumped down from the stage to look for Charrita Luz. They were fed up too, and wanted to end the music once and for all, which equated to ending the party. They would propose this to Alma Santacruz, see what she thought, and then head back to their hotel to sleep, hopefully in each other's arms, like the pair of lovers they were. On the way to find Alma, like a quirk of fate, it occurred to them to ask a murderer if he knew the whereabouts of Charrita Luz, singer with the Malaspulgas: "Have you seen her?" they asked him, "she's a striking mulatta?" "I think we've killed her already," said the man in the hat, who played his own part in the irony, for he believed Cecilio Diez to be another member of his band, the band of shadows: he'd been fooled by the black hat Cecilio was wearing. And as soon as he realized his mistake, he burst out laughing, commenting on the misunderstanding to other approaching shadows. Their furious mockery encircled the musicians, dumbfounding them: what was this about having killed Charrita Luz already? The response came in the form of their own deaths: members of the band of shadows executed the members of the band of musicians, first Momo Ray, flautist, in front of Cecilio, and then Cecilito himself, who struggled vainly, terrified. Within the crowded grounds of the garden, his screams became lost in the breakneck fandango being performed by the surviving musicians.

* * *

Inside the dining room, the knife wielders assumed that Judge Arquímedes Lama had hidden under the table. In reality, they discovered, he was sleeping, and they woke him up in order to kill him; he was followed by the three honorable judges, who had arrived at that very moment to take him home. These ladies were united by their passion for their colleagues' parties, but they had never imagined they would meet their deaths at Ignacio Caicedo's anniversary. They were executed simultaneously, and then deafening screams began to take hold of the dining room, which was assailed everywhere by the men in hats. Such was their speed and eagerness that, wherever they passed, screams were extinguished and replaced with only laughter, lewd comments. Screaming cannoned off the walls. To the delight of the murdering shadows, the only men to offer any unexpected form of resistance were the Púa patriarchs: grandfather and great-grandfather. Finding themselves threatened with knives, they pounced upon the nearest shadow, knocking him to the ground and resting their knees on his chest: "Bandit," they yelled, "show some respect for life!" This was as far as they got; they did not possess the strength to match their manliness: the selfsame marauder they had toppled sprang up, seemingly embarrassed, and did away with the patriarchs, beheading them over the table.

There was a vain attempt made by José Sansón, cousin to the magistrate, and Artemio Aldana, a childhood friend, to escape through the door, not simply surrounded by women but also disguised—who knows when they managed it—as ladies; they were trapped by their petticoats, tortured, then dealt the coup de grâce. So drunk were the teachers Roque San Luis and Rodrigo Moya, discussing sex in a corner of the dining room, that they were yet to even notice the carnage taking place around them. One of them was repeating his most celebrated phrase, stating that, while men are always looking at women's asses, women always look at each other's asses. This is what he was saying when black night poured mist into his eyes, as well as those of his listener.

And more innocents continued to drop to the ground, still perplexed by the blood on the walls: the two Davides, throats slashed over their guitars, those nicknamed Ingenuo and Sexenio, clubbed to death, Sexilia and Fecunda, impaled in front of everyone, the aguardiente exporter Pepa Sol, flogged, her husband Salvador Cantante, his trumpet shoved down his throat, and then there was a sensation caused among the shadows by the woman nicknamed The Hen, who had believed herself capable of seducing the youngest of the men in hats, promising him riches if he spared her: they lopped off her head. And yet something took place with the decapitation of The Hen, something undefinable, barely seconds later, as takes place with hens sacrificed during Christmas feasts: once the beheading had been carried out, her mountainous body raced from the dining room, as the eyes in her head looked on dubiously and her mouth opened to say something no one could understand. This led the crowd to become overwhelmed by an ancient fear, but only for an instant, like a brief respite. The Barney sisters, who had once wished to set themselves on fire, were set alight, and members of entire families—the Florecitos, the Mayonesos, the Calaveras, the Pambazos, the Carisinos, the Mistéricos, the Pío del Ríos, and what remained of the Púas—were mercilessly terminated, whether on the pyre, at the gallows, or by garrote, Chinese water torture, the descabello, the puntilla, throat slitting, walling in, drowning, or stoning.

Luciano Caicedo and Barrunto Santacruz were tortured to death over a low flame—and they had almost perished sooner, of heart failure, while forced to watch in disbelief as the deaths continued to pile up around them. All their lives they had spoken of a violent country, all their lives they had disputed whether it would not be better to call it a murderous country, and yet now it befell them to suffer their country in the flesh, now they came face-to-face with it, now they understood it: this was a country of victims. It's said that there was a discussion of sorts between Barrunto and Luciano and the men in hats, before the roasting. It seems one of the uncles, Barrunto, stepped forward, spreading his arms before the executioners and asking, genuinely amiable but intrigued:

"Why are you doing this?"

The frankness of this question, its pure innocence, like that of friends meeting on a street corner, in the tone of a confessor asking about sins, flattered the executioners, prompting them to look for an answer:

"It's a harebrained operation, that's true."

"We're following orders, that's what we're here for."

"They pay us. Ever since we started messing around in this, we've been in it for the money. We'll save a bit and get out."

"But many of us have grown used to it. You develop an appetite for this dance, you see."

"We aren't forced to suffer through revolutions or liberations or endless fighting. We aren't liars, and we aren't supermen either."

"When the Comandante decided to involve himself in bigger business, things got real tasty."

"We didn't know each other. But we were in the same place, waiting to get picked."

"Ready to stop existing."

"We'd be coming or going."

"But to come or go was the same."

"We followed the path."

"Never slept."

Barrunto and Luciano didn't understand a word. But they tried to fuel the conversation, eagerly coming up with further questions, and yet the men in hats turned deaf ears, tired of talking: they had probably never talked so much in their entire lives. Uncle Luciano went crazy, taking his toy Trojan horse out of his pocket and setting it spinning and whinnying on the floor, as if believing the mere sight of the horse would spare them from death. It didn't. The men in hats weren't amused by the whinnying horse. They had no souls, and proceeded to roast those who'd questioned them alive.

3

Curiously, the waiters, the sweet and diligent errand boys, the tutors, drudges, and caregivers, all harnessed the youth in their legs to make a dash for it. They fled like rabbits from the dining room, fled from the garden, fled just like the musicians—although the musicians soon bowed out and offered up their souls. The survivors were an army that didn't realize what it was. Finding the central corridor of the house besieged by shadows—the corridor leading to the front door, to salvation—they ran instead to the kitchen, where the cooks were already hiding amid a commotion of screaming and bumping bodies, of voices as terrified as they were rebellious: "For fuck's sake, we're getting screwed in the ass here!"

If only half of the waiters and cooks had decided to fight for their lives, they would almost certainly have defeated the murderers—in spite of their weapons, in spite of their proficiency in the art of raising and burying knives without sentiment. The cooks and waiters were greater in number, and no weaklings, familiar in their own way with the art of knives—though it's true they only employed these in the art of carving up chickens and goats—and they could have attempted a successful coordinated attack, could have imagined they were defending themselves from unruly piglets, that these were possessed hogs they were carving up. But they never elected to fight. Such a thought never crossed their minds, only that of fleeing.

Their blood had run cold.

To begin with, they crammed inside the kitchen, but, as they didn't all fit, they soon fled to the small patio at the back, the location of the apartments of the deceased Zambranito, Juana Colima, and the raped and strangled Iris Sarmiento. The waiters and cooks took refuge in the two apartments, some perched on top of others like bread rolls in a bakery, so pale and cramped did they appear—in addition, fright had turned the hair of many of them as white as flour. Once the rooms were crammed with their trembling hearts, they shut the doors and there they crouched, in icy suspense, looking out for the killers who were attacking all over the house, amid a commotion of gunshots and knives.

They were coming.

They were coming.

Yet the only person to appear outside the doors of the apartments was Uncle Jesús, the black sheep of the family, screaming for them to let him in, I'm the brother of the lady of the house! I'm Jesús Dolores Santacruz! However, he could no longer squeeze in, they attempted it once, but he didn't fit, so they repelled him and shut the doors. And through the windows they were able to glimpse the arrival of the shadows, the deranged shadows that laughed and encircled Jesús. He wasn't permitted to speak. He wasn't permitted to call upon inspiration. They watched the fatal knives surround him, watched how they abused Jesús, watched how they sawed through his skull, squeezed out his brains, and ripped his now-cold heart from his chest—just like in the poem Jesús had been able to recite from memory. And everyone noticed how, from inside Uncle Jesús's skull, something resembling a sewer rat emerged.

In the garden, the tables were no longer loaded with victuals but with the remains of maids forcibly unmaidened, some half-dressed, others completely naked, in the most improbable positions, static dolls celebrating who knows what macabre festival.

Fleeing between the tables, Juana Colima was searching for somewhere to hide. Armed with a copper frying pan, as gutsy as she was terrified, Juana had almost brained the first shadow that attacked her in the kitchen. Then she'd grabbed hold of a jug of lemon extract, poured it into the eyes of another shadow, and fled to the garden. Now she was trying to climb into the wine barrel adorning a nook of the "kids' corner" beneath the balloons and streamers, between smashed polystyrene giraffes, the enormous barrel she had spent her whole life wanting to fill with earth in order to plant chrysanthemums, and which now, because she had never planted them, led her to trust in a miracle from God, the barrel where she could hide until the killing hour was over, a barrel where she could pray for Señora Alma, who—where could she be? This was Juana's final thought, for at that moment black night surprised her in the form of knives in the back: it was the two shadows, the quasibrained one and the blinded one, who had come out in search of her. They used the barrel to hide Juana's corpse. They slid her in with a push, effortlessly; neither of the shadows noticed there was already someone at the bottom of the barrel: little Tina Tobón, scared to death but alive. She did not survive. She was suffocated by the weight and abundance of Juana Colima's body—as well as by her own panic.

Overseeing the two shadows was Doctor D, still stroking Uriela's cat in his arms: "So you were almost bested by that old hag, you pair of sissies." Then, with a cry intended to surpass Comandante Cadena's bleating, he gave the order:

"Let's get on with killing!"

This is how he incited them to rampage through the house, dealing out more coups de grâce among the multitude.

Wrathful hands dispatched Principal Dalilo and Marilú, owners of the Magdalene School for Girls. Dalilo, a psychiatrist by profession, realized the barbarians were incited not only by a thirst for killing, but also an appetite for girls in the highest state of terror, and, to his shame, he committed the ignominy of requesting they spare his life in exchange for the virginity of the students at his school—the most beautiful girls in Bogotá, it's claimed he even told them. It was to no avail: Dalilo died along with Marilú, as did Pepe Sarasti and Lady Mar, who drew their last gasps on the pyre, as did the twins Celio and Caveto Hurtado, animal impersonators, who bleated and squawked and rolled back their eyes, leaving this world with a mortal squeal—though their souls fluttered noiselessly, very close to the soul of the art teacher Obdulia Cera, who was brought down with clubs but didn't let out a whimper. And a source of laughter and disdain were the champions—lecturer, magician, and cyclist—big, strong men who could have defended themselves, but instead hugged the knees of their executioners: in a plea for his life, the lecturer

Manolo Zulú confessed it was his birthday, though he hadn't wanted to share his secret with anybody; the cyclist Rayo howled, revealing he was a newlywed, with his wife expecting a child; the magician Olarte struggled in vain to make a bouquet of flowers appear from the ears of one of the murderers; all three bayed like lambs as they were sacrificed. Yupanqui Ortega was different: surely owing to his role as a mortuary makeup artist, owner of a funeral parlor, a thanatologist accustomed to the dead, he had used a table knife to defend himself, managing to wound a barbarian on the left nipple, and yet it was not a lethal wound, more laugh-inducing, and, in punishment, he was felled emphatically with a sharp pike. Aunts Adelfa and Emperatriz had taken refuge behind the statue of the Baby Jesus, in a corner of the corridor leading to the kitchen, a corner that, due to the quantity of tinsel and candles, almost resembled a private temple. They were discovered there, on bended knee before their Baby Jesus. The ladies assumed, hopefully, that the shadows would rape them inside their own temple, but they simply killed them, having first examined them from head to toe, without their dresses on: the work they'd got done was clear to see, their buttocks like pumpkins, their tits like balloons, their stomachs like craters. Face down, rigid, their cavernous open asses caused great hilarity among their executioners. In this way, the guests perished, following one after another, just like the days; in this way, their turns came to step through that final door, in this way, they succumbed without any great struggle or opposition, perhaps because they had nothing more to offer, or simply didn't want to, or couldn't, in this way, they dropped dead, keeled over, kicked the bucket, packed their bags, bowed their heads, gave up their souls, bit the dust, snapped their necks, left this world, drew their last gasp, and closed their eyes. Out in the garden, solid screams could be heard falling like spears, before sinking into the grass and going silent.

Doctor D roamed like Master of the Gallows and the Knife, overseeing the men who killed, ensuring the good order of death, with no setbacks. He wandered with the cat dozing in his arms. All of a sudden, he wrung the animal's neck and flung it far away, and this was because he had spotted Roberto flying through the garden, in the blue half light of the morning. He aimed his pistol: "This is what we call shoot-the-parrot," he said, and fired. The parrot was a burst of green, its body a husk, and, amid the shock of floating feathers, it hit the ground before it could even squawk country.

Nevertheless, the shadows—the handsome and the brave, the bloodthirsty Attilas, the butchers and the slashers—brought an end to the killing with the dawning of the new day. Exhausted amid the blood, amazed at themselves, they again sat down to drink and eat the leftovers of the feast, alongside banter and sinister recollections. Nobody went up to the second floor of the house: these were Doctor D's orders. From afar, Blondie understood that Comandante Nimio's impulse had been to seek out the magistrate's wife and satisfy his revenge. It would be a case, she supposed, of finding the proud lady, screwing her, and then tearing out her guts. Yet it had already been a long time, and, disregarding Doctor D, Blondie instructed Pork Rind and Tick to make a sweep of the second floor, to find out why the Comandante was taking so long or if he needed assistance. While her two minions carried out their task, Blondie continued to direct the killing, the antipode to Doctor D, a fierce competitor. Around her shrieking voice, the rivers of blood ran; around her voice, so very many perished reluctantly, falling and continuing to fall like bedbugs. Mystic of pain and blood, archaic priestess, Blondie crowed about all the ones she had left with a Colombian necktie, all the ones she had bled dry. About how many throats she'd slit, about how many she had erased from the book of life.

<h1>4</h1>

Furtive faces appeared in the second-floor windows, the ones overlooking the garden, faces as pale as candles in the morning chill. From the garden, there came only silence, and not the silence that follows music, but that coming after torture, the iciest of silences. It was suffered by Armenia and Palmira, whose rooms looked on to the garden. Not so much incredulous as horror-stricken, the two sisters ran to hide: one crawled under her bed, the other shut herself in the wardrobe, and, tucked away, they waited heart in mouth for their fate to be decided. Neither Armenia nor Palmira ran in search of their mother. Palmira was regretting having ended up alone, without her unexpected admirer, whom she had given his marching orders following their lovemaking, while Armenia was nothing but a bundle of nerves: she didn't recognize herself. On witnessing the spectacle of blood, the sisters had been unable to even cry, from sheer panic. They knew that Francia's room was next door, but neither thought to call to her. In any case, Francia Caicedo was fast asleep in her bed, with Ike lying beside her—on the floor.

Señora Alma's bedroom, which overlooked the street, had not been reached by a single moan, a single scream, and even the silence appeared no different. There, lying on the bed with Uriela, Señora Alma was talking about her life, about the extent of her love for Nacho Caicedo, and recalling, distraught, episodes from their life together, oblivious to what was going on downstairs, in her enormous house, the deadly events being repeated in the garden. Only the lady of the house was talking: Uriela was asleep. Now Señora Alma turned to praying out loud, she, the irreligious one, as though she'd had a presentiment, and, from the outset of the prayer, she began loading the cylinders of her revolver, in case Monsignor Hidalgo was still in the house; she smiled mordantly on remembering how that man of God had fled, bounding down the spiral staircase. She seemed genuinely transfigured, reliving her volley of gunshots in the presence of the monsignor. She felt dispossessed of her own self, or possessed, but in any case happy, happy about the sacrilege, happy about her sin.

And she did not imagine—she never imagined, how could she?—that on the other side of her door, sitting in an armchair, was Comandante Cadena, savoring her conversation with herself, her lover's nostalgia, her prayers, as he drank, rejoicing in the vengeance that would soon be carried out.

"This party must be brought to an end," is what Alma was saying to herself.

Carrying the gun inside her bra, as she knew her grandmothers had done, she made for the corridor, going as far as to imagine herself heading down the stairs, arriving in the garden, and telling Cecilito the party was over—one gunshot and that would be it, the guests would leave.

To her misfortune, none of this occurred.

Alma Santacruz recognized him immediately: "I know who you are, you're Nimio Cadena," she told him, as if dragging his name up letter by letter, "you have my husband, give me back my husband, what have you done with my husband?" Weeping as she spoke, her hand reached between her breasts, and, to both their surprise, she fired. They were briefly blinded by a billow of smoke. Then they continued to stare into each other's eyes, acknowledging each other. Nimio Cadena laughed, but he'd turned pale; he hadn't been

361

expecting this. The bullet had passed straight through his neck, though it can't have hit any major veins, because he remained standing, his goat voice emerging perfectly, along with its bleating: "Ah, so you plan to kill me?" "I already have," said a stupefied Alma. "And if you like, I can go on killing you." "Not quite yet," replied Nimio, and he took a step forward, moving a hand toward his knife—or did it seem he was offering her his hand in congratulations? Or planning to embrace her? Alma found herself unable to understand, unable to take a step backward; she knew that Nimio Cadena would grab hold of her revolver, and that she would do nothing to prevent this, rather, she would hand him the revolver, saying kill me please, make it quick, and, as she prayed—she who never prayed—Alma discharged all the remaining bullets into the goat face of Nimio Cadena. Incredibly, only one of the bullets hit its mark, right between his eyebrows, as with the forehead of the jaguar.

Alma Santacruz allowed the gun to fall, then allowed herself to fall, unconscious, into the arms of the late-arriving henchmen who'd surrounded her: a knife forced its way inside her chest, killing her instantly, without a cry, her corpse alongside that of Comandante Cadena. They lay curled up on the floor, facing each other, their arms stretched out and almost touching, as if on the verge of embracing.

With the unforeseen death of the Comandante, Tick and Pork Rind hesitated between taking the news to Blondie and opening the closed doors that surrounded them—almost an invitation.

5

Uriela had listened to her mother for a while, lying next to her in bed, but was eventually conquered by sleep. When, in the midst of her torpor, it seemed she heard her mother begin to pray, laughing, and when she believed she saw her again loading the revolver as she prayed, Uriela shook herself and decided to get up and find her sisters so that they could take charge. She even considered going to ask the guests to leave the house herself. She couldn't move: her drowsiness was a spider's web encasing her. And she dreamed that she was getting out of bed: she dreamed she was knocking on her sisters' doors, talking to them, warning them about the revolver, she dreamed she was calling the police and reporting her father's disappearance: "Don't bother," came her father's voice, from some distant place, "to them it'll be a simple robbery with corpses." And when she woke to find that she'd only been dreaming, she tried to resist, jump out of bed, go through with the dream, but slumber closed her eyes again like a prodigious hand dragging her by the hair into the abyss.

It hadn't been too long, a matter of minutes. Beside her, the voice of her praying mother filled Uriela with an eternal somnolence. This wasn't rest for her; lethargy plunged her into a nightmare of nightmares: distinct faces loomed toward her, distinct voices, screams—were they screams from the nightmare? Uriela was sinking into a fever, she wished to say something, wished to howl, to rebel against the inexplicable, and yet she was unable to do even the first thing: to open her eyes. Señora Alma didn't notice Uriela's stirring arms, her hands twitching as though fending off fateful birds. Alma Santacruz was speaking about how much she loved her husband, claiming that, when he returned, she wouldn't know whether to embrace him or knock him head over heels for having caused her all that suffering. This is what Alma was saying out loud, in the stony silence of the second floor, as the shadow of Nimio Cadena listened avidly. Nimio was all too aware that the magistrate was no longer a denizen of this world, but this woman still was, the proud lady he remembered so well, and he need only open the door, present himself, and inform her of the magistrate's demise for his vengeance to be complete. Nevertheless, he abandoned this intention. It was something unheard of for him. He stood up and finished his last drink. He was leaving the second floor, having already reached the top of the staircase, when the bedroom door flew open and Alma Santacruz emerged like a squall or a moan or a ray of light, and then what happened happened.

Had Alma Santacruz not appeared, the Comandante might well have suspended the sacrifice and ordered a retreat.

This didn't happen though, because it didn't happen.

In her nightmare of nightmares, Uriela heard voices that didn't rise to screams, they were the voices of her sisters, their murmurous questions, and then, in the end, their actual screams, followed by cursing and banging furniture. Was her dream real? Uriela began descending the stairs, finding only corpses, stair by stair, corpse after corpse, and, at the bottom of the stairs, in the corridor, a mountain of skulls rising infinitely, a woman's laughter, her putrid breath. She left the house and came upon the sunrise: blood red, like stage curtains. Uriela raised her arms, hands open, and felt pour down over her a rain of eyes, of ears, of arms, of legs, of screams, of protestations, these were physical laments, firm, but sounding elongated, infinitely long, this was the third stomp in the depths, the final call at the theater, the beginning of the tragedy. Uriela became drenched in that rain of blood, and her face and hands, her thoughts, fused with the devastation, dispersing with it.

6

Uriela opened her eyes and sat up in bed, hands trembling, a cold sweat at her temples, her heart pounding: her mother wasn't there with her, where had she gone? To the bathroom? The garden? With that revolver? Uriela left the room and was greeted by darkness; there were no lights, only shadows; she could hear no music, only sporadic moans, cries, protestations, just like in her dream, as if the long hand of the dream had stretched into reality and was again gripping her by the hair. This terrified her, but she launched herself into the gloom, walking over the bodies of her mother and Nimio, without seeing them, without tripping on them; she paused outside the closed door of the sitting room where the children were sleeping, opening it and switching on the light: the children were asleep. She switched off the light, closed the door, and propelled herself toward the stairs, glimpsing or sensing in the dim morning that her sisters' bedrooms were open, a coldness emerging from them.

She raced down the spiral staircase, having scarcely reached the bottom step, in that crepuscular half light, when she walked straight into Blondie, who was heading up. Their faces almost came together. Blondie's face smelled of boiled sausages. She was unknown to Uriela, and yet also known: Uriela had only just dreamed her, had smelled her, had heard her laughter. Blondie stood staring at her, her eyes examining Uriela quickly, voraciously. They were standing face-to-face, blocking each other's path. Blondie smiled: she thought how much she liked these prudish young girls, as if taken from a fairy tale, their delicate bones crunching like those of newly hatched chicks, these young girls, she thought, and then gave a start: they were the same age, and they even looked alike, except that Blondie was blonde and Uriela had dark hair; Blondie's smile grew even wider, and she was about to grasp Uriela by the neck, hear it crunch like chicken bones, when Uriela glanced at a point behind her and cried: "Watch out!" Blondie immediately turned to look, on the defensive, and in that instant Uriela shot past her like a flash of terror, slipping away down the corridor to the living room. Blondie licked her lips, perplexed, because Uriela was already running off in the distance. Uriela even turned to look back for a moment, finding Blondie beckoning to her, laughing, like an invitation to the circus: she would never forget that laugh; she would carry it in her heart, to her regret, forevermore. Blondie shook her blonde head in disbelief at the deception, *she got away from me*, she thought, *what a gutsy girl, apparently brave women do still exist.*

And she went upstairs to check if the news about the Comandante's death was true. If he really was dead, she would need to order the retreat herself, for now nothing could be expected of Doctor D, drunk as a lord: he had been seen amusing himself on top of the corpses of young women.

On the second floor, she recognized Comandante Nimio and cursed him. She wondered if the dead woman beside him was the lady of the house. That's how it seemed, and next to the woman she discovered a revolver that almost resembled a toy gun: it must surely be the weapon that had delivered death to the Comandante; *this woman is even gutsier,* Blondie told herself, sincerely, *I would've liked to kill her myself.*

And she ordered the retreat.

The men carried Doctor D out through the air, like a bundle, having tied a checkered tablecloth around him by way of a bib. He was gurgling words like a lunatic, and, as such, resembled a Roman emperor hoisted triumphantly by his soldiers. The men cracked jokes as they carried him, and he stroked their blood-soaked heads and even pissed himself; the entire group steamed with still-warm blood. They were advancing down the corridor padded with the dead, sometimes firing into corpses just for kicks, the impact causing the bodies to bounce around as though dancing another bullerengue, another cumbia.

And they were now departing victoriously from the house, climbing single file into the truck, carrying bottles of aguardiente, while slices of elderflower cake, fillets of fish, and chicken drumsticks glistened and slid around inside their mouths. "Thanks for the party!" a big guy called out to nobody. Others were heard calling him Wardrobe, were heard telling him off, grumbling that he might be a strangler by trade, but he was a circus clown on Sundays. Another one they called Black Darwin, and another Blue Sky, two men who were drinking and hugging each other. Amid that kind of procession of hallucinations marched Tick and Pork Rind, both satisfied by the Caicedo sisters, by the memory of their faces, the terror in their beds, the scent of those necks in their hands. Hidden behind the living room door, Uriela watched them go by, before rushing over to the windows to witness them depart inside a long black truck like a funeral casket. Then Uriela became aware of the deathly silence in the house. She thought of the children sleeping in the sitting room, wondering, horrified, whether they hadn't perhaps been sleeping like the dead. She thought of her father. She thought of her sisters, the ice of their open doors. And when she thought of her mother, she could bear it no longer, believing she was going mad.

Then she ran out into the street.

7

Uriela was treading on the cement street as if rolling down a precipice. She believed she could peer through to the other side, the side of the dead, see their diaphanous faces made of glass. She felt as if an insect were pricking her mind: the dead were a multitude, they couldn't get stuck, couldn't get in the way, they turned transparent, walked through each other as if passing through air; the dead were hundreds of thousands of faces that surrounded her. In her stupor, she felt she too was drifting away from herself. Her delirium was fascinatingly clear: she believed she was thinking backwards, speaking from back to front, her mind disintegrating; if, in that moment, she were to look at herself, she would see a bird or a fish or a chair, but she would not see herself, she would have vanished into thin air. Then, she heard the voice of Juana Colima, fleetingly, as though pulling her back from the abyss: "This peeler doesn't peel," it said. "Barefoot, I won't set foot on that floor." Uriela's derangement was a white line dividing her eyes, half her face one color, the other half another, she struggled against the delirium. In this kind of rapture with herself, the shadow of a dead person kissed her mouth. The white line of madness now penetrated her mind, segmenting it. She closed her eyes, thinking that she was stronger than this, she had to be. Within the deepest recesses of her mind, her thoughts rebelled against the delirium, but the faces asphyxiated her, tipping her into the void. All the dead of the universe were there with her, in the street, and all the dead of the universe had emerged from her house, just as she had, but I'm not dead, she repeated to herself, I'm alive, I'm still, still, still alive. She was locked in a struggle with herself, one side of her against the other, one living, the other dead. The dead called to her by her name, offered their opinions, their voices filling her. She was with the dead, in a place where it wasn't nighttime but wasn't daytime either, a place where everything just *seemed*. Then one of the dead—her father?—placed a hand of air on her shoulder: "Goodbye," he said. Her mother was with him. They were linking arms like a couple of kids. Her mother said: "There's something we need to go wait for." Suddenly, the air split open and the dead began entering another place, another space: they were disappearing. Uriela was left alone, by herself. She saw herself in the half glow of dawn. I'm alive, she said, believing she had won, that she was returning to herself, and yet she had her arms raised, feeling pour down over her a rain of eyes and ears, of arms and legs, of screams and protestations, these were physical laments, firm, but elongated, infinitely long, this was the third stomp in the depths, this was the final call at the theater, this was the beginning of her tragedy.

FRIDAY, JULY 24, 2020

New Directions Paperbooks — a partial listing

Denise Levertov, Selected Poems
Li Po, Selected Poems
Clarice Lispector, An Apprenticeship
  The Hour of the Star
  The Passion According to G.H.
Federico García Lorca, Selected Poems*
Nathaniel Mackey, Splay Anthem
Xavier de Maistre, Voyage Around My Room
Stéphane Mallarmé, Selected Poetry and Prose*
Javier Marías, Your Face Tomorrow (3 volumes)
Bernadette Mayer, Midwinter Day
Carson McCullers, The Member of the Wedding
Fernando Melchor, Hurricane Season
  Paradais
Thomas Merton, New Seeds of Contemplation
  The Way of Chuang Tzu
Henri Michaux, A Barbarian in Asia
Henry Miller, The Colossus of Maroussi
  Big Sur & the Oranges of Hieronymus Bosch
Yukio Mishima, Confessions of a Mask
  Death in Midsummer
Eugenio Montale, Selected Poems*
Vladimir Nabokov, Laughter in the Dark
Pablo Neruda, The Captain's Verses*
  Love Poems*
Charles Olson, Selected Writings
George Oppen, New Collected Poems
Wilfred Owen, Collected Poems
Hiroko Oyamada, The Hole
José Emilio Pacheco, Battles in the Desert
Michael Palmer, Little Elegies for Sister Satan
Nicanor Parra, Antipoems*
Boris Pasternak, Safe Conduct
Octavio Paz, Poems of Octavio Paz
Victor Pelevin, Omon Ra
Fernando Pessoa
  The Complete Works of Alberto Caeiro
Alejandra Pizarnik
  Extracting the Stone of Madness
Robert Plunket, My Search for Warren Harding
Ezra Pound, The Cantos
  New Selected Poems and Translations
Qian Zhongshu, Fortress Besieged
Raymond Queneau, Exercises in Style
Olga Ravn, The Employees
Herbert Read, The Green Child
Kenneth Rexroth, Selected Poems
Keith Ridgway, A Shock

Rainer Maria Rilke
  Poems from the Book of Hours
Arthur Rimbaud, Illuminations*
  A Season in Hell and The Drunken Boat*
Evelio Rosero, The Armies
Fran Ross, Oreo
Joseph Roth, The Emperor's Tomb
Raymond Roussel, Locus Solus
Ihara Saikaku, The Life of an Amorous Woman
Nathalie Sarraute, Tropisms
Jean-Paul Sartre, Nausea
Kathryn Scanlan, Kick the Latch
Delmore Schwartz
  In Dreams Begin Responsibilities
W.G. Sebald, The Emigrants
  The Rings of Saturn
Anne Serre, The Governesses
Patti Smith, Woolgathering
Stevie Smith, Best Poems
  Novel on Yellow Paper
Gary Snyder, Turtle Island
Muriel Spark, The Driver's Seat
  The Public Image
Maria Stepanova, In Memory of Memory
Wislawa Szymborska, How to Start Writing
Antonio Tabucchi, Pereira Maintains
Junichiro Tanizaki, The Maids
Yoko Tawada, The Emissary
  Scattered All over the Earth
Dylan Thomas, A Child's Christmas in Wales
  Collected Poems
Thuan, Chinatown
Rosemary Tonks, The Bloater
Tomas Tranströmer, The Great Enigma
Leonid Tsypkin, Summer in Baden-Baden
Tu Fu, Selected Poems
Elio Vittorini, Conversations in Sicily
Rosmarie Waldrop, The Nick of Time
Robert Walser, The Tanners
Eliot Weinberger, An Elemental Thing
  Nineteen Ways of Looking at Wang Wei
Nathanael West, The Day of the Locust
  Miss Lonelyhearts
Tennessee Williams, The Glass Menagerie
  A Streetcar Named Desire
William Carlos Williams, Selected Poems
Alexis Wright, Praiseworthy
Louis Zukofsky, "A"

*BILINGUAL EDITION

For a complete listing, request a free catalog from New Directions, 80 8th Avenue, New York, NY 10011
or visit us online at ndbooks.com